Bronwyn Scott is a communications instructor at Pierce College in the United States, and is the proud mother of three wonderful children (one boy and two girls). When she's not teaching or writing, she enjoys playing the piano, travelling—especially to Florence—and studying history and foreign languages. You can learn more about Bronwyn at www. nikkipoppen.com .

Aug 12

D1559947

Don't miss these other Regency delights from Mills & Boon® Historical romance's bestselling authors!

REGENCY PLEASURES
Louise Allen

REGENCY SECRETS
Julia Justiss

REGENCY RUMOURS
Juliet Landon

REGENCY REDEMPTION
Christine Merrill

REGENCY DEBUTANTES
Margaret McPhee

REGENCY IMPROPRIETIES
Diane Gaston

REGENCY MISTRESSES
Mary Brendan

REGENCY REBELS
Deb Marlowe

REGENCY SCANDALS
Sophia James

REGENCY MARRIAGES
Elizabeth Rolls

REGENCY INNOCENTS
Annie Burrows

REGENCY SINS
Bronwyn Scott

REGENCY
Sins

Bronwyn Scott

MILLS & BOON

All the characters in this book have no existence outside the imagination
of the author, and have no relation whatsoever to anyone bearing the same
name or names. They are not even distantly inspired by any individual
known or unknown to the author, and all the incidents are pure invention.

Mills & Boon, an imprint of Harlequin (UK) Limited,
Eton House, 18-24 Paradise Road, Richmond, Surrey TW9 1SR

REGENCY SINS © Harlequin Books S.A. 2012

The publisher acknowledges the copyright holder of the individual works
as follows:

Pickpocket Countess © Nikki Poppen 2008
Notorious Rake, Innocent Lady © Nikki Poppen 2008

ISBN: 978 0 263 88742 6

052-0112

Harlequin (UK) policy is to use papers that are natural, renewable
and recyclable products and made from wood grown in sustainable
forests. The logging and manufacturing processes conform to the legal
environmental regulations of the country of origin.

Printed and bound by
CPI Group (UK) Ltd, Croydon, CR0 4YY

Pickpocket Countess

For Jeff and Diane Clausen and Ellen Holt,
who are great fans and even better friends.

As always, for my awesome family.

Chapter One

Near Manchester, England, Early December, 1831

Even in the darkness, he could sense the subtle alteration of the chamber. The room had been disturbed. Brandon Wycroft, the fifth Earl of Stockport, muttered curses under his breath. Damn, The Cat had been here.

The irony of the burglary was not lost on him. While twelve distinguished men of the district met downstairs in his library, smoking his fine cigars, drinking his expensive brandy and plotting how they'd catch the latest menace to the peace, that very menace had prowled free upstairs, daring to invade his most private sanctum: his bedroom.

It was only due to his keen hearing and the location of his rooms over the library that he had heard the faint scraping of a chair on the floor at all and had gone upstairs to investigate.

Curtains stirred at the window, calling his attention to the source of the winter chill permeating his quarters. The window was open. A slight movement behind the curtains gave away the intruder.

Brandon's eyes narrowed. His body tensed. He amended

his earlier thought. Not 'had prowled' but 'was prowling'. Standing in the doorway of his chambers, he knew his instincts were right. The Cat was still in the room.

Brandon's dissatisfaction transformed itself into a sense of vindication. After a month of burglarising the wealthy of Stockport-on-the-Medlock and other potential investors in Manchester who supported the proposed textile mill, The Cat's reign would come to an abrupt end tonight. He would catch The Cat right now and be done with the blustering investors downstairs who had been more interested in kow-towing to the nobleman in residence than concocting a worthy plan. Then he could get back to Parliament and the contro-versial reform legislation that awaited him in London. But first, he had to catch the man behind the curtain.

A figure emerged from the shadow of the heavy curtains. The figure did not bolt as Brandon expected, but stood brashly at the sill, letting the moonlight outline her silhouette.

Her? The Cat, the daring intruder who stood between him and the success of the mill, which he needed to save Stockport-on-the-Medlock from the ignominy of agricultural penury, was unmistakably a woman. A provocatively dressed woman at that, Brandon conceded, raking his gaze over her form.

Loose folds of a dark shirt draped over the swell of promising breasts. Glove-tight black breeches showed off a slender waist, encasing shapely hips and long-booted legs.

The woman was alluring, but that didn't change the fact she was a thief intruding on *his* private domain and now she was entirely at his mercy. Brandon crossed his arms and affected an air of negligence. He leaned against the door frame, letting his tall form fill the space as an obvious blockade.

There would be no escape through the door as long as he lounged there. The only other option was the impossibly high window that dropped two storeys to the ground, begging the question of how the thief had managed to gain entrance to the house and make her way unnoticed upstairs to his bedroom.

'I am afraid I have cut off your escape route. That is unless you favour the window.' Brandon drawled the last with a touch of sarcasm, knowing full well how inaccessible it was, set thirty feet from the ground. He could not conceive of a way anyone could gain access to it, let alone escape through it. The room's inaccessibility was one of the features he liked about his chambers. A man needed his privacy and Brandon guarded his with dogged determination.

The woman shrugged, indicating a lack of concern over the latest development. 'The window served well enough as an entrance. I am certain it will suffice as an exit.'

Brandon scoffed. The statement was a fool's bluff. 'You came in through the window? Forgive me if I find your claim bordering on the preposterous. Aside from the window's height, I have trained men patrolling the area. I am prepared to ward off an army if necessary.'

'Exactly so, my lord. You were prepared for an army. You weren't prepared for me. It is much easier for one person to slip through the defences than for many.'

Brandon did not care for the cocksure way she dismissed his careful patrols. 'You are overly confident for a criminal who is about to be caught. You will face imprisonment, perhaps transportation, for the crimes you've committed. With the right judge, you may face hanging.' The thought of this audacious woman facing such punishment suddenly sat ill with him. She exuded a wildness that he sensed would not do well behind bars. Her very presence radiated an elemental quality that drew him, unwilling though he was, into her game. He recognised the signs. She was flirting with him, challenging him to catch her.

She laughed as if his warning was nothing more than witty repartee over lobster patties at a dinner party. 'A fine pass England has come to when feeding the hungry is a punitive offense. There are others more deserving of punishment than me.'

Unbidden, Brandon felt a thin smile cross his lips. She thought to outwit him with her brazen statements. Well, she would find him more than an equal match. If there were two subjects in which he excelled, they were women and repartee. 'Who would you recommend?' He took a step towards her.

Six steps remained between them.

'Men like you.' She spat the words at him.

Five steps.

The minx was in dangerous territory now in all ways. How dare she assume she could label him along with the rest of the aristocracy? He'd spent his adult life distancing himself from the *ton* and its pack of gossiping wolves. 'What does a common burglar know about men like me?'

'I know you let others starve in the name of progress.'

Ah, so the vixen was another radical with ill-gotten ideas about the mills and factories that had become the lifeblood of the English economy. 'Manufacture is the way of the present and the future.' The fact that he believed the statement he'd just uttered was proof enough of the distance he'd tried to create between himself and others of his class, where a gentleman was judged by the extent of his idleness. With few exceptions, aristocrats didn't meddle in trade, but, then, few of them actually understood or cared about the impending downturn of the agricultural economy which supported their overindulged lifestyles.

Four steps.

'The textile factory your industrial friends propose to build here is a guarantee of death! Families count on the extra money their womenfolk make on weaving. Your plan will replace their efforts with machines and fewer men to run them. People are already out of work. Families cannot afford food or fuel to see them through the winter while you sit in your fine house cosy with other rich men, plotting how to make life more miserable for those less fortunate.'

'And all the while, *you're* robbing *us*. Funny, that.' Brandon managed a chuckle, enjoying her temerity even if it was mis-aimed and at his expense. The impertinent baggage went too far in making judgements about him.

Three steps.

'I take little enough and you can easily afford it.' For effect, she held up a gold ring, a woman's ring, which glinted, showing off the amethyst set in the band.

Brandon sucked in his breath. Of all the things in the room to seize, it was the one item he was most loathe to lose. 'That ring has special meaning to me. Give it back now.' It was not a plea, but a command.

Two steps.

Brandon held out his hand to receive it, automatically assuming his demands would be obeyed. It had been ages since any woman had dared to refuse the Earl of Stockport.

'No, I don't think I shall give it back. This will feed two families.'

'At least two,' Brandon growled. 'I said give it back, you little thief. I have no wish to harm you.' He took the last step. He was close enough now to make out the half-mask she wore that hid the upper portion of her face.

Glittering green eyes, too like the cat whose moniker she bore, defied him. A dark kerchief tied pirate-style swathed her head. Undaunted by his nearness, she reached up and tugged at the kerchief's knot. It gave easily and she pulled it off in a fluid motion. With a calculated toss of her head, she let a bounty of midnight waves fall to her waist. She postured provocatively, tempting him with curves and curls. A slender hand rested on her hip. 'Very well, I expect compensation for the ring. I will turn it over to you in exchange for something of equal value.'

Her gaze swept the length of him, giving Brandon the uncomfortable feeling of being a Tattersall stud. Usually it was the other way around. Those women who dared to ogle him—and he knew there were several, that was the price of being a highly eligible and titled bachelor who'd reached the age of five and thirty without springing the parson's mousetrap—did so from behind painted fans and coyly downcast eyelashes. Never had he been so boldly assessed, not even by the mistresses he took to his bed.

'Not too bad. Not bad at all,' she said, satisfied with her bold perusal of his body.

Not too bad? Brandon jerked an eyebrow in disbelief. He'd never been found merely 'not too bad' in his whole adult life. He knew himself to be in top physical condition thanks to rigorous training at Jackson's on a daily basis when in town.

'Would you care to check my teeth while you're at it?' he offered coolly. It wouldn't do to let her think she'd scored a cheap hit by attacking his masculinity.

She smiled wide and wetted her lips in a provocative gesture. 'An excellent suggestion, my lord, I think I shall.'

With that, she closed the remaining gap between them, claiming his mouth with hers and silencing whatever protests waited there.

Brandon gave her compliance. Despite his intentions not

to be lured by the minx, his mouth opened of its own accord, tasting the saltiness of her probing tongue as surely as she tasted the brandy-flavoured warmth of his own. The temptress pushed her advantage, crushing her luscious form against him, shirt-draped breasts erotically pressed against his chest. Brandon's groin leapt to life independent of his mind's urge to the contrary.

He moaned. His entire body betrayed him. The seductive hum of her low laugh indicated his arousal was not his secret alone. He felt her hands in his hair, capturing his head on the odds he'd pull away before she was done. Small chance of that occurring, he was in her thrall. Not because the kiss was the most skilful he'd ever received, but because the kiss conveyed more than cold proficiency. It contained heat. It didn't take long for him to realise this woman was kissing him not solely as a ploy, but because she wanted to. In his cynical world, that was a rare pleasure indeed.

Brandon shut his eyes and gave himself up to the momentary bliss found at the pretty thief's lips. He let her tongue taste and torture by turn. He let her hands roam where they would, finding their way beneath his linen shirt where they stroked the planes of his chest, thumbs teasing his nipples until he was in true ecstasy.

'Touch me again and I'll be lost,' he thought numbly, unable to decide in his bemused state if that was a plea for her to stop or a prayer that she continue.

She continued.

She moved a hand lower… That did it. He wanted to be lost, and he wanted her to be lost with him. She'd been in control so far, having used her brash kiss to seize the advantage. That was about to change. With his desire mounting fast, Brandon angled his mouth to deepen the kiss, his hands firmly splayed at her hips, thumbs beginning a languid caress of the bones just above her pelvis.

The Cat sucked hard on his lower lip and released him, pushing out of range of his arms. Brandon could not remember a kiss having so thoroughly aroused him. He tried to speak in an attempt to bring the situation under his control, but the cool reserve and quick tongue that had served him so well in the House of Lords for so long failed him. He found he could utter not a single word in the wake of her spontaneous seduction.

'What's the matter?' she taunted in a husky-voiced purr. 'Cat got your tongue?' She managed a wink from behind the demi-mask.

Without warning, she turned and vaulted easily to the sill and assumed a crouching position. Before Brandon could react, she leapt to the sturdy oak branch seven feet away and several dangerous feet above the ground.

Brandon darted to the window, fear for her safety overriding the more logical action of raising the hue and cry over the intruder. He peered out to where he'd last seen her. There was no sign of her in the branches of the big tree or of a black form moving stealthily across the grounds. She was gone. He had let her escape.

Cold reality doused him. What had he done? His reaction was inexplicable. A known thief had violated his home and made off with a prized possession and he had *allowed* it to happen. He turned back from the window. Something glinted on the carpet. Brandon bent and picked it up. She'd left the ring. So there was a scrap of decency in the thief after all. His hand clenched around the ring before placing it back in the velvet casket he kept on a table.

Impulsively, he realigned the little casket which had been

knocked off-centre. He'd send his valet to set the room to rights. Who knew what else might be missing? Brandon glimpsed himself in the mirror above the washstand. His immaculate shirt was wrinkled and his cravat ruined. He looked thoroughly well used, and he had been. He would have to change shirts before returning downstairs.

Thankfully, he had a dozen pristine shirts like the one he wore waiting for use in his dressing room. Changing would buy enough time for the fully kissed puffiness of his lips to go down. It would not do to appear dishevelled in front of the men waiting in the library, especially when he had decided to tell them nothing in regards to what he'd discovered upstairs.

Nora bent over to catch her breath, easing the stitch in her side. She'd run hard after she'd shimmied down the oak tree and hit the ground. She hadn't stopped until she was well away from the arrogant bounder's estate and deep into the sheltering boughs of the forest.

Only now, ensconced in the safety of the trees, could she give her thoughts full rein over what had transpired. She'd kissed the Earl of Stockport, known in the less-judicious circles of the demi-monde where The Cat had done her research as the Cock of the North.

Nora concurred that the nickname was justly earned on all fronts. He had demonstrated all the well-dressed arrogance of a rooster preening his fine feathers before the hens. He was a fine male specimen and he knew it. No man spent time cultivating an immaculate appearance without being sure of the results, and no one was surer of himself than the Earl of Stockport.

Nora laughed out loud in the darkness. The look on his face when she'd declared him 'not bad' had been the highlight of the evening. Then he'd given her the perfect opening with his quip about checking his teeth. He'd thought she'd back down when he raised the stakes. Men like him didn't expect to be challenged. But she hadn't survived this long without being caught by doing the expected. She knew how to do the unexpected and his opening had been too much to resist.

She should have resisted. He wasn't called the Cock of the North simply for his excellent sartorial habits. She'd thought to use the kiss as a means of disarming him, stunning him until she could get away unscathed. She was out of her depth with such a master. She had waited too long, indulged herself too much, letting herself be seduced by the clean smell of him, sandalwood and spices mixed with the starch of his fresh-washed shirt. By the time she realised the tables were turning on her, it was almost too late.

At the last moment, she'd felt the slight shift of his mouth as he took over the kiss, felt the erotic pressure of his thumbs against her hip bones. She'd taken the only defensive line left to her and recoiled, grabbing the opportunity to speak first, knowing that whoever did so would control the outcome of the interaction. Then she'd run.

The evening's visit had proved dangerous in ways she and her two comrades had not expected, but by tomorrow afternoon, the danger would be worth it when news circulated that The Cat had hit Stockport Hall *while* the Earl was within planning The Cat's capture.

She and her two comrades had been watching the house for a week after learning that the local neighbours had sent an urgent summons to the Earl, dragging him out of the Michaelmas Session of Parliament early so they could hold a meeting to nab the thief. Breaking into the Earl's house while they discussed The Cat would be a bold coup—breaking into the man's private rooms would be even more so.

Those rooms were as elegant as his reported personality. Table tops and dressers held myriad expensive accoutrements of a well-groomed gentleman, from expensive ebony-inlaid combs and brushes to silver-handled shaving gear. She should have stolen them. Those items would have brought enough money to keep a family in food until summer. But her eye had been drawn to the velvet casket and she couldn't resist looking inside.

The ring was a bounty. She'd taken it and then realised it was such a small item the Earl might not notice it was gone for weeks. But the ring was all she needed and The Cat prided herself on not taking more than was necessary—one of the many lessons she wanted to teach these gluttonous industrial barons.

Still, if the ring wasn't noticed missing immediately, its theft wouldn't help her cause. She wanted more from Stockport than his valuables. She wanted him to know she'd been there and when. She'd begun to disarrange the room, intuitively knowing that such an act would get his attention more completely than taking other conspicuous items.

As with all her robberies, the larger implication of her work was twofold. First, she wanted to be an annoyance significant enough to make them re-think the building of the factory. Second, she wanted to prick the social consciousness into action regarding the sorry status of a factory worker's life. Unsafe working conditions had cost her parents their lives. She'd be damned if it would hurt others.

Her plan had gone well enough until she'd bumped into a chair sitting in a dark corner. It hadn't made much noise, but it made enough to catch his attention since his chambers were over the library. She'd relished the confrontation that had followed.

She had gloried in his reaction. He'd roused to her. Unfortunately, that was all she had to show for the night's work. Something beneath his terse command to release the ring had touched her and she'd traded the ring for an ardent bout of kissing. Arousing the Earl of Stockport might be a satisfying touch of one-upmanship, but it wouldn't feed families.

Determined to rectify that aspect of the evening, Nora became practical. She needed pickings and the night was still new. She'd cut cross country to Squire Bradley's house and help herself to another piece of silver from the butler's pantry. The Squire's night watchman was pathetic. In a half-hour he'd be asleep or drunk or both.

Two hours and a successful stop at the Squire's later, Nora let herself into an unremarkable grange house and crept silently upstairs to her bedchamber. A light shone beneath the door. Nora smiled. Hattie, one of her two co-conspirators who masqueraded as workers in her modest household, had waited up. Nora pushed opened the door.

'A successful evening, I take it?' Hattie asked, reaching for the bag of goods Nora carried in her right hand. 'Shall I hide this in the usual place?'

'Yes and yes.' Nora pulled off her mask and plopped unceremoniously into a chair.

'Did everything go the way Alfred and I laid it out? Was the tree branch a good entrance into the house?' Hattie moved efficiently around the room, laying out Nora's night things.

'The plans were accurate, as always.' Nora paused before adding, 'I met the Earl.' She hadn't wanted to tell Hattie that part, but the household needed to be prepared. News of the break-in at Stockport Hall would circulate the village tomorrow and Nora wasn't sure how the Earl would present the story. It wouldn't do for Hattie or Alfred to discover her encounter second-hand. There was no question Hattie wouldn't hear of it. She heard everything.

Hattie turned from the dresser. 'Did you, now? No wonder you were so late. Got into a bit of a scrape?'

'Nothing I couldn't handle.' Nora passed off the incident with a wave of her hand, when in truth she'd been in over her head. 'I had to go to Squire Bradley's or I would have been empty-handed. That was why I was late.'

Hattie clucked her disapproval. 'That was dangerous, Nora. We've hit the Squire's home too many times. One of these days he'll be on to us and there will be trouble.'

Nora tightened her jaw at Hattie's censure. 'We must have funds for the Christmas baskets. We're running out of time and so many people are in need this year.'

'Still, you're no good to the people if you're caught.'

'I won't get caught,' Nora said in a conversation-ending tone. She softened. 'Off to bed with you, Hattie. It's been a long night.' Hattie had been with her through too much for her to be cross with the redoubtable lady for long.

'Should Eleanor Habersham expect visitors tomorrow?' Hattie asked from the door.

'Wednesday tea as usual with the ladies.'

'And the Earl? When should we expect him?'

'Not for a while. I would be very surprised to see him tomorrow. He has no reason to come looking for Miss Habersham,' Nora said confidently.

'Good night, then.' Hattie shut the door quietly behind her.

Nora undressed quickly, careful to conceal her black garb in the false back of her wardrobe behind the mounds of ridiculous gowns belonging to the persona she showed to the town, the eccentric spinster, Miss Eleanor Habersham. Miss Habersham was a silly, giddy lady with a penchant for gossip.

By four o'clock tomorrow afternoon, Nora expected Miss Habersham's tiny parlour would be overrun by local ladies exchanging the latest tittle-tattle about the night's escapades.

Nora forced herself to doze. It wouldn't do for Miss Habersham to appear with dark circles when everyone in town knew the spinster had no call for such sleeplessness in her mundane life. But sleep was hard to come by. Usually after such sprees, Nora's mind was occupied by the results of the evening and the valuables stashed with her disguise, myriad questions running through her head: how would it be dispersed, how much more would be needed to help those in the most desperate straits? There was never enough to go around. Her raids had become bolder and more daring in attempts to narrow the gap.

Tonight, the disturbing memory of Stockport's hot mouth and the firm fit of his body against hers consumed her thoughts. She had played the wanton in hopes of distracting him to ensure her escape. She'd not expected his active participation or her own enjoyment in the act. There was something erotically compelling about a virile man's compliance.

She had made her point tonight. There would be no reason to go back to his estate. It wasn't an easy target. His patrols were harder to elude than she'd admitted. The safest course would be to put tonight's episode behind her. Yet, the thought of doing so left her feeling strangely empty. She knew she'd go back, for the sake of the challenge if nothing else.

Chapter Two

Brandon took his seat at the table in Stockport Hall's cheery informal dining room. He breathed deeply. There was nothing quite as comforting as the smell of scrambled eggs and breakfast ham mixed with the aroma of fresh-brewed coffee. He was pleased to see *The Times* beside his plate, pressed and ready, relieved at last to have his mind on something besides the impassioned episode of the prior evening.

He'd spent the dark hours with his groin in a perpetual state of anticipation, alternately reliving the encounter with The Cat and cursing himself for a fool. He'd let the perfect opportunity pass him by. Not only had he ruined a chance to capture the thief, he'd ruined any chance of identifying the woman in the future. It would have been easy enough to remove her mask either by surprise or force when she'd been in his arms. He had done neither.

He reached for the paper and folded it to the financial section. He had barely engrossed himself in the investment news when his butler, Cedrickson, demanded his attention. 'My lord, Squire Bradley inquires if you're at home.'

Brandon looked up from the pages, fighting the urge to

scowl in obvious contempt. 'Where else would I be this time of day but at home? What kind of man calls at nine-thirty in the morning?' In town no one dared a call before one o'clock and only the intrepid dared call before eleven. But this was the country and he would do well to remember that the rules were different here, less intense. He would not sway the village in favour of the mill by being snobbish.

'He seems quite agitated, my lord, if I may say so.'

'Did he state his business?'

'He did. It's about The Cat.'

Brandon set the paper down. 'Then you'd best show him in. Have an extra place set.'

The Squire did look quite overset, Brandon conceded. His florid face was pale and his usual bluff nature subdued. He had the good manners to apologise for such an early call as he waved away the offer of breakfast. 'This is fine fare, to be sure, although I don't have the stomach for it this morning. We had a difficult night over at the house. It seems that while we were scheming at your place, The Cat struck at Wildflowers. It's the third time. My poor wife was in fits.' At this, the Squire stopped to mop his forehead with a large handkerchief produced from a jacket pocket.

'I can imagine,' Brandon offered as sincerely as he could manage. Indeed, he could picture just what an uproar the Squire's wife had produced. The woman was exactly the kind of flibbertigibbet he avoided whenever possible. 'What was taken? Are you certain it was The Cat? The items haven't simply been mislaid?'

The Squire waved an arm. 'A set of silver candlesticks and the petty cash for household expenses are missing. Only my wife has the key to the silver cabinet. The lock had been picked and the usual calling card was left behind.'

That grabbed Brandon's attention. 'I hadn't heard this before. What calling card?'

The squire reached into the pocket of his waistcoat. 'These abominable things.' He handed Brandon a card.

Brandon studied it. It was cream coloured and Brandon suppressed a smile. The irony of someone who called themselves 'The Cat' using cream paper was not lost on him. He doubted the squire would see the humour in it. Nor would the squire appreciate the mocking wit in the thief's use of a calling card when 'visiting' the homes of gentlemen.

Except for the cream colouring, the card was otherwise nondescript. Bold, black ink on one side proclaimed 'The Cat of Manchester' and nothing more.

'Everyone receives one of these? Witherspoon and the other investors didn't mention it last night,' Brandon said, handing the card back. The Cat obviously hadn't had time to leave one behind when he'd caught up to her last night.

'Well…' the squire cleared his throat '…it's embarrassing to admit. We've all got one. Some of us have more. We have three of them now,' the squire grumbled. 'I am at a complete loss over what to do. We seem to be a regular mark. I can't imagine why we've been singled out.' The man sighed heavily in exasperation.

Because you're an easy target, Brandon mused uncharitably. Out loud he remarked, 'Do you still have that same night watchman? I say change the watchman and the nightly routine and The Cat won't be so eager to come around.'

'Or, we catch that criminal and put an end to the need for night watchmen altogether,' Squire Bradley said with an uncustomary vehemence. 'The only house that hasn't been hit is yours.' The squire seemed to sense he had crossed an invisible line. This might be the country, but respect was still respect. He gave a cough to cover his embarrassment. 'Begging your pardon, my lord.'

Brandon glossed over the breach of social politeness and his opportunity to confess the events of the prior evening. 'As I said, patrols and quality watchmen will go far as a deterrent to crime.' He found it interesting to learn The Cat had hit another house after leaving. His valet had not found anything else missing from his rooms, only an irritating lack of order.

The rooms had been thoroughly disturbed, but nothing more. There were other valuable items to steal such as gold cufflinks, diamond cravat pins and pocket watches. His clothes alone would bring considerable funds for a thief intent on converting stolen goods to cash.

Jewellery and fine garments in their original states wouldn't do much for the people The Cat professed to helping. But if the stolen items could be sold and changed to pounds, her mission would be successful without giving the authorities anything to track. Brandon made a mental note; it would be useful to work out where or to whom The Cat sold her goods. No one was truly invisible.

'Well, I am done with such guarded measures. The sooner that menace is caught, the safer we'll all be.' The Squire huffed. 'That's the other reason why I'm here. I want you to help me start looking for him. We've been passive too long. Now that you've arrived, we can take direct action.'

Brandon drank from his coffee cup and set it down before answering. 'I mentioned last night that I am as eager as anyone else to see the matter settled. However, I am not sure where to start. We don't know what this person looks like. Did your watchman catch a glimpse of the intruder?' It wasn't *exactly* a lie. They *both* didn't know what the thief looked like, only he knew.

'We know he must be from around here, because he has

knowledge of upper-class homes,' the Squire countered, showing more intelligence than Brandon had previously given him credit for.

'Is there anyone new in the neighbourhood since these robberies began?'

The Squire thought for a moment. 'That's the one drawback with progress. Since we've been planning for that textile factory, there have been lots of new men in the area—workers, supervisors, architects, engineers, investors, the whole gamut.'

'If it's too difficult to think of new people, think of a motive,' Brandon suggested, shifting in his chair. The sooner the Squire was placated or given the illusion of action, the sooner he'd leave and Brandon could get on with his day, something he desperately needed to do. Talking about The Cat was creating an interesting side effect in his nether regions. 'Who would have reason to rob certain wealthy homes while leaving other potential homes untouched? Perhaps someone is not happy about the factory and believes it will cost people their jobs?' Brandon shamelessly hypothesised, borrowing liberally from The Cat's argument the prior night. He hoped to plant the idea firmly in the Squire's head.

'That's ridiculous. There isn't anyone who believes that kind of nonsense!' the Squire blustered, nonplussed by the very idea. 'Why, that sort of thinking is not English!'

Bradley's intelligence quotient fell back a notch. Brandon schooled his features to hide his disbelief. Surely the man didn't believe the issues that had sparked Peterloo twelve years ago had actually been resolved? If anything, the intervening years had created a stronger, better-organised working class.

The coming of widespread industrialisation had changed everything, including the need for different representation in

Parliament—the very issue he'd been debating when the message had arrived in London regarding the burglaries. No wonder Bradley was having trouble coming up with motives. The poor man couldn't fathom the political realities of the day.

Brandon returned to his previous suggestion. 'Perhaps names would be the best place to start after all.'

The Squire leaned forward, frustration evident in his tone. 'My lord, I don't think you understand. Your suggestions are theoretically sound. However, there haven't been any new-comers who've taken up long-term residence in Stockport-on-the-Medlock recently except for the investors from London.'

Brandon raised his eyebrows. 'None beyond that? I find it unlikely since all the expansion in Manchester has put the out-skirts of the city a mere five miles from the town. I would have expected other hangers-on to be arriving in order to capital-ise on the new economies that will be opening up.'

Bradley fidgeted. Aha, Brandon thought. There was someone. 'We mustn't discount anyone, Squire,' he encouraged.

'Well, it's just that the newcomers seem highly unlikely suspects.' Bradley drew a deep breath. 'The vicar's new since you've been here, but he's a man you've personally appointed so there's no point in looking that direction. The new indus-trialists in town have nothing to gain from committing rob-beries against themselves. In fact, their homes have been hit the hardest.'

'Out with it, man,' Brandon urged, sensing the Squire was holding back. 'Is there no one else?'

'The only other newcomer isn't a man at all, but a spinster, Miss Eleanor Habersham.' Bradley shook his head as he said the name. 'It's hardly right to even bring the sweet lady's name up in such a conversation. She's quite a silly thing, although the ladies adore her. My wife is going for tea at her place this afternoon. Apparently, Miss Habersham serves the most delectable cakes. I have to take my wife's word for it. The vicar and I both tried to call on her when she first arrived to be neighbourly, but she'll have nothing to do with men. Men intimidate the poor dear, I suppose.'

'Is that so? The woman sounds quite vulnerable to me,' Brandon suggested, hoping to lead the Squire to a particular conclusion.

'S'truth, she's a shy lady on her own. I dare say she knows little about the ways of the world,' the Squire agreed, appearing to mull the thought over for a moment before reaching a decision.

Brandon pushed his point. 'It may be that Miss Habersham has nothing to do with the goings-on around the village, but there might be someone in her household who does. Perhaps someone in her employ has pulled the wool over her eyes and is committing these crimes behind her back.' That scenario seemed most likely since the woman he'd encountered last night definitely didn't look like a spinster or, for that matter, act like one.

The Squire seemed genuinely horrified at the possibility. 'Oh the poor dear! I hadn't thought of that. How awful for her to be in the midst of such danger and be completely unaware of her jeopardy. We must do something.'

Brandon had the Squire where he wanted him. Without an entrée, he could not insinuate himself into a ladies' tea hosted by a painfully shy woman and not appear heavy handed. He needed the Squire to go with him and provide a casual introduction. 'What's our next step?'

'Perhaps we should attend the tea today as well. We can use my wife's invitation to Miss Habersham's little circle. It's all for the dear lady's own good.'

'A capital idea!' Brandon agreed. 'I think it is time the lady in question got over her fear of gentlemen callers and high time the Earl of Stockport met his newest neighbour.'

Nothing Squire Bradley imparted about Stockport-on-the-Medlock's resident spinster adequately prepared Brandon for afternoon tea at Miss Habersham's. To start, the poor dear had the misfortune of living at the Old Grange, a nice enough middle-class manse in its day, once having played home to a comfortable gentleman farmer, but which now had fallen into apathetic neglect. The Old Grange was not faring well if the bleak gardens and straggly front lawn were indications. December made it worse, Brandon thought, dismounting from his bay stallion.

At the door, Brandon gave the dour manservant his card and mentally eliminated him as a possible suspect simply because of his gender. The Cat was *definitely* not male. The manservant gave him a distrusting glance that said men were a rare commodity in Miss Habersham's milieu and reluctantly led the way down a short narrow hall to the front parlor.

Feminine voices reached Brandon before he stepped into the room. It was a good thing too, otherwise he'd have thought he'd stepped into a chamber of mannequins. Upon his appearance, all conversation halted and teacups stopped halfway to lips as they took in his masculine presence with extreme shock. Brandon could imagine the gossip that would circulate town tomorrow—the Earl of Stockport calling on the local spinster in the midst of her weekly ladies' tea.

Brandon squared his shoulders. There was nothing wrong with his actions. He'd correctly kept his hat and gloves with him to indicate this would be the briefest of duty calls. No etiquette expert could fault him for calling on Miss Habersham first since it was the higher-ranking person's duty to initiate a call on lower-ranking persons. After all, he didn't have the time to wait for her to come to him. The faster this business of The Cat was concluded, the sooner he could return to London.

'Good afternoon, ladies.' Brandon bowed to the room in general. 'I did not mean to disturb you, but Squire Bradley will be along shortly and he assured me this was the best place to make the acquaintance of every important woman in town.' He flashed a practised smile sure to dazzle, while inwardly he was quite peeved Squire Bradley was not already there helping to pave his way.

Brandon cast his gaze about the room for a woman likely to fit Miss Habersham's qualifications. The woman who rose to meet him was a walking juxtaposition, putting his politician's senses on high alert. She might dress like a spinster in that ill-fitting brown serge but no spinster in the history of the world had a body like that.

Of course, he probably wasn't supposed to notice such a fine figure thanks to the camouflage of the hideous gown and the severe hairstyle, which was most likely designed to call attention to the heavy glasses perched on Miss Habersham's nose— a delightfully pert creation if one got past the spectacles.

The glasses not only obscured her nose, they also obscured her eyes; that made Brandon uneasy. In his line of work, he preferred to see a person's eyes. Eyes were the only true indicators of trustworthiness. Something was not right.

'My lord, you honour us with this unexpected visit. Allow me to introduce myself, I am Eleanor Habersham.'

The lady in question spoke with a grating nasality to her voice. Brandon fought the urge to cringe—no doubt most did. Such a nagging tone would be a sure deterrent against holding protracted conversations with the lady.

'The honour is all mine.' Using his considerable drawing-room charm, Brandon smiled over her hand as if she were a diamond of the first water. He expected her to titter and play into the fantasy that he found her attractive. After a smile or two, with his eyes firmly fixed on the woman he was addressing, women usually did. This one did not.

'What brings you to the Grange?'

Was that a touch of steel he heard beneath the nasal-pitched voice of this insecure spinster who could hardly meet his eyes?

'I've come to greet my new neighbours,' Brandon offered congenially, overlooking the defensive nature of the question. He winked at the assembled ladies and directed his comment to the group at large, 'Also, I am here to gather information about The Cat. Everyone knows you ladies are the eyes and ears of the village.'

At that, the room began to buzz with voices eager to tell their tales. Alice Bradley's voice rose above the din and she waved a lace handkerchief to silence them. 'La! I don't know what the world is coming to when decent country folk can't sleep peacefully in their own homes. This is the third time we've been robbed. So many of us have suffered!' She waved her handkerchief again to indicate other ladies in the room. Those who nodded in distress were apparently wives of the men Brandon had met with last night.

Alice turned back to her hostess. 'Miss Habersham, that gives you and his lordship something in common. The two of you are the only ones whose homes haven't been visited by The Cat.' She eyed Brandon speculatively. 'It is strange your home hasn't been targeted since it has been unoccupied these last weeks. Pardon my bluntness, but you've got far more to plunder than the rest of us.'

'Ma'am, I am sorry to hear of your loss last night. I passed the morning with your husband, trying to deduce who might be behind these attacks. Miss Habersham and I must count ourselves fortunate thus far. However, I would rather catch this thief than see how long my luck holds,' Brandon offered neutrally. At the moment he was far more interested in Miss Habersham's reaction.

Behind her thick lenses, he noted that Miss Habersham's eyes widened in surprise at the reference to The Cat and she'd actually dared to look up at the mention of their two homes being untouched. Granted, it was only the briefest of glances, but it had revealed to Brandon a pair of sharp ice-green eyes that suddenly seemed too lively to belong to the shy woman awkwardly standing beside him.

Brandon let the conversation swirl around him as the conversation moved on to discuss the Squire's upcoming Christmas masque. It gave him a chance to study Miss Habersham in further detail.

During his tenure as Earl, Brandon had learned the difficult lesson that, more often than not, people wore disguises. He'd developed a knack for seeing beneath the exterior façade to the truths people hid within. He wondered what kind of disguise Miss Habersham wore and why she wore it.

He would bet good money the glasses were unnecessary. They were thick on purpose to distort the size and shape of her eyes, making them look unnaturally bug-eyed. They also offered an excuse to keep her gaze downcast. She probably couldn't see straight ahead at all with them on. Her hair was another matter, worn in a dun-coloured brown mass scraped back into a tight, unbecoming bun that emphasised her face and the unattractive spectacles.

An ordinary man might have been daunted by the nature of Miss Habersham's appearance, but Brandon saw the idiosyncrasies. Miss Habersham's skin was smooth alabaster with not a mark to mar its perfection. For all her professed nervousness, her mittened hands were steady when she held her tea cup. Her submissive posture belied a striking height. If she stood up straight, Brandon wagered she'd stand over five and a half feet.

Her figure didn't speak spinster either. For all her prissy mannerisms, she was a woman in good shape. Her waist was trim, her legs long beneath the brown skirt, her torso lean and her bosom impressive despite the efforts of her undergarments to the contrary. No, there wasn't a dry brittle bone beneath the ugly gown.

His fifteen minutes for a polite afternoon call were up and the Squire had not appeared—so much for masculine loyalty. Brandon turned to his hostess and took his leave. The other ladies near them discreetly drew back, allowing him a semi-private moment with her.

'Could I persuade you to walk with me to the door?' he asked, taking advantage of the opportunity. 'I want to talk with you about your safety. Since it has been pointed out that your home has not yet been a target, I am worried that it soon will be. Do you have adequate protection? I can send men to stand watch.'

'That will not be necessary,' Miss Habersham said in a dismissive tone that frankly shocked him. He had not expected to be declined.

'I must protest—' Brandon began.

'No, my lord, it is I who must protest. The Cat would not be interested in my home. Look around, you can see that I possess nothing that would appeal to a burglar of The Cat's calibre. There is no silver to steal, no china of merit, nothing but a few knick-knacks and souvenirs. I am a woman of modest means.'

'Burglars are not careful of station, Miss Habersham. They

are common thieves,' Brandon lectured. This woman was too naïve by half to think she'd go untouched. She might not be a woman of great wealth, but no doubt there was a trinket or two of some value waiting to be discovered within these walls. She was a woman who had the means to live on her own no matter how modestly. 'It may be true that you have nothing of merit, but The Cat doesn't know that. The thief may strike anyway.'

They reached the door and Brandon knew Miss Habersham was glad to be rid of him. Her farewell was curt and skilfully put the interaction back into her hands.

'Thank you for the warning. I will let you know if I change my mind about your offer.' No polite pleasantries followed, no gesture was offered to visit again, no opening to make sure she saw him again.

Brandon swung up on his horse, disgruntled with the outcome. He'd expected an entrée into Miss Habersham's life. What was wrong with him? The better question was what was wrong with *her*? Miss Habersham didn't add up. It wasn't just his ego, it was a well-known fact in his London circles that no woman could resist his charm. It was galling to think that a spinster of Miss Habersham's unfortunate disposition would succeed so thoroughly where other more sophisticated women had failed. That in itself was a red flag.

Eleanor's rejection of him was quite telling. Sure of his charm, Brandon had expected the woman to drool with anticipation at the thought of an Earl's attentions, no matter how inconsequential. Instead, she had refused his attentions and his offer of protection.

The afternoon visit had not gone as planned, but he had not come away empty-handed. The squire might quickly discard Miss Habersham as a potential suspect, but Brandon knew what the squire did not. The Cat was a woman. It seemed an odd co-

incidence that The Cat and a woman masquerading as a spinster
would take up residence in Stockport-on-the-Medlock simultaneously. If he'd learned anything this afternoon it was that
Miss Habersham wasn't a spinster. She was a mystery.

Chapter Three

Nora sagged against her bedroom door. Escape at last! She'd thought the ladies would never leave. Usually the Wednesday tea lasted for an hour and a half. Today, the ladies had stayed until half past six, dissecting every moment of the Earl's visit.

She tugged at the pins holding her wig in place and freed her head with a sigh. Who would have imagined a wig could be so tiring to wear or so hot? Even in December she managed to sweat beneath it. Nora shook out her hair and let it fall freely. She walked to her vanity, placed the glasses in a small drawer and rubbed the bridge of her nose.

The tea had started off well enough. Alice Bradley had been eager to recount the doings at her place. Thanks to Alice's tendency to gossip, The Cat's legend grew with each robbery. The Cat needed that kind of exposure if she was going to succeed. If she were a big enough menace, the threat of The Cat's presence would be enough to warn off the investors in the textile mill. In the meantime, if the investors continued to take up residence in Stockport-on-the-Medlock, she'd gladly pilfer their wealth to feed the people they were putting out of work.

Then Stockport had shown up, looking devastatingly handsome in his immaculate clothes. She'd felt his excellent physique the prior night but the perfection of his face had escaped her notice in the dark. In the afternoon light, she could better appreciate the strong jaw set off by a razor-straight nose, classical cheekbones and deep blue eyes. His good looks commanded attention and she wasn't the only one who noticed. Every woman in the room had their eyes riveted on him. They hung on each word the black-haired, blue-eyed devil uttered.

His presence would have been a piece of luck if he'd told everyone about the burglary. Yet when given the chance to admit Stockport Hall had been robbed, he had ignored the opening and perpetuated the belief that his home was un-touched. That made him a liar.

His omission hadn't helped her cause either. The whole point of going there last night had been to make a statement, but if he didn't tell anyone the point was moot. He was supposed to react like everyone else and shout his frustration all over town. That was the problem. He wasn't like everyone else. She'd discovered that last night, although her brain had failed to comprehend the impact it would have on her escapades.

Nora plopped into the chair in front of the vanity and began brushing out her hair. Last night, she'd thought the kiss was a stroke of bold brilliance, despite its risks. Now she saw it as a mistake. No wonder he hadn't told anyone of her visit. What was he to say that wouldn't make him look like a fool? 'The Cat put her tongue in my mouth, ripped open my shirt and cupped me through my trousers until I thought I'd burst?' A lesser man might have enjoyed circulating that juicy tit-bit over ale in the taverns but there was nothing lesser about Brandon Wycroft.

It was clear enough from the way he'd smiled and doted on the ladies today that he thought highly of himself. He was a prideful man who was completely aware of his effect on people. His self-conceit would not allow him to admit a thief, and a woman at that, had provoked such a base reaction from him.

The kiss had been her first mistake. Her second mistake had been leaving the ring. Nora was certain that, if she'd taken the ring, he would not have hesitated to mention her presence in his home. He would have gone to great lengths to put word out about the ring in case anyone saw it. That ring meant something to him and he would not be parted from it easily.

Nora tapped her fingers on the vanity, an idea surfacing in her mind. Stockport might go so far as to declare a reward for the ring if it were missing. Even if he didn't, she could blackmail a ransom of sorts out of him. That settled it. She would go back tonight for the ring and to set the record straight. By tomorrow morning news of The Cat at Stockport Hall would be common knowledge in the village.

Stockport Hall was dark except for the lone light burning in the library window as Nora approached from the south shortly before midnight. She was not surprised. Her information was highly reliable. Stockport lived alone when he came to the country and kept late hours in the library, which had a convenient entrance from the garden on the south side of the estate. She wouldn't use the entrance to go into the house. She had a stop to make first. She would climb up the tree to Stockport's bedchamber and retrieve the ring first, but later she'd need an exit after their little tête-à-tête.

Nora scaled the tree easily, her arms and legs recalling the toeholds she'd found the previous night. The tree wasn't the hard part, although it was tall and climbing it was no easy task. The hard part was getting from the tree to the window.

Nora climbed the tall oak a level higher than necessary so that she looked down on the window. Lying on her belly, she inched out along a wide, sturdy branch that effortlessly took her weight, a much more reliable branch than the one below it onto which she'd exited the night before. She took the coil of black rope from her belt and securely looped it about the branch in an intricate knot. She gave it a tug and was satisfied it would hold. She double-checked her watch—ten minutes before Stockport's highly trained patrols would pass this way, plenty of time to reach the sill and pop inside.

Taking a deep breath, Nora levered herself onto the rope. Her arms took the initial weight as her legs found their grip. Then she began the process of lowering herself down the rope length until she was level with the window. She halted and took three more deep breaths. Now it was time for the fun.

Swinging back and forth, she gained enough momentum to launch herself over to the window ledge. The ledge was only six inches wide, hardly wide enough for a strong foothold, so Nora steadied herself with one hand on the rope, using the other hand to grope for the broken window latch while her feet balanced against the sill.

Victory! In his pride, Stockport had failed to have the lock fixed immediately. No doubt he'd guessed The Cat wouldn't strike again so soon or by the same method. The window slid up and Nora scrambled inside. She gave the black rope a yank and reeled it in behind her. It took only a moment to see that the room had been righted and the casket holding the ring was in the same place.

Nora lifted the lid and found the ring couched among the purple velvet cloth. She reached for it and suffered a momentary lapse of conscience. She squeezed her eyes shut and pictured the people the ring could help. Little Timmy Black, youngest of seven children, would have hot porridge until spring. Widow Malone, bereft of a husband because of a careless maintenance error in a Manchester cotton mill, would have clothes to warm her three children. There were others too numerous to mention. She grabbed the ring and shut the lid of the box before she could change her mind. Stockport would get the ring back, she reminded herself. It wasn't as if she was stealing it permanently. She was only temporarily borrowing it for the greater good of humanity.

Feeling better, Nora slipped the ring into a small pouch around her waist and tucked it securely inside the band of her trousers. She squared her shoulders, allowing a small smile to creep across her lips as she contemplated her next task: a visit with Stockport. She was looking forward to giving him a piece of her mind.

The trip downstairs to the library was uneventful, which ironically only served to provoke her irritation with the man. She passed down the darkened major staircase and met no one, not even a footman. What a crime it was for one man alone to command all this space when families crowded together in single-room dwellings!

Nora gained the library. The door stood ajar, affording her the luxury of studying her quarry undetected. Stockport sat behind a large mahogany desk, diligently applying himself to letter writing, documents spread across the desk top. The light caught at his hair, giving it the polished gloss of obsidian. If he wasn't such a prodigiously arrogant man, she'd consider him handsome.

He lifted his head from his correspondence, giving her a glimpse of his remarkable blue eyes, behind spectacles that rode the bridge of his nose. Glasses? The Earl of Stockport wore glasses? Nora found the image before her hard to reconcile with the picture her research painted of the Earl as a man about town who had a way with women. But she had been warned that while Stockport had a well-earned reputation as a lover, he also had a reputation for responsibility.

Stockport stilled, his eyes probing the darkness beyond his door. He took off his glasses and pinched the bridge of his nose with thumb and forefinger before returning his gaze to the door. Had he guessed she was there? For a moment Nora slipped back into the shadows. She scolded herself. The Cat didn't hide. The Cat went where she pleased and when she pleased.

'Is someone there?' His voice held the steel of challenge.

Nora stepped inside the doorway before he could rise and come investigate his suspicions. 'Good evening, Stockport. You and I have unfinished business.'

'You! How did you get in?' He snapped, recognition firing his eyes with the intensity of blue coals.

Nora savoured the fleeting look of surprise that skittered across his face. He was not a man who liked surprises unless they were his. Responsibility and control were two attributes that went hand in hand.

She made herself comfortable in a large leather chair, draping her legs over the arm. 'The same way I got in last night. You're not as smart as I thought. The lock on the window was still broken.' She gave him a pointed, flirtatious look, 'I hope you don't make it that easy for other women to get into your bedroom.'

'A smart thief doesn't return to the same haunt the next night,' he countered.

Nora smiled wickedly, 'I am not a *smart* thief. I'm a *brilliant* thief, and a brilliant thief knows how to do the unexpected.'

Stockport rose from the desk and she knew a flash of uncertainty as he walked to a sideboard holding a collection of decanters containing varying shades of amber liquid. A bell-pull's tassel lounged dangerously nearby. One tug would bring assistance. From her relaxed position in the chair, she would be hard pressed to gain the French doors leading into the garden. She was betting on her usually reliable instinct and Stockport's desire to keep the robbery of his home a secret that he wouldn't call for help.

'Am I supposed to be impressed with your criminal antics?' he asked coolly, his long hands deftly skimming from decanter to glass. The moment of danger passed. He wasn't going to call for help.

Nora breathed a mental sigh of relief. 'You're already impressed.'

Stockport turned from preparing his drink, dark eyebrows raised in censure at her saucy tone. 'Why ever would you think that?'

'Because now, when you could catch me, you have made no move to summon help. Is that brandy? Pour me a glass, a double measure, neat.' *That* shocked him, as she'd meant it to. He needed to be reminded the world didn't always run according to his standards.

He delivered the glass and resumed his seat behind the desk. 'You have your drink, now on to your unfinished business. I don't have all night and neither do you. I presume you have to go rob the Squire's house again.' The last was said derisively.

'You've told no one The Cat burglarised your house last night. I want to know why,' Nora demanded, her eyes fixing him with a hard stare.

Stockport smiled knowingly over his glass. 'I told no one

because you so clearly wanted me to tell everyone. It would make your *coup* complete. However, I do not cater to the whims of morally deficient thieves.'

Nora swung her legs to the floor in a show of anger. 'I do not lack morals!'

'You take what isn't yours,' he accused.

'For a purpose. From people who have more than they need,' she countered evenly.

He scoffed at that. 'You fashion yourself to be a modern-day Robin Hood. I suppose you expect me to believe you give it all to the poor?'

'I told you as much last night. I keep nothing for myself. If this was about money, I wouldn't be limiting my raids to mere candlesticks and petty cash. If you don't believe me, ask Miss Habersham about the orphanage in Manchester or the families living in the poor part of town. They'll tell you all about The Cat.'

His attention perked at the mention of Miss Habersham. 'What does the shy spinster have to do with your elaborate charade?'

'No more than any of the other ladies in the village. At times, they are unknowing conduits for The Cat's loot in the form of baskets for the poor. Especially around Christmas, the need is great. The ladies go into Manchester the third Tuesday of every month to do their good deeds.' The last was said with a touch of cynicism.

Stockport was quick to reprimand. '*They* have found an honourable way to do good deeds.'

'One day a month doesn't do anything beyond making the ladies feel superior,' Nora retorted. She'd probably said too much, but she doubted Stockport would tell anyone. He'd kept her secret so far. She rose from the chair and stalked towards the desk, turning the conversation away from herself. 'What are you working on with such devotion that it demands late hours from you?' She snatched the top sheet off the desk, narrowly escaping his futile swipe to reclaim it.

'Ah, Parliament work. The Reform Act? It's a step in the right direction, but I am sure the House of Lords will never stand for it since it weakens them considerably.'

'I am surprised you know about it.'

'I steal for a purpose,' she reminded him. 'Until the government takes care of the lower classes, someone must represent them in whatever manner they can.'

'It shouldn't be much longer if Prime Minister Grey has his way.'

'You're quite the optimist. The bill has been defeated twice in the House of Lords. I don't see anything happening to change that, no matter how many times the House of Commons passes it.'

'You are surprisingly well informed for someone who exists on the other side of the law,' Stockport commented wryly. 'Still, I can see where passing the bill complicates things for you. You'll be out of work.'

'Hardly, my lord, I've discovered there is always someone to rob, always a cause to fight for. The lists of injustices in this world are quite extensive.' She leaned over the desk until their faces were only inches apart. His lips opened a slight fraction in anticipation. The vain man thought she was going to kiss him again. She gave a mocking half-smile and moved back. 'No, I don't think I will kiss you.' She gave his form an obvious perusal. 'Although, from the state of things, I'd say you need kissing badly.'

Nora backed to the French doors, not taking her eyes from him, and clicked open the easy lock. 'Thanks for the brandy.'

'You will be caught, if not by me, then by someone else,' Stockport said.

'I doubt it.' Nora pulled out the little pouch from her waist-band, waving it in victory as she fired her parting salvo. 'I'd get the window fixed upstairs if I were you.' She bowed theatrically. 'I give you goodnight, my lord.'

Brandon stared at the spot where she'd stood. Damn! Not again. He took the stairs to his room two at a time, a lamp in one hand. She had come back for the ring! He should have known when she said she'd used the same entrance. This was the second time she'd been in his house and caught him unaware. Perhaps she was a brilliant thief after all. He certainly hadn't expected her to return and he'd hardly expected to discuss politics with her over his best brandy. Whoever she was, she had too much education to be from the dregs of society.

He lifted the lid of the casket and confirmed his fears. The ring was gone.

In its place was The Cat's cream calling card, just like the one the Squire had shown him. He turned it over and found a message scrawled on the back: *The ring shall be returned to you in exchange for three hundred pounds. I will collect the money in two weeks' time at the Squire's Christmas ball.*

Ransoming his ring was a neat trick and an audacious one, nothing less than what he'd come to expect from this particular burglar.

He had to have that ring back. However, there was no question of paying the three hundred pounds. The Cat had made a serious misjudgment if she believed him to be a man who would succumb to the unscrupulous practice of blackmail. He would not be The Cat's whipping boy. The mill and the financial security of the people who depended on him were at stake, to say nothing of his considerable pride.

It irked him immensely that he had been called away from Parliament to play catch The Cat when so much depended on his presence. The latest correspondence from John Russell and other prominent Whigs intimated how much he was needed there.

Brandon crumpled the card in his hand with vehemence and silently declared war on The Cat. Her latest antics demanded nothing less. She would learn at the Christmas fête who ran things in this part of the world, if he didn't catch her sooner. Already, the inklings of a plan were forming in his mind. He couldn't find The Cat, but he could find her trail and Eleanor Habersham seemed the most likely place to start. The Cat had mentioned her by name and Eleanor had all the signs of a woman who had something to hide.

Adrenaline still coursed through her as Nora slipped into the Grange's kitchen. That had been fun! She'd pricked Stockport's temper *and* his interest, if those parted lips were to be believed. He'd *wanted* her to kiss him.

'Where have you been?' Hattie's stern tone sapped Nora's smugness. Her post-raid elation faded at the sight of Hattie standing in the kitchen doorway, arms folded and foot tapping in irritation.

'I've been to Stockport's for the ring, just as I told you.' Nora tried a smile and jiggled the soft felt pouch containing her prize. Hattie was not fazed.

'It took much longer than anticipated,' Hattie continued her interrogation, moving to the stove to heat a kettle of water.

There'd be no escaping Hattie's questions now if the woman had her mind on tea and conversation. Nora knew the signs and humbly took a seat at the long work table. 'The Earl and I had a little chat,' Nora confessed.

Hattie slapped a plate of sugar biscuits down on the table next to Nora and sniffed. 'From the smell of it, I'd say you'd had a drink, too. Getting above yourself a bit, aren't you, drinking with the likes of him?'

Nora bristled. 'What is your point, exactly? The man needed taking down a notch. You should have seen his face when I drank down his fine brandy in a single swallow.'

Hattie put down the tea things and stood back from the table, hands on wide hips. 'My point is, why did you do it? You could have gotten the ring without Stockport knowing you were there. Instead, you risked everything for a few prideful moments of confrontation. What if he'd called for help?'

'He didn't call for help. I knew I'd be safe or I wouldn't have done it.' Nora dismissed Hattie's complaint with a heavy sigh. There was no sense in confessing to the moment's trepidation she'd felt when he'd gone to pour the drinks with the bell-pull hovering inches from his hand.

'Safe? Because he let you go last night? Pardon me for saying so, but you're getting dicked in the nob if you think you're ever safe with a man like him. Those men think they own the world and everyone in it.'

Hattie poured herself another cup of tea and turned her thoughts in a different direction, apparently done with scolding. 'We have to be more cautious than ever. Our goal is in reach. The Cat is succeeding. While I was doing the shopping today, I heard that more of the investors are on the brink of pulling out. They're worried about the security of the mill. They fear that if The Cat can get to them so easily, The Cat will get to the mill and sabotage its construction. They aren't willing to risk their money further.'

'Or their reputations,' Nora said wryly over the rim of her teacup. 'Are Cecil Witherspoon and Magnus St John getting edgy finally? They have the most to lose as long as I am free.'

That comment earned her a reprimand from Hattie. The woman shook her finger. 'You know I don't hold with blackmail. I've never liked the idea of you taking those documents out of Witherspoon's safe.'

'It's not blackmail. It's insurance,' Nora protested. 'Those documents prove the mill is unsafe and the contractors are deliberately cutting costs by using substandard products.' Nora smiled, remembering the thrill of the night she'd broken into Witherspoon's study and cracked his safe.

A reliable source from town had sent word he'd overheard a rumour about something murky on the mill's contract. He'd been right. From there, it wasn't a large leap of logic to see that Witherspoon had an insurance scam on his mind. He'd build the mill with substandard materials and after a year or two have the building succumb to an 'accidental' fire. He and the other investors would be waiting to claim the insurance money. The scheme would never come to pass if Nora could prevent it.

'I wish I could have seen his face the next morning, don't you, Hattie?'

'No, I don't,' Hattie said briskly, gathering up the tea things. 'He was furious then and he's still furious. You've made an enemy of a very dangerous man. The Cat might be succeeding, but the risk is going up. It's not just the investors who are angry now. Some of our own wealthier residents are disappointed too, like the Squire. The news is that they mean to redouble their efforts to catch The Cat. They're convinced as soon as The Cat is caught, the additional investors will come.

'It might be for the best that no one knows you raided Stockport's. It would put them over the edge. I fear we're out of our depth here. We've never gone up against a man like Stockport before. He's not one to be trifled with,' Hattie fretted.

Nora covered Hattie's hand with her own, hearing the unspoken plea in the woman's scolding. 'I won't get caught. You and Alfred taught me to be a good thief. Eleanor Habersham has to go into Manchester tomorrow to conduct business. I'll take a look at the situation first hand, if it will make you feel better. Alice Bradley and her daughters are going into the city tomorrow too for shopping and they've offered Eleanor a ride. Alfred can take a note up to Wildflowers in the morning to say I'll join them.'

Hattie looked at her with concerned eyes and Nora braced herself. 'These days I wonder if I should have taught you to be something else. Maybe then you'd be settled with a home, children and a husband. You're only six and twenty. It's not too late for you to have a real life, Nora.'

'It is too late. This is my real life. I made that choice a long time ago, Hattie. Besides, if you recall, I tried marriage once and found it sorely lacking. I discovered men are highly exaggerated commodities, both in and out of bed.' Even as she said it, her thoughts wondered back to Stockport, his ardent kiss, his firm body and the stack of papers on his desk. Perhaps there was an exception to be had. She had to be careful not to overrate him. One good act and a handsome face did not dismiss the reason he was here. She had made that mistake with her brief marriage to the handsome but incurably lazy Reggie Portman when she was seventeen. Well, she wasn't that impressionable any more thanks to the two years of disappointments that had followed.

Nora said goodnight to her long-time comrade and made her way to bed, her mind plagued with the new information she'd discovered that evening. She wished she knew more about Stockport's motivations for siding with the Reform Act.

It seemed an odd position for a man of his rank to take. If successful, the Reform Act would redistribute the seats in the House of Commons and lower electoral qualifications, making it possible for much of the middle class to vote. The House of Lords would be weakened considerably. She had yet to meet a peer who would willingly give away legal power. Yet tonight, it seemed she had.

She couldn't help concluding The Cat wasn't the only one who wore a mask. Stockport was becoming a conundrum and riddles intrigued her. The reputed Cock of the North was more than a well-dressed womaniser. This evening, he'd shown himself to be a politician, who had unusual convictions for a man of his rank and experience.

The Cat had pierced his outer shield with her kiss. Stripping away the rest of his urbane façade and revealing the man beneath was a scintillating concept to fall asleep on, leaving Nora with jumbled dreams of a hard-chested man rousing to her touch wearing little else but tight-fitted trousers and a mask that kept eluding her when she reached to untie it.

Chapter Four

Eleanor Habersham stepped down from Squire Bradley's covered carriage in front of the Blue Boar Inn and thanked Alice Bradley and her daughters for the ride, waving aside Alice's suggestion that she conduct her business in their company.

Several times during the short trip into Manchester, Alice had invited her to join them for the day. Her daughters had echoed their mother's sentiment. Nora had refused all requests politely on the grounds that she didn't wish to hamper their fun and that there was nothing unacceptable about a respectable, middle-class spinster conducting errands on her own.

She did, however, promise to meet them at the inn for tea later that afternoon and to join them on the return to Stockport-on-the-Medlock. Nora had no intention of looking a gift horse in the mouth. In the cold winter weather, it would be the height of foolishness to make the five-mile trip home on foot and carrying her purchases to boot.

Nora pulled her winter cloak close about her. It was a solid, although inexpensive, affair, made of wool and lined with rabbit instead of the other more luxurious furs worn by the Squire's wife and his daughters. But it was what she could afford without taking funds away from the truly poor who couldn't lay claim to even the middling garments she wore.

She pulled her hood over Eleanor's dun-coloured wig and clutched her reticule and shopping basket close, glad to be off on her rounds. The winter had been especially cruel so far and many people would be happy to receive the relief The Cat offered through the conduit of Eleanor Habersham.

The Cat could not afford the risk of making deliveries in person often for fear of increasing her chance of exposure. If she was too liberal in flaunting her identity, it wouldn't be long before someone turned her over to authorities.

Early on, she had taken great pains to set up her network by identifying reliable and trustworthy merchants who would convey The Cat's offerings to those in need. They'd learned to recognise Eleanor Habersham as The Cat's messenger.

Nora hadn't gone far when the strange sensation of being watched caused her to pause and reassess her surroundings, which until that point had been filled only with other people going about their daily business at the shops. Someone was not what they seemed.

Cautiously, so as not to give away her awareness of being followed, Nora glanced around, quartering the area with her gaze. A woman with her young children entered the green-grocer's. A street-sweep cried out his business on the corner. A hackney waited for his next fare. Then she saw him. It was no more than a glimpse before he fell back into the crowd of people moving through the streets, but it was unmistakably him. Stockport was following her.

Nora cautioned herself not to jump to conclusions. He was a busy man. He might very well have his own reasons to be in Manchester. It was, after all, a thriving city and Stockport was a man interested in enterprise and industry. She had no proof yet that he was here simply to follow Eleanor Habersham, a spinster of meagre means, on her errands. He had given no indication of having seen her beyond her intuition sensing his presence.

Yet, his presence sounded an alarm. Nora looked up and down the street. While it was possible that he would be in Manchester for his own purposes, it seemed unlikely that a man of his calibre would be on this particular street, which was devoted to grocers and food shops of various sorts. An Earl didn't procure his own foodstuffs. This was a section of town frequented by the servants of the wealthy and those who couldn't afford servants of their own.

There was only one way to find out if his being in town was coincidence or something more. Nora smiled to herself. Forewarned was forearmed. She would put him to the test and still get most of her duties accomplished right under his nose.

Nora deliberately walked down the street, giving him a chance to spot her if that was his intention, and entered her first stop, the bakery.

'Good day, Mr Harlow. I've come to get some of your excellent sticky buns. Hattie would have my head if I returned home without them.' Nora exchanged pleasantries with Mr Harlow and wandered to the front window while he wrapped up her order. Her initial concern had been warranted. Stockport was occupying himself with a newspaper vendor across the street while keeping the bakery in perfect view.

If he was waiting for her to exit the warm shop, he was going to get extremely cold. There was nothing worse than standing still in the cold unless it was knowing the person you waited for was keeping warm inside. Confident in her strategy, Nora launched into an animated discussion with

Mr Harlow regarding the merits of white bread crumbs versus brown in Manchester pudding.

Good God, what could she possibly be talking about that would take so long and demand so much gesticulation? Brandon stamped his booted feet in a feeble attempt to generate some warmth and movement in his legs. Despite his caped greatcoat, muffler, gloves and fur beaver, he was not impervious to the cold.

He fought the urge to check his pocket watch one more time. He had already made the mistake of dragging it out of his waistcoat pocket once. Getting the timepiece out required removing his shearling-lined gloves and parting his greatcoat to reach inside. The newspaper tucked beneath his arm was warmer than he was. Short of going into the bakery and declaring his presence to the spinster, he had no choice but to wait, since the alternative would be to abandon his plan altogether.

Admittedly, the plan was hastily concocted. He had ridden over to Squire Bradley's to discuss some brief district business regarding the assizes and learned Eleanor Habersham was riding into Manchester with Alice Bradley. The opportunity was too good to pass up after his 'visit' with The Cat the prior evening. What better way to determine if there was a link between Eleanor and The Cat than to follow Eleanor about town? It had seemed a plausible idea at the time. Now, he had his doubts. If he had to wait any longer, he'd have frostbite to add to his growing list of regrets.

He did not usually tolerate being relegated to a watch-and-wait role. There was no reason he was tolerating it now. Brandon decided he'd had enough. If he was going to have regrets over the Spinster Habersham, they would be of his making and not hers.

Miss Habersham tucked a package into her shopping basket and reached in her reticule. Brandon came alert, straightening his posture from the slouch he'd adopted against a lamp post. At last! He watched eagerly as Miss Habersham handed over payment for whatever she had purchased. It was his cue to move in.

'Miss Habersham? Is that you? I thought it might be.' Brandon strode forward, touching his hand respectfully to the brim of his hat. 'It's a cold day to be out. Let me take those packages for you.' He didn't wait for an answer, which would have assuredly been 'no', and relieved her of the cumbersome shopping basket.

'Lord Stockport, what a surprise,' Miss Habersham responded, making a brilliant recovery from the initial look of surprise that had washed over her face. That look bore speculating on, though, Stockport thought.

She'd been surprised, but not in the way someone is startled out of the blue. It was almost as if she'd known he was there. Her look upon his approach bordered on perplexed and annoyed. She had not expected him to announce his presence and she was annoyed that he had. Brandon mused that, if she had known such a welcome would increase his desire to stick close to her, she might have schooled her features better.

'What brings you to town, my lord?' she asked in her nasal-pitched voice.

Brandon waved his gloved hand dismissively. 'Some business that I quickly wrapped up. It was nothing all that important, just something that needed doing. And you? Do you have other stops to make?' He peered into the basket, filled only with the wrapped buns, trapping her into completing the errands he believed still remained. She'd only just arrived in town and one did not travel five miles simply to visit the bakery. In essence, he knew what he was doing. He was coercing her into the spending the day with him.

Gamely, Miss Habersham took the bait. 'Why, yes, I do, Lord Stockport. It would be absolutely wonderful if you could accompany me.'

Ah, the victory was too easily won, but Brandon took it anyway. Since he'd met The Cat, his victories had been more like draws, something he wasn't used to. However, as expected, the easy victory was not without price. Brandon was hard pressed to distinguish whether Eleanor Habersham was being herself with her excessive chatter and tittering or deliberately trying to run him off.

The second stop was the butcher's, where Brandon was exposed to Eleanor's protracted conversation with the butcher on the virtues of redcurrant jelly sauce as an accompaniment to an amazing array of game dishes. Brandon hadn't thought there was that much to say about the subject. She tittered as she confessed to using a naughty dash of cognac brandy to sweeten the sauce. Brandon immediately felt guilty over his pique. Regardless of the woman's potential connection to The Cat, the poor woman had little to look forward to in her drab life, supplemented as it was with the most modest of means.

For a woman of her limited income, there were no new dresses to look forward to, no excitement of taking in the entertainments offered in London or other large cities, no luxury of permitting oneself a splurge here or there. Every penny in her possession was likely budgeted with the strictest of care. If discussing currant sauce gave her day meaning, broke the mundane routine of her life, he could tolerate it. After all, he had invited himself on her errands.

Still, Brandon was glad enough to move on once she finally reached in to her reticule and paid the butcher for the beef.

His relief was short-lived. The roast she dropped into the basket he carried weighed down his arm considerably.

'That's not too heavy for you, is it?' Miss Habersham inquired innocuously, her eyes wide behind the thick lenses of her glasses.

Brandon smiled easily, assuring her with a lie that the basket wasn't too heavy. Whatever charity he had felt for her a few moments ago vanished. The woman must have bought the largest roast in Manchester. He was utterly persuaded by her overly innocent inquiry that she'd done it on purpose too. Eleanor was playing a secret game with him. Very well, he would play one with her. Spinster or not, all bets were off.

Brandon redoubled his charm. He bought her a bag of roasted chestnuts from a street vendor and plied her with stories of London. As if in retaliation for his kindness, she stopped at the poulterer's and added a chicken to the basket.

The afternoon turned into a polite, unspoken tug of war. The more she bought, the more he smiled when she piled the purchases into the full basket. The more inane her chatter became, the more he flirted shamelessly, subtly letting her know that it would take more than insipid conversation and a heavy basket to drive him off.

She made two more stops, paying in cash at each one and tucking her wrapped purchase into the basket. Brandon was cold, his arm aching, when they turned down the avenue heading towards High Street and the clothes shops. Brandon breathed a sigh of relief. At least that section of town had arcades and he'd be a shade warmer.

She chose a large haberdashery and Brandon thanked the fates. The shop was warm and roomy. The long counter at the back looked to be a likely place for him to put down the basket for a bit.

'Feel free to browse, my lord,' Eleanor said. 'I have some private things to take care of.' She blocked the way to the counter, making it clear that he was not to follow her.

'Of course, Miss Habersham, take your time. Let me know when you're done.' Brandon said in his best gentleman's tones. Although disappointed at being denied a resting spot for the onerous basket, Brandon was jubilant. He had been waiting for this all day. He was certain if Eleanor was going to make her move, it would be now. This was the only time all day they'd been in a shop large enough to lose oneself in and the only time she'd been eager to be out of his company.

He selected an aisle and feigned interest in some plain muslin. Out of the corner of his eye, he noted Eleanor making straight for the counter as he suspected. She said something to the bespectacled clerk behind the counter, sending him scuttling off and bringing back another employee, a woman, a few moments later.

Gleeful triumph filled Brandon. His day was not spent in vain. Asking for a particular clerk must signify something of import. Brandon edged his way closer to the counter, putting himself in earshot of Eleanor's conversation.

Come a little closer said the spider to the fly. The old children's rhyme paraded through her mind as Nora eyed her prey from her position at the counter. Stockport had walked right into the web she had spun. This little outing had been inordinately entertaining and enlightening in its own way. She'd been surprised Stockport had stuck with Eleanor Habersham so diligently. It wasn't any man who could tolerate her insipid prattle and titters all day long.

It was quite a testament to Stockport's fortitude and something of a warning to herself as well in regards to the type of man she was dealing with. Had he stuck with Eleanor because he was a gentleman and, once pledged to a lady's company, could not simply cry off? Nora couldn't quite believe he'd endure the entire day at her side all for the sake of honour.

It was more likely he'd stuck by her side because he suspected something. Perhaps he was following up on The Cat's reference to Eleanor that night in the study. Perhaps he was trying to earn his way into Eleanor's good graces after her not-so-covert rebuffing of him at the ladies' tea. She would soon find out.

If he was simply playing the unsuspecting gentleman doing a good deed for the local spinster, she would be able to give him the slip here. If not, the stakes in the escalating game they'd played this afternoon would be raised. The gambler in her almost wished for the latter. All the politics aside, matching wits with Stockport was proving to be far more enjoyable than she'd imagined.

Raising her voice slightly to ensure Stockport could hear, but not so loud as to be obvious, Nora said in her annoying Eleanor Habersham voice, 'Jane, I would like to look at some flannel for, er, um…' she paused to intone just the right amount of embarrassment in her request when in truth only Stockport would be embarrassed, as any rightful gentleman would be '…winter undergarments. I find my petticoats won't last another season.' She gave an old maid's giggle.

'Would you like me to bring out our flannel bolts?' the clerk asked.

Nora's hand flew to her throat in shock. 'Oh, no, I couldn't possibly look at such goods in public.'

'Of course not, Miss Habersham, come to the back with me. Kenneth can watch the counter.'

Smugly, Nora walked behind the efficient clerk to the storeroom. No gentleman would dare consider following after overhearing such an exchange. There would be no plausible explanation to offer if he was found out and there would be no way Stockport could live the episode down if Eleanor Habersham caught him. It would only take Eleanor telling a tearful story to Alice Bradley on the way home and the news would be all over the village by the next day.

Nora shut the stockroom door behind her and turned to Jane. 'We must act quickly.'

'Why? Is something wrong? Usually you don't ask to come to the back room.'

'I'm being followed by Stockport himself.'

Jane sucked in a worried breath. Nora dismissed her concern. 'I'm not in danger, not yet anyway, but I need to make the delivery to Mary Malone. She needs the food desperately. I couldn't get to the apothecary's today, but I have money in small coins.'

'Her oldest boy works at the William Plant hat factory. I'll go myself, right away before it gets dark,' Jane said resolutely, although Nora knew Jane hated venturing into the Anacoats neighborhood.

'No, I wouldn't ask you to do that. I know how you detest it. I'll go. I just need you to cover for me while I slip out the back door. It will serve Stockport right for dogging my steps all day.'

'What will I tell him?' Jane looked more concerned over facing Stockport than venturing into Anacoats.

'Tell him I wasn't feeling well and had to leave immediately. Thank you, Jane.'

Nora flipped up her hood and slipped out into the alley behind the shop. She headed for the street and rounded the corner, only to run straight into the brick-hard form of the Earl of Stockport.

'My dear Miss Habersham, it seems you've left without

your purchases.' He dangled the heavy basket with one hand, which must have qualified as a feat of superhuman strength given all that was in it. He made it look easy.

Nora righted herself, breathing slowly to regain the breath she'd lost in the impact. What did the dratted man know? He stood there, all gentlemanly assistance with her over-heavy basket, acting as if nothing was amiss. It was more than bold to stand there and pretend that the woman who'd dragged him all over Manchester hadn't just been caught trying to dupe him.

Nora studied the basket, searching for a retort that would cover these awkward circumstances. Nothing came. She'd not ever been caught so blatantly red-handed before. Her eyes fell on two packages in the basket she didn't recalled purchasing. Perhaps they would provide a distraction.

'Ah, those,' he said before she could ask. 'Since you were in such a hurry, I took the liberty of having the clerk wrap up some materials for your winter undergarments. I wasn't sure what you had decided on, so I made some decisions of my own. I had the clerk measure out a length of the white satin,' he stated amiably as if he assisted spinsters with their intimate apparel on a regular basis.

'Satin?' Nora gulped. Stockport had picked out satin for Miss Habersham?

'Absolutely. I have it on good authority from my lady friends that there is nothing like the feel of satin against one's bare skin.' He gave a roguish wink.

Nora wanted to slap him. The bastard had no call to treat poor Miss Habersham to such a revealing discussion. Unfortunately, Miss Habersham would never slap an earl. She would merely blush and be embarrassed. That was proving easy enough to manage. All the embarrassment she'd anticipated for Stockport was now hers.

Still, there was work yet to be done. Never mind that the stop at the haberdashery had backfired miserably. Mary Malone didn't have the money for her medicines. Nora could not leave Manchester without seeing to that last chore.

'My lord, you are too kind. I confess I am feeling better now. Perhaps the fresh air has helped,' she improvised quickly.

'And the quick walk too, no doubt,' Stockport commented wryly.

Nora chose to ignore the veiled jibe. She had to get back inside and leave the money with Jane. Jane would see that Mary got the funds. 'In any case, I am feeling better and I would like to return inside for just a moment.'

'Certainly, whatever you would like, Miss Habersham. I am completely at your disposal.'

'Ohhhh, you're such an agreeable man.' She gave a giddy laugh. 'Wait for me outside, I'll just be a moment.'

'Would you prefer me to wait at the back door or the front?'

'The front would be fine, my lord.' It was all Nora could do not to slap the insufferable man. He had caught her and they both knew it, although he didn't really know what he had caught her at. It was small consolation.

What had he caught her at? Brandon wondered, waiting for her return from the shop. She had meant to give him the slip, but to what purpose? Was she merely trying to win the little game being played between them or was she attempting to keep an assignation on The Cat's behalf? He'd gone around back to wait for her because he'd been trying to win. When she'd disappeared, he had felt certain she was up to no good.

In hindsight, he wished he'd let the scene play out a bit longer. He could have followed her and known with surety where Miss Habersham was going and what her connection to The Cat was. It wasn't like him to exchange short-term successes for long-term goals. But the look on her face when she'd collided with him had been worth it. Even more priceless was the abject horror on her face when he mentioned the satin. It wasn't nice to tease spinsters. But this one hadn't played fair all day and he had the sore arm to prove it.

True to her word, Miss Habersham reappeared out the front door of the shop after only five minutes. Her hands were empty, for which Brandon was both thankful and suspicious. He'd half-expected Miss Habersham to buy a whole bolt of flannel just to spite him. Since she hadn't, Brandon could only conclude that whatever business she'd needed to conduct had been done quietly and had most likely been for The Cat.

Miss Habersham took a moment to look at the watch pinned to her dress beneath her cloak. 'Oh, my, it's four-thirty already! My, how the day flies. I promised Alice Bradley and the girls I'd join them for tea before we set off back home. I thank you for your help today, my lord. It's been a rare treat. I can't wait until I write to my friends and tell them all about my day with an Earl!' Miss Habersham enthused. 'Good day, my lord.'

Did she think he could be dismissed that easily after all they'd been through today? 'I'll walk with you. Where are you meeting them?'

'The Blue Boar,' Eleanor said. 'But you needn't bother. I am sure you'd enjoy something more fortifying like a hot toddy at a gentleman's club.'

'Oh, tea would be just the thing on such a cold day. Thank you for the invitation, Miss Habersham.' Brandon jumped on the opening with alacrity. She could not protest now without looking like she was retracting an invitation. He wanted to crow with victory. The fleeting look on her face was enough to know he was the last person she wanted to have tea with.

His victory was far too brief. He'd been prepared for an hour of Alice Bradley showing off her daughters' wifely talents. He had not been prepared for Miss Habersham's latest gambit.

'Girls, the Earl has been regaling me with all kinds of tales about London during our shopping today. Perhaps he can share with you the latest fashions.' She fixed him with a knowing stare that said she knew exactly what she'd unleashed.

Brandon wanted to strangle her. For the next hour he was peppered with questions: Did he prefer hats with ribbons or feathers for trimmings? What were all the ladies in London wearing for the Little Season?

Finally it looked as if the girls were satisfied. His torture was nearly over when Miss Habersham gushed insipidly, 'Oh, my lord, you haven't told them about the satin yet.'

Brandon shot her a quelling look. At what point had he lost control? For a spinster of limited experiences, Miss Habersham had quite a large amount of the devil in her.

Stockport Hall had never looked so welcoming. By the time he returned, Brandon was more than willing to put himself in the very capable hands of Cedrickson and his valet, Harper. They knew exactly what he needed—a hot drink and a hotter bath to thaw him out.

Brandon gratefully sank into the steamy retreat of his large copper tub and gave himself over to the luxury of being warm. He let his mind wander over the events of the day while he soaked, eyes shut. Sometimes he thought better when his musings didn't take a particular direction, but were free to wander along their own paths.

There was something that niggled him about each of Miss Habersham's interactions. He had it! Brandon's eyes popped open and he sat upright, sloshing water on the floor. Money. He'd spent a considerable amount of time thinking about Miss Habersham's financial situation, how carefully budgeted her funds were. Yet she was shopping in Manchester for items that could easily be obtained at stores in Stockport-on-the Medlock.

Going into the larger city for fashionable clothing or rare food items was understandable, but those were not the items Miss Habersham had spent her day shopping for. Brandon focused his thoughts with a probing question. Why would someone with few funds make the effort to travel to a large city and pay more for items that could be bought at local shops?

Brandon squeezed his eyes shut and sank back down into the water, now actively replaying each visit to the shops. What had she done at each stop? Was there a single habit she had repeated each time? Each visit did follow the same pattern: she'd give the shopkeeper her list, she'd carry on some overlong conversation and then pay for her purchases. In his mind's eye he could see her handing over her banknotes for payment. Nothing unusual there. Wait.

He slowly opened his eyes as if not to lose the threads of his idea by rushing. Not once today did he see her receive any change. He saw her reach into her reticule, but never did he see a shopkeeper move to a cash box for change or go to a back room and retrieve smaller notes. It seemed highly unlikely that her purchases all came to exact amounts that she carried on her person. Assuming he was correct, what did it mean?

That answer was much easier to come up with. He had worked often enough with ledgers and finances in regards to his estate. He'd caught a dishonest steward once who had thought to pocket some of the estate's profit by recording less than the actual profit in the estate ledgers. The same principle worked in Miss Habersham's case, only in reverse.

Brandon drummed his fingers on the side of the tub. In her case, she overpaid for the goods received. It was a perfect way to conduct business for The Cat in plain sight without anyone noticing. Of course, his conclusion assumed that Eleanor Habersham was somehow linked to acting as an accomplice to The Cat.

He realised he was making some large leaps of logic here. Eleanor might not be connected to The Cat in any way. She might have other reasons for dressing as she did. It was entirely possible that she had no fashion sense, that she found her gowns pretty.

How to find out if his suppositions were correct? He couldn't ask Miss Habersham without giving away what he knew. If she was connected to The Cat, she'd alert The Cat to his suspicions, making it that much harder to catch the wily burglar.

Another wild hypothesis was starting to take shape in his mind as well. If Miss Habersham was wearing a disguise, what was she hiding? Why not simply go around as herself? People went around in disguises because they didn't want to be recognised. Was it possible that Miss Habersham was The Cat?

The idea was not without merit. Miss Habersham had arrived in the district at the same time The Cat began making appearances. Miss Habersham did indeed disguise her looks for a currently unconfirmed but still suspicious reason. The Cat knew Miss Habersham; had made specific reference to her in a conversation.

Those were good facts to start building on, but the best fact of all was Miss Habersham's wit. The interplay between them today had been similar to the repartee he'd enjoyed with The Cat on both occasions. True, The Cat sparred with him verbally while Miss Habersham sparred with him on a different, less direct, level. It made sense. It would have been out of character for a woman of Miss Habersham's background to make flagrant challenges that were so second nature to The Cat. Still, both The Cat and Miss Habersham duelled exquisitely in their own ways.

Brandon slid deeper into the fragrant water, chuckling to himself. If Miss Habersham was indeed The Cat, he was doubly glad he'd bought the satin.

Chapter Five

The merriment of the Squire's Christmas ball swirled around him in a cacophony of festive scents and noises while Brandon surveyed the ballroom in all its festooned glory. Throughout the ballroom, young couples in masks stole fun-loving kisses under strategically placed boughs of mistletoe.

Everywhere he looked, the room was alive with colour from the evergreen branches to the swags of rich claret silk draping the walls. Masked women in expensive brocades and velvets twirled past on the dance floor, partnered by elegant men in black. Overhead, the chandelier caught the spark of jewels and diamonds. Brandon already knew the refreshment tables in the other room groaned under the Squire's largesse, sporting all nature of sweetmeats and cakes and silver.

It was a night of plenty and of possibility. Everyone was masked and no one was paying attention to anything beyond their own pleasure. The Cat would be in her element. Brandon was counting on it.

Tonight, she'd promised to give back his ring. The three one-hundred-pound notes were safely nestled in the breast pocket of his evening jacket. He didn't intend to turn them over to The Cat. They were simply there to serve as bait. He planned to lure The Cat into a semi-private place under the guise of making payment and then give the pre-arranged signal to alert the four hired undercover guards who mingled undetected in masks around the room. His victory would be swift and decisive. Tonight it was his turn to surprise The Cat.

The Cat had been busy since her last visit to Stockport Hall two weeks ago. He might not have seen her, his forays to uncover where she fenced her stolen goods may have revealed nothing, but he'd heard about her.

She'd struck several times, always limiting her targets to those who had invested in the textile mill and her name was on the lips of every villager. There were tales that painted her as an angel to the poor, bringing medicine to the sick and food to the starving. To hear the citizens of Manchester's slums talk, The Cat was a veritable paragon.

Brandon had difficulty reconciling this shining example of civic welfare with the brash bandit who taunted the law with her break-ins. None the less, he was intrigued beyond good sense. The dichotomous halves of her personality posed the question, was The Cat sinner or saint?

In an attempt to unravel the riddle, Brandon found himself developing an annoying habit of rising each morning and searching out news of her escapades. He'd begun riding into the village just to overhear conversations in hopes of catching even a snippet of news concerning her latest chicanery.

He was dangerously close to becoming obsessed with her. It was frightening to think of the hold she had taken in his life after only two unorthodox meetings. He was torn between the dread of rising in the morning and hearing she'd been caught and the inexplicable relief he felt upon hearing she was safe one more day. He told himself his relief was because he wanted to be the one to catch her. Not because he needed the reward the investors were offering for her capture, but because he wanted answers.

It was a sad commentary that London's untouchable Earl could be brought to such depths by a kiss and a caress in the dark from a masked figure. Against his will, he dreamed about her, his imagination conjuring up variations on the theme of their first encounter in his bedroom. When he climbed the stairs to his chambers, he looked for her in the night-shadows of his empty mansion, inexplicably wanting her to be there.

These were not the emotionally detached behaviours he cultivated in his relationships with women. Never had he let himself go, mentally or physically, as he'd let himself go these past two weeks. No situation or woman had ever gotten to him like The Cat.

In a short while, he'd see her. His body was alert on all fronts as he scanned the room. Even if she'd been inclined to break her word to him, she would not be able to resist the lure of such a bold undertaking. Entering the Squire's house as a masked guest and making free with his unguarded hospitality was a temptation too great to resist for a thief of The Cat's calibre.

She was among the crowd, somewhere. He'd been watching for her—for midnight hair and cat-green eyes. It unnerved him to think she was in the room and he did not know it. He wanted to find her first before she found him.

Across the ballroom behind the protection of her black-feathered mask, Nora smiled with satisfaction. Stockport was looking for her. Oh, not obviously. No one would guess he was waiting for someone. His gaze gave nothing away, but his other body movements did. There was a certain tension to his posture and his long fingers beat an impatient tattoo against his thigh. It was apparent to her that he wanted to find her first. Not yet. She was having too much fun dancing, wearing a pretty ballgown and being herself for a few hours.

Well, the gown was a heavily remade cast off from a brothel and she wasn't really being herself. Tonight she posed as Adelaide Cooper, daughter of a potential investor in the new textile mill project. Everyone would assume she was here on someone else's invitation and no one would expect to see her in the future.

'Miss Cooper, may I have this dance?' a voice politely asked beside her.

It was the Squire's son, Frederick, a kind enough young man with his father's bluff country looks. Nora favoured him with a smile and accepted. The dance was a hearty polka she loved. After this she'd get to work. Frederick could even help her get started.

'Who is that man over by the pillar?' Nora asked as they spun around the floor, pretending ignorance of the masked man's identity.

'That's the Earl of Stockport, but it's a masked ball so we aren't supposed to know. Really, who could mistake him for anyone else? The local lads and I all admire his style.' Frederick supplied, quick to oblige the reportedly rich, pretty daughter of a man who would make his father even richer if the investors could ever enlist the last two people needed to complete their financing.

'Not many aristocrats would deign to dirty themselves with trade, but this man sees the possibilities, he admits to the future.' Frederick would have kept going, clearly suffering from a case of hero-worship for the Earl's wardrobe and his progressive ideas.

Nora cut him off with a coy toss of her head, uninterested

in hearing the benefits of a dirty mill extolled in her presence. It was time to confront Stockport. 'Do you think you could introduce me? I've never met an Earl.' She added a débutante's silly giggle for good measure.

Within moments the dance ended and Frederick unknowingly escorted her straight to the side of her adversary. He made the introductions and eased the way into conversation with small talk.

Nora noted Stockport was polite, but distracted. He made cursory responses, doing only the minimum required to sustain the conversation without appearing rude. Just as he had politely borne the conversational forays made by the Bradley girls during the carriage ride from Manchester, tonight he was unaffected by Adelaide's efforts. He was no more interested in young Adelaide than he'd been in the Squire's daughters.

His indifference prompted the curious question—what kind of woman would interest him? The answer was suddenly obvious. He *liked* The Cat. Her boldness appealed to him. She did not stand on ceremony and she challenged him. It was the only way to explain why he had not taken the opportunity to apprehend her on the two occasions they'd met.

Of course, being attracted to The Cat's bold sensuality was no more than a courtesan's allure. A man of his position would never seek to make such a woman his Countess.

Wife? She had to stop her wool-gathering immediately. It must be the ball that made her so fanciful. Either that or Stockport's excellent physique. Surely a girl was entitled to a little fantasy now and then as long as she understood that's all it was. If fairy tales were real, he'd be the living embodiment of the handsome prince. Frederick was still going on inanely about the fashion of men's clothes, oblivious to Stockport's neutral apathy on the subject. Nora took the chance to indulge, covertly studying Stockport.

Nora had long thought men's evening clothes were the epitome of uniformity. The black trousers and tailed dress coat left little room for individuality. Indeed, the last bastion of uniqueness lay with the waistcoat and cravat.

Stockport had done well with both ends of the dressing spectrum. His broad shoulders filled out the dark coat appreciably. The snowy fall of his elegantly tied cravat and the pristine linen of his shirt peeking from beneath the cravat's fall, reminded all lookers that only a gentleman could afford to wear immaculate linen on a regular basis. She had yet to see him in anything less.

His cravat gave way to a waistcoat of tasteful claret brocade, which was neither too garish like the peacock colours worn by the younger men present, nor too plain like the ivory or grey tones favoured by the older country gentlemen. Tasteful and smart, Nora reflected. He did not flash his town bronze overtly in these people's faces, but chose a rather subtle way to state his rank. An expensive gold chain spanned his waistcoat, boasting a single watch fob, which was also very classic and discreet, not overdone like Frederick's crowded, fussy watch chain.

His trousers fit over naturally narrow hips and waist that needed no corseting to give the impression of athleticism. Nora forced her eyes to stop there. She could not afford the distraction of contemplating what lay between his strong thighs. The memory of cupping him was still potent, even though two weeks had passed since that night in his bedroom. Two weeks only! She felt she had known Stockport longer than that.

'What do you think, Miss Cooper?' Frederick asked, breaking into her not-so-pure thoughts about Stockport. She had no idea what they were discussing specifically.

Nora raised her pretty fan and flapped it in front of her face and said in her best insipid tone, 'I try not to think too much. Mama says it's not attractive.'

Frederick bought the act. 'Right-o, that's what a pretty girl has a gentleman for.' He patted her hand, commending her comment as if it were the wittiest thing he had heard in a long while.

Nora hazarded a glance at Stockport. He was not so easily gulled. She offered a simpering smile to reinforce her vacuous image. Damn him, he had caught her looking at him. Her little performance hadn't fooled him in the least. If anything, he was more alert. He studied her hard for a moment and then moved his gaze beyond her shoulder.

Nora followed his eyes as they lit on four strategic points around the ballroom and the four men in those locations. She took their measure instantly. Ha! Stockport thought to hedge his bets and call for reinforcements. She had to admire the man for his confidence that all would go as planned. But he was dealing with The Cat.

It wasn't too late to melt back into the crowd and disappear. Although Stockport might have his suspicions aroused, she could still stage a quick getaway by faking a visit to the ladies' retiring room. But Nora didn't seriously consider the option for long. Five against one might be unfair, but it wasn't insurmountable.

With acuity, she calculated what needed to be done. First, she would confirm her presence to Stockport and then she needed to create a distraction to get them out from under the watchful eyes of Stockport's hired men.

Nora went into action, flapping her fan again. 'I am hot and need a glass of punch.' Smiling sweetly, she dispatched Frederick to the crowded refreshment room.

She turned back to Stockport, all traces of the sugar-sweet innocent gone, replaced by the self-assured poise of a temptress confident in her abilities. 'I believe you're looking for me, or rather you're looking for this.' Nora produced a small felt pouch from the beaded reticule hanging from her wrist. She didn't need to open it. They both knew what it contained. She had his attention—now for the distraction. She held out her hand. 'Dance with me, Stockport.'

Stockport cast a meaningful glance at Frederick's retreating back. 'Have you no compunction about dancing with people you rob?' he asked archly.

'If I didn't dance with people I rob, I wouldn't get to dance at all. There'd be no one left.'

Stockport tightened his jaw at her cheeky banter, causing a tic to jump in his perturbation.

Nora grimaced. 'I thought the remark was witty.'

'I am not here to trade clever repartee. I am here to conduct a business transaction.'

'Standing amidst all these people?' Nora queried, enjoying baiting him. 'Not here where everyone can see.' She nodded towards the dance floor, where couples took their places for the set of waltzes that preceded the midnight supper, and reissued her invitation to dance.

Stockport led her to the floor without further conversation and swung her into the dance, skilfully manoeuvring them about the floor.

He waltzed impeccably, which didn't surprise Nora. The man was all about flawlessness, from his perfectly combed hair to the toes of his spotless boots. However, he also waltzed with a passion that astonished her. His precision was not an empty effort.

A surreptitious ferocity lurked beneath his well-polished

surface, practically undetectable except to another kindred soul who shared the same love for dance. Nora sensed it in the turns he took a shade too quickly at the top of the ballroom and in the press of his hand against her back as he signalled his instructions.

Nora looked into the sharp blue eyes that peered out from behind his dark demi-mask. They were daring her, but what the dare was, she could not immediately place.

Stockport leaned close to her ear, his voice low and melodious. 'Can't you do better than this? I would have thought The Cat was capable of more,' he taunted.

Now she understood. He was daring her to match his passion. She smiled back. If she took his challenge, she would have the distraction she needed. 'I was just making sure you were up for it,' she countered. She leaned close to his ear, taking in his clean scent of soap and spices. 'You want to fly, I can feel it.'

Stockport laughed, drawing a few stares. 'This is dancing, not sex.'

'Is there a difference? That's why the waltz is so scandalous, isn't it?' Nora sparred wickedly.

Stockport inclined his head, eyes glinted mischievously. 'Then by all means, shall we?' Without waiting for reply, his hand on her back made a small adjustment and drew her up close to him until she could feel the flex and give of his muscled thighs against the fabric of her gown.

'You do talk scandalously,' Nora flirted for good measure, enjoying entirely too much the feel of his body as he whirled them through the turn at the bottom of the ballroom.

'I do more than talk.'

'We're attracting attention. Can you afford the gossip?'

'I'm the Earl. I'll simply say it is how we do it in London.'

His eyes left hers for a moment to stare down a passing couple with wide eyes. To emphasise his point, he increased his speed and turned her sharply, leaving her gloriously breathless.

Their bodies blended perfectly. Nora met him step for step, giving herself over to the exhilaration of the moment and the man. It had been ages since she'd danced like that and even then it had only been in a small country-town assembly hall. But never had she danced with such a master.

Stockport unleashed was a sight to behold.

It struck her there might be a third reason he'd earned his dubious moniker. The Cock of the North was an energetic Scottish reel. She could only imagine how invigorating it would be to dance it with him.

When the dance ended, she was smiling ridiculously. She could feel the grin across her face. She was suddenly aware that Stockport was smiling too—a real smile, not like the political ones he'd bandied about at the tea. This one altered his face entirely.

For an instant the adversarial nature of their relationship was suspended. He was smiling at her as if he *enjoyed* her company, as if the two of them shared some secret knowledge the rest of the world did not. Without warning, the smile was gone and he remembered where he was, who he was and who she was. The spell was broken. Others milled about them, making their way to the supper room and the unmasking.

He gripped her gloved wrist and Nora tensed. She did not want him to ask her to go into supper with him. Surely he knew how impossible the request was? Everyone would unmask. She could not afford that with Stockport, although she could probably fool the rest of the village.

She intuitively knew Stockport would know immediately that The Cat and Eleanor Habersham were one and the same.

His gaze had been too piercing the day of the tea, as if he could see in one short visit what the villagers had not ascertained in the four months she'd lived among them in her spinsterly guise. Of course, she had to give the villagers their due; enemies and friends of The Cat alike were all looking for a man. Only Stockport knew he was looking for a woman. That made him doubly dangerous.

'I am not going into supper with you,' she said with a supercilious air that brooked no contradiction. The amicable atmosphere of the dance floor was gone.

'I am not asking you to. I prefer not to eat with common thieves,' Stockport replied with equal coldness. Was it possible she'd imagined the man he'd been on the dance floor?

'Then you will starve tonight, since this room is full of them,' Nora retorted angrily, her temper rising. How dare the hypocrite refuse to acknowledge that there were other ways to steal? She only stole objects and material goods, all of which could be replaced. Others in this very room stole livelihoods. His textile mill would put him in the same category as the rest. The thought disturbed her. She didn't want him to be like the others. The realisation that she wanted him to be different was more disturbing.

Furious with herself for letting her thoughts run in such a direction, Nora abruptly shoved them to the back of her mind. She would do best to remember that dealing with Stockport was nothing more than a game, one she played well and had played often enough in the past without entertaining such notions in her head.

She gestured toward a set of doors leading out to the verandah and he acquiesced. The cold night air provided an antidote for the heat of the ballroom. The contrast provoked a shiver.

'Would you like my jacket?' Stockport offered, shrugging out of it in a perfunctory manner that suggested his offer was more reactionary from years of training than a heartfelt gesture.

'I'm a thief, remember?' Nora snapped, irrationally disappointed that the magic on the dance floor had been replaced by an iciness that matched the weather.

'And I am a gentleman,' Stockport rejoined, draping the jacket about her shoulders in spite of her resistance. He reached up to untie his mask and tuck it into a pocket. 'That's better. I can't stand these dratted things.'

Stockport moved closer, turning his head to see her better. Nora met his unnerving stare, locking her eyes to his blue-eyed scrutiny. She felt the heat building between them as it had on the dance floor, but she didn't dare back down.

Stockport whispered with husky cynicism, 'How much of your purported proceeds for the poor went to the purchase of this gown? Do you think they'd feel this was worth it while their bellies go hungry?'

'How dare you impugn my honour. I got this dress from a brothel, a prostitute's cast off that she was willing to donate. I scrounged up the trimmings too. I think it turned out quite nicely.'

'You're a regular Cinderella,' he said, unconvinced.

She changed the subject with a dismissive wave of her hand. 'Enough talk. You didn't bring me outside to discuss fashion. We have business to attend to.'

'I want my ring. You indicated you'd be prepared to deliver it to me tonight.'

'In exchange for three hundred pounds.' Nora tapped a gloved finger against her chin, playing the coquette who had her beau dangling. 'But that was two weeks ago. I've decided the conditions for the ring's return have changed.'

That got a reaction out of him. 'This is extortion! We had an agreement. You cannot simply alter the rules and expect to get away with it.'

'Why not? You did. The four men stationed around the ballroom are yours, are they not? I presume they are awaiting a signal that you planned to give when you handed over the money.'

'I may still summon them,' he said darkly.

'To do what? Watch you court Adelaide Cooper on the balcony? The Squire's son will vouch for my identity and I will drop the ring over the railing before your men can arrive. There will be neither an exchange of money nor any incriminating evidence for them to seize. That assumes, of course, that they have located you since your departure from the ballroom. For all you know, they may have gone into supper, concluding that you wished some privacy in which to woo your pretty dance partner.'

Nora watched his stoic features fight for mastery against the emotions roiling within him at her deductions. Was he disappointed this meeting had come down to nothing more than extortion? Had he hoped for a nobler conclusion? He didn't believe she actually used the funds for the poor. In his study, he'd accused her of having a Robin Hood complex. And tonight he'd implied she used the money for her own needs. Well, that much at least she could disprove.

She outlined her offer, thinking quickly. 'These are my conditions—meet me where Stockport and Hyde Roads meet tomorrow morning at ten o'clock. You will come alone and on horseback. No fancy carriages or outriders shall be with you. You shall accompany me into Manchester and make the rounds with me, after which you will return to the crossroads and go your own way. You will make no attempt to follow me or discover my identity. The following day, I will have the ring delivered to you.'

Stockport looked at her, scepticism narrowing his gaze. 'What guarantees do I have that you'll do as you say? Who's to say you won't lure me into an alley where you've prearranged to have some thugs kill me or beat me senseless? These conditions sound suspicious to me. Perhaps the ring isn't worth such a risk.'

Nora feigned nonchalance. She hadn't expected Stockport to give up without a fight. 'It is of no difference to me. I can sell the ring back to you for the price of a visit to Manchester or I can sell it for cash to someone else. Either way, I get something I want.'

'What do you get from the visit that is as profitable to you as cash?' Stockport queried suspiciously.

He was wavering, Nora noted with satisfaction. She stepped away from the railing, inching back towards the doors leading to the now-empty ballroom. 'My lord Earl, I get to take your measure—a look into your soul, and you get a look into mine if you're willing to peek. Now, I bid you goodnight. I'll expect you in the morning.' She felt the smooth brass of the door handle beneath her hand and turned it a fraction. She raised her other hand to her lips, blowing Stockport a kiss as she vanished into the ballroom.

Damn, that woman had a way of disappearing and this time she'd disappeared with his good coat in tow. He had others, but that one was his favorite. The coat! Deuce take it, the three hundred pounds were still in the breast pocket. That made three things he'd lost to The Cat tonight: his coat, his money and his ring. Arguably, by agreeing to her counter-offer, he'd lost a fourth—his sanity.

The evening had taken an unbelievable twist. He'd gone from the security of retrieving his ring to the insecurity of a dubious trip to Manchester with The Cat. By nature, he didn't like cat-and-mouse games, especially when he was the mouse, and he was definitely the mouse here. The Cat had him dangling.

To be honest, not all of him minded. Not because she'd been alluring in that gown she'd worn or because she flirted audaciously, but because she challenged him with her wit, her insights and sense of daring. He had no doubt that tomorrow would be full of such tests as well and not all of them would be hers. His would not be the only measure taken.

Chapter Six

Morning arrived stark and cold. Standing on the wood planks of the bedroom floor in her nightshift, Nora drew back the curtains to view the dreary day spreading before her.

Christmas morning ought to look different. It ought to look special. It didn't. It looked like every other morning in the long English winter. Bare trees raised dark silhouettes to the grey sky. Everywhere she looked, the earth was devoid of colour beneath the frost. The heart of winter carried with it a sense of desperation.

The empty landscape made it difficult to believe spring would come again. Nora could well understand why chieftains of old had contrived great Christmastide festivities for their people. Conceivably, they'd been as anxious as she to drive the cold winter away and create a splash of colour in otherwise colourless lives, if only for a moment.

Even the austerity of her bedroom mirrored the colourless winter. The room was ascetic and clean, fitted only with the most rudimentary of furnishings: an iron bedstead, washstand and wardrobe. By necessity, her lifestyle required an existence as bland and colourless as the landscape outside. The Cat's successes depended on remaining aloof. She had to be able to pick up and leave at a moment's notice. She couldn't do that if she formed attachments.

Her personal road through life was a lonely one. By choice, she spent her life gathering what hope there was in the world and giving it to others. She saved no hope for herself.

That was the purpose of her trip into Manchester today; to give hope to others, a break from the tedium of their lives as they struggled to survive in a world gone grey. And because she couldn't bear the thought of donning the façade of Eleanor Habersham and frittering away the day sitting in front of the Squire's fire with knitting needles, watching young people play silly parlour games.

Nora rummaged through the wardrobe, nimble fingers finding the catch that revealed the hidden chamber in back. She drew out a heavy cloak she kept for just such occasions. The Cat was well received in the slums, but she still needed to be agile and alert in case of trouble. She could not afford to be numb or sluggish from the cold.

And it would be cold. That was a guarantee. She'd told Stockport not to bring his coach. It would attract too much attention and make people suspicious. The ride to Manchester would be a frozen one carried out on the moderately sheltered bench of her closed wagon, loaded with baskets and gifts for those who had nothing.

She dressed quickly and went down to the warm kitchen for a sweet roll and hot tea. She let Hattie fuss over her and wished them Happy Christmas. They'd have their own celebration tonight when she returned. Alfred, Hattie's husband and, superficially, Eleanor's man-of-all-work, had already gone out to hitch up the wagon and load its cargo. They both walked Nora out to the yard.

Alfred volunteered to come with her and Hattie urged her to stay home altogether after feeling the bite of the wind. But Nora would not, could not, be swayed from her mission. She seated herself on the bench of her plain wagon with its wooden sideboards and clucked to the horse.

Nearing the crossroads where Hyde and Stockport Roads met on the way into Manchester, Nora paused before the last corner to tie on her mask and to lower a heavy veil over her face. Checking her veils and mask one last time, Nora turned the corner, surprised to see Stockport already waiting there. He sat atop his big bay, garbed in mufflers that covered him up to his blue eyes and a greatcoat, his gloved hands resting negligently on the reins at the horse's neck. He appeared to be at ease, feeling none of the nervousness that roiled around in Nora's own stomach.

The nerves were due to the dangerous nature of this adventure. To ask her nemesis to accompany her on such a trip was more than bold. There would be little to stop him from taking advantage of their situation and forcing her to reveal her identity. All that stood between her and exposure was his gentleman's creed. Her protection depended on it and in her intuition about his nature.

'Good morning and Happy Christmas,' Stockport called out, surprisingly cheery after the late evening. 'I thought you said no carriages.' He gestured to the closed wagon.

'I needed a way to carry my supplies and keep them protected from the weather.'

'Well, then, at least let me drive. I doubt you can see well at all through that veiling.' Stockport dismounted and tied his horse behind the wagon, oblivious to her protests. Within minutes, he'd secured the horse and climbed up beside her on the wagon seat.

Nora had not counted on such close proximity. She'd thought he would ride silently alongside the wagon. Even then, the bench had looked like it would hold two, but that was proving to be an illusion. Stockport was a large man, a fact amply demonstrated by the space he took up next to her. His thigh rubbed against her leg and his arm brushed her sleeve, conjuring up hot images of the way he'd held her on the dance floor. She could not create another inch between them. But she could make a buffer.

Nora fussed with the lap robes, tucking one around her legs and offering the other to Stockport. He ruined that plan too.

'We'll be warmer if we share them.' To demonstrate, he took the lap robe she offered and shook it out. 'There, it's plenty large enough to cover us both. Layer yours over the top and we'll each have two robes to warm us instead of one.'

What could she say? It was too cold to deny his good sense, so she found herself neatly tucked under the robes, bouncing along the Manchester road next to Stockport, his muscled thigh pressed against hers. The intimate contact didn't seem to bother him in the least, but Nora couldn't help wondering if she'd gone completely mad to put herself into the hands of the one man who could stand in her way. As long as she remembered the old adage 'keep your friends close and your enemies closer' she'd be fine. It was only when she started thinking of him as an ally, like she had last night on the dance floor, that she got herself in trouble.

The trip to Manchester was accomplished in short order and without mishap. The Hyde and Stockport Roads entered the city through the elegant suburb of Ardwick. A few people hurried along the cold residential streets paying Christmas visits to neighbours, but for the most part families were tucked up in their homes.

She had counted on that. It was the reason she'd opted to come into town on Christmas Day instead of a few days before when the streets would have been filled with last-minute shoppers. But today, in spite of Nora's precautions, no one was interested in the plain wagon and the barely visible veiled woman who sat beside the driver.

Peering into windows as they passed, Nora could see people in the midst of their celebrations, faces wreathed in smiles and dressed in fine clothes. The occasional smell of roasted goose and winter treats wafted out to the wagon. There would be none of that where she was going.

The bustling streets of Manchester were deserted. The business centre of town was locked up tight and the factories for which Manchester was becoming famous were shut down for the day. The city looked almost ghostly in its desertion, as if she and Stockport were the only two people in it.

Nora pointed out directions to Stockport and he steered the wagon away from the wide avenues of the merchant homes into the narrow, broken-cobbled streets of the poor. The smells were not so pleasant here, nor were the sounds. The cries of hungry babies reached the streets, mingled with the shouts of angry men who lashed out any way they could against life's injustices. It could have been just another day of the week for this part of town.

She stole a glance at Stockport to see how he was taking their surroundings. His firm jaw was set tightly, causing a tic to jump in his cheek. His eyes peered straight ahead and there was a rigidity to his posture that suggested he was on full alert. As well he should be in these parts, Nora thought.

To his credit, he'd had the foresight to dress in nondescript clothing. His dark riding breeches and greatcoat did nothing to deliberately attract attention, but there was no mistaking the expense of his boots and the care they'd been given.

In a world where greatcoats were a sign of status, often handed down father to son for generations before they finally wore out beyond repair, there was no hiding the fact that the man with her was a gentleman of the highest calibre.

Their first stop was the Hulme neighborhood, once a peaceful area of town, now destroyed by the influx of industry. Bordered on three sides by the Medlock, Irwell and Cornbrook Rivers, Hulme had become a prime location for factories dependent on water for operation. All placidness was gone, giving way to pathetic slums and dense overpopulation.

'Park the wagon over there.' Nora gestured to a spot next to an entrance to a tenement. 'Wait here with the wagon while I go in and let them know we're here.'

Stockport looked sceptically at the building. 'Are you sure you'll be safe alone?'

'Absolutely. These are The Cat's people.' There were those who didn't like The Cat, but they were outnumbered by those who did. It was an unspoken law of the tenements that any attempt to expose The Cat would be met with ruthless retribution.

'Ah, the queen and her loyal subjects,' Stockport remarked as if he'd found a chink in The Cat's democratic armour. She knew what he thought. He thought this was an egoboost, a thrill of power, that The Cat did this as self-promotion. He couldn't be more wrong.

'Oh, I don't rule them in any way, but I provide for them as best as possible, which is more than I can say for the other monarchs in their lives; their landlords care only for rent, their bosses care only for labour and the King himself cares naught at all about these subjects.' Nora's tone was bitter. 'These people have their own code of loyalty. Don't forget that today. You will have safe passage because you're with me and no other reason.'

'Is that a threat?' Stockport raised an elegant eyebrow.

'It's a reminder. You're in The Cat's territory now,' Nora said sharply and jumped down from the bench. 'I'll be right back.'

When all was ready, Nora returned to the wagon with a boy to watch the horses and another boy to help carry baskets. She was almost certain Stockport looked glad to see her. It served him right to be at least a little bit uncomfortable in his surroundings. However, she wasn't about to mistake uncomfortable with vulnerable. The set of his shoulders indicated he was fully prepared to defend himself if the need arose.

To his credit, Stockport swung off the bench and joined in, loading himself down with the heavier baskets. Well, she'd see how much he was truly willing to participate once they got inside.

Nora led the little group to the first floor and stopped in the dingy hallway. She gave orders regarding the delivery of the baskets and sent them off. She motioned for Stockport to follow her.

They went from door to door, delivering packages from the baskets, sometimes food, sometimes a tiny pouch of coins, sometimes oranges and wooden toys for children. At each stop the cry was the same, 'God bless The Cat', or a similar variation of the phrase.

It tore at Nora's heart. There was so much need and her baskets were empty far too quickly. It was tempting to bring in the other baskets, safely covered up in the wagon, but then there would be nothing left for the other neighbourhoods she must visit.

They didn't stop at every door and Nora wondered if Stockport would notice the doors without the discreet marker that indicated The Cat was welcome.

Not everyone was receptive to her aid and reciprocally, not everyone was deserving of her efforts. Nora had decided ages ago that there were some who her efforts could not help— drunks and ne'er-do-wells who didn't lift a finger to help their families or change their lots in life.

Climbing back up on the wagon, amid cries of gratitude and wishes for a Happy Christmas, Nora gave directions and they drove on to repeat the process. The day passed rapidly as they moved from slum to slum, stopping in Chorlton-on-Medlock, and Beswick, the neighborhoods all looking the same with their uniformly terraced workers' houses.

The last visit was Anacoats, the poorest section of all, where she stopped at Widow Mary Malone's.

Nora knocked on the door. Excited voices of children whooped and shouted on the other side, followed by a light scolding for manners and a fit of coughing. Her heart sank. Desperation seized Nora and she gathered her strength for what lay beyond the door. If she didn't think of some way to help the widow recover, the children would be orphans by spring.

'What is it?' Stockport asked quietly, coming up beside her, so near she could feel the heat of his body next to her.

'It doesn't sound like Mary Malone has got better. She took sick in November and that cough has been lingering.'

'Has she seen a doctor?'

Nora shot him an incredulous look. 'If they had that much money, she probably wouldn't need one in the first place.' She pushed open the door and entered, leaving Stockport to follow in her wake. No matter what lay ahead, the kids deserved the best Christmas she could manage for them. Originally, she'd felt very good about the entire basket she'd put aside for the Malones. But now, Nora felt like the basket was inadequate. She should have done more.

The moment she entered, children ran to her, dancing around her skirts and begging to be picked up. She picked up the smallest, a blonde-haired girl of three with huge brown eyes that gave her an irresistible doll-like appearance. 'Anna, have you been a good girl?'

The little girl nodded solemnly, sucking on a dirty thumb. She pointed at Stockport. 'Who's dat man?'

'He's my special helper today,' Nora said, setting her basket down on the one table in the room. The two older boys looked at the basket in anticipation and Nora gathered them to her. 'I've brought treats for a Christmas dinner. I'll need your help getting everything ready. I might even have a few presents.'

She assigned the boys their tasks, set aside her figure-disguising voluminous cloak and veiling and rolled up the sleeves of her dark blouse. She looked around the room for Stockport, amazed to find him deep in conversation with Mary Malone. He'd discarded his greatcoat and had rolled his own shirtsleeves up. He nodded at something Mary said and leaned over to tuck a thin blanket about her knees.

Nora put a kettle on over the fire to warm the hearty soup she'd brought and set to sweeping. Mary did the best she could, but since her illness, she'd been less able to keep the two rooms clean. All her waning energies were spent on providing food and meals for her three children. By now there had to be very little money left from her husband's death settlement.

Nora worried what Mary would do when the money ran

out. She certainly couldn't work in her condition. Her oldest son, eleven-year-old Michael, was working at the hat factory, but the two shillings and three pence he brought home weekly would barely be enough for bread, let alone rent or other living supplies.

Nora cast a quick look at Mary's younger son, Robert. He was six and old enough to work as a scavenger, one of the many children who crawled beneath the machinery at the cotton mills to gather up loose cotton. She shuddered at the thought. The little money he would make doing such a perilous job would not be worth the risk. Each year children died, crushed beneath the heavy machinery if they slipped or were too slow. At best, Robert would end up crippled or permanently stooped from the demands of the job.

Behind her mask, Nora shut her eyes briefly and whispered a prayer. She would find a way to help the Malones. She thought of the three hundred-pound notes she had discovered in Stockport's breast pocket last night when she undressed for bed. It had been tempting to keep them. It was tempting now to give them to the Malones. Three hundred pounds would be a fortune to them. She fought the temptation. The money wasn't hers to give and she had given up her right to it when she dared Stockport to come with her today in payment for the ring.

If she took the money, it would confirm all the ills Stockport thought her capable of, and for some reason that rankled. It was inexplicably important that Stockport did not find her lacking.

Nora finished housekeeping and busied herself laying the table. Little Anna came to help put on the cloth Nora had brought, knowing that Mary appreciated such touches of domesticity. Out of the corner of her eye she saw that the boys had discovered Stockport's greatcoat and Stockport let them.

He was even playing with them, using sticks of firewood for swords, looking quite boyish himself.

The sight of him romping with the children was mesmerising. Nora had difficulty tearing her gaze away. His dark hair was uncharacteristically messy and his shirt was coming out of his waistband as a result of his exertions. And Stockport was smiling! Actually smiling the way he'd smiled for the brief moment on the dance floor.

He looked her way and Nora knew she was caught. She must be more careful. Even with her mask on, she felt exposed. He whispered something to the boys and swept her a bow that made the boys laugh before turning back to them.

Nora lit a pair of candles and called everyone to dinner, satisfied that the table, with its cloth and tallow candles, looked well enough to set the day apart from the rest.

The children gathered around the table on barrels and crates serving as makeshift chairs. They looked hungrily at the feast spread before them and Nora tried to see the fare through their eyes. Hattie's hearty soup with meat and vegetables filled their bowls, while plenty more hung over the fire, drenching the musty room with its rich aroma. Freshly baked loaves of bread sat on a wood board in the centre of the table next to a small crock of butter. The luxury of milk filled their cups.

Stockport escorted Mary to the table and Nora noted how much the young widow leaned on his arm for support. Mary sat and looked around at the expectant faces.

'Who shall ask the Christmas blessing?' she asked.

'Brandon!' the boys chorused, pointing to Stockport.

Stockport was surprised, but accepted and competently performed the duties. Everyone closed their eyes while Stockport blessed the food and spoke a few words about the sacred day.

Nora stole a look at him while the others had their heads

dutifully bent. She should have kept her eyes safely downcast. The moment she gave into the little temptation she knew she was lost. In the candlelight, he looked angelic—like an archangel she'd seen painted in the cathedral in Manchester, a unique mixture of power, strength and justness with his sooty lashes swept over his sapphire eyes and his broad shoulders obvious through the white cotton of his shirt.

He was handsome and he did not disappoint. Today, he'd been all she had anticipated when she'd asked him to accompany her. It would be easier to dislike him if she'd been wrong about him, if he had stayed glued to the seat of her wagon, if he hadn't carried baskets with her, if he had simply refused to come at all. In all honesty, he'd been better than good. It was more than she'd hoped for.

'Amen,' Stockport said solemnly. All heads came up. The children began to eat and exclaim about the food all at once.

Stockport kindly chided them. 'Eat slowly or it will come back up again.' Then he launched into a tale from his boyhood about a time when he'd eaten too many apples, making the boys laugh with his gestures and little Anna grin at him with her eyes wide.

He would make a wonderful father. Nora mentally recoiled from the thought it. She was getting positively henwitted if Christmas brought out such a reaction in her. This was the second time she'd had uncomfortably sentimental thoughts regarding Stockport.

He looked down the table at her and winked, bringing her into the new story he was telling. Nora gave herself up to her fantasy, rationalising that it would be her little gift to herself. For the duration of the meal, she pretended she had the right to call him Brandon; that he could call her Nora; she didn't have to eat dinner with him behind a mask; that they had a supper table filled with children around it who he would make laugh with his tales over the evening meal; two happy people living a simple life in a simple cottage somewhere, with happy children. It had been her ultimate fantasy since she was very young, part of a life she'd once had, but then lost. She took a deep breath and pushed down the memories that thought threatened to dredge up. She couldn't risk the pain. It made her vulnerable, something she could not afford with the Earl of Stockport hovering so near.

When the meal was over, her daydream was too, firmly locked into its place in the depths of her heart. It was too dangerous to let such a powerful dream linger too long.

After dinner, Stockport roped the children into helping him do the dishes and storing the remaining food, leaving Nora a chance to speak with Mary alone.

'You've done too much. I can't imagine how you managed all this and I know you've brought baskets for so many others,' Mary said when they were seated near the fire.

'I've done very little.'

'Everyone will be grateful.' Mary coughed into a worn handkerchief.

'How are you, Mary?' Nora asked cautiously.

'It is taking me a long time to get over this,' Mary confessed.

'Should I send a doctor?' Nora didn't know how she'd manage that. She had spent all the money from her robberies on the baskets and rent was due on The Grange. Even if she could find the money, she didn't know how she'd find a doctor who would be willing to come to such a neighbourhood.

'This is nothing sunlight and country air can't cure.' Mary waved a dismissive hand that looked skeletally thin in the firelight.

Along with hot food, clean living conditions and freedom from worry over an insecure future, Nora mentally added. Out loud she said, 'I'll send more food over later this week. The soup and bread should last a few days.'

'I wish I could say we won't take your charity, but I have nowhere else to turn and I am grateful,' Mary said sadly. Mary nodded to Stockport as he sat jiggling Anna on his knee and telling the children a story. 'Is this man your beau? Does he know who you are? He's lovely to look at and there's something in the air between the two of you.' The thought of love added a soft spark to Mary's eyes.

Nora shook her head. 'He's not my beau. I thought there might be something in it for us if he came today.' She was saved from saying more when Stockport's story came to an end and the boys clamoured for presents.

Nora rose and clapped her hands for attention. 'Gather round over here and Brandon will bring the basket. There might be some presents in there.' *Brandon*. The boys had called him by his Christian name and it slipped as easily off her tongue as it had theirs. Perhaps her daydream wasn't as tightly locked away as she thought. Most likely, it was due to the shirtsleeves' intimacy of the afternoon.

Brandon placed the basket in front of her and Nora distributed the gifts. There were oranges for the children along with a wooden toy for each of them. For Mary there was a small leather pouch that jingled with coins. Her eyes glistened with tears.

Too soon it was time to leave, but Nora had one more stop to make. Bravely, she hugged the children and made promises to Mary to send more food, wondering all the while how she'd manage it.

Chapter Seven

Stockport watched The Cat make her farewells, the children clinging to her and to him. Anna had him about the legs. He'd had a surprisingly good time with the children. He'd been moved by their delight over the simple fare and gifts. But those had been smaller revelations compared to what he'd learned about The Cat.

His sharp-tongued thief was the very soul of compassion, reaching out with all she had at her disposal. He felt something of a cad to have so verbally doubted her motives. Guilt gnawed at him. He couldn't help but compare the extravagant and wasteful largesse of the Squire's ball to the simple surroundings he found himself in today.

The Cat, a common thief, had provided for these people. What had he provided? He had far more at his command and what had he done?

The Cat intrigued him more than ever. He wanted to know who she was. The secret of her identity was creating a feverish mystery he was desperate to solve. But he was no closer to that answer than he'd been last night. She hadn't trusted him enough to remove her mask all day, although the veiling had come off briefly at Mary Malone's. *As well she might*, his conscience reminded him sharply. *What would you do if you knew who she was?*

It was a valid question, one for which Brandon did not have a ready answer. He should place her under arrest. That had been his plan less than twenty-four hours ago at the Christmas ball. Had his plan succeeded last night, these people would have been denied the happiness she brought today. He thought of the Malone boys delighting in the simple wood toys and Mary Malone's gratitude for the hot meal. In one fell stroke, he would have taken all that away from them.

It was a sober reckoning to grapple with. When had the villain become the hero? Somewhere between playing swords with the boys and watching The Cat stir Christmas soup over a fire, his priorities had begun to shift. He was no longer as interested in exposing The Cat as he was in protecting her.

Brandon turned to the remarkable woman beside him when Mary Malone's door finally closed behind them. 'You've given them something special today; something to take into the morning.' To his disappointment, her veils were back in place.

'We've given them a moment. That is as far as our meagre influence can reach.' The self-deprecation in her voice stunned Brandon. She believed her efforts were minimal at best.

He offered reassurance. 'Yet you went and offered that moment anyway. It is more than most people would have done.'

She said nothing and Brandon let the conversation die. Outside, enough rays of daylight were left to see them out of the tenements and back to the wide avenues of affluent Manchester, but the trip home would be conducted in the dark. Not that Brandon was worried. On Christmas night the short road between Manchester and Stockport-on-the-Medlock would be devoid of highwaymen.

They didn't speak until they reached the wagon and paid the boys who had gathered in shifts to watch the horse. Brandon spoke first in a low, tight voice. 'Why did you bring me today?'

'You want to build a mill in bucolic little Stockport-on-the-Medlock. Are you prepared for all this as well?' The Cat made a sweeping gesture to indicate the slums they drove through. 'You see how fleeting my efforts are. Mary has her older children and they can barely scrape together enough to pay the rent and buy food.'

Brandon felt duly chastised. He knew children worked in factories. Many mill owners had no scruples when it came to labour. He'd read the reports that came across his desk. Children could be paid less. Before today, he'd never come to face to face with the reality behind the papers. He had seen much of the world, but not that world.

'The mill in Stockport-on-the-Medlock won't employ children,' Brandon blurted out.

The Cat cocked her head in his direction. 'We'll see how long those noble principles last when your investors learn of the profit they could pocket if they were to use child labour. Adults must be paid ten times more than a child's salary.'

He expected the news to please her. He'd intended his statement to be an olive branch of sorts to The Cat, something that bridged the differences between them. He'd wanted to prove they weren't as dissimilar as she thought.

His temper rose. 'Nothing is ever enough with you, is it?'

'That's because there is never enough of anything!' she snapped in quick reply. 'There isn't enough money for Christmas baskets for everyone who needs them. There isn't enough money to send a doctor to Mary Malone. There isn't enough compassion in the world to help those who really need it. There are five-hundred-and-sixty cotton mills in the Lancashire area. One factory not employing children isn't enough to change anything.'

'It's a start,' Brandon barked, rising to the fight.

She huffed, 'And in the meanwhile?'

'It's the best I can do.' Brandon muttered something inaudible and turned on to the wide streets of the affluent neighbourhoods. The Cat had elected to return that way, knowing the streets would be empty and everyone still at home.

He changed the topic, hoping for better. Didn't the woman understand he was only one man? 'You said last night that you intended to take my measure today. Did I measure up?'

The Cat was silent, seeming to weigh her answer. 'I will say that, for the most part, you did not disappoint.'

'Where was I lacking?' His chagrin was petty, but he thought he'd done very well considering the circumstances.

'You did very well for one day. What will you do for the next three hundred and sixty-four?' she answered coolly.

The last vestiges of Brandon's restraint vanished in the face of her charge. 'We can't all be like you and burglarise homes for our livelihoods.'

They were cruel words and he regretted them instantly. He spoke them in anger but it wasn't anger, directed at The Cat alone. Her words shamed him. It was difficult to admit to one's hypocrisy. The Cat risked her very life for those less fortunate. Certainly, he advocated worker's legislation in Parliament, but compared to The Cat, he did painfully little in his daily life to act as a true champion of the cause. That was about to change.

Brandon yanked on the reins and pulled the wagon over to

the side of the deserted street. The sounds of music and singing filtered out of the houses in fits and starts.

'Wait here.' Brandon leaped down from the wagon, the flaps of his greatcoat flying behind him. He strode up to the largest house on the street and knocked.

Fifteen minutes later, Brandon returned and settled on the wagon bench, clucking to the horse. When he spoke, his tone was gruff. 'Are you happy now? That man owns a number of shops in town. I have asked him to send ready-made clothes and shoes along with foodstuffs to your families. They will be set until spring.'

The Cat said nothing.

Brandon let silence grow between them as he mulled over his recent action. When he'd leapt down from the wagon and arranged for supplies, he'd only thought he was acting of his own volition. It was clear to him now that it was the reaction The Cat had been angling for with the request that he visit Manchester, the very outcome she had been seeking when she changed the nature of redeeming his ring. He had never met a more manipulating minx.

Brandon chuckled softly into the darkness, his breath hanging in the frosty air. 'That's why you wanted me along today,' he said, referring to the purchased supplies. 'It's quite a gamble you took, wagering a guaranteed three hundred pounds against my merit.'

The poor of Manchester were blessed with a resolute bene-factor whether they knew it or not. What a comfort it must be to be cared for with such dedication. For a moment, Brandon gave in to the fantasy building in his mind—one where the resourceful Cat turned her devotion on him.

Brandon cast a cautious sidelong glance at the woman who

sat next to him, staring straight ahead into the gloom, her posture rigid, her features hidden by the dark and her veils. What was she celebrating—her triumph or was she simply satisfied in knowing she'd helped the ones she cared about?

'Why do you do it? Sooner or later, it will end badly. You can't walk this road for ever,' he asked softly when it was clear she wasn't going to remark on his action.

'As long as it's later rather than sooner, I won't mind. I'll have my satisfaction.'

'Or you could stop now before it's too late.'

She gave a wry laugh at the suggestion. 'It's already too late, Stockport. The Cat can't ever stop. Did you really think I could? Stopping would serve no purpose. Even if I didn't rob another house, my past would still condemn me.'

What could he say to that? It was Brandon's turn to embrace the silence. Perhaps silence was best. Darkness had a way of encouraging the exchange of confidences, but, this day aside, they were still adversaries. Tomorrow, he'd still be building the mill and she'd still be robbing his investors in an attempt to undermine his efforts.

At the crossroads, he handed her the reins and jumped down to untie his horse. 'You'll be able to see well enough in the dark?' he inquired politely.

'Yes. The ring will be sent to you tomorrow.'

'Good.' He could feel them revert back to their former roles. The Christmas truce they had implicitly negotiated was already evaporating.

'Stockport,' she called. 'Why did you do it?'

Brandon pulled his horse alongside the wagon. 'I did it for you. You won't have to rob any houses for a while.'

'Then you can't catch me,' her voice teased.

'Exactly. Happy Christmas.' He kicked the big bay into a gallop and set off, leaving The Cat to contemplate what kind of Christmas wish he had granted her.

When the intersection disappeared behind him, Brandon slowed his bay to a cautious lope. It wouldn't do to have his stallion step in a rabbit hole because he'd acted foolishly. He'd hoped the cold wind generated by his brief gallop would have had a sobering effect. He desperately needed it.

There was no escaping it, he had allowed himself to be caught up in the emotions The Cat had evoked in him. As a result, he'd acted rashly. What if someone discovered he'd knowingly spent the day with The Cat and had done nothing to fulfil his legal obligations? Those ramifications would exile him from polite society for ever, if not see him tried for a miscarriage of justice.

To top off the list of questionable decisions he'd made, he had just granted The Cat immunity. Immunity! What had he been thinking back there at the crossroads? He didn't have to search long for his answer. The Cat might have uncouth methods, but, from what he had seen today, her heart was pure gold. She had not lied to him about why she stole.

No matter what he'd experienced today, there was no future in pursuing The Cat beyond his capacity as the local magistrate. He detested the dichotomy it put him in. He detested the idea that his success relied on her demise. Unless…

An inspiration began to form. Brandon's pulse raced as the possibility took shape. Perhaps there was a compromise between their situations if he could convince her to give up the mad game. She'd have her freedom. He'd have his mill. But for his plan to succeed, he had to figure out who she was. He could not protect her otherwise.

While he learned much that day about The Cat, he had no further clue as to her identity. The only link was through the whiny spinster Eleanor Habersham. The correlation between the arrival of a handsome spinster, who hid her form in ugly gowns, and the appearance of The Cat four months prior could not be ignored. The only way to confirm that would be to question Eleanor directly.

Eleanor might have routed him from her house, but she could not rout him from someone else's home. The thought brought a smile to Brandon's lips as he pulled into the stable yard. He didn't know where The Cat would be tomorrow night, but he knew with a fair amount of certainty where Eleanor Habersham would be—Mrs Dalloway's card party. The matron had mentioned it at the masquerade. He had not thought to attend, but circumstances had changed. Instead of wanting to avoid the boring card party, he was starting to look forward to it.

Mrs Dalloway's card party was complicating her plans immensely, Nora groused, jabbing at a ripped hem with her needle as she sat in front of the Grange's fireplace, turning over the dilemma in her head. Eleanor was expected at the party, but The Cat needed to return Stockport's amethyst ring that evening or he'd think she'd welshed on their agreement.

Technically, Stockport was expendable. There wasn't much Stockport could do if she didn't return the ring, but it bothered her that Stockport might think the worst of her, especially after what they'd shared yesterday.

Nora pricked her finger and muttered a curse before sucking on the wounded digit. Her stitches were as unbalanced as her thoughts. Stockport was getting to be a hazardous distraction.

There was nothing for it. The Cat would have to return the ring herself. She would go after the card party. Nora's heart sped up at the prospect of encountering Stockport. Already, she was anticipating the inevitable sharp-edged conversation. Perhaps they would sip brandy together as they had done before.

She might allow herself to kiss him again. After all, once the ring was returned, The Cat would have little reason to seek him out. The Cat must turn her attention in the New Year to other investors who could be more easily influenced to abandon the factory project. Yes, tonight would be The Cat's farewell to Brandon Wycroft and it would be for the best.

Chapter Eight

Nora, dressed in her frumpiest Eleanor Habersham finery, concluded the evening was not going as planned a few hours later, after finding herself partnered at whist with none other than Brandon Wycroft himself.

'What did we bid?' Nora asked for the thousandth time that night in Miss Habersham's nasally voice, hoping that her irritating mannerisms were enough to distract Stockport from the fact that they were on the brink of winning their second rubber.

She was certain a man like Stockport would never believe a silly woman like Miss Habersham could be so canny at cards. However, Nora could not bring herself to cheat at cards simply to live up—or down, as the case might be—to Stockport's notions. If there were two things Nora could not abide, they were cheats and liars. She would not make herself both just to reinforce Stockport's beliefs about the card-playing abilities of a spinster. So she spent the evening across from her self-sworn nemesis, tittering behind her hand of cards at Stockport's polite conversation while soundly routing their opponents with astute play.

'We bid spades,' Stockport said with commendable

patience while Nora made a production of peering at her hand through her thick lenses.

Nora tossed a card on the table, intensely aware of Stockport's cobalt gaze fixed on her. 'What is it, my lord? Have I misplayed?'

'Quite the contrary, Miss Habersham, I think you want to fool us into underestimating you.' Stockport smiled another of his drawing-room smiles, polite, charming and yet somehow slightly mocking—of who or what, Nora could not divine.

'There is nothing to underestimate,' Nora offered smoothly, playing a trump.

'I think there is. You've shown yourself to be an outstanding card player this evening,' Stockport complimented. He turned the conversation towards the woman seated to his left. 'Mrs Tidewell, is Miss Habersham always so capable at card parties?'

The woman blushed and thought for a moment. 'I suppose she is. Miss Habersham is always winning, but 'she's so humble we forget how handily she plays.'

'I am fortunate in my partners,' Nora responded, gathering the last trick. 'There, my lord. We've made our bid. You can speculate all you like about my card playing, but I say it is merely luck and good partners.' Nora rose and stretched, grateful that the other two tables were finishing their hands and that the tea trolley had arrived.

Tables began to break up and guests milled around the tea service, Stockport among them. Nora was glad to be out from under his sharp eyes after enduring the evening under their scrutiny. Within the hour the party would reach its conclusion and she could get on with her business.

Nora took a seat on a nearby couch and tried to look unobtrusive. She failed completely. Within minutes, Stockport's sharp eyes found her. Damn.

'Miss Habersham, would you like some tea?' She'd expected Stockport to join some of the male guests present but here he was, dancing attendance on the village spinster, a delicate tea cup in each hand and looking handsomely at ease with the difficult manoeuvre. How the London ladies must swoon over him, Nora mused, thanking her stars that *she* was made of sterner stuff.

'Thank you.' Nora took the tea he offered, trying to ignore the empty space on the couch next to her.

Stockport smiled gently. When she didn't invite him to sit, he invited himself. 'Miss Habersham, may I join you?'

'Oh, certainly,' Nora fluttered, covering up for her lack of manners. 'Although I am surprised you are not seeking out the company of your friends.'

'I already know them, Miss Habersham. I don't know you. This is the perfect opportunity to get to know my newest neighbor. How long have you been at the Grange?'

Drat, the man could rise to every occasion. That spelled trouble. His benign question immediately aroused her suspicions. In her experience, there was nothing as perilous as seemingly harmless small talk, particularly coming from this man.

No matter how well cultivated his drawing-room manners were, nothing changed the fact that he was positively lethal, much more dangerous than any of her information made him out to be. She must tread carefully.

'There's not much to tell. I am a simple woman. You've already seen that I live a simple life.' She tittered and stared into her tea cup. That would not be enough to put Stockport off, so Nora deflected his burgeoning inquisition with a tried-and-true trick. 'I am sure it's much more interesting to talk about you.' In general, most men were *always* diverted by the opportunity to expound on themselves at large.

She'd forgotten Stockport was not most men. It was the second time in their association she'd made that mistake. The first time, she'd kissed him. She would do well to remember it. He wasn't even half the men she knew. He had a category all his own.

He narrowed his remarkable eyes now and furrowed his brow, looking as if he struggled with an unseen puzzle. A *frisson* of alarm went through Nora. 'What is it, my lord? Have I said something wrong? Oh dear, I'm always putting my foot in it.' Nora wrung her hands dramatically, making a show of muttering her stupidity under her breath while her mind raced, trying to catch her error.

What had triggered Stockport's reaction? He looked like a man who had heard or seen something familiar, but could not place it in context.

Stockport mastered himself. 'No, you've done nothing wrong. It is just that your conversation reminded me of another I had not long ago. I assure you, it's not what you said, merely how you said it. I see you're finished with your tea. Come, stroll about the room with me.'

Nora stared at Stockport as if he had two heads. The spinster walking about the room with the Earl? She had not expected this, but then she hadn't anticipated anything that had happened so far tonight. There was no way out of it, so she placed her hand on his sleeve and consented to the stroll.

Stockport kept up a stream of seemingly innocuous small talk. She supposed other women would find the singular attention flattering. She found it worrisome. 'Before tonight, Miss Habersham, I knew two things about you. First, you live at the Grange. Secondly, your cook makes the best teacakes in town. Now I have discovered a third. You play an outstanding game of whist. I am sure there is more to know.'

'I assure you, those are the sum of my attributes,' Nora said as rudely as Miss Habersham might dare with such a man.

'We shall have to agree to disagree on that point, Miss Habersham,' Stockport said in nonchalant tones that left her unprepared for the dangerous words that came out of his mouth next. 'Ah, we approach the verandah. Fresh air, Miss Habersham?'

The hair on the back of Nora's neck prickled in forewarning. She had waited all night for the other shoe to fall and now it had.

Victory at last! He had the nasally Miss Habersham right where he wanted her—private and alone, where he could confront her with his growing suspicions. He had worked all night for this moment, suffering through endless hands of whist and meaningless village gossip.

It had been highly enlightening to watch the lady in question play so ruthlessly. She was a far better partner than her conversation at the table indicated, which served to support the growing pile of evidence that Miss Habersham did not simply *know* The Cat. She *was* The Cat.

The previously reticent Miss Habersham had not been so timid during cards. Over cards, Miss Habersham had demonstrated a tenacity that seemed out of character for her, but not for The Cat. The Cat and Miss Habersham had sharp tongues. The whiny spinster had found the spine on two occasions now to reprimand him when he pried too closely into her personal life.

There were other characteristics they shared as well. They both had those piercing ice-jade eyes. Beneath the frumpy gowns of Miss Habersham there hid a delectable figure to rival the one The Cat flaunted. Now it was his turn to have the upper hand. He would make The Cat squirm before he pounced.

'I must apologise, Miss Habersham. I find that I have

business we must discuss and I'd rather do it privately.' He wanted to laugh while Eleanor fussed with her glasses, pushing them up higher on the bridge of her nose, doing her best to look discomfited by such male attention. Didn't she realise the game was minutes from being over?

'If you want to bring up the issue of security at the Grange again, I must stick to my initial position and decline your offer,' she began with characteristic nervousness.

Ah, very astute. Stockport gave her points for quick thinking. One of the conversations he'd had with 'Eleanor' had been about security, unlike the conversation he'd held with The Cat yesterday.

'I am afraid I have a slightly different topic in mind. What do you know about The Cat?' Brandon said without preamble.

'Why, only what I hear in town,' Eleanor said. 'Why would you ask such a thing?'

'Your house hasn't been touched. I find that odd,' he pressed, not allowing himself to be gulled by the wide-eyed shock and the hand flying to her throat in horror at his question.

'Neither has yours, I understand,' she retorted archly. 'Perhaps I should be asking what *you* know about The Cat?'

Brandon smiled. 'My point, exactly.' He leaned intimately close. Perhaps if he could fluster her, she would forget herself. 'Miss Habersham, I do know quite a lot about The Cat. I thought it was time for us to share what we know.'

His plan to discomfit her was failing. Eleanor made a great show of her chagrin. 'Are you insinuating I am harbouring a fugitive? Take me inside at once. I find this conversation very unseemly.' She was all Miss Habersham. So convincing was her outrage, his instincts faltered. Had he guessed wrongly about her identity?

All the signs couldn't be wrong. Brandon pushed onwards.

'What if I don't?' Two could play this game within a game. There was no harm in it since Miss Habersham didn't really exist. He was ninety per cent sure of it.

'I would scream,' she said in high dudgeon worthy of any thespian.

The other ten per cent of him almost believed her.

Brandon bowed in mock-surrender. 'I doubt you'd do either, but things will be as you wish. I'll escort you inside.' He stepped aside to let her pass ahead of him, taking the opportunity to audaciously whisper in her ear, 'When the night began I knew three things about you, Eleanor. Now I suspect a fourth.' It would serve her right to let her stew over the possibilities of what he knew.

An hour later, Brandon let himself into Stockport Hall and lit a brace of tapers left on the entry hall sideboard for his convenience.

He walked to the study, letting his candles cast shadows on the walls. He peered inside. Disappointment swamped him. His light illuminated nothing but emptiness. He'd thought she would be here. He had made sure that Eleanor had left the card party before him, giving the masquerading spinster plenty of time to change guises and sneak into the mansion.

This was rich! The Earl of Stockport plotting an assignation with a thief. What depths he had fallen to if the highlight of his social calendar was a clandestine rendezvous.

It was the final stroke in the evening's débâcle with Miss Habersham. Doubt was beginning to replace his earlier confidence. At the card party, Eleanor had used the same deflecting technique in their conversation that The Cat had used at the Christmas ball. It was proving to be a ridiculous connection.

He must be more affected by The Cat than he'd thought if

he was seeing the elegant, stealthy Cat in the dowdy form of the village spinster. He'd been so certain of his instincts on the verandah.

Brandon reprimanded himself the length of the stairs. Still, he had been so sure! But he'd also been sure The Cat would keep her word and return his ring. It was after midnight. The promised day of arrival was gone. For a man used to being right, he'd been wrong about a lot lately.

Brandon pushed open the door to his sitting room. A fire burned low and warm in the grate, assuring him from its glow that the room was empty.

He strode to the low table holding a decanter of his best brandy. He poured a glass, making a mental note to have his valet fill it in the morning. He did not remember drinking so much of it, but apparently he had. The decanter looked to have poured a glass or two.

Brandon headed to bed, tumbler in hand, eager to put the evening behind him. He raised his glass to his lips and halted at the threshold of his bedroom in disbelief.

'Hello, Stockport. I'd offer you a drink, but I see you already have one.' Rich tones purred from the bed where The Cat reclined in semi-darkness against the pillows, clad in her customary dark garb.

Ridiculous elation buoyed Brandon. She had come! He tamped down his relief, determined to play it coolly while heat flared within him. 'Don't you ever knock?'

'Occupational hazard.' The Cat uncurled her long limbs and rose from the bed.

Brandon took a swallow of brandy, trying to ignore the effect The Cat's sinuous walk was having on him as she crossed the room to stand before him. There was something different yet disconcertingly familiar about her attire, but his jangled mind was too busy focusing on her presence in his bedroom to place it. 'What are you doing here?'

She held up the small pouch for him to take. 'That should be obvious. I am returning your ring and something else that belongs to you. You should keep your money in a safer place.' She patted the breast pocket of her jacket. Only then did Brandon recognise that the coat she wore was his.

His heart leapt in victory. All the chastisements his logical mind had whipped him with as he climbed the stairs faded. She had kept her word to return the ring *and* she had returned his jacket from the Christmas ball *with* his money still tucked inside.

Stunned, he stood there, dumb in amazement. The Cat was purring about an affront to her dignity. 'Should I be flattered that you're surprised to see me or should I be insulted? Did you think I wouldn't keep my word?'

'If I am surprised, it is over finding you in my bedroom. I am not used to women making free with my private chambers. It's usually the other way around.'

His urbane scolding did nothing to daunt her. She stood mere inches from him, her low voice making him hard as she spun fantasies with her words. 'I wanted to arrange something special for our last meeting.'

'Last? Are you leaving?' He hadn't thought buying supplies for her needy would drive her out of town. He found he didn't want her to go. Maybe there was time to cancel the orders.

She gave one of her throaty laughs and he discarded his irrational thought. 'Of course not! I still have investors who need my particular attentions. But since you fail to play by my rules and announce Stockport Hall has been burglarised, I must spend my time elsewhere on more likely subjects.' She ran a finger lightly down his cheek along his jaw line where late-night stubble was starting to grow. 'I need the publicity.'

Her continuation of the robberies did not bode well for his plan to dissuade her from her criminal activities. 'I thought I'd provided enough supplies for your families to last until spring.' Brandon was thoroughly confused. He'd believed he'd kept her out of harm's way with his purchases. Apparently, she was addicted to danger.

'You did. But that doesn't change the fact that plans for the mill are still going forward.'

'No rest for the wicked, eh?' he said with a flippancy he didn't feel.

'None, and I am very wicked.' She stood so close to him now that the tips of her breasts pressed against his shirt. He wanted to forget the game they played over his mill. He wanted to throw her down on his bed and play an entirely different game, one that didn't involve clothes or masks or secrets or politics; well, maybe sexual politics, he amended.

Brandon did not believe it was possible for him to get any harder and survive intact. He fully expected it to explode shortly. In a hoarse voice, he tried to turn the conversation down a neutral venue. 'It's foolishness to continue at this rate. You must slow down. Do you want to be caught?'

Her eyes glinted with mischief. 'It depends on who is doing the catching.' A nail lightly raked his chest where his shirt opened in a vee, causing him to shiver in aroused delight.

She continued, 'I have no intentions of being caught by silly Squire Bradley and those nabob investors who have ponied up their pounds for the privilege of associating with you, my lord. I certainly shall not surrender to the pompous St John or that young braggart, Witherspoon.'

She smiled coyly at Brandon, making him feel that the cat had already licked the cream. 'Tell me, my lord, haven't you ever *wanted* to be caught? It can be invigorating with the right person.'

'Yes,' Brandon managed. They were no longer talking about catching The Cat. One moment they'd been talking about traps of one type and in the next were talking about traps of entirely another sort. An inappropriate sort. The sort that made him want to throw back the very proper damask cover on his bed and take her on the red satin sheets that hid beneath.

He groaned his lust as The Cat ran her nails down his chest. Her deft hands found their way inside his shirt to the hard planes beneath the fabric. Brandon sucked in his breath. Never in his intimate relationships had he been so stimulated and he had yet to remove his clothes.

'You see,' she whispered sensually, 'it is nice to be caught.'

His groin swelled painfully. He wanted her to catch him. It didn't take long for his thoughts to head in the reverse direction. *He* wanted to catch *her* in the manner she'd intimated.

His mind ran riot with all nature of exotic visions. He imagined a primal coupling among his scarlet sheets that would leave them both sweat-drenched and slaked. He imagined her sleeping and rumpled in the middle of his big bed, her dark hair fanned out against the crimson clad pillows. He imagined for a moment that The Cat and all her passion belonged to him alone. If he took her, it could not be otherwise. He was a man used to power and the responsibilities that went with it.

She stepped back and arched an eyebrow that both insinuated a dare and mocked his ardour. With languorous movements, she stepped away from him and took a chair, crossing her long, booted legs. 'It's clear from the look on your face, and dare I say "other parts", that you think you are man enough to tame The Cat.'

Brandon's blood was already hot. Her insouciant manner pushed him the rest of the way until he fairly boiled. It was time for this impudent wench to learn a lesson about what happened when she played with fire. 'You need taming badly.' He advanced towards her, hands on hips.

'You think you're that man?' The Cat queried from her relaxed position in the chair, unmoved by his proximity.

He leaned over her chair, his hands braced on each of the arms. He inhaled. The scent of outdoor air with the tinge of winter on it still hovered about her. She hadn't been there long ahead of him. 'Damn right I am.'

'Many men have tried and most have failed.'

'I am not most men.' He was impressed. She hadn't flinched once.

'No, you're an Earl. There's, what, roughly fifty of you?' She rose from the chair, her movements forcing him to step back and aside.

She still wore his jacket. She made a great show of taking it off and laying it aside with all the care of a man preparing to engage in fisticuffs. 'Well, my lord, are you going to come tame The Cat or stand there all night trying to figure out who the other forty-nine are?'

He saw her game and it was over. He would not suffer defeat twice in the same evening, nor would he be cowed into retreating by her brazen tongue.

'I call your bluff. Consider yourself caught.' He gripped her forearms and covered her lush mouth with his in a kiss that conveyed the power of his desire—a desire that both transcended the base need to be the sole possessor of such a wild creature and encompassed the primal need to protect what was his.

Indeed, whether she knew it or not, she was his—his equal in wit, in sensual gambits, in passion for a cause. In all the ways that mattered, she was his. His tongue probed the warmth of her mouth and she responded wholeheartedly, giving herself over to a complete embrace and, for once, letting him lead. Her body pressed against his. Her hands twined about his neck to pull him close. Her hips fitted against his jutting erection. At such contact, Brandon knew an elation as old as Adam.

Confident in himself and in her response, he moved his hand to rest in the provocative space between her breast and ribs. She sighed encouragement into his mouth and he cupped her full breast through the cloth of her shirt. Then he was falling backwards onto the bed, taking the weight of The Cat with him. In a flash he found himself pinned, The Cat looming above him, straddling him at midsection.

She changed her grip so that she imprisoned both of his wrists with her right hand. The charming smile on her lips persuaded Brandon to lay still and see where her shenanigans led. If she required the illusion of control, he could accommodate her whim.

With her free hand she pulled his cravat free and wound it around his wrists, her actions compelling her to stretch over his head so that her breasts were mere inches from his mouth. With a flick of his tongue, he could lick the nipples through the linen of her dark shirt. His sense of fair play startled him back to consciousness. He had not mistaken her motions. She was tying him up with his own clothing.

'What are you doing?' he inquired, a douse of sobriety cooling some of his ardour. He tried to make sense of the amusement playing across her masked features when she leaned back from her efforts.

The Cat leaned forward to sprinkle tantalising kisses against his jaw. 'Have none of your other lovers ever invigorated you like this?' Her hand drifted to his member and grasped it firmly, stroking him through the fabric, her thumb teasing its sensitive head.

'I didn't think so.' The Cat laughed—a deep throaty sound men would pay handsomely to hear in the night. She tugged his shirttails from his waistband and popped the buttons of his shirt open to reveal his bare chest. Brandon knew his nipples were erect with need.

'Still think you can tame The Cat?' She took one erect nubbin in her mouth and laved it with her tongue.

Brandon moaned. If this was failure, he'd like to fail more often.

The Cat sat back on her haunches, smiling broadly. She swung off the bed and studied his long legs for a thoughtful moment. Then she began to tug. Off came his boots. Off came his trousers. His member stood at rigid attention for them both to see.

The Cat stepped away from the bed and walked backwards towards the door, her face still wreathed in her grin. 'Consider yourself caught.' She used his own words.

'Where are you going?' Brandon strained again to sit upright.

'I'm going home.'

'Going home?' The implications slowly dawned on him. 'Wait. You can't leave me like this!'

'Yes, I can.' She fired her parting volley, 'Hasn't anyone ever told you not to trust a smiling cat?'

Chapter Nine

In the end, the bonds hadn't been tied so tightly as to prevent escape without calling for assistance. He silently thanked the vixen for that small consideration. It would have been far too embarrassing to call for his valet. How would he ever have explained this to Harper?

Brandon hoisted his form up and loosened one of the knots with his teeth. His hand slipped through the growing loop and he was quickly free. He recognised the favour for what it was—this private game of point and counterpoint was just between them. It had taken on a life of its own. It had somehow become separate from the fight over the mill.

Tonight, she'd meant to win their game, but not to make him look the fool. He'd wager the crown jewels she'd known he could get out of the bonds with little effort. Well, he was glad to give her the small victory. It was only fair after he'd cornered Miss Habersham on the balcony. They were even. For now.

Still, the loose knots had effectively prevented him from chasing after her. She was gone until the next time—and there would be a next time. There was unfinished business between them.

In the heat of their play, he had not confronted her with his thoughts about her identity or about his plan to see her stop the robberies. The Cat definitely addled his wits.

It was time to call for reinforcements. In the morning, he would send a note to his close friend, Jack Hanley, Viscount Wainsbridge. Between the two of them, they'd crack The Cat's secrets.

Discovering her identity was for her own good. In spite of her games tonight, he recognised that he liked her too much to see her hang and she liked him.

No matter how much she protested to the contrary with her sharp tongue and daring innuendos, she was not impervious to his kiss or his touch. His experience with women told him she had enjoyed the naked passion of the evening as much as he. She had been pliant and willing in his arms. He had felt the moment she gave herself up to her own longings and their burgeoning mutual desire.

He was a man who knew how to get what he wanted, and, in spite of her tricks, he wanted her, wanted her beyond reason and against all good sense. Brandon recognised trouble when he saw it and he was in it up to his neck. Jack had better come quickly.

Dear lord! She'd tied the Earl of Stockport to his bed and left him there naked, or nearly so. The ramifications of her actions burned Nora's cheeks all the way back to the Grange. He'd be furious and all because she'd let her temper get the better of her.

Tonight, The Cat had gone too far. But she'd felt it necessary in order to throw Stockport off the scent that Eleanor and The Cat were one and the same. She hoped to convince him that such disparate personalities could not reside in the same person.

Stockport's insinuations to Eleanor at the card party had left her distinctly uneasy. He wouldn't behave in such a shocking manner if he hadn't been sure he knew Eleanor Habersham was a fiction. Coupled with the impudent gift of satin for undergarments, she could no longer dismiss Stockport's knowledge of The Cat. What he had once guessed at, he now felt he knew with almost absolute certainty.

Nora let herself into the kitchen, thankful for the dark interior. It meant Hattie hadn't waited up. She was in no mood for a lecture tonight, not when there was so much to sort through. Her new knowledge about Stockport was like a flame—both illuminating and dangerous at the same time. A person was better off without some things. Knowing the enemy on a human level was one of them. The quickest way to get burned was to fall in love with one's mark.

That bore thinking about, but not until she was in the sanctuary of her own room. Nora took the stairs quickly, avoiding the squeaky floorboard on the fifth tread. Slipping inside her own private domain, she let the thought loose. If she was to be a good thief, she had to be objective. She couldn't protect herself if she lost perspective. Was she in love with Stockport?

Nora had little to work with from her disastrous, short-lived marriage. From her recollections of conversations with other women, people in love had pulses that raced when the object of their affection was near. They spent hours thinking about their adored one.

If that was the criteria, she was safe. Certainly, she experienced adrenalin rushes at the thought of seeing him again, but that was due to the prospect of matching wits with a commendable foe. No rules of engagement said a thief couldn't *respect* the target. She definitely did not spend hours idolising him. All of her thoughts focused on how to best him. That was not love-like in the least bit.

Nora breathed a little easier after her examination. She was not falling for Brandon. Stockport, she corrected hastily. Thinking of him by his first name was an unaffordable luxury. This venture didn't need any more personalisation to confuse the issue. Besides, developing soft feelings for *Stockport* was tantamount to treason.

Industry had seen to the ruin of her family and tossed her into a life of chaos. She could not compromise her cause by forgetting Stockport was at the heart of the project to build the textile mill.

Her only sin was that she'd dallied too long with Stockport. He'd been a means to an end, but he had not reciprocated by ranting about The Cat all over town. She'd meant it when she'd told him she would not visit him again. There were other, more compliant, subjects and she had to hurry. Ground had been broken and the foundations laid. She had to keep the investors wary, worrying about when The Cat would strike next.

Nora fingered a small pile of post that lay on the vanity, sifting through it until she found a particular envelope. She opened it and smiled. Perfect. Inside was an invitation. Out of a sense of polite obligation and an acknowledgement of the social limitations a village like Stockport-on-the-Medlock presented, Eleanor Habersham was invited to a New Year's Eve fête hosted by Mr Flack, one of the industrialists hoping to expand their fortunes with the new textile mill. The party would provide the ideal staging ground for planning her next move. Eleanor would be able to learn much in unguarded moments.

No one thought a spinster had a brain in her head. She might even manage to eke out a little excitement. Stockport was certain to attend. It would be an opportunity to ferret out what Stockport truly knew about Eleanor Habersham and The Cat.

'This sleepy place is what you traded for the fireworks of Parliament?' Jack Hanley, Viscount Wainsbridge, waved his ornate walking stick in disbelief at the village spread before him. 'I raced from London for this? I left mere hours after getting the message and made excellent time because your letter indicated the situation was dire. This isn't "dire", my dear friend, it's "boring".'

Brandon stepped down from the carriage and stood beside his friend. He tried to see the little town through Jack's jaded eyes. To a man used to the intrigues of London, Stockport-on-the-Medlock no doubt appeared harmless without a hostile bone in its civic body.

It was an outer image only. In the five days since Jack's hasty summons, Brandon knew differently. The white-steepled church, well-kept shop fronts and neatly cobbled streets were superficial signs of prosperity—a prosperity purchased at the expense of others. Beneath the bucolic façade, there was another story, too—a story about farmers struggling to hold on to land that no longer produced the profits it once had, and agricultural workers who once hired out their labour and were now forced to leave their families to seek work in Manchester because their traditional jobs were gone.

The town was at war with itself, divided between those who wanted the new textile mill and those who did not. The Cat led the latter faction and, by merit of his rank and association with textile mill, he led the other.

'If Stockport-on-the-Medlock was in truth what it seemed on the outside, I would not have called for you, old friend.' Brandon clapped Jack on the back. 'We'll walk the streets as

long as we can stand the cold and then we'll dine at the Cart
and Bull. There's no place finer in town for learning the news.'

A few hours later, Jack Hanley sopped up the last of his
hearty rabbit stew with a thick chunk of bread and leaned back
in his chair, ready to make his pronouncement. 'I am beginning to see what you mean.'

They had spent an hour touring the shops and another hour
over a pint of ale in the public room of the inn before retiring
to a private parlour for luncheon. Brandon waited impatiently
for Jack's verdict.

If anyone knew how to see beyond the face of things, it was
Jack. He made an art form out of being a man who dressed elaborately and acted the dandy in order to make people forget the
shrewdness of his clever mind, a talent that King William frequently put to good use for the crown. It was that talent Brandon
called upon now to help him unravel the mystery of The Cat.

'How many people support The Cat?' Jack asked.

Brandon shrugged. 'It is hard to say. I do not believe
anyone openly champions The Cat, but the support is there,
especially from the lower classes.'

'An army of one?' Jack raised a cynical blond eyebrow. 'I
cannot believe one person could so easily tie a town up in
knots. The Cat must have assistance.'

'In Manchester, The Cat has a network.' Brandon
grimaced, remembering the day he'd spent shopping with
Miss Habersham. 'But here, the support is less obvious,
although I am sure there are plenty who quietly support The
Cat. In town, the issue of the textile mill has been met with
strong minority resistance.'

'I can see why.' Jack reached for the decanter of red wine
and refilled his glass. 'The countryside is perfect for grazing.

The river has made the area ideal for sheep. It is hard to convince people to give up on a known way of life that has been successful for generations.'

'They don't understand they're not being asked to trade one for the other. I want them to see that the old and new ways can co-exist. We need sheep wool for the factories. It is an incredible benefit to the cost of production if the mill doesn't have to import the raw wool from long distances.' Brandon warmed to his subject.

Jack steepled his hands against the tidal wave of Brandon's vigorous assessment. 'Your ardour for the subject is sincerely touching, but, philanthropy aside, one cannot forget the reason you're doing this. You need the mill.'

Jack's cynicism did not sit well with Brandon. 'Of course I need the mill. I need a secure source of income to ensure the family coffers survive into the future. You needn't make it sound as if I am hoodwinking the village into something that only benefits me. The mill is a good idea for their future too,' Brandon argued. 'Agriculture will not be able to sustain the estate alone in years to come. I am thinking of the Earls who will come after me.'

Brandon leaned over the table and lowered his voice to a near-whisper. 'I am very sure the project will turn a profit. Why else would I so obviously sully my "noble" hands in trade? Once the factory is a success, the *ton* will overlook my eccentricity.'

Jack gave a bark of laughter. 'I wouldn't worry about that. You can do no wrong, with your elegant manners, good looks and glib tongue. Gawd, man, you're like a woman's Midas.'

Brandon refused to be provoked. 'As I said, I have responsibilities that take all my attention these days and I need your help.'

Jack poured another glass of wine. 'Speaking of responsibilities, you missed the best part of the session when you high-tailed it up here. The House of Commons and the House of Lords are at each other's throats over reform of the boroughs. If the reform bill is to pass the House of Lords, an Earl is going to have to cross party lines and it will have to happen this spring while the momentum is still there.' Jack raised an elegant eyebrow in query. 'What will you do?'

Brandon wanted to laugh at the irony of the situation. The Prime Minister was hoping he would be the one to set a trend and vote for more liberal policies concerning the middle and lower classes. The Cat thought just the opposite, that he was a highbrow peer unwilling to use his power for the benefit of the masses.

'Enough about my politics, Jack. Tell me what you have discovered about The Cat.' Jack had access to all sorts of information that might shed some light on The Cat.

'That's a very abrupt conversational parry,' Jack noted. 'You are losing your touch.'

'Enough, Jack. Now, tell me what you know.'

Jack leaned in close despite the privacy of their dining room. 'The Cat of Manchester is not exclusive to this area. I think there is reason to believe that the moniker comes from the fact that The Cat is merely *from* this area. There are reports of similar burglaries taking place in Birmingham, Leeds and Bradford. As you know, those are cities whose situation is much like Manchester's. They are highly industrialised and face the same social issues.'

'Could it be that there are several people who call themselves by that name?'

Jack shook his head at the conjecture. 'The timing of the burglaries does not suggest that there is a group of people acting in tandem. The timing would support that there is only one person and that the one person moves around from place to place. The only constant is the reference to the name. Wherever this thief goes, the name is the same as well as the cause.'

Brandon drummed his hands on the table, taking in Jack's findings. 'How long has The Cat been operating?'

'Reports indicate three years. But that only indicates how long the name has been showing up. This person may have been active for years under different aliases.'

'Are there any leftover Luddites still practising?' Brandon knew the chance was slim. The Luddite movement, an organisation started by craftsmen who opposed the replacement of manual labor with textile machinery, had been wiped out years ago, but one never knew.

A sickening feeling formed in his gut. It was one thing to rationalise The Cat as being a misguided local with a Robin Hood complex. It was entirely another to know he had fraternised with a hardened criminal. The Luddites had used violent means to demolish machinery. Such behaviour had led to their downfall. How far would The Cat go to make her point? Would robbing lead to other crimes? Would she go as far as to destroy the mill if her earlier ploys failed to bring about the desired results? The truth was, Brandon didn't honestly know.

Jack shook his head. 'I checked the records from the 1813 Luddite trials in York. It is not likely that The Cat was among the group and is still rebelling nearly twenty years later. For starters, it would make The Cat awfully old for carrying on the shenanigans you've written to me about.'

'What about Eleanor Habersham?' Brandon asked the question he dreaded most. Once the connection was firm, he had no more excuses, but at least he could feel less guilty about his behaviour at Mrs Dalloway's.

'I have found nothing, which also means nothing. Your spinster is either what she claims to be and there are simply no records on her because she's of no criminal threat to England or she's a persona The Cat has conjured up. I can't see why the burglar would do that. It makes no sense to create a spinster unless The Cat is a woman.' Understanding dawned on Jack's face. 'You think The Cat is a woman, don't you?'

Brandon nodded. 'I *know* The Cat is a woman.'

'How do you know?'

Brandon put a finger to his lips. 'Wait until we get home.'

'I need a drink.' Jack poured himself a brandy and resumed his seat, where he'd sat riveted at Brandon's encounters with The Cat. 'I find it peculiar that you haven't told anyone. Care to explain?'

'At first I was embarrassed. I'd let The Cat get away.'

'And later?' Jack prompted.

'Let it suffice to say that, later, catching The Cat held little novelty for me.' Brandon took a swallow of brandy.

'That must be how she gets away with it.' Jack smiled triumphantly, gloating a bit at his friend's discomfort. 'Men don't want to turn her in. If she's caught, she simply cajoles them into compliance just as she's done with you.'

'She is not a trollop!' Brandon protested, although he had nothing to base that claim on and plenty of evidence to the contrary. Jack's comment had done its work.

'I've yet to meet virgins who tie men to beds. Good lord, Brandon, do you think you're the only man she's tried this on?' Jack pressed, then softened his tone. 'You're making no sense. You say you want me to help you catch The Cat. Now you're telling me the opposite. Which is it? Do you want to catch her or not?'

Brandon said nothing. Jack's eyes glinted with knowledge. 'Ah, so that's how it is. You want to catch her for yourself. Why? Jealousy? Can't stand the thought of another man under The Cat's thrall?'

'I am not under her spell,' Brandon argued, incensed by the implication that a thief could buy his loyalty with her charms. The claim to jealousy rankled. Was Jack right?

'Then how do you explain this urge to protect her?' Jack shook his head. 'You should know already you can't tame a wild thing. You can't tame The Cat, Brandon.'

Brandon looked down into the remains of his glass, suddenly inundated with vivid memories of his last meeting with The Cat. 'I suppose you're right, Jack. Still, she'd be better off in a cage of my making than a cage of society's making. If the investors catch her, it's off to prison for certain. If what you believe is true and she's guilty of robberies elsewhere, no judge can overlook three years of indiscretions.' He recalled her comment Christmas Day that there was no sense in stopping the robberies because of her past.

'So it's a race and you believe you have the inside track because you think The Cat is Eleanor Habersham the spinster.' Jack began sorting through the pieces of the puzzle aloud. 'You believe this because of a slip in a conversation you had with Eleanor at a card party?'

Brandon stood up and began to pace. 'For other reasons too. The spinster is a disguise, I'm sure of it. Well, I was sure of it until I blundered a few nights ago at the card party. I wrote you about it in my note.'

Jack nodded at the reminder. 'Your account was deuced hilarious. When do I get to meet this paragon?'

'Tonight, at the New Year's party, but, Jack, don't alert her to our suspicions. If she bolts, we're back to nothing.'

* * *

The New Year's celebration was in full swing around her as Nora sat unobtrusively with a few ladies of Eleanor's acquaintance. The display of wealth tonight was more than lavish. It was garish, almost as garish as Eleanor's dress with its large red rose print against a cream background. The material might have done well for curtains, but definitely not for a dress. As Nora intended, the large pattern distracted the viewer from further scrutiny.

The women with her tittered and fanned themselves, exclaiming over the gowns and jewels of the investors' wives. One of them raised her voice over the others and gestured to the doorway of the ballroom. 'Oh, my, the Earl of Stockport has come after all and he's brought a friend. I heard talk that his friend's a Viscount. They had lunch at the Cart and Bull this afternoon.'

Nora diverted her attention from the conversation. Stockport's eyes swept the room, giving her the distinct feeling of being hunted. He was looking for her. For once the guise of Eleanor Habersham offered no protection. He had reason to mistrust Eleanor as much as The Cat after their exchange at the card party.

Damn him for looking so handsome. She took in his dark evening attire. His toilet was flawless, not a hair out of place, or a hair visible on his clean-shaven jaw.

Her cheeks burned at the memory of him a few nights ago, looking less than perfect, but no less delectable in his state of undress, stubble staining his jaw. It would be something of a trial for Eleanor Habersham to remain aloof, but nothing else would do. The last meeting between them demanded no less. Eleanor should still be upset over his treatment of her on the verandah. Of course, there was always the possibility that Stockport would not bother to seek out a lowly spinster.

But this wasn't London and the distinctions of class were more easily blurred. Within minutes of greeting his hostess, Stockport began the long walk to the cluster of chairs where she sat. It would take some time. Everyone was interested in making Stockport's acquaintance. It wasn't often an Earl mixed with such a bourgeois grouping of people. The opportunity was not to be missed.

If she was so inclined, Nora could remove herself from her group, but Stockport would find her wherever she went. There was no sense in delaying it. She reasoned it was far better to confront him with a group of others around instead of risking an encounter where he could get her alone and press his suspicions.

'Ladies, may I present to you the Earl of Stockport and the Viscount Wainsbridge.' The hostess made the introductions. The dreaded moment was upon her. Nora met it head on. She was putting too many constructions on the encounter. Stockport would attribute any awkward behaviour on her part to their encounter at the card party.

The interaction proceeded quite harmlessly until Nora realised it wasn't Stockport who posed the threat. It was his dandified friend, Viscount Wainsbridge. There was an aura of oddness about the gentleman. His gaze was too penetrating when he looked at her. The hardness in his eyes belied his easy manners. His clothes were overly foppish for a man of his broad-shouldered physique.

Well, it took one to know one. Nora recognized the look of a disguise when she saw it. This man might not be masquerading as *someone* else like she was, but he was masquerading as *something* else. She didn't have to think long to come up with motivations for such a show. Her own motivations served well enough. People confided the most amazing bits of information to those whom they believed had no brain and Viscount Wainsbridge was giving a very good impression that he had left his at home.

A man Nora recognised as one of the mill investors approached Stockport and drew him aside. Nora's senses went on full alert. Her suspicions were justified when Stockport returned to the group and took his leave.

'I regret I shall have to leave you. The investors and I are having a short meeting in the library. It seems there is a new plan to catch The Cat.' Stockport looked straight at her, causing her to readjust her earlier thinking. What did Stockport know? Had he looked at her on purpose? Nora wished she could be The Cat tonight. The Cat would deal swiftly with Viscount Wainsbridge and ferret her way into the meeting to overhear the plan.

Stockport's next words caught her by surprise. 'I trust Wainsbridge will be safe in your company, Miss Habersham. If it is not too importunate, I was hoping you might honour him with a dance?'

It wasn't really a question. In an instant, Viscount Wainsbridge was next to her, soliciting for the next dance just starting up on the floor. In front of the group, Nora had no choice but to accept. Nora smiled gamely at Stockport. Apparently, he wanted to play cat and mouse. She would remind him just who was the cat and who was the mouse. If Stockport thought he had her cornered, he would be disappointed. He had no idea just how poorly Eleanor Habersham danced.

Chapter Ten

Brandon eyed the five other gentlemen assembled in Flack's walnut-panelled library over the rim of his brandy snifter with a certain amount of trepidation. Three weeks ago he would have thought this meeting to discuss further action against The Cat nothing more than due process.

That was before he met The Cat. Now, he was hard pressed to take an interest in any plan that might condemn her. Regardless, there still remained the issue of the mill. She had to be brought to heel before the mill failed, but he could not abide the image of her behind bars or, worse, hanging from a gibbet like a common thief. There was nothing common about her.

Tonight, Brandon found himself in the awkward position of trying to protect The Cat without tipping his hand, all the while trying to cope with the comments Jack had made earlier. How had he got in to such a deep game with her? He swallowed his brandy as Cecil Witherspoon, the mill's leading investor, cleared his throat and called the meeting to order.

'Gentlemen, I dislike having to interrupt the festivities with business, but the situation regarding The Cat cannot be allowed to continue. Since we are all together this evening, we can make the most of our time by discussing the issue.'

The men—Squire Bradley, Magnus St John, Stephen Livingston and Jonathan Flack—all nodded in accord. Brandon kept his nod minimal and slightly aloof. He heartily disliked Cecil Witherspoon.

By rights, the tall, slender, blond man should have garnered his respect. Witherspoon was an ambitious, self-made man in his late thirties with a shrewd eye towards investments, very much like himself. But Witherspoon's pale blue eyes were icy windows into a glacier soul.

Brandon found that, throughout their brief business association, Witherspoon was ruthless and utterly lacking in compassion for his fellow humans. Witherspoon was cold blooded now as he laid out his plan for capturing The Cat.

'St John and I have tracked The Cat's circuit of break ins and we believe we have cracked the pattern. We feel confident that The Cat will stage a robbery of St John's place next. We also have divined that the robberies take place on evenings the home's residents are out at social functions.

'This means The Cat will target St John's home for a Wednesday night when he and his wife are regularly out playing cards at Squire Bradley's.' Witherspoon gestured pompously to St John, his crony in crime. 'Magnus, take it from here.'

Magnus St John, dark, bearded and bluff of manner, coughed and began. 'I propose we all meet at my home for a dinner, during which The Cat will show up and be mightily surprised by our presence.'

That was his brilliant plan? Brandon almost laughed out loud. Even more ridiculous was the blind acceptance of the other men in the room, who were nodding their heads sagely and chortling over the planned surprise.

'My lord, is something amiss?' Witherspoon gave him a cold stare. Apparently, he hadn't disguised his amusement well enough.

'Do you think The Cat will simply walk into a dining room blazing with lights or will you spend all night sitting in the dark waiting for the thief to show and then shout "surprise"?' Brandon said. Surely that much was an obvious flaw?

'We won't light the chandelier. We'll use candles. They wouldn't be visible until it was too late,' St John said staunchly and far too seriously for Brandon to mistake his answer for a humorous joke.

'And the "trap" part?' Brandon pressed.

Witherspoon suppressed a condescending sigh as if it was his lot in life to work with less intelligent persons. He tolerated the question only because it came from the Earl. It was no secret that Witherspoon had invested heavily because of Brandon's involvement. Witherspoon was grasping for acceptance into high society. Brandon suspected he would pay any price to ingratiate himself to an Earl of good standing.

'My lord, the trap is that The Cat is expecting no one to be home, but this time we'll all be there, waiting to drag the insufferable bastard off to jail.'

Brandon left it at that. If they wanted to try their plan, they were welcome to it. Still, a trap was a trap and the element of surprise could not be underestimated. There was also the issue of numbers. One lone thief against five men was not the most favourable of situations.

Brandon gave him a thin smile. 'I will be anxious to hear about your results.'

'Oh, my lord, you must be present. You'll dine with us that evening, of course,' St John interjected. The man was no better than Witherspoon. St John would dine out for months among his Cit companions in London on the tale that he entertained an Earl.

'Well, that's settled then.' Brandon inclined his head with a graciousness he did not feel. What was not settled was what he would do with his information. He could tell The Cat of the trap, assuming he could find her or that she would find him. His other choice was to say nothing and let events take their own natural courses.

Therein lay the rub. There were two possible 'natural' outcomes: first, The Cat made fools out of them all, or, second; The Cat was caught. That outcome did not sit well with him.

'Quite right, that's settled,' said Livingston, brushing his hands against his thighs. 'The plan has got to succeed. I didn't count on this type of interference when I paid into this scheme. My wife can't sleep at night for fear of The Cat. She's already talking about returning to London.'

'Here, here,' concurred Flack, a weak-chinned man with little in the way of looks to recommend him, but possessed of a financial acumen that more than compensated. 'It isn't prudent for any of us to put up more cash for the venture. We need two new members and I say they will not come if The Cat is on the loose.'

Witherspoon smiled coldly. 'It seems we are all in accord, gentlemen. I propose a toast.'

The gentlemen all lifted their glasses in toast to their venture. Brandon joined in reluctantly, not missing for a moment the murderous gleam in Witherspoon's eyes. His toast was chilling. 'To The Cat. May the trip to the gibbet be swift.'

The game The Cat played had just grown more dangerous. Brandon wondered if she knew. Did she understand the peril posed by a man like Witherspoon, who would stop at nothing? Brandon set his glass down and made his excuses, quickly leaving the room before he said something rash to Witherspoon.

He was suddenly desperate to see how Jack was faring with Miss Habersham. It was more imperative than ever that Miss Habersham admit to her connection with The Cat. The spinster was the only link he had. If he didn't succeed in winning her trust, he had no guarantee of being able to warn The Cat in time.

Brandon stopped in the dimly lit corridor leading back to the party and drew a deep breath, taking time to contemplate his decision. *He was going to tell The Cat.* How quickly he reached that conclusion! Just like that, Brandon knew it was true. He was going to tell her just as soon as he could, Jack's aspersions on her character aside.

'It's not fair,' Jack moaned, sinking back against the squabs of Brandon's well-sprung coach. 'You get to match wits with a tempting seductress who ties you up and I'm left wooing the ugly spinster.'

Brandon set his fingers to his temples in an attempt to massage away a growing headache. 'There is *no* spinster. Eleanor Habersham is a fiction,' he said in a weary voice as if he'd explained it a dozen times already. It was nearly dawn of the first day of the year and his head hurt from too much champagne and too much knowledge. He fervently hoped it was not a sign of how the year would evolve.

'She didn't feel fictitious when she was stepping on my toes,' Jack groused. 'I thought you told me she was a divine dancer. Your standards have changed drastically.' Jack flexed his foot. 'Damn, the lengths I go to for a friend. I may have done myself a permanent injury.'

Brandon gave a short laugh at his friend's exaggeration. 'I'm sure it wasn't as bad as all that.'

'No one else danced with her twice. The whole town will be waiting for me to call on her and declare my intentions.'

'If it's any consolation, your efforts were not without results.'

'I don't understand what was gained from the sacrifice of my toes.'

'Confirmation. Eleanor dances deplorably. The Cat dances very well. Everything The Cat does, Eleanor does the opposite. It's a case of the lady doth protest too much.'

'What you're saying is that there's no chance Eleanor Habersham is going to sneak into my bedchamber and tie me up,' Jack said glumly, but a spark of humour flared in his eyes.

'Essentially, but in less crass terms.'

'You're certain?'

'As certain as I am going to be in the amount of time I have left. The investors are hungry for blood.'

'And if not? What happens if The Cat goes unchecked?'

'Then I am sunk before I've even begun. My largest investor, Cecil Witherspoon, leads the charge for The Cat's arrest.' Brandon sighed. 'Not only do I need those last three investors, I need current investors to stay. Even though the earldom's coffers are solid, I cannot lay my hands on a hundred thousand pounds in currency at a moment's notice. It would mean liquidating a few of the estates not under the protection of the entailment,' Brandon explained.

'Is there a chance of them deserting?'

'It will be inevitable if The Cat hits their houses again. Livingston is ready to walk and Flack may be right behind him. They didn't bargain on a risky venture. None of us did.'

Brandon closed his eyes. The meeting had brought everything to a head. He could not offer guarantees of safety for the investors. Nor could he offer guarantees of new investors coming forward. The current investors, particularly those with more invested, were anxious to stay on schedule and start framing the mill within the month.

'The Cat should be pleased,' Jack observed, idly twirling his walking stick between his hands. 'You have to choose between her and the mill. It is interesting to me that there's any choice at all. What do you think it says to you, that you're even considering this woman's safety above the financial well being of Stockport-on-the-Medlock?' Jack paused, the look on his face indicating he was debating the wisdom of his next words.

'What is it, Jack? Apparently you have something more you wish to say?' Brandon said grumpily.

'Hell, here it is, but remember we're friends.' Jack pointed the walking stick at him for emphasis. 'You don't think The Cat has real feelings for you, do you? She *wants* you to desire her, even fall in love with her. She is counting on it for her success. She knows that anything more between the two of you is not part of the game.'

'Stuff it, Jack,' Brandon growled. He wanted to say more. He wanted to say that whatever she had done in the past with other men or other ruses was different than what lay between he and she. What they felt for each other, the consuming heat of their passions, was real.

For the first time, Brandon realised how inane that explanation sounded. Was Jack right? Jack was an astute assessor of character. He would be a foolish man indeed if he rejected the very wisdom he had asked Jack to bring.

Across from him, Jack groaned. 'Egads, you did think she had feelings for you. Your face says it all.'

The coach turned down the drive to Stockport Hall. Jack raised a curtain and peered out into the early grey morning. He let the curtain drop and sighed heavily. 'Enough about your love life. I am going to bed for the remainder of the day. When I awake, I am going to take a long soak to alleviate my poor feet. Happy New Year, my friend.'

Happy New Year, his foot. Brandon cursed as he watched his friend sail through the doors into the warmth of the house without a care in the world. He knew it was something of an act. Jack had plenty of cares. He just didn't let on about them. All the same, Jack didn't have a seductive villain to subdue, a mill to build, a fortune to protect and a bloodthirsty Cecil Witherspoon to keep in check before someone got hurt or, worse, killed. Brandon could not remember a new year that had gotten off to a more ominous start.

He hadn't a clue what his next move was. The only piece of luck he had was that The Cat hadn't struck since Christmas Day. However, it was simply a matter of time before that bit of luck ran out. She'd assured him that night that she wouldn't stop her raids.

Perhaps, like him, she was watching and waiting to plot her next move. The one certainty he had was that she would strike again and, if the investors were correct in their guesses tonight, he knew where and he knew when. He could prevent it if he could verify that Eleanor Habersham was The Cat.

To his way of thinking, there was only one way to find out quickly. He would have to take a leaf from The Cat's own book and pay her a nocturnal visit of his own. If he was wrong and Eleanor was really no one more than Eleanor there would be hell to pay. But these were desperate times.

When to strike next? Nora paced the small parlour of the Grange, scanning the list of investors she held in her hand. The Cat was close to success. All the news she'd gathered at the New Year's ball confirmed it; two investors were still needed and the others were getting nervous enough to consider pulling out. If she could keep up the steady pressure, the textile mill would become a moot development.

Once her work in Stockport-on-the-Medlock was done, she could move on, just like she'd done in Leeds, Bradford and Birmingham. The Cat of Manchester never stayed in any one place too long. It was her key to ensure The Cat lived all nine of her lives.

Eleanor Habersham could cease to exist. A new character could be created and the game could begin anew somewhere else where her efforts were needed; and there was always somewhere else. With approximately five hundred and sixty factories in the Lancashire region, employing one hundred and ten thousand workers, she had an amazing amount of job security—as long as she didn't get caught.

The thought of accomplishing her goal and moving on did not fill her with its usual satisfaction. Instead, it left her feeling empty. Brandon Wycroft would be out of her circle of influence for ever. She would be responsible for his ruin and whatever feelings The Cat had aroused in him with her sensual games would be gone in the wake of his embarrassment and loss of face.

She did understand completely what he risked. A peer meddling in trade was highly uncommon, no matter how practical it might be. His failure with the mill would make him a laughingstock. The consequences he potentially faced sat poorly with her. It was becoming more difficult as the days passed to justify sacrificing one individual for the sake of many.

These were dangerous thoughts. She was too close to the Earl, developing real feelings for a man who should be her adversary. If she had any good sense at all, she'd seriously consider leaving Stockport-on-the-Medlock right away before the projected hazards became realities.

The mantel clock struck ten. Gracious! How long had she stood there, wool-gathering over Stockport? She glanced down at the list in her hand. St John's would be her best option. It was time to hit there again and keep his fear alive. He was a big investor and, if he grew too complacent, he might decide to increase his level of financial commitment. She would go on Wednesday night when he and his wife were out at the Squire's playing cards.

That decision made, she decided she could indulged in the luxury of going to bed early.

In the deep part of the night something or someone else found her too. Years of training had taught her to awake alertly and surreptitiously so as to rob the intruder of the element of surprise. Nora fought the urge to open her eyes. Instead, she let her other senses take in the alteration of the room. It might be nothing more than a branch scratching the window, but it always paid to be cautious.

She inhaled, her nose searching for a smell that verified the presence of another. The tang of spicy soap reached her nostrils. Stockport! *He* was burglarising *her*, the stubborn man.

If the situation wasn't so dire, she would roll over and laugh at him, but now he had complete proof that The Cat at least lived with Eleanor Habersham, if not proof that they were one and the same. The dratted man must have been very sure of himself to have dared such an entrance.

Thankfully, she slept on her side, one hand under her pillow. Stealthily, she slipped that hand around the smooth handle of the small dagger she kept there for just such occasions.

The scent of his spicy soap intensified and Nora began to calculate how close he was. He must be very close for the smell to be so obvious. She listened for the sound of his breathing to affirm her guess. Yes, he was close, right next to the side of the bed at her back.

Nora tensed beneath the quilts and rolled, using the force of her arm beneath the pillow to fling it up and backwards, into Stockport's startled face.

'Stockport!' She leapt out of bed, keeping the bedstead between them and brandishing her dagger.

Stockport staggered back a step under the surprise of the pillow and righted himself too quickly. She'd hoped he would trip or catch his foot on the bed, anything to slow him down and enhance her advantage. What she intended to do with that advantage, she had no idea. She was making this up as she went along. It didn't help that Stockport looked completely collected.

'Hello, Cat,' he drawled in maddeningly smug tones, 'Or should I say Eleanor? It's hard to tell. That nightrail is definitely Eleanor's, but the rest of you is all Cat.' The conceited man let his eyes peruse her body in an all-knowing manner that made her feel exposed.

Nora tightened her grip on the dagger, desperately trying to quell the heat rising in her. 'What are you doing in my bedroom?'

'I've come to return your calls. It's only seemly to reciprocate a call. I regret that I've been so tardy in doing so. You came to my bedroom and now I've come to yours.' He smiled wolfishly and began to move.

'Stay there. I won't hesitate to use this,' Nora warned as he circled the bed. She didn't remember him being this large in their previous encounters. Tonight, she was fully aware of his height, the power of his broad shoulders.

'I am not here to do you an injury, my dear Cat. I am here for proof.' He bent to the lamp she'd left on the vanity and brought up the light until the room was visible.

'What will you do with the proof?' Nora asked warily. She had not believed until this moment that he would assist in her capture.

He grinned at her discomfort. 'I rather like having you at my advantage for once. As to the proof, I want it so that you and I can strike a deal without any of your chicanery involved. I want you to know explicitly that I know The Cat and Eleanor are one and the same.'

Nora smiled at that. It was as close to conceding a small victory as she was going to get. Men like Stockport didn't admit outright when they'd been gulled. She gave a small laugh. 'So I did have you convinced that night at the card party. What changed your mind?'

Stockport looked up from a drawer he'd opened. 'Nothing. Until I saw you sleeping tonight, I wasn't fully certain my guesses were right.'

Nora raised her eyebrows at that, a smart retort rising to her lips. 'Really? It is fascinating to speculate on what you might have done had you been wrong.'

'I would have crawled back out the window and left poor Eleanor in peace. Aha!' Stockport reached into the vanity drawer and pulled out her spectacles. 'Eleanor's glasses.' He held them aloft and peered through them. 'Just as I suspected, these lenses are hugely distorted.'

'Satisfied?' Nora lowered the dagger and moved towards him, wondering if her wiles would work dressed in unbecoming white flannel. She felt out of her element, not dressed for the part.

This time, Stockport was ready for her. 'Not a chance. I might have proven to myself that I was correct about the connection, but this only proves to the public that Eleanor wears a wig and glasses. Where's The Cat's garb?' His blue eyes darted around the room, seeking a likely hiding spot.

'The deal you propose is nothing short of blackmail,' Nora accused.

'Tsk, tsk. Blackmail is such an ugly word. I prefer "protection".' His eyes lit on the wardrobe. 'There's a likely hiding place. Let's see what Eleanor hides behind her bevy of ugly dresses.'

Nora experienced a moment of true panic. He strode towards the wardrobe and she knew it was do or die.

Chapter Eleven

Nora flung herself across the door.

Stockport laughed. 'You might as well admit to the hiding place if you're going to be so obvious. Step aside.'

She didn't mind him finding the costume. He knew already. But she did mind him finding other items like the list of investors and the small amount of loot she had hidden there, waiting for a chance to change it into pounds.

'I will not step aside, Stockport. However, I will admit that The Cat's costume is inside. No gentleman would force his way into a lady's closet.' She hoped the appeal to his sense of propriety and honour would work. She looked up at him with a gaze of wide-eyed innocence known to have been the undoing of other men before him.

'*Touché*, madame.' Stockport put a hand over his heart. 'Your appeal to my honour has me at a disadvantage.'

Nora dropped her pose, all business again. 'Now that's settled, tell me your bargain, Stockport.'

He had the gall to smile grandly as if he were enjoying this nocturnal visit far too much for his own good. 'Call me

Brandon. Since we are to be accomplices of sorts, we should be on first-name basis, Eleanor.'

'Don't call me that,' Nora snapped.

Brandon raised his eyebrows in query. 'What shall I call you? I can't call you Cat.' He tapped a long finger against his chin. 'I know, I shall call you Ermentraude. Yes, that's precisely the name that comes to mind when I think of you, white flannel and all.'

'Stop your teasing. This isn't a game, *Brandon*. I have no wish to hang.' Nora brought up the dagger once more, tensing.

'Tell me your name,' Brandon demanded.

'It's Nora,' she ground out through her teeth. She stepped close to him so that the blade pressed against his white shirt. 'I will thank you to take me seriously.'

Something akin to mischief flickered in his eyes. 'Perhaps *you* will thank *me* to take you—preferably horizontally over seriously, but we can work with that. I'm told I am quite skilled at a variety of positions.'

Nora's free hand shot up and slapped him with resounding force across the planes of his gorgeous face. 'If that was the deal you were coming to negotiate, you can climb back out of the window right now.' She gave an expert jab with her blade, slicing off an onyx stud from his shirt front to emphasise her point.

'Ouch, that pricked, you vixen!' Lightning quick, he grabbed her wrist holding the knife. Nora kicked him hard in the shins, succeeding only in raising his ire.

Instantly, she felt herself lifted off the ground and slung over his shoulder. He took two long strides and she was tossed on to her bed. Stockport followed her down, imprisoning her with the sheer size of his looming frame and forcing her to meet his impossibly azure eyes.

Her breath came in pants, her anger quickly turning to

something more lethal than the blade limp in her hand. By all the saints, he was gorgeous and at close range he was nigh on irresistible.

'How dare you?' Nora berated. 'I don't like fast men.'

'I don't like conniving women.' He was nearly as breathless as she.

She gave a throaty chuckle. 'You do too. You like the way I do things, otherwise you wouldn't be here.' She twined her arms about his neck and brought his lips to hers in a searing kiss.

Nora could feel the pressure of his erection hard against the juncture of her thighs and felt her body thrill to it. She wanted him. Negotiations and deceptions suddenly seemed secondary in light of the primal need surging through her.

He drew back, resting on his knees, straddling her at the thighs. Nora cast him a questioning glance at his retreat.

'I want you, Brandon,' she said bluntly in case he had somehow misunderstood her body's invitation.

'I want you too, but not at knife point.' He jerked his head towards her right hand. 'Drop the dagger.'

'Deal. Drop your trousers.'

'Deal.'

The dagger clattered to the floor, followed shortly by the softer shush of trousers.

Negotiations were complete.

'Say it again, Nora. Say you want me,' Brandon murmured quietly as he resumed his position over her, hands on either side of her head, his lips flicking fire-hot kisses along the column of her neck.

She could barely think, let alone speak, but somehow she found the wherewithal to whisper it again. 'I want you, Brandon.'

'No games?' His hand gently kneaded a breast through the flannel. His body might be ready, but his mind was sceptical, no doubt recalling the last time they'd played along these lines. He'd ended up tied to the bed.

Hungry for his full commitment, Nora offered the reassurance he sought. 'It's no game, not tonight.' She leaned up to kiss him again. 'Tonight, it's just you and me, no politics between us.'

He studied her face, a sudden tenderness present on his own countenance that startled Nora. 'Truly?' he asked in near-reverent tones, indicating this was no game for him either.

'Yes.' She nodded, reaching for him once more and growing tired of the delays. With her two hands she reached up and rent the fabric of his shirt and pushed it off his shoulders. Then she began tugging at her nightgown.

'Oh, no, you don't, turnabout's fair play.' Brandon gave a sensual laugh and reached for the gown himself. 'Do you have many like this?'

'Two others.'

'Good. Then you won't miss this one.' He grabbed up the fabric at the hem in both hands and ripped. Slowly. Revealing her to him inch by aching inch.

He was a torturer of the highest order. Nora closed her eyes against the onslaught of desire that took her the moment his lips caressed her exposed calf and moved their way up to her thighs. Never had she been so thoroughly or successfully wooed. His skill had not been exaggerated.

Nora tried to keep a part of her mind detached, focused on something else so that she would not be wholly consumed by the act she and Brandon were engaged in. She tried to think of her next robbery, tried to visualise the floor plan of the St John house, tried to remember Brandon was her enemy, and while there could be an objective moment of shared pleasure between them, there could be nothing more.

She failed utterly.

Her mental exercises were no match for the musky scent of his maleness and the clean spicy smell of his soap. His hands caressed and his kisses worshipped as he made his way up her body, laving and revering by turn until she was at last bare to his gaze.

With a lazy finger, he traced a circle about the aureole of her breast. 'You're beautiful,' he said simply.

Her heart sang at the plain compliment. It meant all the more for its lack of adornment and her desire mounted. She could feel her own slickness welling and she prayed it wouldn't be long before Brandon brought his sweet brand of agony to an end. Nora writhed against him in encouragement.

'Patience, Nora.' He laughed softly before calming her mouth with a kiss. 'I would not rush this and have it over so quickly.' He tested her with a gentle finger and even that small, intimate invasion left her gasping.

His erection prodded the entrance to her soft core and she opened to it, spreading her legs wide to accommodate him between them. His heat was contagious and she was seized with an urgency to have him inside.

The sooner this exquisite distress was over, the sooner she could find her balance. She was fighting futilely and frantically now to save herself from complete capitulation.

He entered her with a sharp push that caused her to gasp and then he sighed, sliding home the rest of the distance. She found his rhythm and raised her hips to join him. Had anything ever felt so divine? Her body pulsed around his shaft, faster and faster until she knew she'd burst from the ecstasy of it. Desperately she strove to hold on to a piece of herself, to not give him everything.

'Let it happen, Nora. We've been moving towards this since

we met,' Brandon coaxed hoarsely. 'There, now, let it go. Come soar with me.'

And she did.

Nora exploded. Her senses were raw and vulnerable. She could feel Brandon's weight as it sagged in satiation against her, having found his release as well. She could smell the musk of their lovemaking. She could taste the sweat of their efforts on her skin. Had she ever been more alive than she was right now?

Brandon rolled to his side and pulled her to him so that her backside lay tucked against him. Not for all the sterling in Britain would she have moved from that position, even if she could have willed her languid bones to do so. Overcome with an odd sense of completion, Nora fell asleep for the first time in years not wondering about tomorrow.

This was not what he had come here for, Brandon mused in the dark, watching Nora sleep beside him. He wished he could rest that easily. He idly fingered a long curl and let it fall against her exposed shoulder. He had come to strike a deal with her. He would warn her about the trap at St John's in exchange for her promise that she would stop the raids. He wouldn't expose her identity. She could move on. Then she would be someone else's problem.

He didn't want her to be someone else's problem. He wanted her to be his problem, and his alone; not Witherspoon's or St John's, just his.

Tonight had complicated matters. He had not come here with any intention to bed her, but, having done so, he was forced to recognise that his attraction to Nora was more than easily slaked lust.

He would be severely compromised if the investors discovered this little liaison. Hell, the investors were the least of his worries. He was the local magistrate and he was bedfellows with the local underworld. Literally. Being with Nora could not happen again.

Nora, Nora, Nora, his mind chanted. At last, his passion had a name and visage beyond the alias and the mask of The Cat. They had made love twice more and each time had served to heighten his desire for her.

She fired his blood like no other. She was not interested in him for his title or his vote like the powdered women of the *ton*. She wanted him as a man and only as a man. The thought was stimulating and highly complimentary if he didn't realise the reality behind it. She could not have him any other way. As a man and a woman, there were no barriers between them. Acknowledging him as an Earl and a mill owner erected plenty of obstacles.

Nora stirred beside him, reminding him that the night was passing and that he could not be caught at The Grange when the sun rose. He doubted his ability to resist another coupling if she awoke.

Brandon reluctantly rose from the bed, careful not to disturb her. He dressed in the dark, the lamp having gone out hours ago. He shrugged into the sleeves of his greatcoat and felt the imprint of the small notebook he carried in his inside pocket. Inspiration struck.

Kneeling by the sill, he took out the small lead pencil and notebook and wrote. He left the paper on the table next to her bed and said a silent farewell before exiting through the window.

He was gone. Nora knew it before she opened her eyes. The bed felt empty. A brush of her hand over cold sheets where he had lain confirmed it. Well, what had she expected? He could have not stayed. He couldn't very well have walked downstairs and declared his presence to Hattie and Alfred or risk being seen leaving the Grange by anyone who happened to be taking a morning ride. It simply wasn't practical.

Of course, 'practical' was merely a rationalisation to salve her wounded pride. He probably woke up and realised how foolhardy their passionate foray had been, just as she was doing now. And it was that—it was the most foolhardy thing she'd done since her brief marriage.

Nora rolled over on her back and moaned. What was it with her and handsome men? They were her Achilles' heel. Her first husband had been handsome, conceited and lazy. She hadn't discovered the last two traits until it was too late. Now it seemed she was on the brink of falling for another handsome face, this one entirely out of her league. A thief had no business giving her heart or her body to a peer of the realm. It would only serve to complicate things between them.

'Hah!' Nora snorted out loud to the empty room. 'It was only sex.' Perhaps saying it out loud would help her put everything into perspective. It wasn't as if she was expecting him to offer for her after their night together—their incredible, exceptional night together.

It didn't help. No matter how many times she said it, she could not convince herself it was only sex. She had wanted Brandon on a higher plane. She'd wanted him body *and* soul. And last night, he'd wanted her too, all politics aside.

Unless he'd been pretending. Doubt gnawed at her innards. Oh, please, no. Was it possible to fake the way he had looked at her? The way he'd seduced her with such reverence as if she were a goddess? Remembering made the doubt worse. Perhaps he thought to ensnare her, lure her close with protestations of love and undying devotion. She remembered his simple words: 'You're so beautiful.'

Nora cringed. Someone trying too hard would have made the mistake of using flowery language, comparing her lips to roses or some other body part to some other ridiculous commodity. Not Brandon Wycroft. He was a master at his craft.

Nora reprimanded herself. She'd willingly eaten from the proverbial tree of knowledge last night. She and Brandon had made love and now there was doubt, slinking like a serpent between them. Before last night, everything had been clearly defined; she wanted to see the mill fail and he wanted to see it succeed. It had all been so uncomplicated.

Nora's eyes lit on the table beside her bed. A note. She reached for it. Nora, do not go to St. John's on Wednesday night. It is a trap. B.

Nora crumpled the small sheet in her hand. The note was short, concise and, after last night, positively deadly. Was he telling the truth and wished to protect her from harm? Was it a lie? Maybe he hoped she would believe the note and forgo the raid. It might be nothing more than a ploy to get The Cat to stop the robberies. If the robberies stopped, the investors would stay. The mill would go forward. He would get what he wanted. He would win.

She hated herself. He had her right where he wanted her—between doubt and disaster.

'She's got you right where she wants you—panting like a stallion around a mare in season,' Jack drawled, sprawled in a chair before the fire in Brandon's library, a glass of brandy in one hand. His growing familiarity with that position was starting to irritate Brandon.

Brandon shot Jack a ferocious glare. 'Don't be crass. That's not funny. I brought you here to help me, not to make jokes at my expense. So far, you've done nothing but drink my whisky and abuse my hospitality.' Looking for insight into his problem, Brandon had confessed his night with Nora to Jack, daggers and all.

'It's not crass, it's true.' Jack twirled the snifter's stem carelessly. 'She beds you...'

'*She* did not bed *me*,' Brandon retorted, his pride stinging.

Jack raised his eyebrows. 'Correction. You bedded her. That's what she's convinced you to think anyway. In return, you spilled the beans and told her everything.'

Brandon stared into the fire. He was mad at Jack for making his time with Nora into something manipulative and tainted. He was mad at himself for partially believing his friend might be right. There was nothing like a little disgust and self-loathing to queer his pitch with Nora.

He was conscious of Jack rising from his chair. Jack gained the door and turned back. 'Tell me, did you ever get a look in that wardrobe she so zealously defended?'

Brandon met his question with stoic silence. No, he hadn't and, worse, he hadn't thought anything of it until Jack brought it up. Whatever she was hiding in there, she had successfully defended. So successfully, in fact, he hadn't even realised she had diverted him until a day later.

'That's what I thought. Now, explain to me again how she doesn't have you where she wants you?'

Brandon sighed and slumped down in his chair. By Lucifer's stones, sleeping with Nora was the worst best thing he'd ever done.

Chapter Twelve

Wednesday night found Nora guiding her horse up the dark Cheetham Hill Road towards the wealthy neighborhood where Magnus St John lived.

She was glad she had chosen to come. She couldn't stand hypocrisy in any form. It irked her endlessly that men like St John and Witherspoon made money off the grime of industry, but wouldn't dare to dirty themselves by living amid the squalor they wrought.

They might think twice about their fortunes if they couldn't look down on the factories of Manchester from their lofty mansions on Cheetham Hill, but instead had to live in Ardmore, a once-elegant, but quickly succumbing, suburb of Manchester or some other such neighbourhood.

The decision to carry out her plans at St John's had been a classic prisoner's dilemma and she'd spent the better part of the week debating her decision.

Go or stay? There appeared no way she could win. If she went and there was no trap, it would mean that Brandon had used their intimate encounter to manipulate her plans. If not, it would mean Brandon held some modicum of feeling for her, but going would put her in significant danger.

Nora knew she should hope the first option was true, but part of her didn't want to believe Brandon could fake such an intense encounter or, even if he could, that he would have done so with her. After all, she'd been honest with him from the start about who and what she was.

While Nora, the woman on the brink of catapulting into love, was tempted to play the coward and renege on her Wednesday raid, The Cat knew her duty. The Cat did not shirk her responsibilities.

Despite the hiccup of her interlude with Brandon, The Cat was succeeding; the investors were scared; word in the village had it that two were asking to pull out. The mill was short on funds. Everything was going according to plan.

Experience taught her that was when the bottom usually fell out of the bucket. Just not tonight, she prayed, please, just don't let it be tonight. Still, in spite of her responsibilities, she might have opted for remaining at home this evening if it hadn't been for the note that arrived Monday afternoon.

The regular food supplies had not improved Mary Malone's health. She desperately needed a doctor and expensive medicines. Nora was her only hope. That Mary had written to *ask* for help indicated how dire her situation must be.

The street on which St John lived in his palatial townhouse was near. Nora turned off and followed the lane behind the fine homes leading to the mews where the residents stabled their cattle. She found a quiet corner behind St John's home, not far from the gate leading to his small city garden where she could discreetly leave her horse.

She'd been here twice before and knew the gardens and house well. The dining room, with its imported Venetian crystal chandelier, was St John's pride. The elegant room could be accessed from the outside by French doors that opened into the room so guests could be entertained by the burbling fountain in the spring. In the winter, the doors were kept shut and the gardens dark.

It would be the perfect entrance as long as the undercook had done her job and slipped the sleeping potion Nora's network had provided into the staff's afternoon tea, the last meal they would have before serving St John's guests. The powder would induce a sound eight hours of sleep before wearing off.

If the potion worked as planned, all the non-essential staff would be asleep, leaving her to deal only with the footmen in the dining room serving the meal. She wasn't worried overmuch. Many of them were hired just for the evening and already had sympathies with The Cat. The others didn't care much for St John and his blustering ways. She was counting on them enjoying the sight of their arrogant master being brought to heel too much to pose any real problem.

Nora dismounted and continued the short distance to St John's on foot. She deftly scaled the garden wall and dropped silently to the ground. Her first task was to unlock the gate. There was no sense in scaling the wall on her way out too.

When she left, she had only to run to the gate, push it open and she'd be in the street with only a short distance between her and the horse. Better yet, should Brandon be telling the truth about the party, the guests would have their carriages and horses hidden from common view. By the time they retrieved their horses to give pursuit, she would be long gone into the night.

Her escape route secured, Nora turned her attention to the house. Customarily, on Wednesday nights the St Johns played cards. She scanned the exterior. Her eyes lit on the dining-room window. The room was dark, the exquisite chandelier dim. Her spirits sank.

She supposed a part of her had hoped to see the chandelier blazing, but that was ridiculous. Witherspoon and St John wouldn't overlook that obvious detail. A lit chandelier would warn off a burglar, a sure sign that someone was dining at home.

She pulled a small watch out from beneath her cloak and consulted its face. Five minutes before nine. St John and company were to have sat for dinner at a quarter past seven. By now they would be finishing their third course, the fowl course, and have had plenty to drink. It was well known that St John served drinks before dinner and kept an excellent wine cellar for his entertainments.

Nora did quick calculations in her head. Her information indicated St John served his meals *à la Russe*. That meant there would be ten footmen in attendance, one for each guest.

Her tallies totalled twenty people in all. Unless Brandon was in the room—then that made twenty-two, Brandon and the footman serving him. The thought drew a shiver from her that she did not dare to contemplate. She had not seen him since their night together. She could not stop to dwell on him now. She had a performance to give—if not to the group quietly waiting for her in the dark house, then for Brandon when she finished here.

She neared the panes and her breath caught. She glanced again and was sure. Candle flames, invisible at a distance, flickered on the dining-room table. Elation surged through her. Brandon hadn't lied. Do not think on him! she cautioned herself, breathing deeply to center her thoughts.

She checked the two pistols and knife she carried at her waist—three weapons, not counting the hidden dagger in her sleeve sheath, the one she'd pulled on Brandon. She thought of Mary's three children and shoved fears for her own safety aside and bravely plunged ahead.

The glass-paned doors that gave out on to the terrace from the St Johns' dining room shattered the polite tones of supper conversation. Women screamed. Men bit off barely restrained expletives at the interruption of their well-ordered evening. A dark form vaulted on to the white-clothed table. In each hand, two deadly, long-nosed pistols gleamed in the dim candlelight.

'I say!' St John half-rose in his seat to protest the intrusion.

'You'll say nothing more until I command it!' came the reply.

Sitting to the right of St John, Brandon felt the tension he'd been carrying between his shoulder blades all evening dissipate in anticipation of what was to come. The Cat had arrived. The trap—laying in wait for The Cat to come—had been sprung, only now it seemed more to her advantage than to theirs.

The investors' plan seemed silly in the wake of the reality playing out before him. They'd thought to catch her by changing the St Johns' weekly schedule and being at home when The Cat came calling. They had not planned for the contingency of The Cat confronting them directly. The servants were supposed to have subdued the intruder.

That worried him. What would she do when the servants stormed the dining room? She couldn't hold off the entire staff. But then, The Cat wouldn't leave such a detail uncovered. Perhaps there would be no staff. Looking covertly around the room, it became clear that the footmen were not going to leap to St John's aid. Maybe no one else would either. Brandon relaxed. The odds were looking up.

Now, the investors' very nemesis danced on the table and held them at gunpoint against the odds of ten to one. Silently Brandon applauded her tenacity but he didn't want to see her hurt and he'd prefer not to be compromised by coming to her defence. Although, at the moment it didn't look like she needed much protection.

His conscience mocked him. It was a bit late in the game to be worrying about compromising situations *now*. Besides, he'd chosen to put himself in this predicament by coming to dinner at all. His curiosity had gotten the better of him; had Nora believed him and used the information he had given her to protect herself or had she been filled with the same doubts that plagued him and come anyway, thinking he had lied for his own benefit?

Tonight would be a litmus test. If she stayed away, it meant she trusted him. If she came... Well, then he'd owe Jack twenty quid and Nora would owe him an explanation about what exactly she thought had transpired between them.

Oh, indeed, his curiosity had led him to St John's dining room. Inarguably it certainly had gotten the best of him. Now, as he watched Nora hold court on St John's damask cloth, he hoped curiosity wouldn't kill The Cat.

With nimble steps, Nora stepped towards St John and presented him with a black bag. 'Pass the bag about the table and deposit your jewellery and effects into it,' she snapped, giving one of the guns an ominous wave.

St John was too flustered to do anything but comply. He fumbled with the ruby cravat pin he wore and put it in the bag. Mister Flack on his left had no such compunction.

'Now see here, you insolent bastard, you cannot commandeer us in such a fashion!'

She cocked the pistol, an unmistakeable sound. 'Can I not?'

'Damn it all, man,' Flack beseeched the host. 'Call for your servants.'

Eyes blazing at the man's insistent mutiny, Nora kicked over his crystal goblet of red wine and let the burgundy stain seep into the pristine cloth. 'Better wine than blood, wouldn't you agree, Mr Flack? At the next interruption, I shoot. Don't take any notions about servants coming to your rescue. They have been effectively subdued thanks to a wee potion in their afternoon tea.' She hoped that sufficiently cowed Mr Flack. She would rather not shoot anyone although, if it came to it, a flesh wound to the shoulder might do some of them good.

The women put up no resistance as she trained the pistols on each guest in turn, causing them to make their donations quickly so that the pistols might be turned on their neighbour instead. The bag came to Brandon last. Her eyes locked on his, compelling him to keep her secret. *Don't make me have to try to shoot you.*

His gaze was riveting and demanded her attention, which almost cost her. In order to keep the bag and Brandon in sight, she turned her attention slightly away from the other half of the table. Brandon's face saved her at the last moment. His sharp eyes slid to the left and she whirled with his gaze, hearing the noise as she did so.

Stinging from the loss of his diamond cravat pin, Mr Witherspoon tried to play the hero. A gentleman's derringer flashed in his hand. Only his penchant for the dramatic bought her the needed extra seconds. If he had shot first and talked later, the outcome might have been vastly different.

'Drop your weapons!' Witherspoon bellowed.

Nora laughed fearlessly. 'Drop *your* weapons, sir!'

'I am not afraid. I don't think you'll shoot,' Witherspoon retorted.

'How willing are you to risk your companions on that bet? For instance, would you be willing to risk the Earl?' She turned one of her pistols on Brandon. Damn the seating arrangement. She had no choice. The shattered door lay to his right—her escape and he was in the way. She wished it was anyone but him. This was the very scenario she wanted to avoid. If she couldn't shoot him, she would have to take him with her.

She started barking instructions while the table erupted into muffled shrieks of horror at the possibility of a murdered Earl. 'My lord, take the bag and start backing towards the door. Do not try to run. I will use my second pistol to shoot you down in your tracks. To the rest of you, I command you to stay seated in your chairs for ten minutes. Do not follow me. My lord is my hostage. It will go poorly for him if you attempt any more heroics.'

To her relief, Brandon moved towards the door. She backed up, using a careful sidestepping motion to keep both him and the table in her line of vision. It wouldn't do for Brandon to play the traitor now. For good measure, Nora fired a shot at the chain holding the chandelier, sending the Venetian crystal confection crashing on to the table, scattering china.

'What do we do now?' Brandon asked once they cleared the house and were out in the street.

'I've a horse hidden down the street. I don't expect those idiots in there to actually wait ten minutes before they come hunting.' She stuffed the guns into her belt. 'Now we run.' Nora sprinted down the street, leaving Brandon to follow, although it never occurred to her that he might not.

Her assumption that he would blindly follow orders and play the hostage-cum-accomplice galled Brandon beyond the point of good sense. The tumult of emotions that had roiled within him all night rose to the fore while he ran after her; all the anxiety of waiting for her to show or not—did she trust him or not?—and the awkward mixture of fear and pride at watching her perform her antics on St John's white-clothed table. It angered him that she would risk her own life to test him.

Deuce take it, he'd worried himself sick on her behalf and she was using him as a hostage. Jack would get a hearty laugh out of that along with his twenty quid. Clearly their night together hadn't meant the same to her as it did to him. Well, she wouldn't get away with it. The game stopped here and it stopped tonight.

They gained the dark corner where the horse waited. Brandon didn't wait a moment longer. He grabbed for her arm, bringing her to a jarring halt. He spun her around amid a torrent of protests and backed her into a wall, both of his hands now fiercely gripping her shoulders beneath her dark cloak. 'Listen to me, you little minx. Whatever game you and I are playing is finished. I could have exposed you back there at dinner and I didn't. You owe me and you're going to pay,' he growled in menacing tones.

'Do you think I'll kiss you for it or perhaps you hope for something more? Would another night between the sheets be enough to cover my supposed debt?' She was all sauce and boldness, making the most of their bodies' close proximity. 'Any debt I owe you has already been paid. I could have shot you for good measure and ensured no one would follow us since they'd be too busy looking after your wounded self.'

Her brassy behavior, coupled with her cocky assumptions, fired Brandon's ire further. 'Stupid fool! You wouldn't have shot me. You were betting on me behaving more like your accomplice than your hostage the whole while.'

'What makes you so sure?'

Brandon growled, 'Because you'd never take an unbound

hostage who has a height advantage of five inches and several pounds of brawn. You'd be setting yourself up to be overpowered. Like this.'

In a fast motion, Brandon pulled her to him, trapping her against his chest. He lowered his lips to claim a primitive kiss while she bucked against him in outrage. He used her in rough fashion, finding an outlet for his earlier frustrations over the danger she'd put herself in by storming the party. He tasted salt where her teeth bit the tender flesh of his lips. He revelled in the fight she posed.

Their mouths duelled. She bit. He nipped. Their tongues tangled. Brandon felt the tempo change as their duel became infused with a heat of a different sort. It wasn't so much the heat of battle that raged between them now, but the heat of passion, of an attraction that, once acknowledged, was not easily quenched. He drew back for a moment to gather breath.

'How dare you!' she cried, remembering to be angry at his advances.

'Tonight, I want something more than kissing from you. I want the truth and I'll have it as soon as we get to safety.' He had more to say, but a glimmer in the next lane demanded his attention.

He was loathe to let Nora out of his sight; however, the appearance of lanterns could only belong to a hastily launched search party. His plans were thwarted.

Brandon jerked his head to the west, calling her attention to the cluster of bobbing lights. 'In the meanwhile, you might want to cultivate some common sense and develop some anxiety over your precarious position.' He was gratified to note a flicker of concern pass through her as she took in the burgeoning scene.

'Unhand me at once. You can stay here. Finding you in one

piece will take the necessity out of their cold evening search,'
she ordered, taking charge again.

Brandon shook his head and held his ground. 'No. We'll do
this my way. I've had enough of your plans for one evening.'

He knelt on one knee and began rubbing handfuls of dirt
into his evening clothes. He smudged his cheek and then proceeded to gather his shirt between his hands and rent the cloth
until he looked thoroughly abused. 'I will go to them and tell
them I've eluded you. I'll show them my wound and ask to
be taken back to St John's for bandaging. That way no one
will be looking for a trail you might have left behind. You will
go on to my estate and await me there. You and I are not
finished tonight.'

'What if I don't follow your dictates? You cannot force me
to show up at your house and turn myself over to your dubious
care. How do I know it's not a trap of your own making?' she
argued coolly, her mind as sane as ever, but Brandon saw the
nervousness in her eyes as she assessed the nearing lanterns
and raised voices.

'You don't have a choice. If you do not comply, I'll call
out the hounds myself. I doubt Eleanor Habersham will appreciate her servants being subjected to the indignities of a
house search, to say nothing of having to explain the oddity
of her own nocturnal absence.'

'You wouldn't dare!' Nora raged in impotent fury.

'Follow my wishes and I'll protect you if needed.'

'There's another consideration you've overlooked. You
don't have a wound,' Nora pointed out.

'Not yet. Give me your dagger.'

Reluctantly, Nora threw back the cuff of her shirt, revealing the hidden sheath and pulled out the dagger, handing it to
him handle first.

He gripped it and quickly flashed the sharp blade across the palm of his hand.

Nora stifled an undignified yelp at the sight of dark blood welling in his hand. He'd cut deep, giving himself a realistic gash. Instinctively, she wadded the hem of her cloak to press against the cut. 'You go too far!'

He stayed her with his good hand. 'Meet me at the estate in an hour and you can doctor me all you wish.' With an impish smile that suggested adventure sat well with him, Brandon took off in the direction of the lanterns. His hand hurt like hell. She was probably right—he'd cut it far more deeply than necessary. But he could not deny he'd enjoyed himself immensely tonight. It surprised him to realise that there wasn't a night in recent memory that he could recall having so much fun despite all that was at risk.

The magnitude of the risk she was taking struck Nora all at once and all too late. She was already ensconced in Brandon's private rooms, wrapped in a paisley robe she'd liberated from his dressing room and sitting before the fire his valet had kept stoked against my lord's return later in the evening, when she realised what she had done. She had trusted Stockport unconditionally not once, but twice that evening.

First, he was right. She had indeed bet that he wouldn't revolt against playing the role of 'hostage' when Witherspoon pulled out his derringer. Second, she actually believed that she would have his protection when he returned to the estate. She believed it so thoroughly she had made free with his chambers, shedding her damp clothing and curling up before his fire in anticipation of the forthcoming conversation.

What was she thinking? At what point had her wits become so addled that she'd started thinking the Earl of Stockport was her ally? In reality, there was nothing to stop Stockport from returning to St John's and leading the company straight to her. After all, he'd told her where to be. It made sense that he was setting her up so he could capture her. Arresting The Cat in front of the people to whom her arrest mattered most would be a feather in his cap. Such an act would go far to restore his damaged credibility over the factory.

As if her doubts had suddenly sprung to life and assumed human form, voices rose from the vestibule downstairs. Stockport had returned, bringing with him unlooked-for companions. Her fears were realised and about to be played out. Being here in Stockport's home was the real trap. The dinner party had merely been foreplay to the true betrayal. Nora's heart plummeted at the sting of it all. She could imagine Stockport telling everyone how he had lulled The Cat into complacency, weaving his own web of deceit around The Cat and fooling her into believing she had the upper hand.

The voices grew strident and Nora detected the seeds of an argument rising between the new arrivals. Stockport's voice rose in protest. He didn't need any further assistance and the men were free to return to their evening. The others with him countered that it might be unsafe to leave him alone while The Cat ran free in the countryside. One of them, probably Witherspoon, suggested a search of the house. Stockport protested again. Nora grinned to herself. Maybe Stockport hadn't told them everything after all. She would wager the contents of the jewel bag she'd collected that night he hadn't told them The Cat was a woman.

The knowledge that he had most likely withheld some information didn't exonerate him from the betrayal he'd wrought by bringing the men here, but it did serve to harden her heart. Brandon had promised her protection this night and he was damn well going to give it to her even if she had to drag it from him in the most compromising of manners.

Nora looked down at the fine paisley silk of Brandon's robe and suppressed a laugh. He thought to show them The Cat, dressed in dark trousers and shirt. He could let Witherspoon and the others search the house. They wouldn't find The Cat of Manchester in residence. Neither would they find anyone hiding away timidly awaiting discovery.

Nora tossed her hair once, giving it a sleep-rumpled look. Feigning wide-eyed innocence, she marched to the top of the stairs, ready to do battle with Witherspoon, Brandon and whatever else fate decreed to throw in her path.

Chapter Thirteen

'Darling, what happened to you?' The siren on the stairs gushed with concern, causing Brandon and the five men with him to stop their conversation in mid-sentence and gaze slack jawed at the vision draped in a man's dressing gown at the top of the landing.

'Your clothes are ruined and your hand—why, you're wounded!' The dark-haired angel managed a feminine gasp of horror and began descending the steps, leaving no ambiguity as to the status of her undress beneath the robe.

Brandon watched her performance in a state of consciousness that hovered somewhere between thoroughly amused and utterly horrified. She was magnificent, so boldly taking them all by surprise. He'd been racking his mind, trying to think of a way to be rid of the men who had insisted on following him home. He'd been unsuccessful. Dismissing them and their offers to search the house for the sake of his safety had proved too difficult to thwart without looking like a graceless cad. From the look of things, he need not have worried. Nora had it all well in hand with her tousled hair and wide eyes.

'My lord…' Witherspoon sputtered incoherently, looking

to him for an explanation of the woman's presence. Witherspoon might be maliciously ruthless, but he was also a prude.

Nora reached his side and put a possessive hand on his sleeve. 'I have discomfited you. I must apologise. I thought Brandon would have told everyone by now.' She playfully tut-tutted him in a chiding manner. 'Before he was called away from London, we were about to announce our engagement. I am his betrothed, Nora Hammersmith.'

Brandon felt his face freeze into a smiling mask. She'd thought *his* self-inflicted wound was too much. This time *she* went too far! Was that her real last name or another alias?

Shockingly, he realised he didn't mind her claim. What bothered him was the impossibility of carrying off such a charade. Did she know all that an Earl's wedding entailed? More importantly, a nobleman's intended would not be alone in his home unchaperoned. Her enticing dishabille cast his entire character in dishonour, suggesting to all assembled that they had anticipated their wedding night not just once, but were in the habit of frequently doing so. It would be much more difficult to wriggle off the hook of an already consummated betrothal.

Nora smiled and blushed, having the good sense to feign modesty. Belatedly, she clutched at the neck of the robe. 'I am so sorry, my lords. I am a simple country girl at heart and seeing my betrothed in such a state has undone my wits. I must beg forgiveness for such a lack of decorum.'

Brandon scrutinised the group, watching for their reaction. He had no need to worry. She had them utterly convinced. Reassurances flowed, followed by congratulations, and a few of the men dared to slap Brandon on the back for finding such a lovely and concerned lady. Others ribbed him about keeping her a secret for so long.

Nora demurely took her leave and retreated upstairs. The men took her departure as a signal for their farewells and Brandon ushered them out of the hall within minutes, happy to see their backs, if only temporarily.

Several of them had assured Brandon their wives would call on his intended come the morrow. To which he had only answered that perhaps such visits were best delayed until his betrothed recovered from her journey.

He shut the door behind the last guest and leaned his head heavily against the solid oak panel. He would worry about tomorrow later. Right now, there was plenty in the present that demanded his attention. The Cat awaited him upstairs and she'd better have a good explanation for her behaviour tonight.

Brandon opened the door to his private chambers, ready to lay claim to those explanations and didn't get a word out before she pounced.

'Protection! You call that protection?' she railed, punctuating her outrage with a well-thrown pillow at his midsection. 'Your "protection" was self-defence at best!'

He schooled his features into a cool expression, a remarkable feat considering the heat she was raising in him, dressed as she was. 'In defence of my actions, I'd hoped to re-direct their attentions to a lengthy search of the countryside. I did not guess they'd feel obliged to accompany me home and search the house or the grounds. If you're angry at how events unfolded, you have only yourself to blame. Let me remind you—*you* told them you were my betrothed.

'Do you know what it takes to pull off marrying an Earl? How will you extricate us from that one?' Brandon pushed a hand through his hair in sign of his evident frustration. 'Your escapades tonight were over the top. Whatever were you thinking to take on the entire dinner party? You could have been captured. Witherspoon's more dangerous than you realise. I shudder to think of what might have happened with his gun if I hadn't been there.'

She pressed the back of her hand against her forehead in a mockingly dramatic pose. 'My hero! Am I such a simpleton that I would have gone into a situation where I had my doubts?'

'Laugh all you want, but, thanks to me, you are not languishing in the Squire's cellar tonight contemplating your upcoming trial.' Brandon's tone was harsh.

He strode to the window and looked out, turning his back to her, his hands fisted in his trouser pockets. He had to keep a cool head when dealing with this virago. He asked the question that had plagued him all night. 'Why did you do it? You knew you were being set up.'

'Did I?' Nora challenged from the chair by the fire where she'd staked out her territory.

'I told you.'

'Why should I believe you?' Nora snapped. 'You might have been trying to keep me away from the investors with the ploy of this invented trap.'

Brandon turned from the window. 'You should know better than to think I would lie to you. You know I am capable of more than cheap tricks.'

'Do I? It's easy to be brave with words and a wagon load of supplies you can afford without troubling your pocket,' she threw at his back.

'I'd say tonight proves all. Do you have any appreciation for what I risked at St John's? If they had realised I knew you or that I signalled you when Witherspoon pulled out his gun, we'd both be ruined. I let you point a gun at me and use me as a hostage to ensure your escape. What does that prove to you?' Brandon barely kept his temper reined.

'It proves what women have known for ages. Men are ruled by their cocks. A man will do anything for a woman who arouses him.'

Brandon swallowed hard. 'Aha, so I am not the only one in this room with "motives". What about you? How am I to believe you're entirely innocent? Perhaps *you* seduced *me* in order to get me to bare my secrets.'

'Then we are nothing more than a pair of double-crossers,' Nora said with smug satisfaction.

He breathed deeply and found clarity in the moment. He saw through her ploy. She *wanted* to drive a wedge between them and she thought this double-edged sword of doubt had successfully put an obstacle between them. Well, then, he would parry with a riposte of his own.

'I can't accept that we are nothing more than two people playing a duplicitous game, Nora.' Brandon lowered his voice, using a trick he often used when speaking in Parliament to gain attention when a loud voice failed to get it. 'I won't quarrel with you tonight. We are not such different creatures despite our disparity in social standing.' Brandon moved to stand in front her chair, bending slightly to gently grip and massage her forearms through the silk.

'Can't you see that we want the same things, Nora?' he murmured in a tone that implied the 'same things' carried a romantic connotation as well as a political one. To emphasise the duality of his comment, Brandon wrapped a dark, errant curl around his finger.

Now that the initial danger had passed, he wanted to remind her in all ways how similar they were, how right they were together, but Nora was still fighting.

'I am your enemy. *You* are building a mill. *I* am trying to stop it. The comparison escapes me,' she argued in breathless refutation of his claim, but her attempt to hold him off was empty.

Brandon felt her breath hitch at his touch. He saw her eyes lose their hardness. They flickered now with uncertainty and he knew what she was thinking—dare she put down her verbal armour? The first time had been a voyage into the unknown, but this time she knew what lay ahead.

Brandon gave a half-smile, delighting in her fire. She was a fighter to the end, but he had patience and whether she knew it or not, the end was very near. 'Poor Nora, you've fought for so long—all you know is the fight, isn't it? My mill will make a difference here. If I don't build it, someone else will, someone who isn't so concerned with the inequities of factory life. Someone like Cecil Witherspoon.'

He dropped the curl he'd been winding about his finger and let it fall against her silk-clad breast. He could practically see the wheels turning in her head as she assessed his words. She was calculating, weighing pragmatic reality against the urgings of her heart. *She wanted to trust him. She cared for him.* But scepticism was a difficult opponent to defeat.

'Why are you doing this, Brandon?' The disbelief he sensed was evident in her words.

Brandon watched her. This was not a moment for teasing; this was the moment for reassurances. He could have told her any number of lies. He opted for the truth, even though it exposed his hand, left him open for manipulation if she chose to do so.

'You fire my blood, Nora. Not just your pretty face, but the whole of you, body and soul. Never have I met a woman with such tenacity or such concern for her fellow mankind. Your passions, all of them, stir me in a way I've not been stirred in a long time.'

Brandon bent his mouth to hers, catching it in a gentle kiss so unlike the rough kisses they'd shared on other occasions.

She pushed against his chest, showing her characteristic stubbornness. His Cat was not easily conquered. But then, any battle worth fighting contained an element of difficulty. 'It's not that easy, Brandon. A few kisses and a flowery proclamation cannot solve what lies between us.'

'You cannot ignore that we're drawn to each other,' he argued softly, drawing her to her feet and bringing her close enough to nibble at the tender part of her ear.

'I don't know what to believe any more.' She sighed.

'You can believe in me, Nora.' Brandon whet his lips and prepared to lay siege.

What if she could believe in what Brandon offered? If they were on the same side of the political spectrum, what other dreams might she dare to give wing? Dare she believe that he might admire her, and that beneath that admiration there might be something more? She would not know if she didn't pursue this thing taking shape between them. It was all she needed to give her desire free reign.

She wound her arms about his neck and invited his lips back to hers. She pressed against him, letting her body say that for which she could not yet brave the words to speak. She tossed back her head and let him trail glorious kisses down her neck, allowing the vee of her dressing gown to dip open until it revealed more than it concealed of her naked form beneath.

Brandon groaned against her, bending to lave her breasts with his hot tongue, and she knew the pleasure was mutual. She felt his fingers tremble as his hands rose to push back the robe from her shoulders. She let the silk slither into a pool at her feet and she let his eyes feast upon her utterly exposed body.

Standing before him, naked, knowing where they were headed, was infinitely more intimate than the spontaneous act between them a few nights ago. This was premeditated.

She felt no shame in her nakedness, or any coveting lust in Brandon's gaze, although it might have been better for her heart if she had. Instead, the look he gave her was full of sincere reverence. At least, in this moment, she was cherished. With that realisation, all barriers vanished.

'Undress me,' Brandon commanded in a hoarse voice filled with awe.

Nora knew what he asked. This was the point of no return. If she disrobed him, they would spend the night consummating the relationship in the most intimate, most complete of ways. There could be no excuses of haste and impulsiveness.

This act was deliberate. As such, it could not be brushed off as a game, an experiment, come the morning. This act would serve to seal an unspoken contract between them and it would bring with it binding implications.

She held his gaze as if she could signal with her eyes her understanding and acceptance of the significance of what they were about to do. The intensity of his stare indicated he understood as well. And he accepted.

'Undress me, Nora,' he repeated, extending the unwritten contract again. He wanted her and he fully comprehended what the price of wanting her meant.

'Patience, Brandon.' Nora smiled, reaching for the placard of buttons on his ruined waistcoat. Now that the decision had been made, she was free, her passions could be hers alone tonight. There would be no worries about manipulation and hidden agendas. Just pleasure.

'Brandon. I like the sound of that. I haven't been simply Brandon for a long time.' His breath caught as she slid back the waistcoat and the panels of his dirty white shirt, thumbing his nipples with her nails.

Her elation increased. He understood! Although it was for entirely different reasons, he too longed to simply be himself, to lay aside the strain of the earldom, of life as a peer of the realm, and to just be.

She bent to suckle him in imitation of his earlier overture. Her hands moved lower to release the fastenings of his trousers. She paused long enough for Brandon to pull off his boots and kick free of his clothes.

Naked and in the obvious throes of full arousal, Brandon held out his hand to her. 'Come to bed with me, Nora.'

She did not miss the import of his words, all designed to set the rhythm of partnership this night. There would be no leading and following. There would be *mutual* explorations. They would learn each other's bodies together with no artifice between them, and at the end of it would be completion.

Chapter Fourteen

The sun had been up for a scant hour when the door to Brandon's study slammed open and bounced off the mahogany panelling of the wall.

Brandon looked up from the papers spread before him on the desk, startled by the intrusion. Jack filled the room, his elaborate cape swirling about his knees in fair imitation of a whirlwind. 'What have you done? I've been away from your side for a mere twelve hours and now the village is on fire with news of your engagement. I hope you haven't done anything foolish.'

Brandon leaned back in his chair, hands folded behind his head while he studied his friend's chagrin. Calmly, he replied, 'I don't believe I've ever seen you this early in the morning before, Jack. Sit down and settle yourself. You look as if you've been up all night.' Brandon gestured to a chair and rang for coffee.

'If I've been up all night, it's your fault. I spent the wee hours in the public house, listening to the latest scandal brewing on your behalf. First, there were harrowing tales of The Cat hauling you out of the dinner party up in Cheetham as a hostage. Then Witherspoon and his friends launched into stories of your delectable betrothed who was beside herself with worry over your wounds.' Jack gave a wry smile. 'What wounds would those be?'

'Self-inflicted.' Brandon held up his cleanly bandaged hand.

'It didn't take me long to add up all the bits and deduce that the supposed intended was none other than The Cat. Deuce take it, Brandon, I've heard politics make for the most unusual bedfellows, but this is beyond the pale.'

Jack might have gone on with his scolding, but a footman entered with a tray of morning coffee and toast.

Brandon gathered his thoughts against Jack's attack. Jack was only the first of many visitors who would demand explanations. He'd left Nora sleeping peacefully more than an hour ago in order to organise his defences, beginning with a missive to Manchester's leading dressmaker.

Jack voiced the most pressing issue facing him as the servants left the room. 'Now that you've got her, what are you going to do with her?' Jack asked over the rim of his coffee cup.

'I am going to play out the ruse and present her as my intended. It will buy some time until everything settles down.' Brandon laid out the plan that had been taking shape in his head. 'It's the only way I can think of to get what I want.'

Jack gave a disbelieving guffaw. 'If it were me voicing those sentiments, I'd know exactly how self-serving that plan was. Humour me, Brandon, and tell me what it is that you want? Somehow I don't think the answer will be the mill progressing.'

'I want to keep her safe. If she goes back to The Grange, she'll try something else just as dangerous as that performance she gave last night at St John's.'

'And you worry that you might not be there to rescue her?' Jack's flippant tone softened. 'You can't keep her, you know that, don't you? The Cat's as wild as they come.'

'Not all of us are as jaded as you, Jack. It's not a character flaw to be less cynical.'

'Still, it's my job as your friend to disabuse you of any foolish notions you might harbour about taming The Cat. It's what you called me up here for,' Jack reminded him.

He gave Brandon a half-grin. 'But I can see my preaching falls on deaf ears. You've got that "morning after" glow about you.' Jack rose and put down his cup. 'I'll leave you to play house with your supposed betrothed and let your ruse run its course.'

Brandon drew a deep breath. 'That's another thing, Jack. I am not sure I want to see the ruse end.'

'Well, it has to eventually, unless you actually—' Jack broke off the sentence. Brandon was rewarded with a view of Jack at his most nonplussed, a feat few accomplished. 'Are you suggesting you would make the relationship more permanent in nature? Make The Cat your Countess?' Jack managed to get out when the initial shock passed.

'Yes, my Countess. I have not forgotten,' Brandon said placidly. 'It is time I marry and look to my nursery.'

Jack resumed his seat, scrubbing at his face with his hands. 'Yes, yes, of course it's time to spring the parson's mousetrap and all that. We're getting no younger, but why couldn't you find a nice débutante?'

Brandon hooted with disbelief. 'A nice débutante? Listen to yourself, Jack. I could no more settle for a nice, white-gowned virgin half my age than you could. Just because I must marry to beget an heir doesn't mean I'll leg-shackle myself to the first débutante and her mother who come along. If that was the case, I would have married ages ago. There would have been no point in waiting. I have standards that must be met. I've waited to marry because no one has yet met them.'

'Until now? Surely you're not in love with her?'

'Until now, no one has provoked me enough to think of a more permanent arrangement,' Brandon said tentatively. 'As for love, well, I'm not sure I'd know exactly what that is, having not ever truly been in love.' He toyed with a pen, avoiding Jack's knowing gaze. Too many people thought love could be feigned if the prize was large enough. He wanted more than that.

Brandon sighed heavily. 'I'm probably not in love with Nora any more than she's in love with me, but she makes me feel alive, Jack, in a way I've felt with no other. When I am with her, life is a grand romp.'

'An illegal romp, don't forget. Surely *that* can't be one of your standards.' Jack was all silky sarcasm. 'I admit I find myself insanely curious as to what those standards might be. What does a thief have that an eligible girl of good family lacks?' Jack stretched out his booted legs and waved his empty coffee cup toward the decanters collected on the polished sideboard. 'I'll need something stronger than coffee, however, to get through this.'

Brandon rose and obliged, pouring a healthy dose of brandy into the cup before adding a splash of coffee from the silver urn on the tray.

Jack sipped and sighed deeply. 'Much better. Nothing like good French brandy to dull the shock that one's best friend has gone completely mad. Now, about those standards.'

'I want a wife who shares my causes and has a passion for the political welfare of the country.' Brandon began ticking his standards off on his fingers. 'I want a wife who cares for people. I want a wife who has a healthy appetite for the bedroom and a sense of adventure. I want a woman who wants me for myself, who looks at me and doesn't see estates, titles, coronets and enormous pin allowances, but sees an intelligent man who thinks and has ideas of his own. In short, I want a woman who will be my partner in all aspects of my life.'

'In short, you want a paragon. The irony of it all is that you think you've found this paragon in the notorious Cat of Manchester, who is robbing your investors blind and hobbling the very ideas for which you want to be appreciated,' Jack asserted.

He shook his head sadly. 'I don't wish to demean your standards. We all want the paragon. In the end, we all settle for the débutante and the glimmer of hope that we might make her blank canvas into someone we can passably spend the rest of our lives with.'

'I don't settle,' Brandon said with conviction.

Jack rubbed his hands on his thighs. 'True enough. I've known you since our school days. You've always found a way to get what you want. It's what I like about you, Brandon. I hope she's worth it. For your sake, I hope she's not upstairs stealing your mother's damnable amethyst ring, again.'

Jack rose. 'I will take my leave of your hospitality. When you decide you need me, I'll be close by. Send word to the inn. In the interim, I wish you well.'

Nora sleepily groped the big bed, searching for the warmth of Brandon's body. Her seeking hands found only cold sheets. Disappointingly, Brandon's side of the bed was empty.

She pulled herself up into a sitting position and scanned the room, looking for traces of him. His clothes were gone. He was up and dressed.

She sighed heavily, flopping back against the down-filled pillows. It was better this way. She could be dressed and gone out the window before he knew it.

The two of them were unsuited for a long-term future together, as much as she wished that could be different. The realisation that she *did* wish it could be different struck her with such force she sat upright, trying to quell her rising emotion.

Her mind cruelly played the 'what if' game. What if there could be more than a short-term relationship between them? What if their passion was based on more than mutually shared lust? What if Brandon had been right, that they wanted the same things?

But they were only fantastical 'what ifs'. In order for them to come true the world would have to be a far different place, a place where Earls married outlaws, a place where The Cat was not needed. That would be a perfect world indeed, an utter utopia where workers were treated fairly, where children did not risk limbs scavenging cotton droppings from under machines.

Those days were far away and probably beyond her lifetime, which might be a short one if she wasn't careful. As much as her body yearned for Stockport, she had no business giving him her trust *carte blanche*. And really, Brandon had no business giving her his. He was in this game up to his neck and she wondered if he realised how deeply he played these days.

She could not allow him to develop a connection to her. It would be too dangerous for them both. She would end up dead. He would end up hurt if he developed a connection to her that could be traced or an attachment of an emotional nature. That was putting the cart before the horse. They had never spoken of love or affection last night or ever.

But sometimes sex did crazy things to a relationship, creating the illusion of something being there that wasn't. Neither one of them could afford that delusion.

The solution was simple. She needed to leave. She dressed rapidly, thrusting legs into her breeches and arms through her shirt. Her hands fumbled on the buttons in her haste. She hoped her absence would send a message. There was no need for him to come looking for her and offering futile explanations for things that didn't need to be explained.

Drat it, where was the other boot? Nora knelt on the floor and bent to peer under an armoire. There it was. She reached out and grabbed for it with a hand. But she was out of time.

'As lovely as your derrière looks in those breeches, I am sure I can find something more suitable for my betrothed to wear.' A familiar male voice broke the quiet of the room.

Damn that boot. If the boot had been handy when she was dressing, she would have been out the window. Now, she would have to face Brandon. From the sound of it, he was not pleased. The last thing she needed right now was a male caught up in some primal sense of protection for the woman he'd bedded.

'Don't get up.' Brandon's voice held a dangerous tone. 'It's the perfect position for spanking, which is what I'd like to do to you right now for even contemplating leaving.'

That was the sound of cold fury. Nora shut her eyes and took a deep breath before rising from her ignoble position on the floor. Her acerbic wit failed her, so she opted for silence, countering his anger with crossed arms and a defiant pose. She waited.

Brandon stared at Nora in disbelief. After Jack left, he'd come upstairs, expecting to find her still abed, still drowsy and on the brink of fully awakening. If he had waited a minute more, she would have been gone.

It was quite a blow to his ego to find that, while he was contemplating some level of serious commitment with a woman, the woman in question was contemplating escape out of a two-storey window. The whole scenario was worthy of a Drury Lane farce: an Earl, rich and handsome, able to have any woman, made sport of by the only woman he wanted.

Brandon shut the door behind him and met her stare evenly. He was gratified to see she was at a loss for words. 'What did you think you were doing?'

'We both know I'm not really your intended,' she said at last.

'We're the only ones who know that.' Brandon folded his arms and settled against the bed post, entrenching. 'You cannot simply make such a claim in front of witnesses and then walk away, leaving me to clean up the mess. How am I to explain your disappearance or live down the scandal of broken nuptials? It's hardly fair to me.' He tried to sound cool, neutral, as if he weren't furious at finding her in the midst of leaving.

'I am sure you'll think of something. Tell them you discovered I was a woman of loose virtue and that I misled you into believing I was something I was not.' Her tone was punishingly devoid of any warmth. They could have been strangers for all that her tone implied. Brandon hated it.

'I don't lie well.' Brandon pinned her with his gaze. 'You are not a woman of loose virtue, but a woman of more honour than any person I've ever known. As for the bit about pulling the wool over my eyes, I resent the implication that I might be capable of being hoaxed. It reflects poorly on my manhood, to say nothing of being highly unbelievable. I fear Witherspoon and others would smell a rat. After all, I am the Cock of the North. I know my way around women, adroitly.'

Nora rolled her eyes. 'Then it's settled. We should definitely let people go on believing in our little deception for the sake of keeping your precious manhood intact.'

Brandon felt a smile crease his lips. This was better. He would rather joust with her wit than shadow-box her silence. 'If there has to be any deception involved, I'd rather deceive others than deceive ourselves.'

'What is that supposed to mean?' Nora fired back.

'You want to walk out of here and pretend last night or the first night didn't happen.'

'For the record, I wasn't going to walk out of here, I was going to climb. And pretending they didn't happen is better than what you want.' Nora bent to tug on her boot.

Brandon smiled wickedly and advanced towards her, making it difficult to look at him and put her boot on at the same time. 'Tell me, what is it that I want?'

Nora gave up on the boot to meet him squarely. 'You want to believe last night meant something, that you are under obligation to protect me.'

'That is true enough. Protection is an issue we must consider. Witherspoon is set on capturing The Cat. We can't risk him discovering The Cat's identity.'

Nora interrupted, caution infusing her tone. 'This is *my* fight. I will not have you entangled. The game has become too perilous.'

Brandon ignored her and forged ahead. 'I will politely debate that point. The moment Witherspoon realises my betrothed and The Cat are one and the same, I am suddenly in the middle of a very tricky situation. I find myself in great need of guaranteeing your safety. The only way we can guarantee your safety is to stop the raids. Once the raids stop, people will lose interest in The Cat.' He braced himself, knowing she wouldn't like it.

'You are asking me to give up my goals. How do I know you are not using the situation to get what you want? You want me gone so your investors won't flee,' Nora said shrewdly.

Brandon nodded. 'You need assurances of my trustworthiness and you already have them. I have had opportunities to turn you in and I have not. Instead, I played out your ruse. Those are not the actions of a desperate man who could take the easy way out.'

Nora crossed her arms over her chest. 'I have to leave at once if I want to live to fight another day.'

Brandon's tone turned sharp. 'There will be no more fighting for you. Consider yourself retired.' He was close enough to touch her.

He reached for her. She let him draw her into his arms, but he could feel the tension of her reluctance. 'Nora, when I said "protection", I meant permanent protection. If Witherspoon doesn't catch you, someone else, somewhere, will. You can't play The Cat indefinitely. The only way to be safe is to stop being The Cat altogether.'

She was ready to bolt and Brandon knew he was on tenuous grounds. 'Nora, don't be The Cat. Don't be Eleanor Habersham or any other bit of fiction you can dream up. Stay with me and let me keep you safe.'

'What did you say?' The pallor of her face did her credit. Her shock was real.

'I said, stay with me.' He felt her tense for a protest. He put a finger on her lips. 'Shh. You can talk in a moment. You told me Christmas Day that you could never stop being The Cat because there would always be the fear of arrest for a past burglary. With me, you would be protected from that. No one would dare challenge you while you are under my care.'

Nora's chest heaved, indicating she wanted to break into the one-way conversation. Brandon shook his head. 'I'm not finished. I haven't forgotten your other reasons. You won't have to give up your cause. All my funds, all my political connections, will be at your disposal, Nora, to do with as you wish. You already know I share your concerns. You know I support the Reform Act. Nora, we would be splendid. Stay with me and know that your fears have been laid to rest.'

Brandon found himself slightly out of breath. He could not think of anything more compelling to add. He watched her face for signs of acceptance. There were none.

'Brandon, all you say is true. It's a good offer. But I won't stay with a man so that he can fulfil an obligation of honour and for other reasons. Please let me go and don't ask any more of me.'

'You cannot expect me to let you go without a reason, Nora, not with the possibility that we've had two opportunities to create a child.'

He had not wanted to push things that far, to use conception as a trump card, but his hand had been forced. He'd not expected her to leave. He'd expected her to stay with him and they'd be able to face that eventuality if it arose in the natural course of time. But Nora had not done the expected. As always, she'd done the opposite.

'Tell me what it is that would drive you away and I will fix it.'

She shook her head slowly. 'You can't fix this, child or not, Brandon. You can't jump down off the wagon box and throw your fortune at it.' It was said with sorrow, without any mocking at his actions on Christmas Day.

Brandon felt a finger of fear move down his spine as he watched her eyes harden. She was steeling her resolve. He was suddenly seized with the desire to retract his statement. He didn't *want* to know.

But the decision was in motion. She was going to tell him. He knew with distressing certainty it would be like hammering the final nail into a coffin. He swallowed hard.

'Brandon, I am married. I will not stay with one man while I am legally bound to another.'

Brandon took an involuntary step backwards, a hand

covering his mouth, his other hand groping for a chair or a bed post, anything with which to steady himself. His world was reeling. The coffee and toast he'd eaten with Jack threatened to come back up.

At last he choked out the word. *'Married?'* This was worse than being on opposite sides of politics and even the law. This was about losing Nora. An Earl could do a lot of things, but he could not be a bigamist. The jealousy he'd so adamantly denied to Jack raised its green head. He did not want to share her with anyone from the past or the present.

'Yes. At least I think so. I haven't seen my husband for seven years.'

A glimmer of hope, then, Brandon thought, as morbid as it was. The rotter might be dead. Deuce take it, what was he coming to when the possibility of someone's death brought him a surge of joy? This whole situation was becoming more ludicrous by the moment.

A knock sounded at the door of his chambers. Brandon had no further opportunity to pursue this latest twist. The present and all its implications reasserted itself.

'This is not over,' he said sternly, waving Nora into the dressing room where she would be out of sight. It wouldn't do to have his servants see her in The Cat's garb.

'Enter,' he called when Nora was hidden away.

'My lord, I have come to inform you that the dressmakers you called for earlier this morning have arrived and are downstairs awaiting your pleasure,' the valet said.

'Excellent, tell them we'll be down shortly.' Brandon reached for a waistcoat and jacket. Shrugging into them gave him time to regroup. When Nora appeared in the doorway from the dressing room, casting him a questioning look, he felt back in control of himself. He had a meagre plan, a delaying action, really, but it was all he had time to come up with as he finished dressing.

'The dressmakers from Manchester are here to help my betrothed restore her wardrobe after the unfortunate mishap yesterday that claimed her luggage,' he explained.

She quirked a brow at the fabrication Brandon was spinning. Brandon didn't give her a chance to respond. 'My dear, you aren't the only one who can improvise.

'Shall we? We have much to discuss between us. You might as well do it in fine fashion. Until we resolve this tangle, I think it is best to see the ruse through,' Brandon said sternly, crooking his arm, knowing she didn't dare refuse. This was a role of her making. She had committed herself when she'd hastily concocted the idea to pose as his betrothed.

Nora took his arm and the challenge he invoked with her customary cockiness. 'The curtain rises.'

'So it does.' With any luck, it wouldn't be the final curtain. As long as he kept her with him, he could protect her from Cecil Witherspoon. He would learn more about this errant husband of hers and send Jack out to find him. In the meantime, he could persuade her about the merits of being his wife, an idea that he was starting to grow fonder of by the moment. He would not let her go without a fight.

Chapter Fifteen

How had he done that? Nora marvelled, standing on a pedestal swathed in fabrics, surrounded by two dressmakers and their assistants. She had thrown her last ace in an attempt to keep an insurmountable object between them; he'd glibly overcome it with a simple sentence to the effect that until this tangle is sorted out, it was best to continue with the ruse.

At best, his option was a delaying technique, but she saw the small victory he'd won with it. Going ahead with the ruse kept her by his side. It bought him time, time to convince her of his proposal's reasonability. But time was dangerous to her. The longer she was in his sphere of influence, the more likely it was she would start to believe him. It would be so easy to capitulate to his logic. Of course, she couldn't capitulate all the way, she did have a husband on the loose out there somewhere in England. And of course, Brandon hadn't asked for the ultimate commitment.

Nora shifted and turned on the dressmaker's pedestal, tamping down the rampant feelings that had begun to surge through her since his proposition. He had not spoken of marriage, merely of being under his care. They were both people of the world. He knew what he meant when he'd couched it in those terms. They both knew what those terms included and what they did not.

She might be an outlaw, but she had standards. She would not flagrantly live as any man's mistress while being married to another. Sleeping with Brandon twice had been bad enough, but that was nothing more than a physical fling. And who could fault her giving into temptation after seven years of celibacy? In her book, it was a small infraction.

Being his mistress was more than an infraction. She wouldn't, couldn't, do it on principle as well as practice. Giving up The Cat and becoming his woman would force her into an emotional realm, a realm where she'd establish an attachment to him, where he'd have all the control, where he'd decide when it was over.

She could not let herself be devastated in such a manner. That day might be months or years off, but it would come and she could not tolerate standing by and watching him marry or take a different lover. And he would. She'd noted during his protestations this morning that he'd not spoken once of affection or love.

Nora was acutely aware that she needed to marshal her resolve and stand against Brandon's ideas of protection. There would be difficult conversations in the near future. Stalling those conversations was the only reason she had permitted herself to be poked and fussed over. As long as she was surrounded with dressmakers, Brandon couldn't begin to broach the many questions that were obviously rolling around his mind.

She hazarded a glance in his direction now. He lolled indolently on a sofa in the small parlour as if he had nothing better to do with his time but help his intended fuss over her selection of gowns. Only his eyes, sharp and shrewd as they took in the developing scene, belied his relaxed pose. She had sparred with him too often to miss the intensity in his gaze. For him, indolence was merely a façade.

The long case clock in the hall chimed the hour. Three o'clock. Good lord, they had been at it all day. Nora's stomach grumbled in confirmation that they'd worked through luncheon.

The dressmaker held up two swatches of silk. 'Miss, do you prefer the cerise or the cherry?'

Nora barely fought back a groan. Was there a difference? 'I prefer green.' She was gratified to see the dressmaker look suitably horrified. No doubt 'green' was too simple of word. A lady didn't wear 'green'. A lady wore emerald, jade, olive or lime, but not plain green.

Brandon swiftly stood up and clapped his hands, commanding all the attention in the room. 'The lady prefers the forest green. I thank you all for your time, but I regret my betrothed grows weary from her exertions. I will expect the first of the gowns tomorrow afternoon.'

Her exertions! Climbing a tree to a two-storey window or breaking glass window panes were *exertions*. Standing still with pins stuck all over like a witch-doll was only *boring*. Nora would have laughed at the thought she had exerted herself if she hadn't been so grateful for Brandon's interruption.

In no time, the women had packed up their goods and exited, bobbing their heads and murmuring effusively 'thank you, my lord' to Brandon.

Brandon shut the parlour door when the last of them had left and rang for tea before sinking back down onto the sofa. 'Tired?' he asked.

'Bored. I can't believe ladies take such a thrill in visiting the dressmaker.' Nora sighed, plopping down into a chair across from him, careful to keep the low serving table between them. 'I had no idea there were so many shades of any given colour. I said blue and they said, "azure, periwinkle or sapphire,"' she offered in fair mimic.

Brandon smiled his commiseration and carried on making small talk. His facile conversation made Nora nervous. She saw it for what it was—an obvious camouflage of the actual issue. He was waiting for the tea tray to arrive before launching into the real conversation.

Never one to put off the inevitable, Nora was relieved to see the tray arrive. The footman put it on the table between them. The door shut ominously in the wake of his departure, signalling the totality of their privacy. Pregnant silence followed while Nora poured out a cup for each of them. It seemed best if Brandon began. So she crossed her legs and sat back and waited.

He sipped from his cup.

He reached for a sandwich from the platter of food that accompanied the tray.

He took a bite.

Chewed.

Swallowed.

He was driving her mad.

She would plant a facer on that beautiful jaw of his if he took one more bite.

'You're not eating. Sandwich?' Brandon picked up the platter and held it out to her.

She met his gaze levelly and took one. It might come in handy as an impromptu torture device.

'So,' he began casually, 'tell me about this professed husband of yours.'

'He's not professed. He is quite real, I assure you,' Nora said, taking a delicate, savouring bite of the sandwich in slow retribution before she delivered any more information. Two could play his game.

She took another bite. 'Delicious.'

'Fine, I'm sorry about the bit with the sandwich. Am I going to have to drag every detail out of you or could you just divulge the story without turning it into a parlour game of twenty questions?'

She supposed that was about as close to begging as he would allow himself to get. Nora put down her sandwich and showed mercy.

'Fair enough, we have moved beyond the point of games,' she said in all seriousness. 'I fell in love when I was seventeen with a man named Reggie Portman. He was handsome and adoring. Back then I still believed in fairy tales.'

It was true. Reggie had not been anywhere near as accomplished as Brandon in bed, but his ardour had meant everything to her young heart and nothing to his. She had not understood at the time that sex was purely physical for men and usually devoid of any emotional connection.

'I sold myself in marriage once. I did not enjoy it. I am not likely to pursue arrangements that would put me in similar circumstances again,' Nora said baldly.

'How do we get from young romantic to hardened cynic? It seems to me that you've left some pieces out of the story.' Brandon was quick to note the gap.

Nora took a sip of tea to fortify herself. 'I was alone and on the run, except for Hattie and Alfred.'

'Are they your parents?' Brandon looked perplexed.

'No. They are not even relatives.' Nora shook her head sadly, staring without seeing at the sandwich in her hand.

Brandon moved next to her, the tea tray forgotten. He took her hand and intertwined his fingers between hers. 'What happened to your parents? How did you come to this?' he asked softly. 'It's time for stories, I think. Nora, you can be yourself with me.'

It was amazingly easy to open up her memories after keeping them closed for so long. Nora found, once she started, that she couldn't stop the flood of remembrances. 'My father was a successful businessman here in Manchester. I was an only child and I had plenty of luxuries, a tutor and a good education. Then, one day, there was an explosion at the factory. My father died trying to save some workers trapped under fallen timbers.

'My mother and I were left well provided for, but I saw what happened to the families of the workers who were killed. There was no help for them to repay them for what they had lost. We tried to help, but it didn't matter. They were destitute and living in the slums before the year was out, through no fault of their own. Investigators later concluded the fire started because an improperly made machine became too hot. Carelessness cost those families everything and they were simply told they were expendable.'

'My mother was ruined in an altogether different way. After my father died, she lost her will to go on. When I was fourteen, she passed away in the night. The doctors could not explain it. Nothing was wrong with her except for a broken heart. I was packed off to my only relatives, a strict aunt and uncle in Bradford.'

Nora shuddered at the recollection. They'd been puritanical in their beliefs and lifestyle. The home, while large, was austere and empty of frills. She was allowed only the most sombre, high-necked gowns, and the smallest modicum of freedom. Many days were spent serving out punishments in her room—punishments she had earned for sneaking out of the house with supplies for those in need. Her uncle believed the poor got what they deserved and her aunt feared the dirt and illness that came with poverty. In a way, she'd been playing The Cat long before it had become official.

'How does Reggie Portman figure into all this?' Brandon prompted quietly when she fell silent.

'My uncle had a marriage planned for me to a man that was stricter than he. I couldn't fathom a worse fate and I couldn't imagine how I would manage living such a life. It wasn't the life I wanted. I felt I was in prison. There was a fair in town, and Reggie Portman was there, a charming and handsome travelling merchant. He offered me a way out. I was desperate and I took it, four days before the official betrothal.'

'And taught you everything you know?' Brandon supplied wryly. 'A good role model.'

Nora grimaced in censure. 'Everything has its place. I use my skills for good, not evil.'

'That's debatable.'

'Not today it isn't. Do you want to hear my story or not?' Nora scolded, back on familiar ground, the hardest part of the telling over.

Brandon acquiesced graciously. 'My apologies, please continue.'

'Travelling with Reggie was exciting at first. But as Reggie and I moved from place to place, I saw the same stories being played out in different towns. The poor got poorer and the rich got richer, not caring who they stepped on to make a guinea. I promised myself I'd do something about it, just as my mother and I had tried to do for the workers at my father's factory and as I had tried to do at my uncle's, especially for children and widows; people who had limited ways of improving their station in life.'

Nora made a face. 'Reggie didn't share my attitude, although I thought he cared enough for me to help anyway, out of affection. But what he loved was making money at any cost. He sold fine fabrics, jewellery, expensive trinkets. He lavished gifts on me and my head was turned. I assumed he would want to use his largesse to help others. But I was wrong.

'Once we married, I discovered he was singularly interested in making a pound wherever he could. His finer goods were acquired through illegal means and the items he sold at discount were so flawed that they were of little use.'

'You married him for his philanthropy and he let you down,' Brandon summarised.

'He was boyishly handsome. He could make me laugh when he made the effort, which was seldom after we courted. His charming was an act. He just wanted someone to trail around the countryside, cooking and cleaning for him.

'The worst part was once I got over the realisation that he was a borderline criminal with his business dealings, I couldn't leave him. The law doesn't allow for a woman to cast off a husband and, even if I had been able to, I had no way to support myself.' Nora paused, letting Brandon assimilate the pieces of her history.

'Then you ran away and became The Cat?' Brandon guessed.

Nora shook her head. 'Not at first. I started small. In the beginning, I left baskets of goods I pilfered from Reggie's stock. He was a terrible book-keeper and kept a shoddy inventory. It was easy to take a length of cloth here and few tins of food there.'

'He never caught on?'

'Not for a while. He was quite angry when he discovered what I had been doing.' Nora cringed at the memory.

'He hit you?'

'He beat me up quite thoroughly. I started carrying the knife in the sleeve sheath after that. One night he came back to our camp site drunk. It was worse than usual. I pulled the knife and, when he lunged for me, I stabbed him in the shoulder. Between the wound and the alcohol, he passed out. I knew I couldn't be there when he woke up.

'I took what was left of his stock, and had the good fortune to meet up with Hattie and Alfred at a fair. They were small-time con artists, but they were getting on in years for such living. They liked the idea of settling in a house, even if it was just for a year or so at a time. After that, I started being The Cat in earnest. When it became clear that I had to have a means of income, I expanded The Cat's range of activities.'

'Incredible,' Brandon breathed when she had finished.

Nora gave a bittersweet smile at the sight of his admiration. 'That is why I can't possibly marry you. I have to be The Cat for the sake of helping others and because I must live in hiding. Reggie is out there somewhere. As long as I keep moving and forgo my true identity, he can't find me. You cannot risk being connected to me.'

'Do you really expect me to let you walk away after knowing that?' Brandon said softly.

'Yes.' Nora stamped her foot in frustration. 'There's nothing for you here but the harbouring of a fugitive.' *Especially since you don't love me.*

Not an iota of affection. She had noticed that he admired her. She fired his blood like no other, but that was all lust and physical attraction. It was the novelty of her. Those things would fade and Brandon would be left wondering why he'd risked so much for so little. And, of course, she'd be left hurt because in the final analysis she liked him a great deal. *A great deal.*

'It should be for me to decide,' Brandon said. 'You are my

responsibility. I will not have you martyr yourself out of some misguided notion that I am the one who needs saving.'

There was that word again: responsibility. She was coming to hate it. She would hate it if it wasn't so important to her too. She understood the power of responsibility all too well.

'Be glad I have the good sense not to take advantage of you. My rejection is a gift,' Nora fired back, relieved to feel her temper rising. Good. She wouldn't dwell on all that she was turning down. She cared for him too much to tie him to her when he did not reciprocate her depth of feeling. When he worked that out, he'd be thankful for her decision.

'You will see reason and you'll know I was right to decline. I cannot abide the idea that you would marry me to fulfil your sense of duty. You cannot wish to be shackled to a woman you don't know for the rest of your days.'

'You're wrong. I know you, Nora. I know you're The Cat. I know you have a criminal past, all for a good cause. I know and I still admire you. When I saw Witherspoon point that gun at you, I knew I couldn't lose you.'

Of course not. You can't stand to lose, you insufferably stubborn man. Nora stared at him, letting silence permeate the room. She took a moment and let the import of his words sink in. It would be easy to interpret them to mean what she wanted them to mean—a replacement for 'I love you'.

Any other woman might be taken in by those powerful words. But in the past month she'd come to know Brandon Wycroft. He was a man who hated to lose and hated to share. She knew what he really meant: he wasn't going to let a chap like Witherspoon call the shots. This was his game with The Cat and his game alone. She understood, but it still hurt.

Brandon chuckled in the quiet. 'Besides, Nora, you can't

leave just yet. I need to produce a betrothed for a reasonable bit of time or else it will look suspicious.'

'How long?' Nora said warily. Letting him determine how the betrothal gambit evolved put her in a tenuous position.

'Two weeks ought to be sufficient.'

'Two weeks and then you let me walk away?'

'Yes, unless you change your mind.'

'I won't. I can't.'

Brandon smiled knowingly with all the confidence of an urbane rake prowling the London drawing rooms. 'We'll see.'

What had she got herself into? Nora wondered two days later, standing in what had become her suite of chambers, surrounded by boxes of hats, shoes, gloves and undergarments of the finest linens. Her wardrobe began arriving the afternoon following the dressmakers' initial visit, providing a signal of sorts to those in the village who felt obliged to consort with the Earl and his intended.

The purported tragedy befalling her luggage and maid held would-be callers at bay for a day, long enough for Brandon and she to sort out what lay between them. For the ruse to succeed, they had to have a united front. Playing his role to the hilt, Brandon had dashed off a letter to his closest sister, inviting her to chaperon.

Now that her new clothing had arrived, the callers were not far behind. Indeed, Nora had been informed mere minutes ago that Witherspoon, along with his wife and sister, were downstairs in the front drawing room, hoping to be received. She supposed she could ask Brandon to tell them she was indisposed, but that would be the coward's way out. Brandon expected more of her. He had performed his role as dutiful husband-to-be quite well.

She must respond in kind. Any believable candidate for an Earl's wife would be an accomplished hostess. Acting like a shy country miss or wilting wallflower would not reflect well on Brandon.

Nora rang for the maid and pulled a morning gown of emerald-printed challis with Medici sleeves from the pile of gowns covering the bed. 'Quickly, Ellie, we must not keep Witherspoon and his guests waiting overlong,' Nora said in her best imitation of the lady of the house, which was what the servants expected of her. In their minds, she was to be the Countess.

Fortunately, she'd spent enough time robbing the rich to know something of their lifestyle and behaviours. She was not without her own resources when it came to avoiding major mistakes and Brandon had been diligently present behind the scenes, making sure she did not face insurmountable tasks alone.

Nora let Ellie drop the dress over her head and straighten it before sitting down at her vanity to arrange her hair in a hasty but tasteful coiffure. Ellie was a genius with hair, gathering Nora's heavy curls into a low knot at the base of her neck that at once gave the admirer an impression of maturity and innocence when studying Nora's face.

As Nora fastened on a pair of earrings, a knock sounded at the door. Brandon peered in and smiled. 'Are you ready to go down? When I heard Witherspoon was here, I thought we could receive him together,' he offered politely.

Nora graciously accepted. Witherspoon was their first visitor—the first of many. Nora knew Brandon wanted to offer guidance and cues so that she could manage well on her own for later visits. No one would expect the Earl to actually be present for the social calls. That was a woman's domain.

There were other reasons she was glad of Brandon's presence by her side. The way Witherspoon had looked at her when she'd descended the stairs the night he and the others brought Brandon home from the dinner party made her nervous, as if he were trying to unravel a great mystery. And, of course, there was the fact that he'd been ready to shoot her the night of the St Johns' dinner party—not that he knew The Cat and Brandon's intended were one and the same. Still, there was something edgy about socialising with someone who wanted to see her dead.

'I don't suppose we can get out of this,' Nora said as they descended the stairs.

'Don't say you're nervous.' Brandon winked. 'I have a plan for avoiding other callers today.'

'What is it?'

'It's called a picnic,' he said in a playful tone of high drama.

'A picnic?' Nora said excitedly, then sobered. 'But it is the middle of winter, Brandon.'

'Did I neglect to say a picnic in the summerhouse? We'll be warm enough, no matter the rain outside. Now, let's dispatch our guests with all due haste.'

'Witherspoon, welcome, it is good to see you.' Brandon shook hands with the tall, blond-haired man, sounding genuinely delighted to receive the visitors. Nora marvelled at Brandon's talent for easy conversation.

Nora stepped forward and let Brandon make the introductions. She saw the ladies seated comfortably on the couch near the fire while Brandon and Witherspoon took the two wing-backed chairs opposite. She probably should ring for tea, but she didn't want to encourage Witherspoon to stay. It would take fifteen minutes to get a tea tray together and another twenty to politely partake of it with company. It was difficult to play the gracious hostess when a picnic in the summerhouse with Brandon loomed on the horizon.

Witherspoon must have sensed the need to expedite his visit. He shifted in his seat to directly face Brandon. 'I appreciate being received, my lord. We did not have an appointment.'

Nora watched his face. The man might sound self-effacing as he kowtowed to the Earl, but his eyes told a different story. She hoped Brandon could see the calculation in them.

'I am always glad to meet if I am at home.' Brandon inclined his head slightly.

'I felt what I have to say cannot wait, considering the state of affairs in Stockport-on-the-Medlock. It has to do with The Cat.'

Brandon affected a look of cool interest. 'Have you heard something?'

'It is something I noticed during the incident at St John's. I think we may have been looking in the wrong direction for The Cat. I think there is reason to believe The Cat is a woman.'

It took all of Nora's self-control to avoid looking at Brandon. Any contact might arouse suspicions.

'Why would you think that, Witherspoon? It's a highly unlikely hypothesis,' Brandon said in an even tone that conveyed only the tiniest bit of inquisitiveness. For all intents and purposes, he sounded like a bored man forced to listen to ludicrous tales.

Witherspoon swallowed hard. Nora was gratified to see that the Earl's haughty demeanour had disconcerted him. Then, Witherspoon gathered his backbone. 'When the intruder turned to watch you with the bag, the cloak fell away enough to reveal certain, ah, womanly parts.' Witherspoon choked out the last.

Nora couldn't resist the jibe. 'You mean breasts?' she asked with an air of innocence. The three guests blanched at the use of such a term in mixed company.

Brandon coughed discreetly. 'I see. We will need more proof, but in the meanwhile it can't hurt to expand our search to encompass both genders. I appreciate your thoughts, Witherspoon.' Brandon rose and held out his hand. 'I am sorry to rush our visit, but my betrothed and I have an appointment shortly.'

'Thank you for your time, my lord,' Witherspoon said, rising too. 'And, of course, we want to extend our felicitations on your upcoming nuptials.'

Nora's head was reeling by the time Brandon shut the door behind their guests. 'He knows The Cat is a woman.'

They'd both lost their appetite for a picnic. The allure of the summerhouse faded in the wake of Witherspoon's visit. In silent accord, they drifted into Brandon's study and shut the heavy door behind them.

Nora settled on the sofa, the whole nasty scene with Witherspoon playing out again in her mind. His revelations spelled disaster for The Cat. 'I think The Cat should rob him blind and force him out. I am sure I could "persuade" his wife to apply some more pressure. She'd decamp to London with a little more effort from The Cat.'

Brandon joined her, sternly denouncing her plan. 'Absolutely not. As long as you're here, you're in retirement. Besides, I need Witherspoon's money.'

'You're hard up?' Nora gasped incredulously, thinking of the fortune that had been paid out for a wardrobe full of gowns for occasions she'd never attend. The ruse was getting dangerously expensive.

'You shouldn't have bought all those gowns. I am horrified when I think of the money wasted on them. Did you know I have six gowns specifically for afternoon tea? I'll never wear them. It will take me some time, but I will pay you for the clothes,' Nora said with resolve.

Brandon rolled his eyes at that. 'By doing what? Robbing

my neighbors? You most certainly will not. A wardrobe will not beggar me.'

Nora furrowed her brow, perplexed. 'But you need Witherspoon's money. You're poor.'

Brandon gave a friendly chuckle. 'Hardly. Poor is a bit over the top. My pockets aren't to let. But it is getting more difficult each year to keep the estates functional. My estates generate enough to support repairs to the tenants' cottages, to buy seed and farming implements for the fields, but there's less and less profit for expansion and other expenses. I fear it will only be a few more years before the tenants will be forced to look elsewhere for their livelihoods. Aristocracy is an expensive career. The agricultural economy hasn't helped.'

Nora saw the pieces fit together at once. 'The mill is your plan for financial security.'

Brandon nodded. 'It's at the foundation of it, the first building block. I need the investors' money to build for the future of Stockport-on-the-Medlock. I can't build that future alone. My pockets aren't that deep.'

Nora felt sick. Her plans would ruin more than his credibility. A few weeks past, such ironic justice would have suited her perfectly. Now, looking at the man across from her, she could barely stomach the thought of all she'd be responsible for. She had to cut ties here before she was too emotionally involved to see reason.

'None the less, Brandon, I am not comfortable being a kept woman,' Nora said slowly. 'Even if you were the richest man in England, I would be reluctant to accept the wardrobe you've lavished on me these past few days.'

'My intended needs the appropriate clothing. No one would believe I was to marry a woman of dubious fashion.'

'I will pay for the gowns,' Nora insisted.

Brandon took her hands in his, squeezing them in reassurance. 'You talk too much. Maybe I'll get my money's
worth out of the gowns. After your two weeks are up, you
might decide to stay.'

Nora sighed. 'I am not free to marry and I won't be your
mistress.'

'If he were dead, you would have a choice,' Brandon
said softly.

Nora drew back. 'What have you done, Brandon? You will
not commit murder on my behalf.'

Brandon laughed. 'Nothing that bad, Nora. Did you
imagine I sent thugs to kill your errant husband?' He sobered.
'I did send my friend Jack, Viscount Wainsbridge, though. If
Reggie Portman is still of this world, Jack will find him.'

Brandon slipped a hand behind her neck, sifting her hair
through his fingers and drawing her close for a deep kiss.
'Until then, we have two weeks to ourselves to wait and see
and enjoy. Promise me, two weeks, Nora. The Cat can take a
holiday,' he whispered against her neck.

'I promise,' Nora replied softly. But it was already a broken
promise. She still had the haul from St John's to pawn for cash
and get to Mary Malone. Brandon kissed her again and Nora
felt a twinge of guilt. He couldn't see the fingers she crossed
behind her back.

Chapter Sixteen

Brandon took off his glasses and stretched back in his leather chair behind the desk. He had been poring over the latest dispatches from London. Even though Parliament was out until spring, dedicated politicos like Earl Russell were still hard at work, trying to lobby support for the Reform Act which would be the focus of the spring session.

Brandon used his break from paperwork to study the beautiful woman sitting demurely in the wing-backed chair near the fire, her neck bent slightly forward as she read a slim volume of poetry, a silver tray containing hot fudge and strawberries next to her elbow. Nora.

After nearly a week of her constant presence, he still couldn't believe his good fortune. She had stayed. She had admitted she cared for him; so much that she would throw away the passion they shared together in order to protect him. It was the partnership he craved, the knowledge that he was not alone. He had found the one person who could bring him the solace his soul demanded, not just in the dark watches of the night but in all aspects of his daily life, from the mundane to the more extraordinary.

Never had his heart been so committed. He could not resist her. She could not resist him, yet she did for reasons he did not perceive or understand. For every obstacle she erected, he countered with a solution and still it wasn't enough to win her capitulation.

Looking at her now with the firelight dancing on her features, her toes tucked beneath her soft rose-coloured skirts, her hair gathered into a loose chignon at her neck, he could hardly reconcile the image with the brazen Cat who had dangled her trousered legs over the same chair and swigged down his brandy like a dockhand a month ago. Anyone seeing her tonight would see a lady of gentle refinement. Of course, it was all an act, a trick wrought of fine clothes and a competent lady's maid.

He liked the illusion. He liked it even more because he knew what lay beneath the soft wool and pearls. He had only to look in her sharp jade eyes and see the truth of her—the keen intelligence, the ardent passion for her cause. That passion made sense now in the wake of her tale. She'd been disappointed by important people in her life and by the world in general. But instead of letting those disappointments overwhelm her, she'd elected to change the world so that others would not be similarly disappointed.

Not so unlike him. He wished he could convince her of that.

She raised those eyes to meet his. 'You're staring, Brandon,' she chided softly.

'Better to look at you than these damnable papers,' Brandon said with a weary tone. 'I swear they tread over the same ground time and again, never gaining an inch. The act has passed the House of Commons three times, but the House of Lords will not admit the need to change.'

Nora rose and put down her book. She came around the desk

to stand behind him, her capable hands massaging his shoulders. 'Was there anything else of interest in the post today?'

Brandon knew what she was really asking. Had Jack come up with any news of Reggie Portman? 'No.'

He reached up and covered her hand. 'It is too soon for him to know anything conclusive. It doesn't matter what he finds. If Portman is dead, you are free now. If Portman is alive, we will petition the courts for a divorce on grounds of abandonment. You will be free either way,' he consoled her. 'It's been seven years—perhaps we can have him declared legally dead.'

'Divorce, Brandon? You cannot consider it. A divorced woman may be your mistress, perhaps, but not your wife. You must not forget your station.' Nora's soft tone carried a warning edge to it. 'Besides, he'd have to be the one to divorce me. The law doesn't allow a woman to sue for divorce. You know that, Brandon.'

There it was again, that damnable tendency to block his solutions. Debating with Nora was as frustrating as his opponents in Parliament; more frustrating, perhaps, because the next minute she was all soft compliance, making him forget how hard-headed she could be.

'Besides, I am free now, Brandon. There is no sense in going through the public display of a divorce if he's alive. He hasn't found me for years. Perhaps you're right and he isn't as bent on revenge as I imagined.'

Brandon drew her around to his lap. 'I would never stop looking for you.' He smiled at the blush rising on her cheek.

He had discovered in their short time together that The Cat might be a tough, saucy-tongued woman, but true flattery was the chink in Nora's armor. A sincere compliment was her undoing. It thrilled him that in many ways he was the first to love her honestly and in the truest sense. It also touched a tender spot deep inside him that this woman, who risked herself so completely in order to give to others, had received so little affection in her life.

'I know, let's play a game, Nora. I've had enough of paperwork tonight. It's called Truth or Consequence. You choose if you want to answer a question or if you want to take a challenge of my making.'

Nora smiled like a cat with cream. Any thought of 'demure' exited his head. 'That sounds decidedly wicked, my lord,' she said in the husky voice he loved.

'It can be,' Brandon conceded. He had played a few bawdy versions of the game before when he and Jack had been in their salad days. 'You go first.'

Nora twisted a lock of hair that had come loose from her chignon. 'What will it be, truth or consequence?'

'Truth.'

'Do you really have a sister? You cannot answer yes or no. You must elaborate,' Nora said.

'Not only do I have one sister, I have four.' Brandon laughed outright at the incredulous look on her face. 'How do you think I got to be such a ladies' man? I learned a lot about the whims of women growing up in a household where my father and I were severely outnumbered and regularly outflanked by the fairer sex. There's Margaret. She's the oldest. Then, Elspeth, she's the scholar in the family. I'm the third child, but, being male, I was instantly catapulted to the head of the line.' That earned him a punch in the shoulder from Nora. 'Then there's Clara and Dulcinea. Dulcinea's the wildest.'

'Was it Margaret you sent for?' Nora asked, referring to the letter he had sent out for a chaperon.

'Heavens, no! She's the most reliable of them all, the

perfect oldest child. She's married with three children of her own. I wrote to Dulci.'

'The wild one?' Nora raised an eyebrow. 'I'm sure she doesn't meet the criteria for a proper chaperon.'

'I wasn't after a "proper" chaperon. But you have broken the rules. That's two questions.' Brandon tapped her on the nose. 'It's my turn. Will it be truth or consequence?'

'Truth,' Nora said gamely.

'That day in Manchester, when "Eleanor" tried to give me the slip at the drapers, where were you going?'

'To Anacoats. I needed to see Mary Malone and give her some money for medicines.'

Brandon's conscience pricked. His desire to catch The Cat in action had prevented her from doing a good deed. 'Did she get them?'

'Yes. When I went back in, I gave instructions to Jane.'

'Outside the baker's in Manchester, did you know I was there?' Brandon broke his own rule and plunged ahead with another question.

'That you'd been following me? Yes.' Nora laughed so hard Brandon had to right her to keep her from falling off his lap. 'I spotted you almost immediately. I confess I was quite mean to you, staying in the bakery longer than necessary. I hope you didn't freeze too badly but you deserved it, sneaking around behind poor "Eleanor".'

Nora reached for his cravat and tugged. 'You were too canny from the start. The day you came to tea at the Grange it was as if you could see right through me. No one in town had caught on after four months of me living under their noses. But you were different. You were too alert and too handsome for your own good. I had to convince you utterly that "Eleanor" was what she appeared to be: a gentry-class spinster with a small amount of breeding, a smaller amount of funds and a ton of missish manners.'

'You should have let me impress you with my manners and good looks, then,' Brandon teased. 'It was your resistance to my charm that put me on your scent.'

Nora pushed at him playfully. 'You arrogant man! All women are dying of love for you, is that it?'

'All but you, apparently. I even risked my neck going into the Manchester slums on Christmas Day with you. There were times while I waited for you that I thought I might lose my boots.'

Nora shook her head. 'You are far too capable for any thug to risk his neck, as nice as your boots are.'

'Capable, am I?' Brandon felt himself growing warm. She smelled of rosewater and lavender as she fiddled with his cravat. The game was going to take a decidedly different turn within moments. 'Is that why you kissed me that first night?' He dipped his head and feathered a kiss along the column of her neck.

'I kissed you because I thought it would be a successful distraction and assist my escape.'

'Why did you think that would work?' Brandon asked, desire mounting in his voice.

'I could tell right away that you were a man used to having his commands obeyed.' Nora traced his jaw with a finger. 'Men who command sometimes like to be commanded.'

'Is that why you tied me to the bed after the card party?' He was completely hard now. He was sure she could feel the progress his member was making beneath her buttocks.

Nora grinned mischievously. 'I tied you to the bed because you deserved it for torturing "Eleanor" on Mrs Dalloway's balcony. That's too many questions for you. We're not very good at following the rules.' She was the absolute coquette. She squirmed strategically on his lap. 'This is harder than I thought.'

Brandon didn't have to ask what she was referring to by 'it'.

She breathed against his neck. 'It's your turn to pick and you choose consequence.'

'Do I?' Brandon asked in hoarse anticipation. 'I forgot, men like me want to be commanded.'

'There are no men like you.' Her hands were in his hair, her mouth at his ear, sucking provocatively on his ear lobe. 'Take me upstairs.'

'Your command is my very wish.' Brandon rose with Nora in his arms and headed for the door.

'If your skill in bed matches your wit, this should prove to be very pleasurable,' Nora rejoined, tossing back her head, enjoying the moment thoroughly.

'One can only hope,' Brandon parried.

Nora adeptly leaned back in his arms and swept up the small silver pitcher of melted hot fudge used for dipping the strawberries they'd eaten for dessert. 'When one cannot hope, there's always chocolate.'

A surge of unadulterated glee ran through him. Never had foreplay been this stimulating. This was an utter romp and had him looking forward to a long delightful night.

A sharp knock on the door of his chambers woke Brandon late the next morning. He was slow to wake, wanting to ignore the knock and focus instead on the warm feminine form curled against him, her buttocks sensuously nestled against his groin. The smells of the night before, mixed with the subtle aroma of chocolate, brought a smile to his face. He wanted the world to retreat so that nothing existed except him, Nora and this room. But Harper, persistent valet that he was, wouldn't let it. The knock sounded again.

Brandon rose with a groan and covered Nora with a sheet

for the sake of decency. For Harper's sake, Brandon reached for a robe and belted it, although it would serve Harper right if he answered the door naked. Harper found unnecessary nakedness offensive in the extreme, the prude.

Brandon called out, 'Enter.'

'Sorry to disturb you, my lord.' Harper bustled around the sitting room, picking up hastily discarded garments and shaking them out.

Brandon smirked. The busybody wasn't sorry in the least.

'I have news that needs your immediate attention,' Harper said, smoothing out Brandon's shirt from the night before and clucking over the missing buttons.

Brandon stiffened in expectancy.

'There was a small fire at one of the tenant's cottages last night and they need you to come inspect the roof.'

The tension seeped from Brandon's body. He had hoped the news might be from Jack. 'I will go at once. Lay out my riding clothes. I'll have coffee and toast downstairs. Tell the groom to saddle my bay.'

It was the last thing he wanted to do. He'd planned to spend the grey winter morning in bed with Nora, but duty called.

Harper finished dressing him quickly and Brandon penned a short note for Nora, who still slumbered on in the bed. The afternoon was just as good. He could spend the morning thinking up inventive things to do with scones and jam—yes, definitely jam.

The door shut and Nora rolled over. She'd feigned sleep. It would have been too tempting to persuade Brandon to come back to bed and ruin her opportunity. In spite of the pleasure she found in their time together, the problem of getting more funds to Mary Malone and the others still encroached. She wouldn't rest easily until she had fulfilled her obligations there. She had her plunder. She simply had to get into Manchester and pawn it.

It was clear Brandon was not going to let her out of his sight, so she had waited for a chance to sneak away. He would be gone until mid-afternoon. That would give her plenty of time to go back to the Grange, don her 'Eleanor' disguise, drive into Manchester and take care of her business. With any luck, she'd even beat him home. If not, she would leave a note saying she'd gone out to pay calls or that she'd gone to run a few errands in the village.

She regretted the deception, but if Brandon knew, he would never let her go. He might offer to give her the money, but that wouldn't be the same. This was her cause and she had to see it through. Her mind made up, Nora put her plan in motion.

Brandon had been thinking about scones and a pot of jam all day. He entered the front hall and stripped off his riding gloves, handing them to a waiting footman. The butler bustled out to meet him.

'Good afternoon, my lord. I am glad to see you. Mrs Bradley is waiting for you in the drawing room.' He delivered his message with a haughty roll of his eyes, suggesting he found Mrs Bradley above herself to importune the Earl with a visit.

'She's waiting for me?' Brandon asked, slightly perplexed. In all the years he had been in residence here, Mrs Bradley had never called on him alone. She usually called with her husband or alone only if one of his sisters were visiting. 'Surely you mean she calls on my betrothed.'

The butler cleared his throat. 'Miss Nora is not at home. She left you a note.' The butler extended the folded white sheet inscribed with Nora's neat hand.

Brandon scanned the note and looked up. 'Are you certain the caller is Mrs Bradley?' The note from Nora said she was hoping to call on Mrs Bradley and run some errands in the village. He found it deuced odd that under the circumstances she would go down to the village. The fewer people who saw her, the better. Odder still was the idea that she'd pay a deliberate call on the Bradleys, especially since Mrs Bradley was here and apparently had no idea that Nora had deigned to call on her.

The butler looked chagrined that Brandon would doubt his ability to correctly identify the neighbors. 'It is Mrs Bradley. I have known her for over a decade.'

'Of course, my mistake.' Brandon gave a curt nod of his head. 'I'll see her right away. Send a tea tray to the drawing room.' He strode to the blue drawing room, keenly aware that *this* was not what he had in mind when he had contemplated scones and jam.

'Mrs Bradley, to what do I owe the honour of your company?' Brandon said congenially, crossing the room in great strides.

'I had hoped to meet your betrothed, Stockport,' Mrs Bradley said.

Brandon wondered if she had any idea that she was far too familiar with the use of his name for London manners. 'I am sorry she is not here,' Brandon apologised smoothly, taking a seat across from her. 'Perhaps there is something I can help with?'

Mrs Bradley smoothed the lap of her skirt and preened under his undivided attention. 'I came to invite the pair of you to the Squire's Valentine's ball. It's a betrothal ball for you, really. This engagement has been so sudden, but it must be acknowledged. We'll do it properly for you and the gel.'

Was one actually invited to one's own betrothal ball? Despite the forward assumptions the woman made on his behalf, the ball would complicate things immensely. Valentine's Day was past the two weeks Nora had contracted to stay for. A smile creased his lips. Perhaps that would work in his favour.

'I will have to consult with my betrothed, of course. I am not sure how long she had planned to stay.' Brandon turned his head towards the door at the sound of light footsteps. Nora was home.

A fleeting look of shock crossed her features when she saw him with Mrs Bradley, the very woman she'd professed to be visiting, which verified that she had been up to something.

She masked her surprise beautifully after that and came sailing across the room, hands extended to Mrs Bradley, apples blooming in her cheeks. The minx had been out riding and for quite some distance to look so ruddy.

'Mrs Bradley, I regret I was not here to receive you. I've been out riding.'

Brandon felt piqued. Not a word of greeting to him. He interjected himself into the conversation. 'I thought you had gone to see Mrs Bradley.' He held up the note.

She smiled. 'You can imagine my disappointment when I arrived at Wildflowers and found I had missed you, then my delight when the butler told me you were here!' With aplomb, Nora turned to Brandon, beaming. 'Darling, what did I overhear about a Valentine's ball?'

Mrs Bradley jumped ahead of Brandon. 'We are throwing you a betrothal ball, my dear.'

'I wasn't sure how long you would be staying?' Brandon put in cautiously. 'It is up to you. I think the idea splendid.' Let her interpret the message and all its import, he thought. It would be tantamount to a permanent declaration.

Nora smiled, but Brandon could see the tension in her lips. 'If you think it is a good idea, then we shall accept the offer.' She nodded at Mrs Bradley. 'You are too kind.'

Brandon grinned. Nora would make a fine Countess if given the chance. Now that she was home, he hoped Mrs Bradley wouldn't linger over tea.

Mrs Bradley reached for a second shortbread scone and dashed his hopes. 'Do you think your sister, Lady Dulcinea, will be able to attend?'

The woman was a gossipmonger of the first water. Brandon swore silently, regretting he had mentioned to the Squire that he had sent for his sister. 'I certainly hope so. However, I am distressed that I have not yet had a reply from her. I fear my letter may have missed her at her current residence,' Brandon said smoothly.

Brandon let the conversation lag, conveying his desire to be done with the interview. Mrs Bradley finished her scone and took the none-too-subtle hint.

The drawing-room door shut behind her, and Brandon turned his attention on Nora. 'Where have you been? I was surprised to find you had been out at all.'

'I went riding. I thought I might pay a call or do some shopping, but I wasn't sure,' Nora offered.

Brandon sensed a lie of omission. She was telling the truth, but not all of it. She had gone riding. The rosy cheeks attested to it. She probably had paid a call and done some shopping, but he'd wager his mother's ring that it wasn't in the traditional sense.

The knocker on the front door sounded and Brandon swore out loud. 'Lucifer's balls, you'd think we were having an at-home.' The day couldn't get any worse. Moments later it did. The butler announced Cecil Witherspoon.

'More tea, if you please,' Nora ordered tersely, obviously steeling herself against the visit.

'We'll need something stronger than that,' Brandon muttered as Witherspoon strolled into the room, looking as if he had a standing invitation to call on a peer of the realm.

'Stockport, I have news,' Witherspoon said with, in Brandon's estimation, an overblown sense of self-importance.

'Please, be seated and share it.' Brandon gestured to a chair with a bonhomie he didn't feel.

Witherspoon glanced at Nora and then sent a Brandon a silent query as to whether or not she would be staying.

'You can speak freely in front of my bethrothed,' Brandon assured him. Whatever Witherspoon had to say, he felt it boded no good for The Cat and Nora had best hear it first hand.

When they were all seated and Nora had poured out, Witherspoon delivered his news. 'I have had men watching the pawn shops in Manchester, you know, in the hope of finding some of the jewellery taken from us at the dinner party.'

Brandon looked up from his tea cup. No, he hadn't known. He didn't let on. He'd thought he was the only one watching them. 'A very sensible idea,' he said noncommittally.

'Indeed. Today, my men found this.' Witherspoon withdrew a ruby necklace. Brandon recognised it as belonging to Witherspoon's wife. She'd worn it to the dinner party at St John's and relinquished it to The Cat.

'I am sure your wife will be glad to have that back, it's a lovely piece.'

Witherspoon smirked and held it up to the light, appreciating the jewellery. 'Yes, it is, isn't it? I had it commissioned for our wedding anniversary. You might try the same for your first anniversary,' he offered pompously.

Brandon fought the urge to punch the condescending tone

right out of the lout's mouth. 'Did your men discover how the necklace got to the pawn shop?'

'That's the best part, Stockport.' Witherspoon replaced the necklace carelessly in his outer coat pocket. 'A woman dressed in a gaudy print gown and wearing spectacles brought the necklace in. My men can testify they saw a woman matching the description of Eleanor Habersham enter the shop late this morning. They sent for me right away.'

'Was Miss Habersham's name on the ticket?' Brandon asked, casting a sidelong look at Nora. He didn't need further evidence to know where she'd gone and what she'd done when she'd said she had shopping to do. Damn her, she had *promised*. How could he protect her when she refused to be protected?

'No, of course her name isn't on the ticket, although my men did look,' Witherspoon said in a condescending tone that suggested he found the Earl to be soft noodled. 'She was clever enough to use an alias. It would be foolhardy to pawn stolen merchandise under one's real name, don't you agree?' Witherspoon paused briefly and then went on to outline his own thoughts on the matter. 'I wouldn't have been suspicious if it hadn't been a necklace I personally knew. After all, the Habersham woman hasn't a penny to her name and she has to live on something,' he said callously, maligning the poor spinster with the implication that she was disgracefully selling off family heirlooms.

Brandon's fist clenched. If Eleanor Habersham had been real, he would have called the man out for abusing the woman with his aspersions on her finances.

Unaware of Brandon's growing agitation, Witherspoon droned on. 'I did some checking. I stopped at the Grange on my way home from Manchester. Do you know what I found?' Witherspoon was delighting in the telling.

'I cannot possibly guess,' Brandon said in a tone he hoped conveyed interest, although he already knew to some extent what Witherspoon had found. Eleanor Habersham wasn't in residence.

'Her man of all work told me Miss Habersham had left a week ago to visit an old aunt in Yorkshire. There's a rat here, Stockport. How could she be in Yorkshire when she's pawning stolen goods in Manchester pawn shops, I ask you?'

'What exactly are you implying?' Brandon asked, feeling heartsick at the man's discoveries.

'That Eleanor Habersham is The Cat. It fits with the timing and *my* discovery that The Cat is a woman,' he said grandly.

Egad, the arrogant man was making himself out to be Christopher Columbus. 'That's quite a hypothesis. You've done a lot of work,' Brandon said.

It became apparent the conversation was going no further. Witherspoon rose awkwardly. 'I thought you should know, as the area's magistrate and as the head of our little investment group.' There was coldness in his tone that implied he thought Brandon was lax in his duties.

Brandon rose with him. 'I appreciate your assistance. I am sure this matter will be brought to a close very soon. I believe The Cat has not struck anywhere since the dinner party. I am hoping that the raids have stopped and that Eleanor had some other reason to be in possession of the necklace. I would not like to taint her name with any unnecessary scandal.'

'We'll see,' Witherspoon said tersely, patting the pocket containing the necklace.

'Are you certain it is your wife's necklace?' Nora asked innocently, entering the discussion for the first time. 'After all, I am sure there's more than one ruby necklace in the world. Are there any markings or special engravings?'

Witherspoon growled at her. 'It was commissioned specially for her. I have the jeweller's papers and original design to prove the necklace is hers.'

Nora appeared to brighten and Brandon was instantly alert. 'How lovely for her that you've retrieved it, then. And how important that necklace will be as a proof should there be a trial. I'd keep it under lock and key. It would be a shame to lose it again.'

'Yes, quite,' Witherspoon said, a bit nonplussed.

'I'll walk with you to the hall,' Nora offered.

Brandon sat down and waited. He and Nora would have a grand discussion when she returned. If she thought she was going after the necklace, she thought wrong. After today's débâcle, he wasn't letting her out of his sight for a moment.

Nora came back in, a look of contrition on her face. At least she had the good grace to feel guilty over being caught in her little deception. He wanted her to feel guilty for more than that, though. Brandon wanted her penitent for have perpetrated the deceit in the first place, not simply for having been found out.

'You are not going after the necklace,' Brandon began. 'If you think I'll let you so much as leave the house unescorted, you're dead wrong. Look at the bumblebroth you caused today.'

'You're absolutely right. I won't leave the house,' Nora agreed readily, far too repentant for his taste. Something was wrong. She hadn't interrupted him. He hadn't thought he would get through the first line of his planned scolding. Now that he had, he couldn't think of anything else to say.

'Do I have your word on that?' Brandon asked warily.

'Yes, Brandon. I give you my word. I won't leave the house to go after the necklace,' Nora pledged solemnly.

Something definitely wasn't right. Her compliance had been too easily won. Not that her word meant anything after her latest exploit. She had already broken one promise. Still, she wouldn't promise away her permission to leave the house. *Unless she didn't need it.* The inspiration struck Brandon all at once. He grinned in spite of himself. 'You already have the necklace, don't you?'

Nora held up the item in question, dangling it from her fingers and laughed. 'He was far too careless with it. I am sure it would have fallen out of his coat pocket on the ride home. It could be laying anywhere on the ground between Stockport Hall and Cheetham Hill.'

Brandon couldn't help himself. He laughed out loud, finding an outlet for his tension after the last two interviews. Witherspoon would be mightily surprised to find his pocket empty when he returned home.

Goodness, he loved his pickpocket Countess. He pulled Nora to him and kissed her hard on the mouth. 'Life with you, Nora, is never dull.' He reached beyond her shoulder for the bell pull, suddenly finding he had a penchant for scones and a pot of jam.

Chapter Seventeen

'What did you do in Manchester?' Brandon asked later as they lay in his big bed cuddled together and drowsily sated. His hand rested on the curve of her hip, his thumb stroking the flat of her belly.

'You know what I did.' Nora sighed. She had known he wouldn't let it go, that he would ask.

'I want to hear it from you.'

'I pawned the necklace and took the money to the apothecary for Mary Malone's medicines. Then I arranged for a doctor to visit her. I stopped in to see her and gave her the rest of the money.'

'That should have been a pretty penny. The necklace was worth a few hundred pounds.'

'It probably was, but pawnbrokers won't pay full price, although I am sure the broker was happy to charge Witherspoon full price for it. The shop was not one I usually use and I find that particular broker less than trustworthy. Witherspoon must have paid him a nice bonus for showing him the ticket too. Those tickets are supposed to be confidential.'

'How is Mary?' Brandon changed direction.

'Worse. I fear she is beyond medicine. She needs a permanent change. Consumption and lung diseases are the bane of the industrial working class.'

Brandon nodded. She knew what was coming next. 'Nora, you could have asked me for the money. You didn't need to risk yourself. I would have given you the funds.'

'No.'

'Why not?'

'You cannot pretend The Cat doesn't exist, Brandon, that you can turn me into a philanthropic Countess overnight. Those people need The Cat. They need what she brings, but they also need what she stands for. It gives them hope that someone is watching out for them, that they are valued. Can you understand that, Brandon?'

'Yes, but there is a better way, Nora, a legitimate way. You know The Cat's days are numbered. Once we are married—'

Nora sat up so quickly the sheet slipped down to her hips. 'Married? We have not reached that conclusion yet, Brandon, and after today, we cannot even think it.'

It was Brandon's turn to sit up. 'What else is there for us to do? Devil take it, Nora, you just agreed to Mrs Bradley hosting our betrothal ball. I assumed when you accepted her offer you were signalling your acceptance of our relationship as well. My protection is limited as long as we remain unwed. You were the one who put the betrothal-façade gambit in motion—you have to see it through, Nora.'

'I only accepted the invitation because it seemed awkward not to. When are you going to realise you don't want to marry me? You want to save me. However, I am completely capable of saving myself.'

'When are you going to realise that you want to marry me?'

Brandon shot back. 'You cannot pretend you are repulsed by the idea of marrying me.'

'I am not repulsed at the thought of marrying you, but I am repulsed by the thought that I could cause your ruin. If people found out you knowingly married a wanted thief and that you assisted her, I doubt your title would protect you.' Nora swung her legs out of bed and reached for a robe, belting it furiously. The man was stubborn to the core. It was all a game to him. It no doubt galled him that the almighty Stockport didn't have her eating out of his hand—well, he did, she just couldn't let him know it. If he'd been talking of love, *true* love, and not honour and protection and duty, she might have been less resistant.

'Don't worry about Witherspoon. I can take care of him,' Brandon assured her with his customary confidence. 'He's been so eager for my friendship, he'll do anything for my approval. Once you're my wife, he'll fawn all over you in hopes of winning my favour. He won't think to connect any of it back to you.'

'We don't know what Jack will find.'

'Jack's findings are the least of our worries. We can manage them. There are other larger worries that deserve our attention, like Witherspoon. Don't go out again,' Brandon warned. 'I'll send for Mary Malone and the children. I have an empty crofter's cottage they can have.'

'She won't take charity.'

'I'll find something for her to do. The oldest boy can work in the stables and I am sure there's work in the kitchen.'

Nora gave a tremulous smile. 'Thank you,' she said softly, touched by his concern. She bit her lip and paused. 'Brandon, I want you to know I wish it could be different.'

Brandon stretched across the bed and took her hand. His voice was quiet, commanding. 'It can be different. You just have to choose to make it so. You've made a difference in others' lives for so long. Now it is time to make a difference in your own.'

The night of the betrothal ball approached, bringing with it, for Nora, an increasing amount of anxiety. Everything was running too smoothly. The interceding weeks between the ball and Witherspoon's visit had gone well.

Mary Malone and her children were established in the cosy cottage. Witherspoon had to eat humble pie and confess Brandon's belief that the raids would stop had been legitimate.

The harder decision was Nora's choice to let Eleanor Habersham take the brunt of Witherspoon's suspicions. She sent word to Hattie and Alfred to close up the house, pack their things and move away. It would keep them safe if anything went wrong; if Witherspoon wanted to believe the spinster had been the thief, she was happy to let him. Eleanor had disappeared and with her, The Cat. Brandon had arranged everything so that her past was tied up into a neat package. She only had to accept it and the book on The Cat was closed for ever. She could start again as a Countess, as Brandon Wycroft's wife, if she chose. That appealed to her more than the title. But there was still one loose end in that regard.

There was still no word from Jack, although she knew Brandon remained hopeful that his friend would turn up shortly. There was nothing to do but wait. The waiting was killing her. Brandon said it was because she was not used to inactivity. The everyday thrills and dangers she had lived with for so long had receded from her lifestyle.

Nora thought otherwise. It seemed the rest of her life hinged on what was to come. She understood completely that the night of the betrothal ball would mark the beginning or the end of what she could have with Brandon. Did she trust him enough to admit to her feelings and reach for the life he offered her? Could she do it knowing that he was offering sanctuary, but not his love?

So she waited impatiently, spending her days with a recovering Mary Malone, reading books in Brandon's well-stocked library and storing up a treasury of memories in case the worst happened. By the night of the ball, she was a bundle of nerves.

'Ellie, we won't need you any longer. I'll help my lady finish with her *toilette*.' The connecting door between Brandon's rooms and Nora's little-used chambers opened, revealing Brandon resplendent in full evening dress.

Ellie, the hastily employed lady's maid, bobbed a curtsy, hiding a nervous titter and the implications of his request before fleeing downstairs to share the latest bit of gossip regarding the master and his betrothed.

Nora's breath hitched as she stared at Brandon in the vanity mirror. The dark clothes suited his commanding presence. He carried with him the urbane aura of the socially astute, but tonight it was coupled with a lethal quality that suggested he was something more than what lay on the surface of his polite veneer.

Danger prowled beneath the surface if one dared to look. That quality had always been there. Nora had seen it the first night she'd invaded his bedroom. She had seen it because he had wanted her to see it. He had hidden it well from the rest of society. Now it was thoroughly exposed, lending him a sharp-edged charm. No matron seeing him tonight would consider him safe for their daughters to cut their flirtatious teeth on.

He must feel it too, Nora reflected, watching him in the mirror. Tonight was a decisive evening. Then he spoke and her hopes and fears were confirmed.

'Jack has returned. He will seek us out at the ball with his news.' There was tightness around his lips.

Perhaps he had already told Brandon. 'Don't spare me, did he say anything to you?'

Brandon shook his dark head. 'No. I asked him to wait until later tonight. This affects us both.'

He moved to stand behind her, lifting the dark curls that fell down her back from an elegantly arranged pile of hair and pearls on top of her head. He let the curls sift through his fingers in a slow cascade so that they fell in a titillating tumble against her bare back. 'You look beautiful, Nora.'

'I'm not dressed.'

'I know.' His hand caressed the nape of her neck sending a *frisson* of longing down her spine. His eyes met hers in the mirror, conveying the promise of wickedness.

'You're dressed,' Nora pointed out, barely able to contain her rising desire.

'I am told opposites attract,' he whispered, bending to nip the tender flesh at her neck. His warm breath blew sensually in her ear. Nora felt herself dampen. Good lord, she'd reach climax before he even took off his trousers. She turned from the mirror and reached for the waist of his trousers. Perhaps they could manage something without wrecking his exquisitely tied cravat.

She tried to be careful, but Brandon would have none of it. 'Damn it, Nora, do you think I can look upon you in that flimsy dressing robe, all that passion darkening your green eyes, and take you gently?'

He pulled her to him, devouring her with his mouth. She hungrily arched against him, ripping and stripping until he was bare with her, skin against skin on the carpet of her boudoir. 'We've never done this in my room before,' Nora panted.

'Then it's high time we rectified that,' Brandon growled fiercely, covering her with his length and plunging deep until she cried out her satisfaction. They plunged and soared over and over, each time soaring a little higher, a little closer, like Icarus to the sun, to the heat that begged to overwhelm them.

'Now, Brandon,' Nora cried, letting the conflagration of their passion sweep over her in hot waves. She let the flames of their climax brand her. There would never be a fire like this again with anyone else.

She fell to earth slowly at first, spent and dreamy. Then with a crash she plummeted the rest of the distance. Was this the last time? The possibility painted the after-bliss of their coupling with a bittersweet brush, explaining the intensity in Brandon's eyes, the wolf-like quality to his stalking seduction, the ravenous frenzy they'd engaged in on the floor without a thought for seeking the comfort of her bed just feet away.

She looked at Brandon, rumpled and ruined, lying next to her. 'You're a wreck. We've destroyed your clothing.' She gave a soft laugh, picking up the limp strip of linen that once represented his finely starched, impeccably tied cravat just minutes ago.

Brandon's blue eyes, still glowing like hot coals from the intensity of their coupling, simmered now with humour. 'It will put Harper's talents to good use, trying to redress me in record time.' He rose up, naked, and sorted through the pile of his discarded garments. 'I have something for you. Ah, here it is.' Brandon pulled a long, flat, blue velvet box from his jacket.

Nora pulled on her diaphanous dressing gown and sat down at the vanity. Her heart beat at the sight of the slender box. It was jewellery. She'd stolen enough of it to know the boxes it came in. She swallowed hard, nervous over the import of the gift.

'Go on, take it,' Brandon urged softly when she hesitated.

'What is it?' she asked gamely, smiling like a woman should when receiving gems. Every man was raised to believe women liked jewellery. She perpetuated the myth with a beatific smile. Brandon would expect it. None the less, she couldn't allow him to fritter away jewels for a lost cause. She would have to refuse them. But first she'd have a peep inside the box.

Nora stared in amazement, forgetting to breathe. A diamond necklace set with emeralds lay nestled among the folds of blue satin, flanked by a matching bracelet and earrings. 'They're magnificent, Brandon.'

'They're the Stockport diamonds.'

It was even worse than she'd thought. He hadn't bought them. They were heirlooms. Nora snapped the lid shut at the import of the jewels. 'I can't possibly wear them,' she said firmly. She held the box out to him.

Brandon took the box and set it on the vanity. He opened the lid and drew out the necklace. 'You can and you will. They are your betrothal gift,' he said with equal firmness, clasping the jewels about her neck.

'Our betrothal isn't real,' Nora reminded him sharply. She laughed suddenly, fingering the diamonds. 'I get it, these aren't real, either. They're paste. Quite good for paste. I haven't seen anything of this quality.'

Brandon looked affronted. 'I assure you, they are real. They've been worn by four generations of Stockport brides.'

'But not by me,' Nora rejoined softly. 'It wouldn't be right.'

Brandon ignored the quiet plea and fastened the earrings gently in her lobes, his hand skimming her bare shoulder where the peignoir had fallen away. 'Everyone will expect to see you wear them tonight.'

Expectations again. His use of the word reminded her that

the handsome, virile man in her boudoir had not forgotten this was indeed a ruse. He had not brought the gems to convince her of his affections. He'd merely brought them to keep up appearances and perhaps to remind her of all she was giving up if she refused his protection.

'Say you'll wear them, Nora,' Brandon cajoled. He pulled her hair to one side, letting the light catch the diamonds. 'They look stunning on you.'

He was still naked. Nora felt his manhood stir against her back.

She couldn't fight his lethal persuasion. If she didn't do something quickly, they would end up back on the floor and hours late for a function in their honour. 'Don't make it harder than it is already,' Nora protested.

Brandon reluctantly stepped back. 'I assume when you say harder you are not referring to me.'

Nora laughed and let her gaze drift lower to where the member in question lay in a state of partial arousal. 'If the reference applies, my lord,' she teased, glad to have the argument behind them if not resolved.

Unabashed by his nakedness, Brandon strode to the wardrobe and sorted through the myriad gowns. 'What did you plan on wearing?'

'It hardly matters since you obviously have a gown in mind. I don't want to end up arguing about it.'

'Afraid you'll lose?' Brandon countered, pulling out the gown he sought, deep green velvet trimmed lavishly with gold braid. The neckline was cut off the shoulders to showcase Nora's shapely collarbones and jewels. Elegant and sophisticated, it was the perfect betrothal gown for a woman past her débutante years.

She gave a quirky grin. 'I never lose. I merely let you think you've won.'

Brandon helped her into the various undergarments the gown required and fitted her into the dress with amazing dexterity. 'Done this before?' Nora queried playfully.

'Give me some credit. Jack could tell you stories about our exploits. I used to be a man about town in my younger days.'

'Rumour has it you still are,' she bantered. The teasing levity between them helped keep the serious issues at bay.

'If the reference applies...' he tossed back easily, using her earlier words.

Tonight was possibly the last night between them. Ostensibly it would be up to her. His offer of marriage still held, but for the wrong reasons. Nora found she didn't want to think beyond the ball.

They dressed Brandon next in a second set of evening clothes, turning him out as pleasing to the eye as he had been before. Nora did a credible job of tying his cravat, even if the knot was simpler than the one formerly devised by Harper.

'How do I look?' Brandon asked, grabbing up his evening cape.

'Hmm...' Nora pretended to study him, contemplating her answer. She tapped a finger against her chin. 'I think I liked you better undressed.'

Brandon flashed a wicked grin. 'Maybe we can accommodate you later this evening.'

'How much later?' Nora batted her eyelashes up at him in flirtatious parody.

'Tut, you're a naughty lassie, already thinking of ways to sneak off to dark corners at the Squire's.'

'Well, first we have to get there.' Nora glanced at the carved wood clock sitting on a side table. It was time to go. As they left the room, Nora felt as if the curtain was going up on the last act of their play, but she still wasn't sure how it ended. If only she could convince herself that Brandon's protection was a valid substitute for his true affections.

The ball was well attended. The squire filled his home with businessmen from Manchester, the investors and the appropriate people of his acquaintance from the village. For a countryman, he was extremely well connected and it showed in his guest list and in the extravagance on display.

Squire Bradley pumped Brandon's hand with bonhomie and began a round of introductions immediately upon their arrival. Most everyone had met Brandon at various functions, but many had yet to meet his bethrothed.

Witherspoon was there, oozing a barely masked jealousy that Brandon had been right about The Cat halting attacks. But Brandon didn't have time for such petty nonsense. He swept the ballroom for a sign of Jack. He found him across the ballroom, gleaming like crystal. Good lord, the man carried fashion to its furthest extreme.

'Lud, man, are those real diamond buttons on your waistcoat?' Brandon asked incredulously when Jack finally wended his way to their group, dressed opulently in evening attire and sporting a highly dandified waistcoat with buttons that sparked beneath the chandelier.

'Indeed so, you've quite the eye for fine things, Stockport,' Jack said smoothly to Brandon while taking Nora's gloved hand and bending over it adroitly to make sure no one missed the *double entendre* of his words.

'Viscount Wainsbridge, it is splendid of you to come,' The Squire, standing next to Brandon, offered.

'Squire Bradley, this is a lovely affair. Your wife has outdone herself,' Jack complimented. 'I dare say a London hostess could have done no better.'

'Why, thank you.' The squire fairly preened under the admiration lavished on him by the foppish Viscount Wainsbridge. 'I'll be sure to pass your compliments on to Mrs Bradley. She'll be thrilled.'

The Viscount turned to Brandon. 'Might I have a word with you, Stockport?'

The Squire jumped in before Brandon could respond. 'We are ready to make the announcement and have our honoured couple lead out the first dance.'

Brandon silently cursed their bad luck. He had hoped the squire would opt to make the announcement before the exit to supper. It would give him time to hear what Jack had to say. Brandon studied Jack's face, trying to guess in what direction his news lay. He sent Jack a silent appeal.

'Ah, Squire Bradley, I had hoped Stockport would have arrived earlier so that I could have conversed with him before the announcement,' Jack filled in. Brandon didn't miss the pointed look Jack cast his way as if to say he knew exactly what Brandon had been up to and why he and Nora had arrived in the nick of time.

The bluff Squire didn't take the hint. Instead, he clapped Jack on the shoulder. 'I am sure it can wait. After all, this is Stockport's betrothal party. He doesn't want to talk business on a night like this.'

Brandon recognised defeat when he saw it. He acquiesced to the Squire's request. At least he could lay plans to speak with Jack in the immediate future. 'Wainsbridge, if you could wait until we open the festivities, I would be happy to speak with you.' He hoped Jack saw the message in his eyes. He understood there was urgent business, but he could not address it just yet without raising eyebrows.

The Squire made his way to the front of the ballroom and

banged on a goblet until he garnered everyone's attention. Then, puffed up with importance, he formally introduced the Earl of Stockport and his lovely bride-to-be, Nora Hammersmith. He made a polite speech about Brandon's dedication to their community, but Brandon heard little of it. He was too busy staring at Nora, drinking in her beauty and pretending in his mind that this was indeed their engagement ball.

Of course, if it was, it would have been held at the townhouse in London, which would have been overrun weeks before the actual event by his sisters and countless second and third cousins, great-aunts and all their progeny. What would his predominantly female extended family have thought of Nora?

Nora looked like a natural Countess in the family jewels, her head held high while the squire prattled on to the crowd. He was proud of her. It had taken consider gumption to carry off her role with such success.

Looking past Nora, he saw Jack standing close behind Witherspoon and a few of the other investors. Whatever news Jack brought, he'd find a way through it. There was always a way. He was a man who knew how to get what he wanted and he wanted Nora. She could not doubt his intentions or affections. Yet he sensed she still wavered. Something unknown to him held her back from committing unequivocally to their passion.

Nora coughed discreetly at his side. 'Brandon, the Squire expects you to say something.'

Brandon uttered some glib nonsense that was met with applause and he gratefully heard the orchestra strike up the opening dance. At a usual ball, the first dance would have been a quadrille, but, in honour of the engagement, the orchestra played a waltz. He took Nora in his arms and made a wide sweeping arc that caused comments to ripple throughout the ballroom.

He smiled as he caught bits and pieces. 'It must be a love match.' 'Look how much he adores her.' 'They make a handsome couple.'

'We've put on quite a show for them, sweetheart,' Brandon said as they took the last turn. Too bad the waltz was over. He'd have to share her with other well-wishers.

'I have to go find Jack,' he said reluctantly as the music finished, relinquishing her to a group of well-wishers. 'Stay here—we can't deprive the Bradleys of all their honoured guests at once.'

Jack found him first and quietly ushered him down the hall to a private room. 'Brandon, things are getting a bit too dicey for my taste,' Jack began before they were even seated.

'What has happened?' Brandon asked cautiously, sitting down in a chair and adopting a casual pose so that any accidental passer-by would think the two gentlemen were lounging and catching up on gossip.

'Witherspoon has been asking questions. He's been talking to Squire Bradley about newcomers to the area. He's been exceedingly interested in the spinster, Eleanor Habersham, and he hasn't been shy in sharing his supposition that The Cat is a woman.'

Brandon nodded gravely, recalling the very similar conversation he'd had with the Squire upon his arrival in December. 'I know. You've been away. This is old news to me. He's already come to me with his information. He found a necklace taken from his wife at the dinner party in a pawn shop and his men identified the woman pawning it as Eleanor Habersham, even though she used a false name on the ticket.'

'That could be damning.' Jack whistled low.

'Not really. Nora's already stolen it back. She lifted it out of his pocket at Stockport Hall before he even got out the door,' Brandon said smugly, lighting a cheroot.

A smile split Jack's usually cynical face. 'You've got yourself a live one, Brandon.'

Brandon only smiled. 'Let's talk about Witherspoon later. I want to hear your news.'

Jack sat down and crossed his legs, adopting a casual pose similar to Brandon's. 'I suppose you do, since there is the issue of bigamy at stake.'

'And is it? Is bigamy going to be a problem?' Brandon drew on his cheroot.

'I should make you stew a bit for all you've put me through this past month, but I find I haven't the stomach for torture. In short, no. She is no longer married to Reggie Portman. Mrs Nora Portman is officially a widow and has been for two years. The bounder had the good grace to die from a stab wound obtained in a tavern brawl.' Jack offered the last with distaste.

Brandon stared at Jack, motionless, trying to separate out the emotions tumbling through him at the news. He'd imagined this moment in recent days. It had always been a triumphant moment in his daydreams. Now that it had arrived, he was filled with conflicting emotions. He did not want to celebrate a man's death. Yet, he did want to celebrate that Nora was free to choose him.

Nothing more stood in their way. Things couldn't be wrapped up any neater. They had packed off Eleanor Habersham and placed most of the blame for The Cat's antics on the spinster's shoulders. The rotter of a husband was dead. He wanted to find Nora immediately and tell her. He wanted to celebrate—not because a man was dead, of course, but because he and Nora had triumphed against insurmountable odds. They'd found a way to be together. But Jack wouldn't let it go so easily.

'The morning we talked in your study, you were besotted with the wench, Brandon. From the look of things tonight, that hasn't changed. You do realise you don't have to marry her, Brandon? Have you forgotten the engagement is just an impromptu ruse? Engineered by her, I might add. Did you stop to think she might have gone so far just to force your hand?' Jack fiddled with his elaborate lace cuff. 'Maybe she knew your honour wouldn't allow you to back out. After all, she gains everything here, Brandon. You gain very little. Have you thought of what could happen if someone finds out sooner or later who your wife-to-be is?'

'It won't happen.' Brandon dismissed Jack's concern.

'It might happen if Witherspoon keeps up his investigation,' Jack warned, leaning forward. 'I think you need to take Witherspoon seriously. He will not let this lie.'

'Then he can chase Eleanor Habersham all the way to York and find nothing at the end of his rainbow,' Brandon retorted fiercely. He would not let Jack's misgivings tarnish his happiness.

Jack would not be thwarted. 'Let me give it to you in plain speech. You've got what you wanted. You've kept The Cat safe. If she's caught now, it won't be on your watch. Your conscience can rest easy on that account.

'Confidence in the mill is restored. I heard you signed the last-needed investor yesterday. The financial security of Stockport-on-the-Medlock is secured.

'Brandon, old chap, you did it. You played two games and won them both.'

'What games would those be?' Brandon answered coolly.

'The Cock of the North beds The Cat and saves his factory. That's audacity if I ever saw it. Now, be smart. Don't stay in the game too long and risk losing everything.'

Brandon's gaze narrowed in dislike of Jack's devil's advocacy. 'It wasn't a game, Jack. It never was. Nora and I are not finished.' He stood and straightened his waistcoat. He wanted to find Nora and catch her up in his arms, swing her around the dance floor and kiss her silly. She would have to say 'yes' now. He was in no mood for Jack's nay-saying. Where was Nora? She should have been here by now.

Chapter Eighteen

'*You played two games and won them both.*' '*Nora and I are not finished.*' Nora froze in the dimly lit hallway at the sound of two male voices. It was definitely Brandon and Jack. She could see the back of Brandon's dark head over the top of a chair.

Brandon had asked her to join them, but now that she had she felt as if she were eavesdropping. Had Brandon meant for her to overhear the conversation? Had he planned this as a cruel goodbye? Or perhaps he hadn't planned for her to overhear it at all. His ominous last words suggested as much. What else did he have in store for her that could be worse than what she'd heard so far?

How could she have been so wrong about Brandon? How could she have lost such a complete perspective on the reality happening around her? Jack's comments horrified her. Tears gathered in her eyes. What he said made sense; there was no refuting his logic. Brandon had deceived her.

Nora sagged against the wall for support as the brutal duplicity of his lies hit her. All of it—the soft words, the afternoons spent arguing politics, every touch, every look, every kiss, every caress—was a lie, a trap meant to ensnare her in the cruellest of ways. All along, Brandon had known what he was doing. She should have shot him that night at St John's.

He'd cleverly used his wit and virility to charm her into thinking of him as an ally. He'd gone so far as to propose marriage and to act as if he meant to see the deed done. He'd given Mary Malone a cottage. He'd lured The Cat on all fronts, pretending to share her cause.

Her stomach lurched. She felt sick. Brandon probably meant to turn her in when he was done with her. But why go through with the public engagement? Why let her wear the diamonds? Wasn't he afraid she would steal them? Merciless reality struck. Therein lay the answer. His motives with the jewels were clear now.

He probably hoped she *would* steal them. Then he could go after her and expose her, or let Witherspoon do his dirty work for him. That was more likely.

She wouldn't let him get away with it. Cold calculation and the chill of heart-hardening anger slowly replaced the ache in her soul. No one used The Cat. She would strike back at the thing Brandon held most dear. Before she left town, she'd pay Stockport and his friends one last visit. He would realise all his contretemps had been for naught. Although he didn't know it yet, he'd been right about one thing tonight: he and The Cat weren't finished yet.

Brandon put a finger to his lips in warning. Jack broke off in mid-sentence, his voice dropping to a low whisper. 'What is it? Did you hear something?'

Brandon gave a slight nod and launched into a discussion of horses in a voice loud enough to carry to the doorway. If anyone had been there, the conversation should prove to be unexceptional to them. Two gentlemen talking about horseflesh was nothing significant. But Brandon couldn't shake the feeling that the person had been eavesdropping. It was no accident someone had passed by the door. Someone had deliberately come looking for him or for Jack. He'd heard the sound when he'd risen from his chair.

Mentally, Brandon replayed the conversation in his head, trying to decipher what might have been overheard and how it might have been perceived. It was a risky conversation to fall into the right hands. The mention of his 'supposed plan' and mention of The Cat would raise eyebrows if the person knew enough—someone like Cecil Witherspoon or St John.

'I think we had better head back to the ballroom before anyone takes our absence seriously,' Brandon suggested. 'If someone did overhear anything damaging, our quick return should put paid to any suspicion that we're running a conspiracy.' He also hoped he would catch a glimpse of those who were mingling in the corridor closer to the ballroom. Perhaps the eavesdropper hadn't had time to get too far.

'You might not have heard anything either,' Jack reminded him as they rose. 'It is just as likely that a branch scratched the window. It is easy to develop paranoia when you keep secrets.'

'I would like to think that is all it was,' Brandon conceded, eager to get back to the ballroom and back to Nora's side. He didn't like the notion of leaving her alone in close proximity to Witherspoon, although she was more than capable of handling him.

Brandon breathed easier as he and Jack gained the brightly lit dance floor. No suspects presented themselves in the harmless crowds mingling in the corridor outside the ballroom. Jack was probably right, the sound he'd heard was a branch brushing the windows. Jack clapped him on the shoulder and melted into the crowd, instantly adopting his

returned and confirmed his thoughts. Nora wasn't there either.

Back downstairs, he beckoned to Jack and informed him of Nora's disappearance in a low voice. When Jack's survey of the card rooms turned up nothing, Brandon sought out the Squire.

'Lost your wife already?' The Squire laughed at Brandon's pensive expression. 'You're in luck. She left half an hour ago. Said she had a headache and didn't want to ruin your fun. She took the carriage and was going to send it back for you.' The Squire scratched his head. 'I assumed you knew. The plan seemed so organised. I thought the two of you must have agreed on it together.'

Brandon suppressed the dread that rose in him. It seemed deuced odd that Nora would leave without joining him first when she knew he'd gone off to speak with Jack on business that concerned them both. He would have thought her curiosity would have compelled her to wait before leaving, no matter how her head felt.

The headache bit niggled at him too. Nora was the halest person he knew. She scaled trees, wielded weapons and ran around the countryside at night. That was not the behaviour of someone prone to evening-ending headaches. It all confirmed what he'd intuitively known earlier. She had been the one in the hallway. She'd overheard Jack's damning remarks. What a cad she must think him, a man no better than her late husband.

'She must have heard us talking,' Brandon said as the Squire moved off to mingle with another group. 'She felt fine foppish demeanour as he effortlessly insinuated himself into a group of people.

Brandon scanned the room for Nora, looking for the rich green gown amid a sea of reds and pinks. He could not find her. He quartered the room with his gaze and tried again. The dress, the diamonds and her above-average height should have drawn his gaze immediately, let alone the fact that he was always aware of her presence. *She wasn't in the room.* He forced himself not to panic. There were any number of places she might be. She could be strolling on the terrace or sitting in the refreshment room. She could be in the ladies' retiring room. *She could have been the one strolling down the corridor and overheard your conversation, or, rather, Jack's cynical diatribe.*

That brought Brandon up short, his panic renewed. What would Nora think if she had heard Jack talking about the plan? Would she realise Jack was wrong? There had never been a plan. He loved her and meant to marry her. But The Cat was not used to believing the best of people. He had to find her fast before she did something that severed their relationship completely.

Affecting a casual stroll, Brandon moved through the ballroom towards the terrace doors. He nodded to those he knew as he double-checked the clusters of people chatting on the sidelines. He studied the dancers whirling past on the floor in a country polka.

groom in, I want to know if she took her horse.' He gestured for Jack to follow him and together they mounted the stairs to Brandon's rooms.

All was as the staff had reported. Her gowns hung in the wardrobe. The personal items he'd purchased for her still lay on the bureau. The Stockport diamonds shimmered on the vanity next to the blue velvet box. Brandon shut his eyes and groaned, not caring if Jack witnessed his distress. The evening had started off with such promise. Now, their vibrant coupling on the floor seemed a lifetime ago.

'I am sorry, my friend,' Jack said softly. 'I can see you're in pain over this.'

Brandon sighed, pushing a hand through his hair. 'The thing is, Jack, I am hurting more for her than I am myself. I cannot begin to fathom the depth of betrayal she must be feeling. The level of deceit she thinks me capable of must be devastating.'

'Now, stop right there.' Jack took a seat on the edge of the bed and looked stern. 'I think you might possibly assume too much. She might have been playing you the whole time. According to your arrangement, your association expired after the ball. For all you know, she was leaving tomorrow anyway. If she overheard us, she might have felt it was safer to leave immediately instead of waiting for you to pull a fast one and have her arrested in the morning.'

'God. I am an idiot.' Brandon swore softly, sinking on to the bench in front of the vanity. When had he stopped thinking about her as The Cat? At what point had he started seeing her only as Nora? He'd been blind to all the nuances outside their relationship. She'd so cleverly used sex and self-disclosure to weave a web of intimacy around them that cocooned him from all else going on under his nose. He had loved her. Had she ever loved him? At any point had she cared for him?

He thought of her resistance to his proposal. He'd been a fool not to see it for what it was—the oldest trick in the book of female wiles. It had been nothing but a clever rendition of playing hard to get. She'd kept him panting after her right up to the end with her bed tricks. Even tonight, just hours ago, she'd writhed beneath him in hot passion on this very floor, making him believe she cared, that she might stay, that she might accept his honourable proposal.

'Brandon, I'm not saying that's how it was,' Jack cajoled. 'I simply believe it bears thinking about. I don't want you torturing yourself with unnecessary guilt.'

A knock sounded and Harper entered. 'The groom's downstairs, my lord.'

Brandon looked up, all business. 'I'll be there in a moment. Have him wait in my study.' Brandon stood up and brushed at his trousers. 'There may be some truth in what you say, my friend,' he said to Jack. 'I suspect we'll know soon enough what The Cat really felt for me.'

'I hope I am wrong.'

'I don't hold much hope at all.'

His words proved fortuitous. By eleven o'clock the next morning, the whole village knew, in spite of the late night of dancing at the Squire's, that The Cat had appeared in Manchester and hit the homes on Cheetham Hill. Not just one house, but three. All three homes were occupied by major investors in the mill and all three of the homes' occupants had been away from home at the Squire's ball in Stockport-on-the-Medlock. Expensive items were missing, far beyond the usual prey of silver candlesticks and small pieces of jewellery.

Brandon speculated as to the reason for such a large-scale robbery. The Cat was getting ready to move on and needed enough funds to start over in a new place. She would need enough time to establish her new identity and to study the terrain. His careless conversation with Jack had forced her to it—or maybe Jack was right and it was inevitable.

Either way, the outcome pained him. He could not bring himself to go into town and hear the news first-hand. Instead, he sent Jack so he could stay hidden away at home, wallowing in self-pity.

Footsteps and a voice in the hallway alerted Brandon that his sanctuary had been invaded. Moments later, the butler announced the arrival of St John and Witherspoon. There was no denying them. He had to see them.

'Gentlemen, please come in.' Brandon gestured to the empty seats in front of his desk. He decided to address the issue head on. It would be useless to pretend he didn't know why they'd come. 'I hear The Cat has been busy again. I had hoped we'd seen the last of him.'

'Or her, as the case may be,' Witherspoon did not hesitate to put in. 'We mean to catch The Cat once and for all. I've spent the morning putting together a watch crew. Each of the investors' homes will be heavily guarded from now on. Additionally, we've organised a patrol to guard the mill. Now that the framing has begun, the construction site is more vulnerable than ever. There's actually something there now that could be burnt down or blown up. St John has organised a little militia to roam the countryside.'

'A militia?' Brandon repeated, trying to sound cool. He trained a gimlet eye on St John with the intent of intimidating him with his hauteur. 'Isn't that word a little exaggerated?' He could only imagine how absurd the farmers would look armed with their pitchforks and scythes.

'Besides, St John, the farmers are *my* tenants. I am the only one who can "organise" them into a fighting force.'

St. John had the good sense to look abashed. 'Of course, my lord. I would not be so presumptuous as to order your people. What Witherspoon means is that there is a group of half-pay British regulars billeted at the inn in the next town over. I've gotten permission to use them. They should arrive late this afternoon.'

Brandon hid his surprise. 'That's excellent thinking, St John.'

'Will you join us, Stockport?' Witherspoon asked, fixing Brandon with an intense stare that gave Brandon the impression of being transparent. What was the man looking for?

Before Brandon could answer, Jack's voice boomed from the hall. 'Absolutely. Stockport would not miss this opportunity for the world and neither would I. Count us both in.' Jack invited himself into the private meeting and drew up a chair.

'Lord Wainsbridge, how good of you to volunteer.' Witherspoon narrowed his gaze, looking Jack up and down in barely disguised disdain, his eyes clearly conveying the impression he thought Jack's services would be negligible at best.

'Glad that's settled.' Jack slapped his riding gloves against his palm. 'If you'll excuse us, Stockport and I have preparations to make.' He smiled, ignoring Witherspoon's chagrin over the abrupt dismissal from someone not even the host.

'Do be ready, Wainsbridge. Tonight, we ride for blood and we shoot to kill. Are you up for such sport?' Witherspoon said from the door.

'Are you?' Jack shot back.

Brandon stood up to intervene. 'Gentlemen, let's save our animosity for another time. We're all on the same side.'

'Are we?' Jack asked after the two visitors departed.

'What do you mean?'

'Witherspoon and St John have mustered a real army. Your

Cat is no match for British soldiers. You heard him. Tonight they're out for blood. Is that the side you're on?'

Brandon paced to the French doors overlooking the garden. He looked out over the bleak winter lawn, his hands clasped behind his back. 'No. I've thought about nothing else all day. When I heard she'd struck, I knew it would come to this. I had hoped it wouldn't be so soon. Who knew Witherspoon and St John could be so efficient?' His attempt at sarcastic levity fell flat.

'Witherspoon is the brains behind that duo. He doesn't miss a detail,' Jack replied. 'Gawd, the man's fanatical. He's awfully emotional over money and for a man who's not the emotional sort, I find that odd, don't you?'

Brandon turned from the doors. 'Are you suggesting there is something else at stake?'

'I honestly don't know.' Jack shook his head. 'But I do know Witherspoon would rather see The Cat dead than caught. If The Cat is caught, she won't live long enough to see a trial.'

Brandon nodded slowly. 'I find that I don't care if she left because it was time to be The Cat again. If she bested me, I accept that. As you put it, I had a prime adventure. My pride is wounded, if I meant nothing to her beyond another conquest. Perhaps I am just another man she's duped into playing the accomplice.

'But whatever anger or hurt I feel, it is not enough to warrant seeing her dead. I can't blame her for my willing participation in what happened between us. She did not force me to keep her secrets or to come to her bed. I could have turned her in at any time and I chose not to. I didn't have to bed her, yet I did. She did not ask for my protection, but I gave it anyway.'

Jack yawned dramatically from his chair. 'You sound so reasonable for a man who's been jilted. Can't you sound a bit angry? You just lost the best sex of your life. Punch a wall or something!'

Brandon turned sharply from the window, his voice a menacing growl that contradicted his dispassionate logic. 'If I am cool and collected, it is because I have no choice. A hot head will get her shot and me incriminated. Jack, what do you think will happen if Witherspoon actually succeeds in capturing her and discovers that The Cat of Manchester looks distinctly like my betrothed? Barring that most likely of calamities, what happens when I can no longer produce a betrothed? How do I explain that my intended has ridden off into nowhere and broken the engagement?'

'Disaster comes to mind.'

'Disaster doesn't begin to cover it, Jack. Damn it, this is no time to be flippant,' Brandon reprimanded his indolent friend.

'Do we have a plan?' Jack said, sobering.

Brandon nodded tersely. 'I have some ideas about where she might go.' He hoped his guesses paid off. Nora was out there somewhere, alone and without any way of knowing what awaited her. 'Jack, it is imperative that we find her first, especially if you're right and Witherspoon would rather shoot than ask questions.'

In spite of his best efforts, Brandon failed to locate Nora by sunset. With great anxiety over what was to come, he and Jack saddled their horses and went to join Witherspoon and his 'militia'.

The night was moonless, forcing the men gathered to search out The Cat to rely on other senses than sight. The blinder the better, Brandon thought grimly. He would take whatever luck he could make or steal. Even the devil's own luck would do tonight. It was very likely the only hope he had left.

During the afternoon, he had discreetly scoured the area, searching out The Cat or any sign of her. He tried the Grange, although it was too obvious a choice for a hideout. He tried tracking her horse. He looked in abandoned cottages.

All of his efforts revealed naught. The Cat was every bit the master she purported to be. If he had any doubt on that score, it was clearly settled now. Any sign of her presence had vanished. He prayed it was sign of safe passage. It was entirely possible The Cat had settled for the loot of last night's robberies and was well away from Stockport-on-the-Medlock without a backward glance. Brandon fervently wished the night would result in nothing more than a wild goose chase.

Dogs bayed in the distance, the growing loudness of their howls indicating they were nearing the assembled group. Brandon cast a sharp glance at Jack.

Jack took his cue. 'Lud, Witherspoon, dogs? This is no fox hunt. A bit unnecessary, I say.'

Witherspoon gave the foppish viscount a cold look. 'What better way to flush out a cat than with dogs?' To all gathered he explained with a dictatorial flourish, 'We've left nothing to chance this evening. Between Squire Bradley's excellent hunting hounds, the British regulars and our own manpower, The Cat will not elude us. Everyone has been given their instructions. Let us ride!' He waved his arm in a forward motion and the teams broke out in various directions.

'Tally ho!' Jack said derisively as his horse stamped eagerly, wanting to be off with others. 'Gawd, the man thinks he's a general. He only lacks a sabre to complete his pose.'

Brandon cast Jack a sideways glance as he wheeled his horse around. 'Self-importance can make a man careless. All the better for us if he overvalues himself.' He kicked his horse into a canter and set off after the two soldiers assigned to ride with him and Jack. 'Keep Witherspoon's group in sight,' he reminded Jack.

Witherspoon's group rode to Brandon's left. The plan was to create a fan, eventually becoming a circle that encompassed the residences of the investors and the mill. If The Cat was in the vicinity, planning to strike, she'd meet with guards at each house. Should she manage to elude them, there would be a living net of men encircling the area to contend with. It would be nearly impossible to get through. The Cat's incredible skill could not compete with the sheer number of men out against her.

Brandon forced himself into a state of heightened alertness. His eyes scanned the perimeter of their search for the flare that signalled The Cat's capture. His ears strained for any sound that someone was nearby in the underbrush. He clamped his thighs tightly around his big bay stallion, trying to feel for any change in the horse's demeanour. If someone unseen were nearby, his horse would give sign of it. He wished he could shake the feeling that The Cat had finally run out of lives.

Chapter Nineteen

Dark at last! Nora rose from her cramped position in the little-used root cellar of the Grange. She ran her fingers through her hair, freeing it of cobwebs and who knew what else. However, she had few complaints. She had leased the Grange specifically for the feature of the hidden room beneath the kitchen floor.

Earlier in the day, the root cellar had served its purpose, allowing her to rest and to hide, both of which had been imperatives. She could not carry out her final mission in Stockport-on-the-Medlock sleepless. Booted feet on the kitchen floor under which she hid proved the importance of the latter.

The intruder's voice belonging to the purposeful steps had been Stockport's. She'd taken satisfaction in his presence. He was worried enough to come looking for her. He had every right to be worried; worried about what might become of his mill if she were allowed to run loose; worried about all the different ways he could be incriminated if she were caught.

It did not escape her that the man was faced with an awful dilemma, either let her stay free and protect his culpability while potentially endangering his precious mill, or attempt to catch her and save the mill while exposing his connection to her. Nora wondered what he would risk, his reputation or his finances. One or the other would have to be sacrificed. He had nothing left to barter with. He'd already sold his soul with the plan he engineered to keep her at Stockport Hall.

Nora struck a match and lit one of the candles stored in the cellar. It was time to get to work. She struggled out of the dirty ball gown, tamping down memories of the nimble fingers that had done up the tiny buttons in the back. She could not afford to let sentiment cloud her thought. Nora shut her eyes tight, pushing back images of Brandon, naked, fastening diamonds and emeralds about her neck, making false promises.

Nora slipped into The Cat's costume, dark leather breeches, black silk shirt, and enveloping cape. The clothing felt like a second skin, comforting and familiar.

The only change tonight in her costume was an expensive dun-colored wig she had decided on at the last minute. She pinned up her hair and tucked it beneath the excellent hair-piece, which looked real and hid her own dark mane effec-tively, before tying the pirate headscarf over it. She wasn't planning on being caught, but, if she was, she wasn't ready yet to expose herself as Brandon's intended. One didn't burn bridges until they were absolutely unnecessary.

Last, she tied on the black silk mask that partially hid her face and emphasised her cat-green eyes.

She went to the crude chest in the corner and lifted the lid, revealing a small cache of arms. With the calculation of a duellist selecting his weapons, Nora tested and rejected a snub-nosed pistol. She hefted the weight of another pistol and found it to her liking. She put it in her belt along with a pouch of ammunition and a skein of dark rope.

She turned her attention to the array of knives and selected a small dagger reminiscent of a *sgian dubh* for her arm sheath and a longer one for her belt. She hoped she wouldn't need any of the weapons.

Nora hung a powder horn about her chest, bandit-style, and grabbed up a medium black bag and matches. Charges were a bit of a nuisance, heavy and weighty.

She did a final mental inventory of her supplies: powder, charges, pistol, knives, matches. She had everything. Her saddle bags, containing the valuables from the previous night, were already at the base of the ladder leading to the hatch. She was ready for her last raid.

Outside, Nora breathed deeply of the crisp night air. It felt good to stretch, to be in the open, after hours in the confinement of the cellar. She put her fingers to her mouth and whistled for her horse. She'd let the gelding roam during the day. The horse couldn't lead Stockport to her if he happened to find it, recognise it and try to track it. If anything, her horse probably led him on a merry chase to nowhere since her horse had no idea where she was.

The horse came to the whistle though, following the bird-call of the night-jar to where Nora stood. She flung the saddle bags over his withers and fastened them with a cinch. She retrieved a bridle and deftly slipped it over his head. It was the only harness he'd wear. Tonight, she'd ride bareback.

Nora set out for the mill, her progress slowed by the lack of the moon, but she appreciated the added invisibility it afforded her.

A short distance from the mill, Nora stopped to survey the structure. A patrol passed by the structure. So, Stockport thought to increase his security. She watched for a half-hour, sure of the guards' circuit. They passed every ten minutes. It would be enough time to lay a quick line of powder from where she hid to the structure and run back to light the fuse. She was counting on the explosion and subsequent flames to create enough distraction for her to make an invisible getaway.

The guards made their pass. Nora went to work, efficiently sprinkling the powder and setting the fuse. She hesitated for a moment upon reaching the mill. When she dropped the match she would put paid to Brandon's dreams. There would be no going back for either of them. He would be ruined and he'd know she was the one who had done it.

Her fingers trembled with the match. She struggled to light it. She tried again. This had to be done. Firing the mill now would save lives and minimise whatever funds Witherspoon would collect in insurance. Brandon would find a way to go on.

No image she could conjure up could persuade her to see it through. Just as she'd known that night at St John's that she couldn't shoot Brandon, she could not bring herself to destroy his mill in a wanton act of violence.

Her heart rebelled at her weakness. *He betrayed you!*

Be fair! Nora argued. *You entered into the liaison knowing his full mettle and he yours. It's not his fault you fell for him. He set the trap and let you decide if you wanted to spring it.*

Nora blew out the match, careful to cup her hands around the flame and the residual smoke. She dropped the extinguished match to the ground. She wouldn't do it. She would get on her horse and ride away.

It would be punishment enough for Brandon to struggle with the remnants of The Cat's presence. The charges were still laid. He would see the last gift she left him. He would know The Cat had won their private game. He would know she could have blown up the mill, but hadn't. He could spend his life pondering why.

Lost in her own thoughts, Nora didn't hear the two stealthy

soldiers approach her from behind. She turned to go and ran right into their scarlet-clad chests.

'Well, well, well, what do we have here?' one of them said in a tone that indicated full well they already knew the answer.

'I think,' said the other, 'The Cat has come out to play for the last time. Fire your flare and get Witherspoon over here.'

An orange spark lit up the night sky. An excited cry issued from the men up and down the search line. After two hours of empty patrols, there was action at last. Brandon's heart leapt. Nora was caught. Without waiting for the rest of his party, Brandon wheeled his horse towards Witherspoon's group, thankful that they were the two search parties closest to the location from which the flare issued.

'We've got The Cat now!' Witherspoon cried in a near-maniacal voice as Brandon flew past him. He refused to wait for anyone. His bay stallion was fast and fresh from a night of slow riding. If he could get there soon enough, he might be able to do something before the others arrived.

He could effect a diversion, but he could not directly aid her without incriminating himself beyond the pale. It struck him that it might not matter. He might be incriminated already. If her mask was off and someone who knew his 'betrothed' had found her, there would be awkward questions to answer.

A thousand thoughts tumbled through his mind as he rode. Was she hurt? Had the men wounded her? If there was any chance for escape, it would depend on Nora being whole. God, he hoped it was men who had found her and not the dogs. She might stand a chance against a pair of malleable young half-pay soldiers. Her wiles would mean nothing to the dogs.

Worried for Nora, Brandon gave the stallion its head, letting it race through the dark, heedless of potential pitfalls.

Every second mattered; it was not a night for caution but for intrepid, decisive action.

It wasn't until the skeletal frame of the mill's structure loomed against the night sky that Brandon realised where the flare had come from. He'd been too full of fear for Nora to notice where he was headed. Of course The Cat would go to the mill—what else could possibly keep her around? It made sense now. She had no more use for baubles after her raids last night. If she was still in the area, it would be because of unfinished business at the factory.

He saw the trio and recognised the cut of the uniform. He called out to them to warn them of his approach. He didn't want to risk a trigger-happy soldier mistaking him for The Cat's accomplice.

Nearing the threesome, he could see Nora standing rigidly, hands over her head. She still wore the mask, but it wouldn't be long until Witherspoon arrived and the secret was out.

She barely looked at him, keeping her eyes and all her attention on the two soldiers, waiting for an opportunity. Brandon silently applauded her. She might give the appearance of surrender, but she had not yet admitted defeat.

Beneath him, his stallion pranced, agitated over having his hard run curbed. It gave Brandon an idea. 'Good work, lads!' he congratulated the two soldiers in an overloud tone that enhanced the bay's sidestepping.

'That's quite a horse you've got there, milord.' One of the soldiers, a young pimply-faced boy, said, eyeing the big stallion with grave speculation and nervousness.

Brandon preened, putting on a show worthy of Jack's dramatics. 'Yes, he's a big brute. I must admit he's almost too much for me to handle on occasions. He's quite high strung tonight.'

Nora's stance grew more alert. Good girl. She'd picked

up on his plan. Would she understand she could trust him? That this was about freeing her, not about protecting his own interests?

The riders closest to the flare and Witherspoon appeared in the clearing. He had less than a minute to effect his plan. Witherspoon would not buy an act of sloppy horsemanship from him without smelling a rat. He knew Brandon rode too well for such an occurrence. But these boys knew nothing of him.

Brandon sawed on the reins, causing the stallion to rear, his great hooves striking the air. The rearing horse created a barrier between Nora and her captors. Nora turned and ran.

'The Cat's getting away!' the soldiers yelled, recovering themselves as the horse settled down. They pointed and gestured wildly as the other riders pulled up.

'This way!' Witherspoon raised his arm in the direction Nora had gone. Witherspoon kneed his horse and took off with Brandon beside him. Brandon knew he hadn't been able to give Nora much of a head start. The riders' later arrival and the brief moments of confusion at the site had bought her a small amount of extra time. He hoped, between the head start and the cloudy night, it would be enough.

His luck was failing. The clouds suddenly parted, revealing a white three-quarters moon. In the distance, he made out her form, running hard towards a copse of trees. Beside him, he heard Witherspoon cheer, still clinging to his belief The Cat was female. 'There she is!'

Brandon spurred his horse on, but Witherspoon's mount was equally as fine and matched the stallion stride for stride. There'd be no breaking away from him in the short run, but if Nora led them on a merry chase, the thoroughbred would tire over time. Behind them, the rest of the pack had fallen steadily back. Jack was with them, somewhere.

Perhaps Jack would coax them into taking a false trail or short cut and leave Nora to the two of them. Brandon liked those odds better.

Nora burst from the copse, mounted low over the neck of her gelding. Thank goodness she hadn't gone to ground. With a lead and horsed, she stood a chance if she rode smartly. Her gelding was a solid horse and good over the long distance. If she could hold on long enough, Witherspoon's thoroughbred would exhaust himself. A sidelong glance at the mount showed flecks of foam already forming at the bit.

'She's horsed!' Witherspoon called over his shoulder. They were closing in on her faster than Brandon liked. They were near enough to see her take a hedge, trying to cut cross country. If the situation hadn't been so dire, Brandon would have taken time to appreciate the fine bit of horsemanship on display.

Witherspoon's horse stumbled briefly and a movement at his side caused Brandon to glance over. Fear gripped him. Witherspoon had drawn his pistol. Recognising that his flashy thoroughbred was tiring and wouldn't be able to catch the sturdy gelding, Witherspoon was opting for a bullet.

'My horse can't catch her, Stockport, but my bullet will. You go on and bring her down when she tires,' he said, speaking of her as if he were bringing down a buck from the hunt.

'You can't kill her,' Brandon yelled over the sound of racing hooves, fumbling for the persuasive skill for which he was reputed to possess. 'There'll be no satisfaction of a trial, no chance to see her punished for her crimes. This should be decided by a court of law.'

'I only mean to wound,' Witherspoon said with cool calculation. He slowed his horse and took steady aim.

Pistols were unpredictable things, Brandon told himself. It was highly unlikely Witherspoon would hit his target at this distance. Short of throwing himself at Witherspoon and overtly fouling the shot, he was helpless to intervene.

Witherspoon's finger squeezed the trigger and time slowed. Brandon edged his stallion into the thoroughbred, throwing it off balance. The bullet fired. Brandon's distraction wasn't enough. He watched in horror as Nora slumped forward into the horse's mane.

'A hit! In spite of your incompetent horsemanship, Stockport,' Witherspoon crowed. 'That should slow her down. My horse is spent. You ride ahead; at least that edgy beast of yours has some stamina.'

Brandon wasted no time. He let Nora make one last effort, turning the gelding towards a forested area where speed would matter less and trickery more. He knew she intended to dismount and hide. He let her, relieved to see that she was conscious and not suffering unduly.

He entered the woods behind her and slid off the stallion's back. 'Nora, it's me, Brandon. Show yourself.' He looked around desperately. He had only a little time. A small cry of pain caught his attention and he followed it to Nora, crouched in the notch of a dead tree, nearly invisible in the dense undergrowth.

'I will shoot without hesitation.'

Brandon's gaze dropped to the pistol in her good hand. 'I am not the enemy, Nora.' He held his hands out at his side. If he ever needed the right words, it was now. 'I know you ran because of what you overheard at the ball. You misunderstood.'

'I heard about your plan, how seducing me was your way of keeping the mill safe,' Nora ground out, her anger apparent in every word.

'Nora, there isn't time to explain. You are wrong. How else can you explain why I am out here risking my neck for you, again? Don't be a fool, Nora, you know what we had cannot be faked.'

Brandon sensed her wavering. The pistol lowered. Had his words been successful or had her arm simply tired of the act?

'Are you hurt badly?' He took a confident step forward, not daring to betray the anxiety inside. The Cat appreciated strength. If she sensed weakness, it would be like blood to a shark.

'It just grazed me. But it's bleeding and it hurts at present,' Nora admitted.

'Unbutton your shirt.' Brandon commanded. It was too dark to see much of the wound, but he pressed around the area to make sure the bullet had not entered. 'You're right, there is no entrance or exit wound. You're lucky. But it's bleeding too much for a simple graze.' Brandon ripped a strip from his own shirt and fashioned a tight bandage. 'There, that should stop the bleeding and keep you from dripping until we get you home. I don't want those dogs to smell blood.'

'I am not going back with you. Everything is over. Finished,' Nora said sternly.

Brandon ignored her. 'I'll stall them here. You go back to Stockport Hall and have Harper tend to you. We'll sort everything out in the morning.'

Nora backed away. 'No. Brandon, be reasonable. There is too much doubt between us.'

'There is too much passion between us for us to let it go. Do you think what we have happens every day?' Brandon was worried. Already blood seeped through the bandage. He had to get her back to the hall.

'I know it doesn't. But The Cat cannot do this. I have devoted my life to helping others, to saving people from lives of industrial slavery.'

'Your husband is dead. I meant to tell you at the ball. You are free to start a new life.' Brandon returned her gaze with a hard stare of his own, closing the distance she'd created between them. 'You cannot start a new life if you're dead.

'Nora.' Brandon reached for her, taking her face between his hands and kissed her lips with all the passion of a lover.

She fell in his arms, limp against him. 'Oh, so now you're swooning, at last,' he joked, not quite grasping the situation.

'That's not funny,' she said faintly, all her strength ebbing. 'Help me, Brandon. Don't let me die. Witherspoon will win, he needs me dead before…' She didn't finish the sentence.

'Nora!' he called out in the shock of holding her slumped form, but she was gone, completely unconscious in his embrace.

He swung her up in his arms and looked about frantically for a place to hide her, but it was futile. The wound and her exertions over the past twenty-four hours proved to be too much.

He heard horses approach and felt his heart sink. Time had run out. Nora lay limp in his arms and he could not protect her. A fine champion he had turned out to be for her.

'You've got her, Stockport.' Witherspoon and his cadre reined in, Witherspoon's voice full of glee at the sight of Brandon with The Cat unconscious in his arms.

Witherspoon jumped off his horse and strode to Brandon's side. He flicked back Nora's cloak, revealing the bandaged wound and the rise and fall of breasts beneath the dark shirt. 'Aha! I was right, Stockport. The burglar is a woman.'

'So you were.' Brandon barely held his temper.

'I wager the woman is Eleanor Habersham.' Witherspoon reached for the mask and head scarf, pushing them off.

'Have you no decency? The poor woman is unconscious,' Brandon rebuked him, 'You're mauling her as if she were a cheap doxy.'

'She treated us no better,' Witherspoon snarled. 'There, it is Eleanor, that tricky piece of baggage.'

Brandon looked down at Nora in his arms, expecting to see her mass of dark hair, but seeing instead the dun-coloured wig. He was safe for the moment. Her forethought bought them both some more time—more time for him to find a way out of this and perhaps another chance for them. Had she worn the wig out of concern for him? To avoid exposing him to censure?

The others turned their horses and began the trek back into the village. Witherspoon and Jack remained behind with Brandon to help him mount his bay with Nora.

Witherspoon flicked a glance over Brandon's torn shirt. 'I didn't want to say anything in front of the others, but you're getting soft. I wonder what else you might have done if we hadn't arrived so quickly. You bandaged her wounds. If she persuaded you to tend her wounds, perhaps she would have persuaded you to let her go.' His eyes gleamed like blue icicles in the dark.

'Speak plainly, Witherspoon—what are you suggesting?' Brandon returned with a cold steel of his own.

'That you've a soft spot for thieves or, if you like, that perhaps the reason you bandaged her wound was that you're in league with The Cat.'

'You're a slanderous fool!' Jack interjected with scorn. 'How dare you suggest such a thing about Stockport. He's an upstanding member of Parliament.'

Witherspoon swung up into his saddle, fixing Jack with an intense gaze. 'All the same, Stockport's house hasn't been robbed.'

'You're welcome to your speculations,' Brandon said curtly, before kneeing his bay into motion and grabbing the reins around Nora's still form.

'I'll be watching you, Stockport. There's something not right about all this,' Witherspoon cautioned.

For Brandon, the night seemed an interminable hell. He rode back to Stockport-on-the-Medlock with Nora in front of him. Gratefully, she remained unconscious.

He argued with Witherspoon over where to take her and won. Witherspoon wanted to take her to the Manchester jail. Brandon argued she ought to be held in Stockport-on-the-Medlock, at least until she was better able to travel and arrangements could be made.

The small town jail, which was nothing more than the Squire's root cellar, would be much better than the dirty city jail.

He stayed with Nora until he saw that she received medical treatment and was regaining consciousness. He ensured her privacy by counselling everyone to get some sleep and promised they'd meet in the afternoon to discuss their next step.

'What is there to discuss, Stockport? I say we hang her. We all know what she's done,' Witherspoon countered.

'There's protocol to these things and it must be followed,' Brandon had responded tersely, wondering how much longer he could keep Witherspoon at bay. It was apparent Witherspoon was starting to believe his favour wasn't enough.

The sun had been up for an hour before Jack and Brandon returned home.

'To bed, then.' Jack stretched and yawned as they entered the house.

'I think I'll stay up,' Brandon said in desultory tones.

'She's going to need you in possession of all your faculties, old friend. It would be best if you slept. Perhaps things will look better after some rest.'

'I hope so, Jack, because right now I am flat out of ideas. But you were right, she's got something on Witherspoon.'

Chapter Twenty

Nora swam towards consciousness, acutely aware that her shoulder was a throbbing, aching mass of pain. How had it got that way? It felt like she'd been shot. She remembered. She *had* been shot. By that bastard Witherspoon too, she guessed.

She remembered being in the woods. Brandon had been there. She'd been in his arms. He'd been frantic. She could hear his voice in her head, begging her to run, to go home with him. Then she had fainted. She had never fainted before in her life. She picked a rotten time to start adopting that womanish behavior.

She opened her eyes. The room was nearly dark, except for a small shaft of light coming in from the crack between two doors positioned above her. She was underground, but this wasn't the root cellar at The Grange. She shifted her position on the cot where she lay and winced at the pain in her shoulder.

Nora forced herself into a sitting position and took in the scene of her captivity. It was too much to hope that this wasn't a jail, that Brandon had somehow whisked her away to a secret underground room. That could only mean one thing. She had been caught. Caught and shot. Witherspoon meant to see her dead before she could tell someone about his secret plans. She had to get out of here, had to live long enough to tell Brandon.

She should have told him earlier. She'd had ample opportunity. She could have told him Christmas Day or any time during the past weeks at the Hall. Now, it was almost too late.

She surveyed the room, looking for an escape route. The room was small, square and relatively clean as dirt rooms go. It contained the cot she was on and a rickety table that held a ewer, basin and a bit of towelling.

The idea of cleaning up reminded her of something. Nora put a hand to her head. How much did her captors know? The wig was still in place and she breathed easier. Brandon was the only potential ally she had at the moment. She needed him safe and above suspicion. If her captors discovered The Cat and his betrothed were one and the same, he'd be unable to help her. There were still unresolved truths between them, in spite of what he'd said in the copse, but he was all she had.

She had no way to reach Hattie and Alfred in Manchester. Only Brandon knew what had happened to her and where she was. Hell, *she* didn't even know where she was. Word would spread, of course, as a trial date neared, unless Witherspoon decided to forgo a trial and take justice into his own clammy hands—a huge possibility.

If there was a trial, Hattie and Alfred would hear of it, but she didn't want them to risk their necks on a rescue mission. She didn't want the Manchester slums to rise up and march to her side. Not that they would, necessarily, but she could well imagine a few of them would try. She couldn't bear to see any of them hurt.

Ignoring her shoulder, Nora pushed herself into a standing position and began pacing the room, working out the stiffness in her joints. The best way to make sure no one did anything foolish was to make sure she wasn't here for a trial. The longer she remained in this room, the more likely it would be that someone might try to play the hero.

There were obviously no windows, but there was a crude, earthen staircase that led to the trap doors. Nora pulled herself up them and tested the doors with her hands. Her experimental pushes met with resistance. As she expected, the doors were barred from the outside.

She shouted a 'halloo', to determine if they had left her alone or if they'd posted guards.

A low, gravelly voice responded. 'Quit yer bellyaching. You'll get breakfast soon enough.' Others laughed.

Nora went back down the stairs. There were guards, at least three or four from the sounds the guffaws. She sat down on the cot to rest from her exertions and to think. How would she get the door unbarred? How would she get past the guards?

Getting the door unbarred would be the least of her worries. From the guard's comment, they meant to feed her. The door would be open once or twice a day when someone brought food. Most likely, a doctor of sorts would be allowed down too, to check on her bandage. She could feign a fever, draw him close to the cot and cosh him over the head with a table leg. Getting past the guards was a much bigger concern.

While Nora sat mulling over her options, the door at the top of the stairs opened. Food was placed on the top step and the door closed again. She made a note of the procedure. Any information at this point would be useful. She would only get one chance to effect an escape.

Nora took the food, a bowl of gruel and dry toast, and a crock of water. She ate all the food for strength and so as not to attract bugs or rodents. The water she saved, unsure if there would be more to drink later in the day or if this was her sole ration for drinking and washing.

The door opened again and a guard called down, 'There's a visitor to see you.'

Nora stood up from the bed, hope mingling with caution. She prayed it was Brandon.

'I trust you find your accommodations to your liking,' a frosty voice inquired with all the warmth of a January afternoon.

The visitor was Witherspoon. Nora swallowed hard and mentally girded herself for battle. Had he meant to come and finish what his bullet had failed to do last night?

She needled him, trying to determine his intentions. 'It's so kind of you to call on me in my home. After all, you've been polite enough to let me have free run of yours all these months.'

'Still cocky, I see.' Witherspoon was dressed impeccably in riding gear, Nora noted as he circled her.

'Truthful,' she retorted, keeping her chin up, trying to ignore the riding crop he kept slashing against his thigh as he studied her.

'I've come for some conversation, Miss Habersham. But I see you're not dressed for it.' Something cruel and cold flicked in his pale eyes.

'My wardrobe is a bit limited at this time.' Nora followed him with her eyes.

'No bother. Perhaps I should have said you're not undressed for it. Take off your shirt, or, if you prefer, I'd be glad to relieve you of it.'

Nora knew trouble when she saw it; right now she was looking at six feet of it. She'd better cut him down to size fast. He'd come to toy with her, not kill her, not yet.

'So, it's like that, is it?' She quirked a saucy eyebrow at him, doing her best not to let him see how much she loathed the idea of being bared before him. 'You've come to torture the prisoner. Certainly, you can't call what you intend to do anything else.' She started moving, swaying her hips as she made her own circling perusal.

Nora gave a husky laugh as Witherspoon realised one can only be circled if one stops moving. No doubt he'd been too shocked by her lack of fear to catch on. Now, however, he was furious. His eyes narrowed, calculating, assessing her game.

'Is this how you bargained with Stockport?'

That was truly alarming. 'What does Stockport have to do with any of this?'

'You tell me. Why does a man bandage up the very enemy who would ruin his financial livelihood? If you ask me, you must know some pretty interesting tricks to please a man like Stockport to such a degree.' He tapped his riding crop. 'I find that I'd like to know what those tricks are, myself.'

'You're not half the man Stockport is. Anyone can tell that by the pathetic way you attempt to curry his favour.'

'You're nothing better than a thieving whore!' he said, his voice rising dangerously with his temper. He started moving too until they were circling each other like prowling dogs.

Nora ignored his comment and returned to her own line of conversation, doing her best to hide her tension. He *would* pounce, that much was inevitable. He would make a grab for her. She just wanted it to be at a time of her choosing.

'Witherspoon, that's an unusual name. Traditionally, English names describe something about a person or their family line. For instance, "Smith", usually refers to smithy work, blacksmiths, goldsmiths, what have you. Wither means to wilt.' She pursed her lips and tapped them with a finger. 'Spoon. Hmm. I can't say I've heard "it" called that before, but I suppose it is possible.'

Despite himself, Witherspoon was drawn into her little monologue. 'What, pray tell, is "it"?' he said crossly, his eyes narrowing slightly, betraying his readiness to spring.

Nora smiled and sprung the trap. Ingenuously, she widened her eyes, an innocent look at odds with the calculated sway of her hips. 'Why, the male member of course. *Witherspoon.*' She made a drooping gesture with one of her fingers and pointedly glanced down at his crotch.

Witherspoon stopped circling, his cold face now infused with an angry red as he grasped the meaning of her by-play. 'You little bitch!'

He lunged. Nora was ready for him. The force of his attack took them both to the cot. Nora grunted as her shoulder rebelled against the fight, but she ignored it as best she could, sinking her teeth into the tender part of his cheek and drawing blood.

Witherspoon reared back, yelping in surprised pain. Nora shoved at him, catching him off balance on the narrow cot, and toppled him to the ground. He grabbed for her and she kneed him in the groin, forcing him to let go of her.

There was a commotion outside the doors and Nora raced up the stairs while Witherspoon writhed on the dirt floor. She started screaming, hoping the guards would remember she was a woman and forget she was prisoner and unlock the door. She didn't want to face an angry, recovered Witherspoon.

'Eleanor!' a familiar voice called with urgency from the other side and Nora wanted to weep with relief.

In moments, the bars were lifted and Brandon's form filled the doorway. 'What happened here?'

It was all Nora could do not to run straight to his arms and beg protection, but that would do neither of them any good.

'He attacked me, milord,' Nora said, trying not to show how upsetting the incident had been.

Brandon's jaw tightened, the only sign of distress he allowed himself to show. 'Guards, get Mr Witherspoon up and see that he is cared for, then see that he has no further admittance to see the prisoner,' he barked.

When Witherspoon had been removed, and the guards were busy tending to him, Nora motioned Brandon down to the rumpled cot. 'I was afraid the guards wouldn't care enough to open the door,' she said in a low voice. The door was still ajar. Apparently, she'd inspired fear regarding the safety of male visitors.

'I doubt they would have if I hadn't been there.'

His hands covered hers and Nora became conscious of them shaking inside his warm grasp. 'I'm all right,' she reassured him.

'I hate that I cannot touch you, Nora. I want to draw you into my arms and comfort you.' Brandon's voice was raw with emotion. 'The guards told me to wait, that Witherspoon was inside already. Then I heard you scream. A thousand fears ran through my head. I swear I would have rammed that door down myself if they hadn't unlocked it.'

'I know you would have,' she said quietly.

'You must have provoked him something fierce.'

'*He* provoked me. I didn't care for his suggestion that I was overdressed for our conversation.'

Brandon tensed and Nora knew she'd better watch her words before Brandon ended up facing Witherspoon at thirty paces. 'The bastard wanted you naked.' He grimaced.

'It didn't happen,' Nora said softly.

'I have to get you out of here,' Brandon said with frightening determination, casting a backwards glance up the staircase. 'There's going to be a trial. I came to tell you that the judge will be from Manchester, but the trial will be here. I am, in part, relieved that I won't be the magistrate hearing the case. Yet, I'd hoped I might be able to find a loophole to declare a mistrial.'

Nora shook her head violently. 'Listen to me, Brandon, you cannot risk such a blatant ploy.' She squeezed his hands to emphasise her point. 'Witherspoon suspects we have some type of licentious arrangement. The only thing that stands between us and his suspicions, frankly, is this blonde wig.'

'That's why we have to get you out of here, fast. We can't rely on that wig holding out for ever. I have an idea. Where do you get your sleeping powder? The one you used at St John's?'

Nora shook her head. 'Brandon, you cannot help me in any way. Witherspoon will ruin you. It will give him the last bit of proof he needs.'

'I will not be commanded in this, Nora. I will not let you hang while I can prevent it. You are my responsibility. You would not be here if you hadn't misunderstood Jack's remarks at the ball. I never meant for this to happen.'

A guard coughed at the top of the stairs. 'Milord, it's been ten minutes.'

'I'll say when it's been ten minutes,' Brandon barked up the stairs. 'I need five minutes more to question the prisoner.'

'You cannot come again, Brandon. You owe me nothing. But I must tell you something,' Nora whispered. 'Witherspoon is deliberately sabotaging the mill for insurance fraud. I have the proof, stolen from his own safe. The papers are at the Grange beneath the squeaky step on the stairs. Get the papers.'

'That's why he wants to see you dead,' Brandon said.

Nora nodded. 'If the worst happens, and I am exposed as your betrothed, you can use the papers to bargain with Witherspoon and protect yourself.'

'I want to explain everything. I won't have you believing

I was going to betray you, that I used our association to set you up. I will come again. I will see you free,' Brandon vowed.

She slipped her hands from his, although it killed her to do it. He was all she had right now. Nora gave a wan smile. 'No, you won't.' Then she screamed, 'Get your hands off me! Guards! Twice in one day—I swear I am not safe from these lecherous gentlemen.'

Brandon was saved. The papers were damning. She watched Brandon's back as he moved towards the door at the top of the stairs. Then it shut and she was alone in the darkness to wait for the inevitable. At least now she could wait with a clear conscience. It was a weight off her mind to know that the people she cared about most—Hattie and Alfred, and Brandon—were protected in case she couldn't protect herself.

Brandon was in a temper by the time he got home. He threw his stallion's reins to a groom and stomped into the house, bellowing for Jack.

'He's in the drawing room with—' the butler began, taking Brandon's riding gloves.

Brandon didn't wait to hear the rest of it. He was already on the way to the drawing room. He was halfway across the room before he realised Jack was with someone.

The woman turned and smiled, a misleadingly sweet smile if one knew her well enough to know. 'Jack has been telling me that I am just in time for a jail break and perhaps a wedding,' she said in pleasant tones.

Brandon would recognise that voice and that countenance anywhere. It was like looking at himself in the mirror, only female. It was the first good thing that had happened in the last forty-eight hours. 'Hello, Dulci. I am glad you could make it.'

Dulcinea Wycroft patted the seat beside her. 'I know you

wrote three weeks ago, but I had loose ends to clear up and you know how the roads are this time of year, all ruts and puddles.'

Brandon grinned at his sister. He didn't want to ask exactly what qualified as a 'loose end' these days. The last time it had been Viscount Gladstone's marriage proposal, which she had rejected in short order. Dulcinea might look like a living, genteel rendition of Snow White, but she did not act like it. Dulcinea meant soft, calm. His sister was anything but placid. Excepting Jack, there was no one he'd rather have with him.

Dulci tossed her raven-black hair and reached for a tea cup. 'Jack tells me a notorious cat burglar is masquerading as your intended. At your behest, I should add.'

'Jack talks too much.' Brandon threw Jack a scolding glance. 'He should be helping me think of a way to get her out. Witherspoon nearly had his way with her today.'

'What stopped him?' Jack inquired.

'Her knee.'

'Ouch,' said Jack, crossing his legs uncomfortably.

'I like her already,' said Dulcinea, looking pointedly at Jack, daring him to respond.

Brandon intervened quickly. Dulci and Jack were known for their legendary battles of wit. 'I don't have time to play spectator to your demonstrations of verbal prowess. We need to think about Nora.' He nodded to Jack.

'You were right, Witherspoon is setting up an insurance scam with the mill. Nora told me where to find the papers. She says I can use them for protection against Witherspoon if necessary. It's no wonder he was so eager to beg for my favour. He was betting on my reputation squelching any potential scandal. No one would dare say an Earl committed such a heinous act.'

Brandon sighed and pushed a hand through his hair. 'She

doesn't think she'll get out. I could tell. She's taken care of everyone, doing "last things" in her own way.'

He heard Nora's own desperation in his voice. He tamped it down and forged ahead. He didn't need Dulci and Jack's pity. He needed their strength. 'Witherspoon won't allow her to stand trial. We can't give him a chance to go back there and finish the job. I have a plan.'

To their credit, Jack and Dulci both turned their attention on him and Brandon proceeded. 'We can slip sleeping powder into the guards' dinner and free her when they fall asleep.'

'And?' Jack asked.

'That's it,' Brandon said, feeling suddenly sheepish.

'That's it? If it were that easy, there would be no one in prison. Everyone would slip powders to the guards.' Jack began to enumerate his concerns. 'First, we have to get the powder without raising suspicions. Second, you, Brandon, cannot go anywhere near her or an apothecary's. Witherspoon smells blood. You've got to lay low.'

'Fair enough. If you're such a genius, what do we do?' Dulci put in, taking an opportunity to rib Jack.

'We use her network,' Jack said simply.

'And I know how,' Brandon said with a smug smile, taking a leaf out of The Cat's book of tricks. 'She once ran me ragged when I followed her on her shopping rounds in Manchester and all the while she was conducting business under my nose.'

In the end, Witherspoon was indeed far too suspicious. Brandon could not leave the house without attracting attention. While the plotting had been his idea, the execution of it was left up to others out of necessity for its success. After putting the plan into motion, Brandon could do nothing more than sit back and rely on others, a role he was not used to.

It was up to Dulci to pass a small note to Mary Malone when she visited the crofters' cottages. It was Mary Malone's son who carried the note to the apothecary's when he went to visit a friend in the old neighbourhood. He carried the prescription for a large supply of sleeping powder when he came home.

It was Dulci who wooed the cook's assistant out of the tray he carried nightly to the guards on duty and dumped the powder in the meals. She sat with the two burly guards and poured them wine and regaled them with bawdy stories until they fell over.

It was Dulci who lifted the heavy bars from the door and raced down the steps towards Nora, who already stood alert at the sound of the door opening at an odd time of night.

'There's no time to explain, but you're free,' Dulci gushed upon reaching Nora. Dulci whipped off her cloak and swung it around Nora's shoulders. 'Brandon was right, we are of the same size.'

'What is going on?' Nora queried.

'Brandon has engineered your jail break,' Dulci said gaily, as if this were all grand fun instead of a felonious crime. 'I am to stay here, so they'll think it's you asleep in the morning when they come with your breakfast. It will buy you a few more hours to get further away. Then I'll tell them I came to collect the dishes last night and you hit me on the head.' With that, Dulci grabbed up the ewer and smashed it into pieces.

'Brandon's not here, is he?'

There was panic in the other woman's voice and Dulci was glad to hear it. Like Jack, she was curious and doubtful about the nature of Brandon's association with the woman.

'No, Witherspoon could not be shaken.'

'Then how?' Nora gestured helplessly. 'How did he arrange all this?'

Dulci smiled conspiratorially. 'He used your network. He told me you led him on a wild goose chase all over Manchester. We did the same to Witherspoon and his men. There were three decoys and one real message. Mary Malone's boy it carried to the apothecary's for the powder.'

'She should not have risked it,' Nora scolded.

Dulci was moved by the tone of the other woman's voice. 'Everyone wanted to help when they heard. You are well loved and not in the least by my brother.'

'You're wrong about that. He has a care for his own hide now that the game has gotten so perilous and he has become implicated so completely,' Nora protested.

Dulci looked at the woman speculatively. 'Well, there's no time to argue that out now. You need to be off. Brandon waits for you and you can sort it all out together. Now, go. Ride to Mary's cottage. Brandon is there. Hurry.' Dulci winked.

Brandon was the only thought crossing Nora's mind as she sped through the night on the horse Dulci had left outside. She had to see Brandon one last time, to thank him, to tell him all debts had been paid, the scales between The Cat and the earl were even.

She'd been wrong, at least in part, about what she'd overheard at the ball. Whatever manipulations she'd held Brandon accountable for, not all could be laid at his doorstep. He'd done his best for her the night of her capture and now he'd engineered her rescue again. These were not the actions of a man who wanted to see her betrayed.

There was still the issue of his motives for complicity. All this effort might simply be for the benefit of clearing his name. Once The Cat left Stockport-on-the-Medlock, he would be out from under suspicion. Still, it seemed to her that an Earl of his magnitude could have found other, easier ways to clear his name should it come to that besides assisting in her escape. It would be easy enough to simply turn against her or concoct some tale at having been elaborately duped by the said betrothed. Perhaps a whirlwind affair that addled his brains? Ha, Brandon Wycroft was the least likely of men to have his mind turned to mush over a woman. Still, he had the papers and could quietly turn those to his advantage. Oh, yes, he had plenty of options. He hadn't needed to free her. And yet he had… It bore thinking about. The impossible suddenly looked more probable once again. Brandon made it easy to believe.

If her mind had been less absorbed with Brandon and the conundrum of their relationship, she might have noticed the two mounted horseman dressed darkly and discreetly following behind. As it was, she was oblivious to all but reaching Brandon and getting through what would have to be their final meeting.

A single candle burned in Mary's window, the usual sign that all was safe for The Cat's approach. Nora swung off the horse and ran to the door. It opened before she could knock and Brandon swept her into his arms, smothering her mouth with a kiss.

'Nora, you're here. You're safe.' Brandon tugged her inside, reluctant to let her go.

The cottage was warm and cosy. Mary was conveniently absent, but Jack was there along with a man Nora didn't recognise. Nora stiffened at the sight of the stranger by the fire. Instinctively, she pulled back against Brandon's hand. 'Who is that?'

'My vicar.' Brandon gestured to the tall, balding man who rose. 'He came to the village the same time Eleanor did.'

Nora relaxed slightly. Upon closer inspection, she did recall the man. He and the Squire had paid a call on Eleanor. 'What's he doing here?'

The man smiled politely. 'My child, I am here to perform your nuptials.'

Nora turned to Brandon. 'What is the meaning of this?' Did he think to marry her to Jack? The thought was horrifying.

'He will marry us, tonight. You will be my Countess and beyond the reach of Witherspoon or anyone else who hunts you.'

Confusion rioted through Nora. 'No. We cannot suddenly marry. Marriage won't make everything right or the past disappear. I thought you understood. Despite the wig, someone could recognise me and put all the pieces together. It is best if I go far from here.'

'I don't care,' Brandon said firmly. 'You would be surprised at what a peer can accomplish.'

'I have no doubts about what you can accomplish. I've seen you in action. Still, marriage is not something to be rushed into. We've not ever spoken of it.'

'What do you mean? We've spoken of nothing else. I asked you to stay with me.' It was Brandon's turn to be confused. 'I have offered you protection, permanent protection under my care.'

'That was not a marriage proposal. It was a proposition. You and I know very well you were asking me to be your mistress. We didn't even know if my husband was alive or dead at that point,' Nora said slowly, trying to piece together this latest misunderstanding between them.

It seemed as if misunderstandings were abundant in this relationship. She was sick of them and sick of the whole game. Nothing was clear any more.

Suddenly, she was angry—wholly, completely, irrationally

angry. She could not have articulated why, but anger boiled up. She wanted to fight with Brandon, thrash it all out until nothing remained but the honest truth, even if that truth stung. Even if that truth was acknowledging that her feelings for Brandon were unrequited. Certainly such hard truth would make it easier to walk out the door. Freedom lay just eight feet away. All she had to do was span the distance and step out into the night.

Jack coughed in the corner and nodded towards the vicar, reminding them both that they were not alone. 'It might be wise if the vicar and I left the two of you alone to sort out this tangle. Come on, my good man of the cloth, I'll buy you ale at the inn.'

The door shut behind them. There was no longer any need for restraint. The proverbial gloves were off. She was spoiling for a fight with Brandon, and from the looks of the sparks glinting in his eyes, he was too.

'You are twisting my words. I will not allow you to justify walking out the door because you think I desired to make a whore out of you,' Brandon responded coldly. 'You think it will be easier to leave if you can convince yourself to believe the worst and not the best about me, about us.'

Nora adopted an aloof pose. 'What exactly is the best? I am unclear on that, beyond the great sex, that is.' She gave him an assessing look that ran up and down his length, hoping the perusal didn't give away her mounting desire. It would be hard to give up this man, body and soul.

'I want to marry you.'

'In case you don't know, you can buy great sex without a marriage licence these days.' She was sarcastic and mocking, desperately trying to create some distance, to show Brandon how much he needed to be rid of her.

'Stop it, Nora. I won't be provoked on this. You want a fight. You've used that strategy before. Well, I won't give you one.'

'Just give me the truth, then.' If he wouldn't argue, she had no choice but to force his hand. 'Do you love me?'

Brandon looked nonplussed and she wished she hadn't asked. If she didn't know for certain how he felt, she could let the illusion of possibility fire her empty nights in the years ahead. Maybes and what ifs could keep her warmer than the cold truth that he had not cared for her, not like she cared for him. With four words she'd thrown away that paltry parting gift.

'Do I love you? Don't you know by now how I feel?' Brandon shoved a hand through his hair in distress and began pacing the room in great agitation. 'Of course I love you. I think I started falling in love with you that night in my study when you dangled your feet over the chair and drank down my expensive brandy in a single swallow.'

'You do?' Her voice was nothing more than a squeak and it sounded very far away to her. He loved her. She had her answer.

'How could you not know?' Brandon's voice was softer now, the frustration of cross-purposes seeping out of both of them. 'What man would do the things I did for you if not out of love, Nora?' He reached for her and she went to him, overwhelmed at his declaration. He kissed her softly, his tongue leisurely tracing the seam of her lips, licking her teeth when her mouth opened. His hands stroked the small of her back, moulding her to him.

'Can I hope, Nora, that you might feel the same? What truth can you give me? I often wondered if I held your affections. No one has ever led me on such a merry chase,' Brandon whispered huskily, moving his lips to the column of her throat.

'I love you, Brandon.' The words were not as hard to say as she'd imagined. She'd imagined the words would make her feel vulnerable. Tonight, she felt only fulfilment. Saying them had not exposed her, they completed her. With Brandon, she was whole.

'Then it's settled.' Brandon's voice was low and husky.

The door slammed open on their intimacy. Brandon clutched Nora to him out of a reflexive need to protect, to shelter.

'Unsettled might be the better word once you've heard what I have to say.' Witherspoon filled the room. Behind him, Magnus St John barred the door.

'What are you doing here, Witherspoon?' Brandon asked in cold, commanding tones.

'The more interesting question is, what are you doing here?' Witherspoon countered, malice and calculation radiating from him as he took in every aspect of the scene.

'My betrothed and I were in need of some privacy,' Brandon responded, daring Witherspoon to contradict his explanation.

He did just that. 'Your betrothed? She's no more your betrothed than she's Eleanor Habersham. Stockport, the ruse is up. You've been caught *in flagrante delicto* with a criminal of the highest order. The woman with whom you've been "settling" things is none other than The Cat of Manchester.' He pointed his riding crop at them for emphasis. 'And you very well know it.'

Nora twisted in his arms to face Witherspoon. He tightened his grip on her, hoping she wouldn't do anything bravely foolish. 'You make unfounded accusations, sir,' she ground out, sounding very credibly like a lady wronged.

Witherspoon's smile turned cruel, his gaze raking Nora. 'St John and I followed you from the jail, my pretty thief. You see, I was curious. Things about Stockport and this situation didn't add up, particularly his behaviour the night of your capture.

He suddenly becomes a dolt on horseback when everyone knows he's a capital rider.'

Witherspoon tut-tutted and slapped his riding crop against his thigh with a series of ominous whacks. 'It made no sense that Stockport was in league with you. He has more to lose on this venture than any of us. But then, I got a good look at you—Nora, is it? I began to see the appeal. I began to think that if I had a woman like you in bed, I might start to think less of my factory and more about my pleasures.'

'This woman is to be my wife. I will not stand here and listen to another word of slander against her. Say what you came to say and get out or face me at twenty paces.' Brandon nudged Nora off to one side, directing Witherspoon's attention to him solely. He would not tolerate another of the man's leers at his wife-to-be.

'Oh, yes, I had almost forgotten my real news. Your factory is burning as we speak and this woman is guilty of it.' The chill of evil was evident in his voice.

'That's not true! I couldn't have set the fire,' Nora cried. 'I've been here.'

Witherspoon drew a pistol from beneath his greatcoat, training it on Nora. 'It won't matter what's true or not. You'll be dead shortly. Your body will be found in the ashes and ruins along with Stockport's unless he's willing to make a deal. There'll be insurance money enough from the fire for the three of us to make out handsomely, Stockport. There would have been more if we could have waited a year or two. But I'll cut my losses in exchange for your eternal gratitude, Stockport. All you have to do is keep quiet.' He jerked the pistol, motioning for St John. 'Take her now, Magnus.'

Pandemonium broke loose in Mary Malone's small cottage. Trusting Nora to handle herself against Magnus St

John, Brandon rushed Witherspoon, grabbing his gun arm in a dangerous gambit.

The two men fell to the floor in a wrestling heap. The battle for the pistol was on. This was no bloody fisticuffs. This was a fight to the death. Witherspoon and St John had come to the cottage intent on one murder, if not two. Brandon knew he was fighting for his life and Nora's. There could be no holds barred.

Across the room, Magnus lunged for Nora. She danced away, deftly putting the cottage's wood table between them. She laughed and taunted as she feinted left, then right, on her side of the table, throwing Magnus St John continually off balance.

The ploy couldn't last for ever. Eventually, St John would tire and attempt a leap across the table. The cottage was a small place. It would be hard to get past St John and the brawling Witherspoon and Brandon. She knew what she had to do. When St John lunged, she had to find a way to disable him for the duration of the fight.

From the other side of the room came the grunting, punching efforts of Brandon and Witherspoon, punctuated by an occasional crash as Mary's furniture or few pieces of crockery were sacrificed to the occasion. It took all of Nora's training and concentration not to glance over at Brandon, to see how he was faring. His situation was more dangerous than hers at the moment. His fight involved a deadly weapon. Her fear for Brandon threatened to distract her—another reason for wanting to subdue St John.

Finally the lunge came. St John dove across the table, swiping at Nora's shirtfront. She darted backwards just out of reach, causing St John to lose his balance and tumble to the ground.

'Bitch!' he roared, furious at having been made to look a fool. He struggled to regain his feet. He never quite made it.

Nora grabbed up a pitcher used for milk and broke it soundly over his head. He staggered and fell. With expert quickness, she shredded a dish towel into strips and tightly bound the unconscious man's hands. If he woke before the fighting was over, he'd be useless. These bonds were not held with easy, playful knots like the ones she'd used on Brandon a few weeks ago. These knots were practically Gordian. He'd only get out of them with the help of a knife.

She sprang from her trussed captive, ready to join the fray against Witherspoon. She wished she had her dagger handy, but all her usual weapons had been taken from her during her captivity. One look at the fight and she doubted it would do any good. The men were brawling close. Each looked as if they'd taken the brunt of the other man's fists.

Brandon pinned Witherspoon's gun arm and was repeatedly slamming it against the plank flooring in an attempt to shake it loose from Witherspoon's grip. Witherspoon punched at Brandon's mid-section with his free arm. Brandon groaned from the impact, incrementally loosening his hold on Witherspoon's pistol arm. It was enough for Witherspoon to force Brandon away from him and scramble to his feet.

Nora screamed a warning.

'Nora, get out of here!' Brandon yelled, not once breaking his concentration from Witherspoon. Brandon, still half-bent from trying to rise, rushed Witherspoon like a bull head down, the force of his muscular body taking the other man up against a wall. Caught between the wall and Brandon's powerful form, Witherspoon lost his grip on the gun. It fell to the floor with an ignominious clunk and misfired.

'Brandon!' Nora cried in fear. Both men were down, Witherspoon's body falling into Brandon's in a heavy slump that took Brandon to the ground beneath it. Neither moved.

'No!' Nora rushed forward, careless of her own safety. Witherspoon was absolute dead weight in his unconsciousness. It took all her strength to heave his form off Brandon. Once she did, she could see plainly where the bullet had struck him in the ribs. It had likely punctured a lung when it misfired. He was dead, beyond her help.

She knelt next to Brandon. Blood soaked his shirt although she fervently prayed the blood was Witherspoon's. She took the cloth of his shirt and rent it in two, too worried about what she'd find underneath to take the time and undo his buttons. She ran hands over his torso, looking for any sign of serious injury or bleeding.

He was battered and would be bruised in the days to come. But he was all right. Nora sat back on her heels, allowing herself to breathe a sigh of relief. He still hadn't woken, but now there was at least the possibility that he would.

'Brandon! Nora! Are you in there!' Sounds from outside caught her attention. Help at last.

Nora went to the door and unlocked it. 'Jack! Dulci!' she exclaimed. 'There's been a terrible fight. Witherspoon's dead and St John is tied up over there. Brandon's unconscious.' She tried to control herself. It sounded like she was babbling, but she couldn't help it.

They went to Brandon's prone form. Jack felt the back of his head and smiled. 'He'll have a goose egg there tomorrow. I would bet he hit his head when he fell. He should be fine in a few moments.'

Protectively, Nora sat down next to Brandon on the floor and took his head in her lap while Jack and Dulci righted the cottage and checked on St John.

As Jack predicted, Brandon stirred shortly. 'Where's Witherspoon? Are you all right?' He immediately tried to rise and fell back in her lap.

'Shh. Everything's fine,' Nora assured him. 'Jack and Dulci are here. They'll take care of everything.'

'You're fine too?' Brandon asked.

'Perfectly.'

'Help me get up. I want to sit at the table and hear what Jack has to say.'

With Jack's help, Nora got Brandon to the table and he laid out the events of the evening for Jack and Dulci.

'I expected as much,' Jack confirmed grimly when Brandon had finished. 'When the vicar and I got into the village, I could see the fire in the distance. At first, I didn't suspect the mill, but the closer we got the more obvious it seemed. I went to the jail for Dulci then. I feared for her safety in case there was a mistaken identity in the dark. We came out here directly. I wish we'd been earlier.'

'We managed.' Brandon smiled at Nora and reached out to cover her hand with his.

'Are you well enough to ride into town and look over the mill, what's left of it?' Jack asked.

Brandon shook his head. 'There's one stop I need to make first. Tonight has been a cautionary tale about the import of time. I find I don't want to wait another minute to make you mine, Nora. Will you come with me to the vicar's?'

Dulci broke in. 'You can't be serious, Brandon. She needs a dress and you should have a big wedding.'

Nora looked at Brandon and shook her head against Dulci's exclamations. 'I don't need those things. I only need you. I'll marry you tonight.'

Brandon rose slowly and held his arm for Nora. His blue

eyes danced with teasing good humour. 'Excellent. I promised the vicar a wedding tonight and I always keep my word.'

An hour later, The Cat retired and Nora became Lady Stockport in a quiet firelight ceremony performed by the vicar and witnessed by Jack and Dulci.

It was an odd wedding as weddings go, but no less heartfelt for its idiosyncrasies. The bride wore black, the groom sported quite a facer and kissed the bride for an indecent length of time. But in the end, the important conventions were followed and Brandon sealed their vows with a ring set with amethyst on the bride's finger.

The vicar left them alone afterwards while he went to gather the necessary licences and forms. Nora held her ring up to the firelight, watching the gem dance. 'It's the ring I stole the first night we met.' She gave Brandon a coy smile. 'Why did you want it back so much?'

Brandon came to stand behind her and wrapped his arms about her, hugging her against his form. 'I always meant for my wife to wear it some day. It belonged to my mother. She was a woman who specialised in making impossible dreams come true.'

'She sounds a lot like her son.'

'I think she's a lot like my wife.' Brandon nuzzled her neck. 'Let's go home, Lady Stockport.'

Chapter Twenty-One

London
Spring, 1832

'I heard the bad news, it looks like the legislation will fail again,' Jack said, deftly swiping two glasses of champagne from a passing footman's tray at Lady Summersby's political soirée.

Brandon nodded grimly. 'Yes. I suppose I should not be surprised. The Reform Act has passed the House of Commons twice, only to be defeated in the House of Lords. I am at a loss as to how it can possibly succeed. We will try again, but I fear it is an exercise in futility.'

Jack sipped his champagne, trying to look as if he hadn't a care in the world. In a serious tone, he said quietly, 'I wouldn't give up. The word at court is that Prime Minister Grey will force success by threatening to create fifty new peers, Liberal peers, of course. And that will carry the bill and much else for years to come.'

Brandon gave a weary chuckle. 'I see. The House of Lords can either bow to this one victory or set themselves up to be slowly eradicated over the years.'

He raised his glass in salute to a group of passing acquaintances and turned back to his conversation with Jack. 'If Shaftesbury would change his vote, I think others would follow without all this need for arm twisting.'

'I thought he believed in reforms,' Jack said, somewhat surprised by his friend's comment.

'I do,' a low voice said behind Jack as Anthony Ashley Cooper, seventh Earl of Shaftesbury, joined them, Nora on his arm. 'I am afraid I've become a bit misconstrued over the past months.'

Brandon fought back a smile. Apparently, Nora had set the Earl on the right path with her brand of hard-to-resist charm. In the last five months since their marriage and moving up to town, Nora had captured many hearts with her beauty and her intellect. Her introduction into *ton*nish society had been seamless. Witherspoon had been found guilty of arson and insurance fraud and the village of Stockport-on-the-Medlock had agreed with Brandon and Jack's theory that The Cat had been Eleanor Habersham.

'Your wife is quite the politician. She does you credit, Stockport,' Shaftesbury said. 'She tells me she's hosting a tea for Earl Russell later this week and that we might all sit down and talk things out.'

Nora nodded, leaving Shaftesbury to stand beside Brandon. 'I do hope to bring all parties together for an enlightened meeting of the minds.' Brandon noted her eyes glowed with impish mischief.

'I think it won't matter, my dear,' Shaftesbury said. 'Rumour has it that the Prime Minister is going to change our minds for us, force our hands to get his way. It will just be a matter of time and you'll have your victory. Still, I applaud your diplomacy. Now, gentlemen, if you'll excuse me.'

* * *

Prime Minister Grey made good on his threat to appoint new Liberal peers and pandemonium broke loose in the House of Lords as people began to rethink their voting options. When voting took place again on the Reform Act, Brandon found himself on the winning side. The House of Lords chose to approve it, under duress, of course, but approval none the less.

Brandon felt buoyed by the victory. It wasn't a complete victory. He wasn't fool enough to believe this alone would change the world. But it was a start, like his experimental textile factory that he and Nora were rebuilding together in Stockport-on-the Medlock with its safety measures, limited work day, and the non-hiring of children.

He had been invited to several rowdy parties, but he found there was only one person he wanted to celebrate with. That was Nora.

The town house was strangely dark when he arrived. To his knowledge, Nora hadn't any plans to go out that evening. He let himself in and found no staff awaiting him. Some of his elation faded. He'd been looking forward to a victorious homecoming. Nora knew the vote was tonight.

Brandon went to the study and poured himself a drink. He mounted the stairs and headed towards their bedchambers. He'd settle in and wait. Wherever Nora was, she'd most likely be home soon.

He opened the door to the bedroom and halted. Something was different. The room had been disturbed. Something moved ever so subtly from behind the curtains. A wicked smile spread across his face. The Cat was here. He liked this game.

Seductive tones spoke from the window as Nora stepped from behind the draperies clad in The Cat's black and looking far too tempting. 'Hello, Stockport. I'd offer you a drink, but I see you already have one.'

'The Reform Bill passed,' he said, raising his tumbler in a half-toast.

Nora came to him and twined her arms about his neck, pressing herself firmly against his body. 'Yes,' she breathed huskily. 'I'd heard reports that a certain Earl was wreaking havoc in the House of Lords over the Act.' She reached a hand down to cup him. 'You don't disappoint.'

Brandon thrilled to her touch. 'By that I assume you mean my oratory.' No legislative victory could make him feel as alive as he felt with Nora.

She expertly squeezed him through the cloth of his trousers. 'Is that what they're calling it these days? I hadn't heard.'

Brandon groaned in pleasure and threw back his head in genuine laughter. 'God, I love you, Nora.'

Nora cocked her head and looked at him with her green cat's eyes. He knew she was going to tease. 'Is that all you can think of to say? I would have thought a great orator like yourself would have something more original.' Nora smiled gamely. 'Or has The Cat got your tongue?'

'She's got more than that. The Cat's got my heart,' he said in a voice laden with heavy passion. 'For ever.'

'For ever,' she confirmed.

Notorious Rake,
Innocent Lady

Chapter One

London, early May 1829

She would not be sold like a prized mare at Tatter-salls! Julia Prentiss's elegantly coiffed head swivelled in disbelief between Uncle Barnaby and Mortimer Oswalt, the lecherous old cit who had come to offer for her. She could hardly countenance the conversation that flowed around her as if she were not standing in the centre of her uncle's study listening, nor had a mind of her own and was quite capable of speaking for herself.

'I would, of course, provide a handsome bride price for your niece. Say, fifteen thousand pounds.' Mortimer Oswalt spread his hands confidently over the purple expanse of his waistcoat, which gave him the appear-ance of an overripe grape. He leaned back in his chair, perusing Julia with his dissipated blue eyes, still blood-shot from a night on the town.

Fifteen thousand pounds! Julia fought back a surge of inappropriate comments. How dare he offer for her in the same manner one might offer for goods on the dock or at an auction house. The force of his vile gaze made her skin clammy. She could not bear to imagine how his hands would feel against her skin. But surely there was no sense conjuring nightmares that would not come to pass.

Julia turned her frantic gaze on Uncle Barnaby. Uncle Barnaby would certainly refuse the offer in spite of how advanced the talks had become. After all, Mortimer Oswalt was not from their circles. Her uncle was Viscount Lockhart, a noted politician in the House of Lords. Oswalt was merely a London merchant. A *wealthy* London merchant, to be sure, but still a merchant, regardless of the fact that his annual income was at least triple theirs. The Lockhart title might not be possessed of a fortune, but they were peers and peers did not marry cits.

'Fifteen thousand pounds, you say? That is quite generous, a very respectful offer. I am sure we can come to an agreeable accord.' Uncle Barnaby gave a resigned smile, carefully looking anywhere but at her.

Julia was dumbfounded. What had possessed him to *sell* her to this old man? She would have dug her toes into the carpet she stood upon if it had had any pile left on it with which to do so. It was time to speak up. This ridiculous notion—nay, this repulsive notion—had gone much too far for her liking. Julia summoned her best manners.

'I respectfully decline.'

Her voice was sufficiently loud to be heard. It cut across the two men's conversation. Incredulously, both men shot her quelling glances and continued their discussion.

'Five thousand pounds now and ten thousand after she is certified by my physician. I will have a draft drawn and deposited for you this afternoon. My physician will return to town in five days. We can do the necessary examinations then and I will write a second draft to you immediately upon his surety of her condition.' Oswalt was all brusque business in spite of the intimacies of his contract.

Julia blanched at his coarse requirements. She stared directly at her uncle and was gratified to see that he wavered over such terms, but only slightly.

'I can vouch for my niece's chastity. I assure you that such indelicate proceedings are not needed.' Uncle Barnaby coughed with embarrassment at such frank discussion.

Mortimer Oswalt shook his bald pate. 'I must insist. I have not made a fortune in business dealings without making absolutely sure of the quality of my investment. Let me remind you, I will be sixty in November. My first two wives were unable to give me the heir I required. My medical advisers confirm that whatever prior difficulties have occurred in that area, a virgin wife would overcome those concerns. I must have an heir quickly. My bride must be of virgin stock and must be quite capable of conceiving and birthing a child in short order.' He fixed Uncle Barnaby with an intimidating eye. 'I will pay the family an extra five thousand pounds upon the birth of my child.'

Julia watched in horrified fascination as her uncle capitulated to the bribe. Well, she was not dazzled so easily.

'I will not consider it!' She stamped her foot for emphasis, making sure the men could not ignore her a second time. 'Uncle, I cannot be married under duress. There are new laws. The Betrothal Act of 1823 allows people to marry out of free will.' It was a weak appeal and she knew it. Legislation was only enforced when one had an advocate or the means to acquire one. She had neither.

Uncle Barnaby opened his mouth to scold, but Oswalt raised a hand to stall his reprimand. 'Lockhart, allow me to explain it to her. She is to be my wife soon enough and must learn to take direction from her husband. Young women are a sheltered lot and must be tutored in the ways of the world.'

Julia fought the urge to cringe. It would be a cold day in hell before she took 'direction' or anything else from the lecherous likes of Mortimer Oswalt. She struck a defiant pose, disgusted that Uncle Barnaby demurred.

Oswalt continued. 'Miss Prentiss, the subtleties of

this arrangement may have escaped your notice. Young ladies like yourself are often not aware of the rigours associated with maintaining the lifestyle you take for granted—the horses, the country home, the gowns, the entertainments and all the fal-lals a young woman expects as her right.

'It is especially difficult to raise a beautiful girl like yourself since it is much more expensive to accommodate her needs. A lovely girl stands out. She cannot afford to be seen in the same gowns as a wallflower who isn't noticed. A pretty girl must always be shown to her best advantage. In short, a lovely daughter or, in your case, a lovely niece, can become an asset to the family.

'Your uncle has fallen into need of such an asset. His coffers are empty. There is no one who will advance him any further loans. He has mortgaged all he can simply to lease this *borrowed* town house and to give you *one* Season. You are the last pearl left to the Lockhart title. Failure to make a financially advantageous match on your part will land your aunt and uncle and cousins in dun territory, to say nothing of yourself. You will suffer the deprivations with them.' Oswalt finished his lecture and began picking his nails. 'They have given you this Season not merely for your personal enrichment, but in hopes of getting a return on their years of investment.'

'Tell me it's not true, Uncle?' Julia demanded, whirling on the poor man. Oswalt's disclosures had discomfited him and he seemed to shrink in the leather chair he occupied behind the desk. Julia's throat constricted in terror at the morbid truth.

'It is true. I cannot deny any scrap of it. Our pockets are to let. We need Oswalt's offer.'

'There must be another way! I do not love him. I will *not* grow to love him. He is a despicable old man to buy a bride in this way.' Julia gave her tongue free rein, not caring that Oswalt sat feet away, absorbed in his nail picking.

'Julia! Hush. This outburst is most unladylike,' her uncle admonished. He craned his neck to speak around her and she could see the fear in his eyes that Oswalt would retract his offer at the display of her temper.

Julia put her hands on her hips, ready to do battle. 'What about Cousin Gray's ship? Surely the payoff from that cargo will see our problems resolved.'

'Gray's venture is fraught with risk. It is a gamble. I would rather bet on a sure thing.' Uncle Barnaby gave her a terse scolding. 'Remember your manners, Julia. It is not good *ton* to speak of money in company.'

'You don't seem to mind. You and Oswalt have divided me up like so many stock dividends on the exchange.' The comment went beyond the pale, but if a temper tantrum got her out of this unholy arrangement, then so be it.

Oswalt was not fazed. He gave Julia all his attention. 'Ah, I've got myself a cinnamon-haired virago, have I? Perhaps all that hot blood is what I need to warm myself. My dear, I welcome your passion and I care not a whit if you love me. I certainly don't love you, nor do I intend to cultivate affection for you. I merely need a well-bred virgin in my bed from a family who will accept my offer. All that aside, it will be exciting to tame you to my hand. Should all go well with my physician, I'll have a special licence in hand by week's end and we'll be wed by Sunday.'

'My wife will want to give the wedding breakfast,' Uncle Barnaby put in, relaxing again now that the deal had not been retracted.

Oswalt gave a gracious nod. 'My new bride will enjoy a last chance to associate with family and friends before we depart.' He fixed Julia with a crawling stare filled with a wealth of meaning. 'I will have no desire to stay in London, where the pleasures of the Season might detract from our marriage. We will journey promptly to my country home in the Lake District. It's very remote and well supplied. We won't be bothered by outside interruptions. Once we have good news to share, I will return to town.'

Julia swallowed hard. His libidinous intent was clear. She was to be locked away in the country. Her only task in life would be to service his base needs and produce an heir for his cit's fortune. She was nineteen and her life was about to be over.

She gave them each a curt nod of her head. 'I give you good day', then she turned hard on her heel and exited the room before either of them could see the fright they'd wrought in her with their thoughtless negotiations.

Once in her room, Julia locked the door and leaned against its solid oak panelling, taking comfort from the thickness of the wood. The little ormolu clock on the table beneath the window suggested the whole reprehensible interview had taken a short twenty minutes. It was barely eleven o'clock in the morning and her life was nearly ruined. The good news was that her life was only 'nearly' ruined.

It could have been worse, she supposed. Oswalt and her uncle could have signed the contracts already. Oswalt could have arrived with a licence and vicar in tow and married her in the study.

Julia shuddered and thought uncharitably that the scenario was unlikely since his coveted physician wouldn't have been on hand to certify her virginal status. Five days. That was all the time left to her, barring the unforeseen circumstance that the physician return to town earlier or that Mortimer Oswalt's need for haste caused him to engage another physician who wasn't on holiday.

This was a time for action unless she reconciled herself to a life under Oswalt's rule and hoped he didn't live very long. It was clear from events in the study that neither protests nor legislation would avail her now. It was true, a law had been passed that allowed people to marry without parental consent, but it didn't *prevent* parental arrangement of her marriage to another.

Her uncle's financial situation had been made painfully clear as well as the reason for her Season in London. She was the one thing her uncle had left to pawn. He'd used her on the Marriage Mart to garner an offer that would save the family from penury.

Not for the first time, Julia cursed her unusual beauty. Ever since she'd turned fourteen and started to come into her womanly form, her looks had held an appeal for men that she could not understand. When she looked in the mirror, she saw a normal girl with green eyes that tilted up slightly at the corners, a mouth that might be described as wide, and a heap of red-brown curls her cousins often teased looked like the hue of autumn leaves. But there'd been local callers aplenty at the Grange where they lived when she started receiving last Christmas and her dance card had been full at the local assemblies. It had been the same in London after her presentation at court.

She knew, although it was difficult to admit, that this proposal from Oswalt wasn't the first time her uncle had used her looks to ward off a financial situation. It had never been as dire as it was now, but he'd sent her to the village on several occasions, telling her to talk to the merchants to whom he owed money, to see if they'd extend his credit a little longer.

Julia paced the chamber, her fright giving way to

anger. She would not allow herself be used again in such a shameless manner. They would have to tie her up and drag her from this house in order to see her wed to Oswalt. She stopped pacing. It would come to exactly that, she was sure of it. Dragging her to the altar, literally, would be just one of the many indignities she would be put through this week if she remained.

Her options hit her with startling clarity. If she stayed at her uncle's rented town house as a virginal débutante, she would have no way to fight her wedding to Oswalt. There was nothing for it. She would have to find a way on her own to break the contract. There would be severe consequences, but she would suffer them.

Immediately, her mind raced over her options. The most obvious option was to run away. Where could she go? Who could help her? She sat down on the bed and sighed. She had no answers to any of those questions, but it hardly mattered. She was far too bright to ignore the reality. If she was discovered at any point, she would be brought back to London and forced to fulfil her uncle's contract.

No, running away wasn't a valid choice. Julia prided herself on being practical. If she was honest now, she had to admit that the prospect of successfully eluding Oswalt, who would most likely hire professionals to hunt her down, was a slim one indeed. She had learned much during her short time in London, but she had not learned enough to hide herself indefinitely, or at least until her twenty-fourth birthday, which marked the end of her uncle's guardianship. Even then, she wasn't certain being four and twenty would nullify her uncle's contract with Oswalt.

She stood up and started pacing again. 'Think, Julia, think. How do you get out of the contract?' She mumbled to herself. She could use the 1823 legislation and marry another. Her uncle couldn't stop her. She discarded that notion immediately. Where would she find a husband in five days who would be willing to risk marriage against a pre-existing contract?

A husband might be too ambitious on short notice, but one didn't need a husband to be ruined. She could cast aspersions on her suitability. That option might work. A plan began to form.

There was a rout tonight at Lady Moffat's. It would be well attended and many of the beaus who made up her court would be there. She would lure one of them out on to the terrace, coax a walk in the garden, flirt with him a bit and make sure they were found in a compromising situation.

Yes.

No.

Julia shook her head. The only way that would work would be if Oswalt cried off in the heat of his anger over being cuckolded before the ink dried on the contract. He might not care. He might not believe her and insist on the examination anyway and the physician would discover her hoax. The idea left too much to chance. Besides, even in her dire straits, she couldn't lower herself to be like her uncle and use an innocent pawn in a deceitful game. She couldn't countenance one of her swains being used so poorly at her whim.

She must be thoroughly ruined in order to ensure the contract would be void. She must be ruined tonight and back in the morning to prove it. Then Oswalt would be thwarted in a very final manner. Julia tapped a finger on her chin. How did one get ruined quickly?

There was prostitution, of course. She could saunter into Covent Garden and offer herself to the first man who came along. But that wasn't much of an option. She knew from a stern lecture she'd accidentally over-heard Cousin Gray give his younger brothers about the importance of being selective in 'satisfying their urges' that people could get infected with sexually related diseases. Unfortunately, Gray had seen her before she could learn much more. But while all the nuances of catching such a disease were beyond her realm of knowledge, she didn't think it was much of a trade to risk infection and what Gray had termed as 'certain lingering death' for being Oswalt's enslaved wife. At least with Oswalt, there was the chance he would die soon. With the other, there was no chance of any redemption on the horizon.

Common prostitution might be out of the question, but the direction was correct. Julia turned at the wall and paced another length of the room, veering around the bed to the window. She'd also heard vague, scandalous references from her male cousins regarding brothels that held virgin auctions. That was a distinct possibility. She didn't know precisely what such an event entailed, but she would *definitely* be compromised.

Julia's stomach clenched and she experienced a wave of nausea at the import of what she meant to do. Could she go through with it? Could she give herself to an unknown man? Would that be any better than the indignities Oswalt's proposal forced upon her?

The truth was, she found her options as abhorrent as marriage to Oswalt. It was positively terrifying to imagine the consequences of her choices. If she chose to run away, she'd be running away from a lot more than Oswalt. She'd be shut out of society for ever. No one would dare countenance a friendship with a woman who had done what she was contemplating. There would be no husband or children of her own in the future. Such action could not be erased. Her family would have nothing to do with her. After this, she would be irrevocably on her own.

She would be free. Entirely left to her own devices.

Julia sat down hard on the bed, momentarily stunned by the revelation. Freedom had suddenly become quite expensive. It was clear now that freedom would cost her more than embarrassment at a brothel and an uncomfortable confrontation with her uncle. Those things would be over in a week. But she would keep paying for the rest of her life, and life, the way she knew it, would be over for good.

Her life would be over for good with Oswalt, too. No matter what she chose to do, it was a certainty that everything was going to change irrevocably this week. She was at a crossroads whether she wanted this to be so or not. She wished Cousin Gray was here to talk things through with her. But Julia supposed she'd better get used to being alone and relying on no one but herself. It was going to be her lot in life. Today might be the last day she had to decide her fate. Would she put her faith in her own capabilities to make her way in the world or would she put herself into Oswalt's hands?

Better the devil you know? Not this time. She would summon her courage and take matters into her own hands.

Resigned and more than a little bit frightened, Julia bit her lip and began to think through the only choice open to her. It would have to be the auction. In her mind's eye, she could see her strategy unfolding.

She would convince her aunt and uncle that she was accepting, even glad of the decision they'd made on her behalf. She would call for the carriage and tell her aunt and uncle that she wanted to share the good news of her betrothal with her friend, Elise Farraday. Hmm. She'd better make sure of the weather first.

Julia drew aside the curtains at the window and peered outside. Good. The morning fog was clearing away to reveal a blue sky of late spring. The driver would believe her if she asked to be dropped a few streets from Elise's home in order to walk and enjoy the lovely day. Then she would make her escape and wend her way through the streets to Covent Garden and from there to the finer brothels of London where she'd make her plea. By morning she would be ruined.

By a stranger.

In humiliating circumstances.

From which there would be no turning back.

It was a plan.

It was her only choice.

Only?

The word gave Julia pause. As a rule, she did not believe in dichotomous thinking. Life was far too complicated to narrow the world's complexities into a mere two categories of black and white, yes and no, true or false, do or do not.

Was there another way? A more private way? Julia felt cowardly to even consider it, but perhaps there was a way to be ruined and to preserve discovery unless forced to reveal her fate beyond the confines of her uncle's contract? If so, she'd much prefer it to the public exposure of an auction and the risk of someone recognising her, the risk of being revealed before the deed could be accomplished. The spark of a counter-plan flickered to life in the back of her mind and gathered impetus.

Another way.

Another man.

None of the young bucks that peopled her débutante's court would qualify. Unbidden, there came to mind a blurred image of a man she had encountered once—she couldn't use the word 'met' for she'd only seen him from a distance at a crowded rout one of her first nights out in London. But whispers about his presence had made the rounds of the ballroom readily enough and for once no one thought about editing their words in front of débutantes. Indeed, the opposite was nearly true. Mothers apparently felt their pristine daughters needed to know about the dangers this man posed.

He was Paine Ramsden, third son of an earl, known in less charitable circles as a dark rake with a reputation so black he could not be countenanced in polite society. Julia had learned quickly that he attended the rout solely as a favour to his aunt, the Dowager Marchioness of Bridgerton, Lily Branbourne, who insisted he was her favourite nephew, regardless of the public outcry against his morals.

Julia smiled to herself. By repute, Paine Ramsden was an irresponsible charmer who was loose with his affections and his finances. There were other reports, too, circling the ballroom that night—darker rumours that went beyond the usual complaints of womanising and wastrel tendencies—rumours of time abroad in foreign lands as penance for his involvement in a duel over a woman. The rumours didn't end there. It was quietly reported that since his return he'd been living hedonistically on the shadowy fringes of the *demi-monde,* having bought a tumbledown gambling hell of his own to support himself.

Julia didn't care two figs for his proclivities. The more debauched he was, the less likely he would be smitten with a case of misplaced honour in the morning. Paine Ramsden it would be. She was sure of her course now. She had only to find him and convince him to ruin her. For the latter, she had her pearl earbobs tucked in a small bag to provide any additional financial induce-ment he would need to see the deed done. A gambler like him would know where to pawn them. Yes, the latter would be easy. Based on his poor social standing, it would be harder to do the former.

She might not know where he'd be, but she had a good idea of where he wouldn't be. He wouldn't be at any of the soirées or *musicales* scheduled for the evening. He wouldn't be at any of the fancy gentleman's clubs or gaming establishments on St James's. The gossip she'd heard maintained that he took rooms on Jermyn Street. There was little chance he'd be there at the time she planned to seek him out, but that was where she would start. A landlady or a neighbour might know his direction for the evening or be able to guide her to one of his favorite haunts. True, she didn't know which of the bachelor establishments he lived at, but if she had to go door to door asking landlords, then that's what she'd do. That time of night, the bachelor tenants would most likely all be out carousing and there would be few home to note her presence.

Julia cast another glance at the clock. Eight hours until dark. Eight hours to convince her aunt and uncle of her acceptance of their decision and that she wanted to stay home that evening to work on her trousseau. No. That sounded too suspicious, given that she despised needlework. Better to go with them and give them the slip at the rout tonight. Lady Moffat's entertainment was bound to be a crush and her aunt and uncle were not vigilant chaperons once her dance card was full.

It should be easy to clandestinely slip away through a back-garden gate without being missed for some time. Her uncle would be in the card room, oblivious to what was happening in the ballroom, and her aunt would be caught up in conversation with her friends. Her aunt would assume she was with the Farradays, who often acted as her stand-in chaperons at such events.

Determined to follow through with her decisions, Julia gave her attention to the massive oak wardrobe standing in the corner. She strode to it and threw open the door, revealing dozens of gowns made of the finest silks and fabrics. She eyed the gowns with a new cynicism. Her uncle had not spared any expense when it came to outfitting his niece for her Season. The reasons for such extravagance were horribly clear.

Now, for the last decision. Julia tapped a long finger against her chin, considering the array of finery spread before her. What did a girl wear to her ruination?

Chapter Two

'I never guessed you held aces!' Gaylord Beaton, the young man seated across the card table from Paine Ramsden, threw down his cards in disgust. 'You've the luck of the devil tonight, Ram.'

The others at the table in the dimly lit gambling hell laughed and threw in their hands. 'What do you mean "tonight"? Ram has the devil's luck every night!' another exclaimed.

'Have you considered I might have something more than luck?' Paine Ramsden gathered his winnings with a swift, practised move of his arm.

'What would that be? A fifth ace?' The table broke into guffaws at Gaylord's bold jest.

'Skill,' Paine replied drily, giving them each a piercing stare before he began to deal. He'd heard the underlying anger in young Beaton's jest.

This was the second night these bucks had been in to play and the second night they'd lost heavily. In his experience, an angry gambler was a dangerous gambler. He'd have to keep his eye on the young man. He'd hoped Beaton had learned his lesson last night and taken steps to preserve the remainder of his quarterly allowance. But apparently Beaton thought those steps involved trying to win back his losses, a common enough mistake and one Paine had made during his own misguided youth.

The five of them were playing high-stakes Commerce. He was winning thoroughly, having won a hundred pounds from each of the four young bucks at the table. Paine should have been enjoying it. Instead, he was bored. No, he was beyond bored. He had been bored three nights ago. Now, he was apathetic.

Paine discarded one of his three cards and drew the queen of hearts. With the addition of the queen, he held three of a kind. They were all going to lose again. He waited to feel the elation of victory. He felt nothing— not the excitement of winning, not the pleasant blurring of the edges of the world from the cheap brandy in his glass, not the spark of arousal from the sassy promises of the lightskirt who hovered near his shoulder. He was numb.

How had that happened? When had the usual thrills lost their abilities to sate him? There had been a time earlier in his return from abroad when simply being in a seedy place like this, several streets away from the well-lit halls of St James's, had been thrill enough to send his adrenalin racing at the prospect of needing to draw the knife secreted in his boot. He'd liked the prospect so much, he'd bought this place from the owner, who was looking to retire.

These days, he was the king of the roost. He'd made the seamy gaming hall his private kingdom. Young bloods looking for racy diversions came to try their hand against him at cards. Hardened gamblers appealed to him for loans when their luck was down. The whores offered themselves to him willingly. He had gone looking for the underworld and now it came looking for him.

He hardly left except to make a rare appearance in the *ton*, as he had done several weeks ago to escort his Aunt Lily to an early Season ball. He genuinely liked his Aunt Lily and her forthright manner. But as for the *ton*, Paine much preferred life outside high society's restrictions and expectations. His time in India had taught him that. The fact that he had grown tired of his current arrangement merely indicated he needed to find a new excitement.

Paine set down his cards to a chorus of groans from the table and began unrolling his shirtsleeves.

'You're not thinking of leaving before we have a chance to win back our losses?' one dandy cried in dismay. 'It is only midnight.'

'Exactly so—' Paine replied, breaking off in mid-sentence. He narrowed his gaze and looked into the smoky gloom beyond the table towards the entrance. There was a commotion at the front. 'Gentleman, if you'll excuse me, there seems to be a problem that needs my attention.'

Paine strode towards the door, aware for the first time that evening of a prick of anticipation growing within him. This was what he needed, something unknown and unpredictable, to spark his enthusiasm again.

'John, is there anything wrong?' Paine asked the doorman.

'Doorman' was a polite word for John's occupation. The hulking man with the crooked nose was charged with the duty of keeping people in who didn't pay their debts and keeping out those who didn't belong to the murky depths of the hell. It was a duty he did well. There was seldom an occasion John couldn't manage. Tonight seemed to be a rare exception. John appeared relieved to see him, although Paine was having difficulty noticing what the trouble might be.

'It's this 'ere chit. She's asking for you.' John stepped aside, revealing what his girth had hidden from Paine's approach.

Paine's breath caught and his member stirred violently. The girl was stunning. One look at her generous invitation of a mouth and his mind was awash with images of bedding her, of stripping her out of the turquoise silk that hugged her curves exquisitely and kissing her until she cried out for all of him. In his veins, his blood began to heat at the prospect. He was alive again.

'It's all right, John. I'll speak with her.' Paine clapped the big man on the shoulder. Was that relief he saw on the girl's face? He was certain he didn't know her. She looked far too fine to be familiar with the places he frequented. And too innocent, he amended. There were no chandeliers or crystal goblets here, but the woman beside him had the carriage and clothing of a woman who was familiar with such trappings.

He gave her one of his rare smiles and offered his arm, drawing her inside. He felt her gloved hand tense where it lay on the sleeve of his linen shirt as she took in the surroundings and he saw the place through her eyes while they wended through the tables; the smell of stale smoke mingled with alcohol and unwashed sweat; the worn garb of the patrons, the faded upholstered chairs and scarred tables.

Belatedly, he recalled he had left his own jacket at the table and that he wore no extra adornments as was his wont when gambling. No diamond pin twinkled in the folds of a nonexistent cravat, no gems sparkled at the cuffs of his sleeves. By *ton* standards he was in extreme dishabille, garbed only in a plain white shirt and tan breeches—a far cry from the expected dark evening wear.

Paine turned down a narrow hallway and opened the first door on his left. It was a small room that served as his office of sorts for when he discussed loans or other private issues. He ushered her inside and motioned that she should sit.

'Can I get you a drink? I have ratafia or sherry.' She shook her head and Paine shrugged, fixing a brandy to give himself something to do. Once he had his glass, he took his customary place behind the plain wooden desk and studied her, waiting for her to state her business.

Beautiful and nervous, he concluded, although she was hiding it bravely. She didn't fidget with her pristine white-gloved hands, but held them clasped tightly in her lap. Her posture was rigid. Despite the control she held over the rest of her body, her eyes gave her away completely. Her eyes were bold, challenging orbs of jade. He'd seen the exact shade in the gem markets of Calcutta, transported from the mines of the Kashmir Vale, an exotic green polished to an emerald sheen. She wanted something.

He could not imagine what he had to offer a stranger such as herself. But whatever she thought he had, she wanted it desperately. The challenge in her eyes said as much.

She did not speak and Paine felt obliged to fill the lengthening silence. 'Since we have not met, let me introduce myself. I am Paine Ramsden. However, you already know that. I feel distinctly at a disadvantage, for I have no idea who you might be.'

'I am Julia Prentiss. I thank you for agreeing to see me.' She spoke matter of factly, giving Paine the unlikely impression it might have been daylight outside and this meeting nothing more than a standard interview.

'This is a rather unusual time of evening for a business appointment. I must admit I am quite curious as to why you're here.' Paine leaned back in his chair, steepling his hands and trying to look as if he weren't fully aroused from the sight of her magnificent figure or the sound of her voice.

He saw the long column of her neck work briefly as she swallowed. For the first time since she'd entered the establishment, he felt her resolve waver. When she did not speak immediately, Paine offered a lifeline. 'Do you need money?' Perhaps she had a gambling debt. It was not unusual for women to wager beyond their capabilities at cards at a ball or house party.

She shook her head, causing the aquamarine earbobs to dance lightly. Too late, Paine realized his faulty reasoning. The earbobs alone could have been discreetly pawned to cover a small debt. Good lord, he'd only known her for a handful of minutes and she'd addled his wits. His manhood strained against his trousers. He hoped she'd get to the point soon so he could begin his own manoeuvres.

'I need you to ruin me.' The words came out in a rush; a light blush coloured her flawless alabaster cheeks.

'Ruin?' Paine quirked an eyebrow. 'What do you mean by "ruin"? Shall I ruin you at the gaming tables? I can arrange to have you lose any amount of your choosing.'

Her gaze met his evenly in all seriousness, her courage having returned in full force now that she'd begun talking. 'I don't wish to lose any money. I wish to lose my virginity. I want you to ruin me in bed.'

His mind warned of danger while his member fairly exploded at the anticipated pleasure being handed to it. Dangerous pleasure—his favourite kind of diversion. 'I am not opposed to such an arrangement, but I would know more,' Paine said coolly.

'I am to marry a man I find completely unsuitable in five days. He will not have me if I've been...' She paused, casting about for a word she could utter. 'If I've been touched by another.'

Paine felt a surge of disappointment. Partnering her in this request had any number of obvious drawbacks, not the least of which was the odds of facing a duel. Danger was one thing, illegal proceedings like duels were another. Still, it needn't end so drastically. It wasn't as if he had a reputation to protect and the chit wasn't looking for him to do the honourable thing afterwards.

'This is a rather rash course of action, one that is irrevocable, Julia.'

He spoke her name, liking the sound of it and the familiarity it implied. He rose and came around to the front of the desk, determined to teach her a lesson about the nature of men. He half-sat, half-stood at the corner, his arms crossed, his lower body exposed so that there was no mistaking his maleness or his arousal, which pressed unmistakably full and hard against the fall of his breeches. Let her see what such a request involved. He would give her one chance to back out.

'Have you thought this through? Is there no chance of resigning yourself to the marriage? Perhaps you will come to rub along quite well with your betrothed in a year or two. Many women find once they marry, have a home and a family to look after, that all else settles itself with time.' Good lord, he sounded like a finishing-school marm.

Fire lit her eyes and she replied, 'I am not a silly chit rebelling against her parents' choice for a husband because I fancy myself infatuated with another. I assure you, I have no desire to "rub along well" with this man. Mortimer Oswalt is a lecher of the worst sort and I refuse to be reduced to nothing more than his legal brood mare! Even if it means I shall not stand a chance of ever marrying.'

Paine felt his heated blood chill at the name. Mortimer Oswalt was well known to him. There was old animosity between them and a vengeance to be repaid over a woman. It would be fitting to ruin the man's betrothed. He was no longer a stripling. This time, Mortimer Oswalt would not be able to manipulate him so easily. This time, an innocent would escape Oswalt's clutches.

He studied the girl before him. Bedding her would be no act of charity. She was a divine beauty and his body clearly wanted her. She was more than beautiful, though. He wasn't so fickle as to be aroused by appearance alone. Julia Prentiss had spirit and courage. Not every girl in England had the power to rebel against a chosen match and to take action on her own. Such passion boded well for what they could share in the bedroom. First, he would ascertain with actions the willingness she professed with her words.

'Stand up, Julia, so that I may see what I am getting myself into.' He held her eyes, noting that her gaze did not flinch from his scrutiny.

She rose, her skirts brushing his legs. The lemon scent of her soap filled his nostrils, conjuring up images of sunlit days in faraway places where trees grew exotic-scented fruits. Paine let his eyes roam the length of her, stopping to rest intently on her firm breasts shown to advantage beneath the aquamarine bodice. He stared long enough to know her cheeks were heating.

Paine stood up from his lounging position against the desk and closed the half-step gap between them. He fitted his hands at her slender waist appreciably. Still, she did not move. He ran a hand up her ribs to cup the underside of a full breast. 'Very nice, very firm. I like that,' he said huskily.

Without warning, a hand slapped him hard across the

face. He took a step back, releasing his grip on her. 'What the hell was that for?' He massaged the stung cheek.

'For trying to scare me off. I see your game and I won't scare.' The coldness of her words matched the coldness Paine saw in her eyes. He'd expected her to be stunned by his vulgar assessment.

Julia delivered a scathing set-down. 'You can't do anything more humiliating to me than what awaits me with Oswalt. At least when I am done here, I'll have my freedom. However, I would still ask that you not treat me like prized cattle.'

Paine gave a sardonic laugh. 'Who's treating whom like prized cattle? You are the one who has marched in here and demanded I play the stud.' He was gratified when she coloured a bit at that.

'Enough. Will you do it?'

She was magnificent in her scolding, her colour rising, her eyes starting to thaw with her temper. He liked that better. He had no use for ice maidens. A wicked grin lit his face. He advanced again, his stung cheek forgotten. There was one final test. 'Darling, have you heard the bedtime story about the princess and the pea?' He whispered, catching her chin between his forefinger and thumb so that her lovely face was turned up to meet his.

'Wh-what does that have to do with anything?' she asked, startled, her eyes widening.

For an answer, Paine bent his head to capture her

luscious mouth with his. He coaxed her mouth open with a light pressure from his lips, letting his tongue probe her mouth, running across the smooth surfaces of her teeth, tasting the fruity sweetness of evening champagne, feeling her compliance.

He opened his mouth wider and pulled back his tongue to offer her an opportunity to reciprocate. She did, tentatively letting her tongue explore him. Paine groaned as her teeth nipped at his bottom lip and she giggled at his response. Paine moved his hands to her waist and pulled her against him, letting her feel his hard member, letting her feel the power she had to summon such a response.

Paine grabbed her hand and held it between them, against the straining length of him. 'Do you feel what you do to me?' he murmured, tearing himself away from the kiss. This was meant to be his test. When had he lost control?

Instead of being embarrassed by the intimate nature of her touch, Julia looked exultant, her face flushed with more victory than apprehension. If she looked this beautiful now, Paine could hardly imagine how glorious it would be to see her after a thorough bedding and know he was the one responsible for such a satisfied glow. There were countless positions and tricks he could show a willing participant.

'Does this mean you will do it?' she pressed, breaking into his thoughts before they could start to vividly itemise the lessons he wanted to give her.

Paine gave her one last assessing glance, not wanting to appear too easily conquered for pride's sake. Whatever rumour might say about him, whatever rumour might have led her here under the premise he was not discerning about his bed partners, Paine knew otherwise. He considered his bedmates carefully and with utmost discretion.

'Yes. Yes, I will do it.'

Paine visibly saw the breath she'd been holding go out of her, so great was her relief. Looking past him, her eyes evaluated the room. He followed her gaze to where it rested on the narrow cot with its drab blanket shoved against the wall. She pursed her lips into a resolute line and nodded towards the bed with dogged determination. 'Then we'd best get on with it.'

Paine thought he heard a note of sadness in her voice, perhaps regret, and he moved to eradicate it. She might be forced to surrender her virginity, but it didn't have to be a degrading experience. His own considerable pride as a lover bristled at the notion. No woman should ever leave his bed feeling demeaned by the experience of his lovemaking. He made a quick decision.

'I think you'll find my rooms better suited for our needs.' He nodded towards the cot. 'I've spent enough nights on that to know it is not even passably comfortable for one, let alone two people engaged in intimacy.'

She blushed and Paine was struck afresh by her innocence. For all her forthright behaviour, she was young and pretty and apparently alone. The last resonated with him strongly. He knew what it was like to be alone and he felt a kinship with her that he had not felt for another person in ages. Something that slept deep within him was waking up.

'My carriage is in the back. We should leave before someone comes poking around,' Paine suggested, moving the interaction forwards. Now that the deal had been struck, Julia had fallen silent, her gaze pointedly fixed on her gloved hands.

He held out his hand. 'It's time to go unless you are rethinking your choices. Once you leave here, there's no turning back.' He gave a small chuckle meant to reassure her. 'I am sure it has come to your attention that I want you.'

Her head shot up at the comment, her eyes blazing with fire. 'First of all, how could you want me? You know nothing about me beyond my name and even that could be a fabrication on my part. Secondly, I haven't had any choices to "rethink" since eleven o'clock this morning, when my uncle sealed my fate with his greed. Thirdly, there's been no turning back since the moment I left the Moffat rout tonight. I don't need your pity. I know exactly what I am doing, but I don't have to like it.'

Paine tossed back his head and laughed, partly out of relief that his vixen had returned and partly at the pert speech. 'You're right. You don't have to like it, but if your performance a few minutes ago is any indication, I bet you will.' He would make sure of it.

Chapter Three

The carriage ride was accomplished in silence. On her side of the carriage Julia seethed inwardly over letting Ramsden goad her. Like it, indeed! She might be an innocent, but she was not utterly naïve. She knew quite well 'it' referred to the sex act. Paine Ramsden was as handsome as purported with his midnight hair and riveting blue eyes and twice as conceited if he thought she'd find pleasure in what she was about to do. In his male arrogance, he'd quickly forgotten she'd been forced to these measures.

She hadn't picked him for his skill. She had picked him for his willingness and she'd been right. He had acquiesced with very little persuasion. She had been prepared to beg, even pay for his services.

The carriage rolled to a halt. Julia sucked in her breath and steadied herself. Paine leaped down and turned back to hand her out. She'd expected to see Jermyn Street with its bachelor residences. Instead, she found herself in unfamiliar territory.

'Where are we?' she asked, casting her glance up and down the street, looking for a marker. A *frisson* of doubt travelled through her. It was the height of foolishness to go with a stranger in a closed carriage without telling anyone of her whereabouts. Should he will it, Paine Ramsden had her entirely at his mercy.

'Brook Street. I just acquired a house here. I have hopes of turning the place into a luxury hotel that will appeal to an elite calibre of clientele.' Paine gestured to the rest of the street where other hotels had recently sprung up. 'The location seems ideal.' Then he winked conspiratorially, 'It's ideal for us as well. We will be less likely to be disturbed here.'

Paine produced a key and proceeded to unlock the door. 'You will have to excuse the absence of furniture. The place is quite bare except for the bedroom upstairs and a little office I cobbled together in the back. I imagine I'll be making good use of the rooms once renovations begin and my presence will be required around the clock.'

Julia gave a forced smile, appreciating his effort to put her at ease. Now that she'd had the space of the carriage ride to review what she was doing, her nerves were doubly on edge. Still, she *must* go forwards, she'd come too far to back out now.

Julia stepped inside, unprepared for the opulence that met her gaze. As he'd warned, the place was empty of furnishings. But it was not devoid of decoration. The richness of the marbled tiled entry with its gilded mirrors did not resonate with her image of Paine Ramsden's financial status. He was a gambler by trade, a man who ran a seedy gaming hell. Those were not the traits of a man with money to spare. Yet, this was a house only a wealthy man could afford to purchase. And it would take a large sum of money to renovate it as well.

They reached a curved staircase and halted.

'Would you like to go straight upstairs or would you prefer to sit and talk in my office, makeshift as it is?' Paine offered, gesturing to a room farther down the hall.

Julia lifted her skirts with resolution. 'Straight upstairs, if you please. I am eager to see this business concluded.'

'Do not be too eager, my sweet. There is much you might discover to be enjoyed if you take time and savour our interlude,' he said in low tones at her elbow.

'You are quite sure of yourself,' Julia responded with disdain. 'I am interested only in seeing the deed accomplished in an expedient manner.'

Paine laughed, a throaty, intimate chuckle that sent an unlooked-for thrill through Julia. She spared him a sidelong glance that lasted long enough to see that his blue eyes danced with smug merriment, giving her the distinct impression that he knew something beyond her comprehension.

She didn't like being so far out of her depth. She was not fool enough to believe that she'd ever held the upper hand in their dealings. He held all the knowledge and all the power. Should he decide not to go through with her request, she had no way to coerce him back into compliance.

They ascended the stairs and she reflected wryly on her earlier thoughts to offer her earbobs as financial compensation, thinking they would appeal to him in his lowly circumstances if she needed leverage. In light of this elegant house, her earbobs seemed laughable. But her powerlessness was not. She had no leverage now if he suddenly found his long-forgotten conscience and backed out. Then again, he was a rogue of the first water. Gossip had it that he seldom slept alone and the line of women parading through his bedroom was endless. He was a man of intense physical appetites. He wouldn't back out. He *needed* sex.

Paine stopped before a panelled oak door and opened it wide, allowing her to enter ahead of him. 'My chambers,' he said without flourish, but she could feel his hot eyes on her, watching her reaction.

She hid nothing in her response to the room. Indeed, she didn't know how she could have schooled her features to remain impassive when faced with the seductive opulence that spread before her. The room was

exotic and utterly unlike anything she'd seen before—
not that she made a habit of frequenting male bedchambers. In reality, seeing one or a hundred bedchambers
was immaterial. She knew instinctively she could view
every bedroom in England and not find one like this.

Candlelight from candelabras placed about the room
lit the place in a soft glow, casting shadows on gold
damask-hung walls. Beneath the soles of her dancing
slippers, Julia could feel the plushness of the carpet, the
thick pile a marked contrast to the threadbare Axmin-
ster rugs that dotted the floors of her uncle's home.
This carpet was of soft wool dyed in rich crimson hues
and accented with gold to match the walls. Julia
doubted anyone else in England would have been so
bold as to decorate a bedroom in deep crimson and bur-
nished gold, but the differences didn't stop there.

Her eye was drawn to the furniture; an ornate cabinet
of ebony stood against one wall, inlaid with gold and
ivory to create a design, perhaps a symbol of some sort.
Low-slung chairs filled with pillows sat at angles to a
low teak table, but what garnered her gaze unequivocally was the bed.

Unlike the high, pillared beds she was accustomed
to seeing, this bed was framed low to the ground, piled
with pillows and silken coverlets. Blankets seemed too
ordinary of a word to describe the lush swathes of fabric
that lay strewn about the bed, vibrant in their shades of
scarlet, saffron and jade. Julia could not resist the temp-

tation to touch the fabrics. She walked to the bed and ran her fingers across the surface of the closest covering, revelling in the smoothness of the silk as it shushed through her hands.

For a moment, she'd forgotten where she was and why she was there. The heat of his gaze on her back served as a searing reminder. She dropped the blanket self-consciously and stiffened.

'It's a magnificent bed,' Paine said from across the room in a slow drawl that indicated he'd watched her every move.

'It's very interesting. I've never seen one like it,' Julia replied stiffly, turning away from the bed.

'Are you sure you wouldn't like a drink before we get started?' Paine offered, opening the inlaid doors of the ebony cabinet to reveal assorted sizes of crystal glassware and an impressive collection of decanters.

Julia was tempted to say no. As a rule, she didn't drink beyond an occasional glass of champagne. But tonight, the thought-numbing properties of alcohol, which she had been warned against as a débutante, might be just the addition she needed to get through the evening. 'Yes, sherry, please.'

Before she could rethink her decision, Paine had the glass in her hand and was gesturing to one of the cushioned chairs. 'Let's sit and talk. It makes these encounters less formal.'

His coolness spoke volumes about his character,

Julia thought. While she was fighting back nerves, he was entirely at ease, as if this were something he did regularly—which, in fact, it was, according to the rumours. He lounged casually in his chair, looking devastatingly handsome and comfortable. The only sign he was in any way affected by the presence of a female in his chambers was the burning intensity of his eyes— eyes that followed her every gesture, every move. She was supremely conscious she was fiddling overmuch with the folds of her skirts as she sat.

Julia sipped from her glass, giving herself a moment to savour the warmth of the sweet liquor as it slid down to her belly. 'You must like to travel.' There. That was a safe topic.

Paine nodded briefly. 'I have found places in the world where I feel at home.'

'Are these pieces of furniture from any of those places?' Julia asked, her eyes sliding to the lacquered cabinet, looking desperately for a safe direction of conversation. She'd hoped he would have said more about his travels than the meagre offering of a single sentence. But the talkativeness he'd exhibited upon arrival seemed to have disappeared. 'Do you know anything about the design on the cabinet? It appears to be a symbol. Do you know what it is?'

'Yes. I know.' Paine followed her gaze to the inlaid panels of the cabinet doors, a smile quirking at his sensual lips.

The dratted man was a rotten conversationalist with his minimal answers. Julia put down her glass and rose. She went to the panels, tracing a portion of the symbol with a slow finger. 'Mr Ramsden, talking to you is virtually impossible since you are not the least bit forthcoming with any information. I feel obliged to tell you that a gentleman is able to make conversation on a diverse array of subjects.' She hazarded a sideways glance at Ramsden to see the effect of her veiled barb.

It had hit the mark, perhaps too effectively. Ramsden rose and came towards her with all the feral stealth of a jungle panther. He paced behind her, giving Julia the distinct impression she was being stalked. She had not meant to strike so deeply.

'Miss Prentiss,' he began in low tones, 'your very comment is a trap from which neither of the answers available shall save me. My dilemma, you see, is that while proving my worth as a gentleman I am at the same time besmirching that title by the same means. If I confess that I am no gentleman, I shall save myself from answering what the symbol is, but at the expense of my honour, which I hold dearer than you might have been led to believe. On the other hand, if I confess what the symbol is and provide an erudite exposition of my conversational skills, I shall vouch for my ability to perform the gentlemanly arts. However, discussing that symbol with any well-bred girl is a conversational topic

that no true gentleman would broach. So I ask you—
do you want to know what the symbol stands for?'

Julia bit her lip and fought the desire to step back,
away from his masculine onslaught. He stood with
hands on his hips hardly inches from her, his blue eyes
penetrating and challenging as he threw down his
gauntlet. She saw his ploy and the detection gave her
strength. He still thought to scare her with his dares and
the promise of blatant sin.

The man was positively aggravating. She was supposed to be the one baiting the hook and yet he'd neatly
turned the conversation to his advantage. 'So you
cleverly choose neither option. Instead, you lure me
with temptation, betting that my curiosity will cause me
to permit you to speak freely, thus absolving you of any
gentlemanly obligation on the subject.'

'*Touché*. You see my ploy too clearly.' Ramsden
covered his heart with a hand in mock hurt.

'You might as well tell me about the symbol,' Julia
prompted. 'After all, I am about to grant you far more
liberties than that of questionable speech.' It was as
close as she would get to admitting her curiosity had
won out. Since he'd made such a to-do over discussing
the panel, she had to know what it was about.

Ramsden's hands came down on her shoulders, his
fingers kneading gently through the thin material of her
dancing gown. He turned her away from him to face the
cabinet, his voice low and soft at her ear. In that

moment, her senses were utterly encircled by his presence; the scent of him in her nostrils, the warm strength of his body against her back, the press of his fingers to her shoulders. He was the centre of her universe, the only person she could see, smell, touch or hear. Julia could scarcely concentrate on the tale he laid out in tones designed to seduce even the most resolute spinster.

'The symbol is known throughout the eastern world as yin and yang, two opposite but yet complementary forces that make up all aspects of life.' His voice dropped a notch lower, speaking now just to her. 'Yin, the dark portion of the symbol, is female. It represents valleys and streams. It is passive and absorbing.' At this, Ramsden ran a hand languorously down her arm, took her fingers between his and led them over the bottom part of the inlay, the ebony smooth and cool to her touch. He guided her hand over the top portion done in ivory.

'This is yang, her male counterpart, representing light and heaven. Yang is penetrating and active.' He pressed his hips against the round swell of her buttocks, letting her feel the possibilities of penetration between her thighs, between them. Julia inhaled sharply at the suggestive display. He whispered huskily, 'Yin and yang express the interdependence of opposites. Without the other, neither is complete. Feel the need you arouse in me, Julia, a need only you can slake. '

Julia felt weak. Heaven help her, she was a wanton to react in such a base manner with a stranger she didn't know beyond a name. Her business proposition was quickly turning to unnamable pleasure. She wanted to sink back against his chest, let his arms close about her and take her weight. She wanted him to fulfil the ancient, earthy promises of his voice. She'd never guessed a simple cabinet could inspire this depth of longing.

One of his hands slid about her waist, drawing her against his hardness, the other was in her hair, slipping through the pins and pearls of her elegant coiffure until her hair hung loose and free. This time when his hardness jutted against her back, she could not even feign shock over his intimate proposal. This time, her inhalation was from pure desire that would not be put off any longer.

She turned in his arms, pressing her body against his, instinctively rubbing her nipples against his chest in a desperate attempt to quell the tempest brewing at her core. She looked up into his face. His blue eyes no longer reminded her of the colour of the sky on a deep summer day, but bore shades of midnight, darkened as they were by his arousal.

Something thrilled deep within her at the knowledge she had done this to him. But her own rising need left little time for contemplation or even a celebration of victory. She was drowning in heretofore unknown sensations and she clung to him for support. Intuition told her only he could provide an antidote to what coursed through her veins.

'Steady now,' Paine whispered to her, his hands on the buttons of her gown, expertly freeing her body from its satin casing. Through the thin linen of her chemise, he traced the silhouette of her body against the candles' flames. His thumbs teased her nipples through the cloth until Julia panted for release. She reached to pull the chemise over her head, suddenly in a hurry to be completely naked, as if by being so she could assuage the pressure growing within her, demanding emancipation.

To her frustration, Paine pushed her hands away. 'Not yet, my eager one.' He bent and swept her into his arms. Julia gasped at the sudden movement, but she hadn't the wherewithal or desire to protest when he laid her on the low bed amidst the silken covers. She made no move to cover herself. She could do nothing but hold Paine's intense stare. She reached for him to pull him down to her, but he stepped back.

'Watch me, Julia.'

Did she have a choice? Julia could not muster the fortitude to look away. Paine's eyes did not leave hers as he lifted his shirt over his head and stood magnificently bare-chested before her, his torso bronzed from years beneath a tropical sun, the strength of the arms that had lifted her evident in the obvious musculature of his shoulders and biceps. Julia groped for a word to describe him. Beautiful came to mind—sublime, masculine beauty, the kind of beauty sculptors carved in stone and for the night it was hers.

His hands dropped to the waistband of his trousers, reminding Julia that he was not done. He was not wearing small clothes underneath and the core of his manhood sprang free of the trousers, straining upright towards his belly in unabashed glory. Artfully, he bent to pull his legs free of the trousers, supplying Julia with an unadulterated glimpse of his backside.

He must be a fabulous horseman, Julia concluded, eyeing the muscled power of his long legs and firm buttocks. The thought was so errant and ridiculous, Julia choked back a giggle.

'What is it?'

'I was just thinking you must be a great horseman,' Julia confessed.

Paine smiled wickedly. 'I know how to ride.'

The cryptic remark puzzled her. She sensed there was a double meaning, but she could not fathom what it was, too enamoured of the sight before her to do anything else.

Seeing her consternation, his smile softened and he knelt on the floor beside her, the knuckles of his hand grazing her cheek in a caress. 'Ah, Julia, my innocent.' He reached for a trifle box on a low table and withdrew an unfamiliar item. Julia watched, amazed, as he fitted it on to his sex.

'It's a sheath to prevent us from making a child,' Paine explained softly. 'Now, we're ready for our true pleasure.'

Julia could not imagine more beyond what she'd already felt but Paine knelt at her stockinged feet and convinced her otherwise. Skilful hands rolled down the stockings and discarded them. Lips kissed the sensitive space behind her knees until she thought she would scream aloud from the sensation of it. Heat built inside her, a heat that was damp and scorching all at once as Paine's hands spread her thighs and his mouth nipped seductively at the tender flesh near her woman's core, his breath hot against the triangle of her curls.

Then he was over her, covering her with the length of his form, his sex strong against her leg. Without leaving her, he reached again for the trifle box and re-trieved a small vial of oil that smelled of lavender when he removed the stopper and poured some into his hand. Julia watched, entranced as Paine moved his hand between her legs and gently inserted his oil-slick fingers inside her.

'You're ready for me,' Paine whispered, covering her again and this time it was his sex that found purchase at her entrance. Julia felt him thrust in, just a little at first, and then, to her dismay, withdraw. She cried out her disappointment. Paine smothered the cry with a kiss and entered again, further this time, and withdrew, then again until Julia realised his rhythm and intention.

Secure now that she was not being teased, Julia fitted her hips against his and joined in the rhythm. She felt him plunge deep, felt a sharp stab of pain. He stilled inside her as she breathed a cry into his mouth and waited until she urged him onwards.

Deep inside her now, their rhythm increased, the pressure grew, spiralled to new levels. Not even his kiss could silence her moans of delight. In this new pleasure, she was free. She was not bound to the earth or to anything on it; beneath Paine Ramsden, she was flying, soaring. When she felt she could not soar any higher, she felt her core fracture into countless pieces, the pressure that had built in her since his first touch finally assuaged. She was boneless and drifting in a new satisfied world, aware only that Paine, too, had seemed to reach a level of fulfilment, contentment. He, too, had cried out at the last and now rested against her, his weight a warm reminder of their intimacy as sleep took her.

Chapter Four

Paine awoke to the scent of lemons mingled with the musk of sex and the warmth of another body cradled against his own, his arm draped over the lush curve of a breast. It was a heady awakening.

Images of the evening came back to him with striking clarity: Julia Prentiss in her delectable aquamarine gown begging him to ruin her, her green eyes shrewdly assessing him as she made her plea; Julia naked on his bed, weeping for his caress as he initiated her to the pleasures of lovemaking; Julia crying out as the final moment of their joining took her to untold heights, her hips arched high into him, her head thrown back on the pillow as she gave way to unabashed ecstasy.

At that moment, all pretence of doing a duty, of thwarting her fate with her madcap scheme, had fled from her thoughts. He'd seen her eyes darken the moment she'd submitted fully to the pleasure between them, when business had ceased. She'd been utterly his, and utterly without artifice.

Everything in that instant had been truth. Not just for her, for him, too. He'd cried out at his pinnacle, feeling his own climax completely, devoid of the usual restraint he practised. It was his wont to give pleasure, not to take his own, not to give in to anything beyond the physical fulfilment of the act.

Last night had been disturbingly different. He'd found he could not hold back the emotional tide that surged at the sounds of Julia's bliss beneath him. He had given into temptation—a temptation that he rarely felt, if ever—and joined her at the height of her rapture.

The act of doing so was somewhat alarming, perhaps a sign of vulnerability in himself that he had thought long suppressed. Perhaps he wasn't as changed by his years abroad, his studies of the human condition, his adventures in far-off lands, as he had believed. There was danger in that. He'd been exiled once before for behaving rashly on behalf of a woman. He'd promised himself not to let such foolishness take him again.

Julia stirred beside him, nesting her buttocks against his groin provocatively in her sleep. He flared to life, his body responding immediately to the inadvertent invitation. He tamped it down. He'd taken her twice more after their first joining. She'd be sore this morning. He should refrain until she'd had a hot bath and soaked away the initial soreness. But neither could he lay by her side, playing the neutral eunuch. If he was to grant her a respite, he had to keep himself occupied.

Paine rolled over and out of the bed in a single, quick motion before his body could persuade his conscience to act otherwise. He would see about some breakfast. His new piece of property might be ideal for a quiet assignation—indeed, he'd only picked up the key two days ago—but as such, it was without staff or supplies. Paine pulled on trousers and shirt. He cast a last glance at Julia, sleeping peacefully, oblivious to the arousal he was fighting on her behalf. He would hurry so that Julia wouldn't awake alone.

Outside, the sun was up, its brightness something Paine realised he hadn't seen in quite some time. The streets were strangely quiet as well, something Paine noticed immediately, so at odds was the deserted scene with the crowded bustle he usually contended with. Of course it was London and the streets were never truly deserted. Even now, vendors and workers straggled down the streets to work.

Paine spied a milkmaid turning at the corner, no doubt seeking out the alleyway leading to the back entrance of a neighbouring mansion. He followed her. Milk would be a good start to breakfast. If the milkmaids were just coming out, he judged the time to be a little past six o'clock. Six o'clock! Hell's bells, it was early!

The stark realisation hit him with a feeling of disbelief. It had been ages since he'd seen the city through morning eyes. Early it might be, yet he felt refreshed and ready to take on the day.

Three-quarters of an hour later, Paine stood in the doorway of his bedchamber, carrying a tray laden with the breakfast treasures he'd culled from the early-morning vendors. He indulged in the sight of Julia dozing. He smiled as she turned over, starting to wake. Paine set the tray on the low table near the bed and eased on to the bed at her side, waving an orange beneath her nose.

'Mmm.' Julia gave a breathy sigh, her eyes opening at the citrusy scent.

'Good morning, darling.' Paine reached out to push a tangle of hair back from her face.

Julia stretched, her movements drawing the loose covering sheet down to reveal a tantalising glimpse of a breast, reminding Paine that his hand had lain against the creamy flesh only an hour ago. The erection he'd subdued with his breakfast errand rose in defiance. She turned her green gaze on him, already sharp, not the least bit dreamy from sleep. 'What time is it?'

'It's a bit past seven o'clock,' Paine said, taken aback by the question. It was not what he'd expected. Most women didn't ask him what time it was when they awoke and saw him kneeling at their bedside.

But Julia had proven last night that she was not most women and he'd do well to remember it. Most women didn't invoke the depth of feeling that had accompanied his climax. He'd been tutored in the arts of the sexual sutras, learning the mastery of yin over yang in the arms of India's exotic concubines. Most women didn't have the ability to unman him as Julia had last night.

'Seven o'clock!' Julia sat upright, the sheet sliding to her waist in her agitation.

'I know it's early, but…' Paine said boyishly, tempted to reach for her and put off breakfast a while longer.

She didn't let him finish. 'Early? How can you say that? It's late. I never meant to stay this long! How could you have let me sleep the entire night away? I thought you understood.'

She was scolding him? She never meant to stay the whole night? She'd meant to slip away after their coupling? Wasn't that his line? This was all backwards. *He* was supposed to be the one leaving in the dark of night. *He* never actually *slept* when he bedded a woman. *He* left as soon as he could. Paine stared at her in utter confusion.

'Julia, whatever are you talking about?'

'I have to leave. I have to get back to my aunt and uncle's. With luck, they won't have checked my room yet.' She threw an accusing glare at him as if this was all somehow his fault. 'I meant to be home by two o'clock, long before they came traipsing back.' With luck, she'd even held hopes of returning to the ball before it was over. The Moffat rout had a reputation for running until dawn.

Her tone pricked Paine's temper. He rose from the bed, hands on hips. 'Dancing, deflowering and back by two. That was an ambitious agenda, Julia,' he drawled.

'It's what had to be done and, now that it is done, I have to go and finish what I have put in motion. Ruination isn't much good unless I go back and prove it.' Julia gave a belated blush and reached for the sheet, making an effort to rise modestly from the bed with the sheet draped about her. 'I will just dress and go, if you don't mind.'

Her haughty tone didn't sit well with Paine. He advanced towards her. 'I find I do mind, Julia, quite a lot. This is my home and my chamber. I will not be dismissed from it like a common servant.' With luck, she'd step backwards and run into the bed. Then he'd have her where he wanted her.

No such luck. Julia stood her ground, even though they stood only inches from each other. 'You can't stop me.' She stared him down, giving no quarter with her challenge.

Paine's eye caught the glimmer of aqua silk heaped in the corner. A wicked smile took his lips. He let his gaze linger on the heap long enough to draw Julia's attention.

She instantly divined the plan that had spawned his devil's smile. 'No, you wouldn't dare.' She barely got the words out and the race for the dress was on.

It was not an easy race. Julia didn't play fair.

Julia shrieked and shoved a chair in his path to slow him down. Paine shoved it aside and reached for her, laughing at her nerve. 'Vixen!'

He succeeded only in grabbing a handful of sheeting as she spun out of the linen and darted to put a table between them.

She was fully naked and panting, her auburn tresses falling over the heaving globes of her breasts as she stared at him across the table top. Paine was gloriously aroused. 'Temptress! Godiva!'

'Call me what you like, but I've got you now!' she crowed, her anger forgotten in the thrill of the race. Near-triumph coaxed a laugh from her throat as she gave over to the exhilaration of victory.

Paine saw the reason she gloated. The dress was on her side of the table. She simply had to make a dash for it and the gown would be hers. He feinted left, then right, keeping her attention while he made his decision. He would not stand a chance if he wasted a precious second going around the small table. He would have to go over it.

Paine lunged, coming over the table and taking Julia to the ground with him. She wriggled against him, struggling, tantalising with every movement.

'That's not fair!' she protested, obviously wanting to be put out by his audacity, but not quite able to void the laughter from her voice.

'You gloated too soon,' Paine teased, enjoying the friction of her naïve movements against the fabric of his trousers where she lay beneath him. He inched forwards and grasped at the hem of the gown. 'I win. I have the dress and I have you right where I want you, right where you belong.' He ground his hips meaningfully against her pelvis, his member in an overt state of readiness that could not be overlooked.

Julia angled her head back to see her discarded gown clutched in Paine's hand. She stretched to reach and take it from him. Paine pinned her gently with the power of his body. 'Do you think I would relinquish your gown so soon after winning it?' Paine tut-tutted.

'Please, give it back to me.' The earlier playfulness was replaced with a plea. He was alert to it at once.

'All right.' Paine sat up, straddling her between his thighs. He needed to be careful not to push Julia too far. Such games of love-play could easily be misconstrued as something more sinister. He didn't want her frightened. That was never his intention.

'You may pay a forfeit.' He kept the tone light to remind her his intentions were not motivated by evil.

'What?' She was all wariness. She wanted to play the game, wanted to trust him, but knew better than to do so. Damn Mortimer Oswalt and her uncle for teaching her such cynicism already. It turned his insides to think of what a month of marriage, let alone a lifetime of marriage to Oswalt, would to do her.

Paine reached out a gentle hand to stroke her cheek. 'The forfeit is simple. Have breakfast with me.' He gestured to the tray waiting on the low bedside table. 'I went to a lot of trouble to put it together. I went out for it.'

'Just breakfast?' Julia queried.

'Just breakfast.'

'I can go after breakfast?'

'If that is what you wish,' Paine answered solemnly. He meant it. He would keep his word, although he hoped it wouldn't be necessary. This would be a breakfast Julia Prentiss would not soon forget.

Julia sat cross-legged on a pile of colorful pillows in the middle of the floor, securely garbed in a satin robe Paine had generously loaned her from his wardrobe. Paine lounged next to her, propped on an elbow, and dressed only in a pair of thin silk Indian-styled trousers, having forgone the wool trousers he'd worn out to find breakfast. He peeled a section of orange and offered it up to her, creating the effect that he was a loyal squire serving his queen. Having such a handsome man staring at her in overt adoration, serving her every need, was highly intoxicating.

It was also highly hazardous. She almost believed she was a queen when he stared at her thus, almost believed a host of other things, too: that last night had been more than a discharge of a duty, a fulfilment of a contract between them; that he'd felt what she'd felt at the end; that he'd stolen her dress and conjured up the forfeit because he didn't want her to go. Most dangerous of all, that there was something real between them, that their night together didn't have to end. That was the biggest folly of all.

'I love oranges. We seldom have them in the country except at Christmas,' Julia confessed, using a finger to wipe an errant dribble of juice from her chin.

'They taste better when someone else feeds them to you.' Paine hoisted himself up to take her head in his lap. He looked down at her with a soft expression in his blue eyes that did strange things to her stomach. He could feed her worms for all she'd care when he looked at her like that—as if she was a divine goddess and he a devout worshipper. This man was far more rakish, far more seductive than any rumour had suggested. He was a consummate master at his trade.

'Is it always like this?' She arched her neck back to see all of his handsome visage staring down at her.

'No, hardly.' He held a succulent orange slice over her mouth and made a show of gently squeezing sweet drops of juice on her lips. Julia felt her breasts tighten in analogy, remembering the way he'd manipulated her nipples with soft pressure until they'd been erect with need.

'I can see why,' Julia said softly. 'If such pleasure was so readily available, I doubt anyone would get much of anything done.' She blushed at her own frankness and Paine laughed again, popping another slice of orange in her mouth.

'How is it that you are privy to such carnal knowledge?' Julia asked between bites.

'I shouldn't tell you. A master never shares his secrets,' Paine flirted. 'But I can hardly have you walking around London thinking just anyone can do this.' He dribbled juice on her lips. She flicked her tongue across her lips to gather the juice and heard him groan at the action, a low throaty groan that had nothing to do with pain and everything to do with pleasure. It was a small, thrilling piece of power to think such a simple motion could affect a man of his experience.

He offered her a slice of orange dipped in ground sugar, sliding it into her open mouth and letting her suck the juice from it. She closed her eyes and sucked hard, wholly unaware at how the sight of her savouring the rare treat with abject delight was pushing the limits of Paine's restraint. His hand clenched in her hair.

She opened her eyes and looked up at him, recognising the intensity of the need mirrored in his gaze. He wanted her. His eyes said it. His body said it. She was sharply alert to the intimacy of his lap, the thinness of the silk fabric. She had only to turn her head slightly to encounter the full dimension of his rock-hard manhood. Julia thought of the orange slice, of its slightly phallus-like shape, of sucking the juice from it. Would Paine like that? The look in his eyes suggested he would. Hesitantly, Julia turned her head. She parted her lips and mouthed him through his trousers.

Paine gave a sharp gasp at the contact. She drew back, worried the idea wasn't to his liking after all. 'Don't stop, Julia, don't stop,' he pleaded, a gentle hand urging her head back to his straining member.

Julia was giddy with power. She sucked hard until Paine made no effort to confine his satisfaction to groans, but gave full vent to his enjoyment with loud cries.

'Julia, pull it out, let me be in you.' He panted, close to his end.

Julia found the hidden slit in his trousers and pulled free the swollen member, slick with its own juices. Her hand clenched about its tip, revelling in what she had wrought. She reached over his head for the trifle box he'd used last night and rummaged quickly for a sheath.

'Now, straddle me, Julia.' Paine instructed, helping her to roll the thin sheath over his sex. 'Take me inside you and ride.'

Julia lowered herself on to him, exhaling in wonderment as she slid on him. He was so large, much larger than she'd thought last night. Yet he fit perfectly, filling up the space inside her. She began her motions and he joined her in a seamless rocking rhythm that teased her, then ultimately fulfilled her as she found the place she'd found last night, soaring in Paine's arms. He drew her down to him as he shuddered his own release, muffling his cries in her shoulder.

They lay together, their breathing slowing in unison as the initial power of climaxing ebbed. Julia wanted to stay clasped against him, warm and sated in his arms, for ever. Reality intruded. If she moved, breakfast would be over. She would have to go. But she no longer wanted to.

She wanted to stay. She wanted to feel this pleasure he'd awoken in her again and again. She didn't imagine such pleasure could be found with Oswalt. She fought a shudder. The horror of doing such intimate things with him escalated against the backdrop of what she'd shared with Paine Ramsden.

'Are you cold?' Paine reached for a throw to wrap about them, misinterpreting the reason for her shudder.

Julia searched for a way to prolong the moment, the minutes of their time together. 'You have not answered my question yet.'

'Mmm.' Paine breathed into her hair sounding like a well contented man. 'There are studies, sutras, in India that teach men and women about sexual congress. Each person has a different task, a different function in the act. There are such teachings in China as well. Remember my cabinet with the yin and yang symbol?' He shifted Julia to the side and wrapped an arm about her, warming to his subject. She waited for him to continue, her curiosity getting the better of her at the idea of such studies.

'In China, the man is the yin and the woman is the

yang. It's the man's task, through lovemaking, to make the woman give up her essence, her yang, without losing his own yin to attain it. When a woman climaxes, her essence is surrendered.'

Julia punched him in the shoulder. 'That sounds completely arrogant and not so enjoyable for the man if he can't—what did you call it? Climax?' She tried out the new word.

'That's the whole point,' Paine instructed. 'Attaining a woman's yang without climaxing yourself makes you strong and it increases your life. It's the mark of a skilled male to be able to claim such discipline. There's tales of men being able to have congress with up to fourteen women before releasing their yin.'

Julia levered up on one arm and searched his face quizzically. 'Last night, and just now, did you, uh, steal my yang, as it were?' She'd felt that he'd held back nothing, as had she. It would be a private disappointment to learn she'd been cheated in a fashion.

Paine smiled. 'No, my enchantress. I gave up as much as I took.' Paine folded his arms behind his head.

'So you've taken my virginity and I've taken your immortality,' Julia said drily.

Paine chuckled. 'I suppose so, but chances are I was mortal already. Those are old teachings. Some say they go back to the third century before Christ. Since then, the Chinese have shifted their focus. They discovered that denying women the yin denied men their heirs. Now, the sexual teachings have been adapted to be more co-operative in their outcome, much more similar to India.'

'Oh, no stealing of essences there, then?' Julia probed, utterly enthralled by such talk.

'No stealing, only giving. In Hinduism—that's the primary religion in India—sexual intercourse is seen as a metaphor for a relationship with the gods. Sex is spiritual and sacred.'

'I think I prefer the Indian way.' The words were out of her mouth before she could rethink the wisdom of them. She regretted it immediately.

Paine would think she meant something by them, something altogether much more personal than she intended their dealings to be. To cover her silliness, she sat up, letting her hair fall over her shoulders. She made no move to shove it back from her face. Its curtain obscured her face, which was just as well. She had what she came for—she was thoroughly ruined by now and fully instructed in more than she'd bargained for. Such knowledge made it hard to leave, knowing that she'd find no outlet for it in the English world.

It was past time to go and Paine Ramsden did not strike her as a man who responded well to womanly whines. Even in her naïvety, she knew he would be a hard man to hold. He did nothing for the sake of tradition and protocol. He operated by an entirely different standard of rules. The rumours about him had been right in that respect, although much else she'd heard did not ring true with what she'd experienced. She should put on her dress and be gone with all the dignity she could find.

Chapter Five

Julia crossed the room to the forgotten gown they'd
tussled over in the early morning. She hazarded a covert
glance at Paine while she slipped into her undergarments. He had levered himself up on one arm, his shirt
open, his dark hair dishevelled. The sight of such blatant,
post-coital masculinity studying her every move as she
dressed was potent. Julia felt her blood fire at the sight.

'What are you doing, Julia?' he drawled.

'Dressing.'

'I can see that. But to what purpose? I will simply
undress you again.'

'Paine, I am leaving.' A rush of anxiety filled her.
Would he let her leave? Would he renege on their agreement? 'You promised me I could go.'

'I promised you could go if you wanted to. Do you
want to?' Paine replied with apparent nonchalance.

'The world often demands we act beyond our selfish wants,' Julia parried, pulling on her stockings, recalling with clarity how they'd come to be off her legs. Would she remember that every time she pulled on stockings for the rest of her life?

'Does it, Julia? What do you hope to gain by going back that you haven't already gained?' Paine gained his feet and strode to her side, his deft hands taking over the working of the buttons at the back of her gown.

'I have to go back and tell them the betrothal is off,' Julia stammered. The heat of his hands provided a very real distraction as they skimmed her back.

'I would think that would be obvious to them by your absence.' Paine chuckled, finishing the buttons. His hands rode at her waist, easing her back against his chest so that she was fitted along his length and his arms encircled her. 'Nothing but sorrow awaits you there. For a woman who seemed to have thought everything through so thoroughly, I am surprised you haven't realised that yet. Even if you break the betrothal with your announcement, they will not let you go again. They'll punish you, pack you off to the country at best. At worst, they will cast you out without a penny or force you into marriage with an unsuspecting dolt from the country just to get you off their hands. They'll have to find a way to countenance your dishonour.'

'I know. I have resigned myself to that,' Julia said stoically, although accepting those consequences was going to be far more difficult now after Paine's education than it was in her imaginings yesterday when she'd concocted her mad scheme. 'Regardless, they'll be worried about me. I owe them the courtesy of letting them know I am well.'

'Worried about themselves is more likely,' Paine drawled with cynicism. 'Don't delude yourself. You cannot simply waltz back home and put paid to the contract.'

His scepticism fired her temper. She didn't like to be laughed at. 'How dare you speak of them like that! You don't know them at all. You've never even met them.' To her embarrassment, her lip quivered and she fought back the urge to cry in her despair.

Her aunt and uncle weren't cruel, only desperate, and, in their desperation, they'd made some poor choices. But surely they would forgive her and see reason. When Gray's ship docked, everything would be put to rights without Oswalt's money.

The thought encouraged her. She shook her head and straightened her shoulders resolutely. 'My aunt and uncle aren't ogres, Paine. They're merely misguided. Whatever they do to me, it'll be better than marriage to Oswalt. I made my choices and I'll abide by them.'

'And the choices you made for them with your actions? Will they forgive you for driving them to the poor house?' Paine queried.

'What do you mean?' She looked baffled.

'I mean, will they get by without whatever Oswalt has promised them in exchange for you?'

'How did you know about that? I didn't tell you.'

Paine shrugged. 'If Oswalt is involved, money is involved.'

Julia looked guilty. 'Money is at the root of the contract. He's promised fifteen thousand pounds to my uncle. But my cousin Gray has a ship he's invested in. The cargo will cover our debts when it arrives and my uncle won't need Oswalt's money any more.'

'Wait, Julia,' Paine spoke slowly, putting his thoughts together as he talked. 'Has Oswalt given your uncle any money yet? An advance, perhaps?'

Her answer was just as slow. 'I don't know.' But then, there was so much she hadn't known just twenty-four hours ago. 'I suppose it could be possible.' The implications hit her full force. She twisted in Paine's arms to face him, hands clutching at his shoulders. 'Oh, no, if he has there's no way my uncle could pay him back. Any funds would already have been spent.' She thought with alarm of the wardrobe for her Season, that no expense had been spared for her gowns.

How had she ever thought her uncle and aunt could have suddenly afforded such expenditures when they'd sent her begging to the butcher to delay the meat bill back home on the estate? 'Now that I think about it, I am sure funds must have been given in advance.'

Paine nodded. 'Oswalt is known for his shrewd

business dealings. If he's given someone money, there's bound to be a contract behind it, something legal done in writing to secure his investment.'

'There is a betrothal contract.' Julia looked frantically into Paine's face. What he said made sense, horrible sense. She couldn't decide which was worse: the cold reality that her actions would create a potential financial crisis for her family or that she had been bought and sold long before yesterday morning. What she'd thought was a prelude to her demise was in reality the finale. She swayed, relying on Paine's arms to keep her upright. 'Then this was all for nothing. My virginity was not a deal-breaker. He meant to have me regardless, just at a better bargain.'

'It is most likely the truth. Your uncle didn't think you'd run. Mortimer Oswalt doesn't care if you run—perhaps he even counted on the fact that you would.'

'Except he's lost his money. Granted, he's not out the whole sum but he's out a few thousand pounds,' Julia said, feeling a bit more herself now that the initial shock had passed.

Paine shook his head. Julia felt his grip about her waist tighten. 'Oswalt isn't a man who loses money with grace. He loses face with even less grace. He won't care if you run, Julia, because he'll find you. He'll count on your inexperience and lack of connections in the city, then will hunt you down and drag you back home in disgrace.'

Julia shook free of Paine's embrace and sank on to the bed. 'I have to go back and bargain with Oswalt. I have to fix this. I can't let my family suffer because of me.' She saw that Paine would protest that 'nice' people didn't sell their nieces.

'Really, they are good people. They've raised me since I was a little girl and I have repaid them with financial ruin.' She'd had her night of passion and got much more than she'd bargained for, a reward of sorts to act as a bulwark against the years to come. Perhaps for her family's sake she could stand it. In the morning light, it seemed to be the only solution in the wake of her transgressions the night before.

Her bravado received no support from Paine. Paine's eyes narrowed. 'I will not hear of it. Your solution is no solution at all. Oswalt is a lecher, but a keen student of human nature. He probably knew you'd run just as assuredly as your dolt of an uncle didn't think you would. This is just another perverse game he's invented for the entertainment of his sick mind. There's no disgrace in eluding him. Oswalt has probably engineered all this like a puppet show, knowing that eventually your sense of honour will bring you back, begging on your knees, and in the meanwhile, he can financially blackmail your uncle.'

Despair rocketed through her. There had never been a chance for her to win. She was playing a game that was far deeper than her abilities, a game that had been well under way, if Paine was to be believed, long before she'd joined it. She prided herself on her sharp mind, but she could not divine the layers laid out by Oswalt. She had no experience when it came to understanding the thought processes of the depraved.

What would she do now? She took quick stock of the inventory at her disposal. She still had a small opportunity and her earbobs. By now, Oswalt and her uncle knew she was gone, but they didn't know where. It was unlikely even Oswalt would deduce she'd gone out seeking someone to ruin her. They would think she'd act like a girl fresh from the country—perhaps seek a way back home or take refuge with girlfriends. They would check the houses of her acquaintances and the posting inns. That would keep them busy. But for how long? Long enough to catch a ship? They would check the docks next when the posting inns turned up empty, but maybe she could beat them.

Julia raised her head and drew a deep breath. She could not save her uncle; perhaps she never could have, even with her marriage. But she could save herself and pray that Gray's ship returned safely for the family's sake.

Her decision made, she could not impose on Paine Ramsden any longer. That was a shame. He seemed to know quite a bit about her betrothed and he made her feel unaccountably safe. 'If I could ask for one last favour, I would ask that you take me to the docks so that

I may find passage on a ship. I have some money and I have my earbobs. I am certain it would be enough to get me a berth of some sort.'

God, the girl had courage. The news he'd imparted to her was dire, but here she was, already rebounding from it and planning her escape. The chivalrous fires she'd stoked in him last night roared to life at her suggestion. There was no way he would deliver her to the docks and leave her to set sail alone. There was no telling what kind of harm could befall a girl of such beauty, travelling without a chaperone on the high seas. No crew he'd ever sailed with would have let her go untouched. It was no credit to the scurrilous company he'd kept over the years, but the truth all the same.

Paine shook his head. 'Where would you go?'

'Anywhere. Whatever ship leaves first is the one I want. I haven't much time. They'll check the houses of my friends and the posting inns first. But they'll check the docks next.' Paine heard the frantic undertones in her voice. Courageous, but still frightened, then.

She took his reticence for refusal. 'I will go on my own if you will not assist me. It is not your responsibility anyway. You've done what I asked of you and that is the end of our association.' Julia rose from the bed, head held high and stuck out her hand. 'I thank you.'

Paine fairly exploded. Courageous, frightened *and* stubborn. The list of adjectives that described Julia

Prentiss was growing rapidly. 'That's ridiculous, Julia. Sit down, you're going nowhere. When you do, it will be with me. You cannot face Mortimer Oswalt alone and you can't go wandering around out there on your own, resourceful as you are.'

He began pacing away his agitation, gratified to see that Julia obeyed. He'd fully expected she wouldn't. It was good to know she could do as she was told. She would need that skill in the days to come if they were to effectively deal with Mortimer Oswalt.

'They.' 'We.' His conscience warned him he was running headlong into all kinds of foolishness on behalf of Julia Prentiss, whom he had known less than a day; the foolishness of entangling with Oswalt again, and another kind of foolishness he couldn't name yet, but had everything to do with why the ancient Chinese warned against a man surrendering his yin.

Julia was peering at him through her thoughtful jade eyes; a cool calculation crept into them, assessing him. 'Why?' she said.

'Why what?' Paine stopped his pacing.

'It has suddenly occurred to me that I know very little about you. *Why* should I trust you? Who's to say that you aren't just as sly or as debauched as he is?'

'You trusted me enough last night,' Paine shot back, angry that she had the gall to categorise him with the likes of Oswalt, although he knew she didn't know better—couldn't know better.

Julia skewered with him a stare, refusing to back down from her inquiry. 'Last night was about a temporary arrangement. It seems the stakes have changed a bit since then. Last night I didn't need to know. Today I do.'

Good lord, the woman was exasperating. Now was the time for plans, not for some parlour game of twenty questions. Paine sighed. Conceding this small victory seemed the quickest way to overcome the obstacle of her obstinacy and move forwards. 'All right, what do you want to know?'

'Only two things. Really, you'd think I was the Spanish Inquisition.' Julia gave a sigh of her own. 'First, let me ask my question again. Why should I trust you? Second, how is it that you know so much about my betrothed when you've only been back in England for less than a year?'

The questions brought Paine's hand to a halt, frozen in his hair where he'd been riffling through it. How had a simple bedding turned into something so complicated? He gave her the only answer he was prepared to give. 'You have two questions and I'll give you one answer that suffices for them both. Mortimer Oswalt is the reason for my exile.'

Julia looked ready to ask a thousand questions. He shot her a sharp glance that suggested she reconsider that angle of conversation. The answer he had given her was by no means a complete one, but it was the truth and it was all he was going to say on the matter.

He watched Julia draw a deep breath, her eyes never leaving his as her mind sifted through his latest revelation, weighing the facts he'd presented like a judge hearing a trial. And he did feel quite like a defendant, waiting to hear the sentence.

He tried to tell himself the verdict didn't matter to him. If she chose to leave, he'd be better off, able to return to his daily routine. If she stayed, upheaval was guaranteed. There would be a past to revisit and old wounds to reopen. Still, he could hear his own breath exhale with relief when Julia said in her firm, resolute tone, 'All right, all things considered, it seems best that I stay for now. But let's get one thing clear, Paine Ramsden, I will not be the subordinate in this. It's my fate and I will have a say in it.'

'Absolutely.' Paine knew that was a promise he couldn't keep the moment the words were out of his mouth, but he would have agreed to anything just to keep her safe. One woman had already fallen to Oswalt's evil wiles because of his failure. He'd make damn sure another one didn't suffer the same consequences.

Late that afternoon, Paine concluded Fate couldn't have sent a more obvious sign than Julia Prentiss than if that wily muse had sent him a letter. It was time to take back his life. The moment he'd decided to return to England, he'd known the day would come. Now it was here. It was time to finish his business with Oswalt and reclaim his place in society.

Not far from where he sat behind the wide, scarred cherrywood desk in the room he'd appointed as his makeshift office, Julia dozed on a clean but old sofa, a book haphazardly in her lap, still open to the page she'd been reading before nodding off. No doubt the activities of the last twenty-four hours were catching up with her. She slept like someone who knew she was safe. Her breathing was deep and even. She slept, knowing she would not be disturbed or rudely awakened by an unpleasant surprise. He envied her. It had been ages since he'd been able to sleep like that.

Paine pushed back from the desk, putting aside the pile of letters he'd been going through and propped his feet up on the desk's surface. Most of it was business correspondence. The grande dames of London had ceased issuing him invitations to their social events months ago. The only invitations he received were through his aunt's connections. London society had as much use for him as he did for it—very little. Until last night, it had been an amicable arrangement. That would have to change.

He couldn't protect Julia and effectively deal with Oswalt without the *ton*'s support. That had been his mistake last time. He'd been rash and overbold. Even though there had been those who had applauded his efforts, he'd done it in such a way and over such a thing that no one could openly champion his interference. He had not understood then that there were boundaries to what people would acknowledge, no matter the motivations.

He would be more careful this time, laying his foundations, establishing his credibility, before going after Oswalt. Paine recognised this was about himself as much as it was about Julia. Oswalt had once attempted to ruin him altogether for his sense of misguided honour. It was time to pay him back.

Julia stirred on the sofa, shifting her position in her sleep. She would have to be careful, too. She'd have to agree to stay in the house and go out only with him until they were ready to draw out Oswalt. It wouldn't do for Oswalt to learn of her location until Paine was ready. Oswalt and her uncle had an agreement for her marriage that could not be overlooked or minimised, no matter what the status of her maidenhead.

It made Paine's blood boil to think of Oswalt laying any kind of claim, even a paper one, to the beauty sleeping on his sofa. Oswalt was more than a debauched old man. He also experimented deeply in darker sexual practices that went far beyond the sacred joys Paine had initiated Julia into.

Twelve years ago, Oswalt had been an anxious man looking for a cure, any cure, for what ailed him. Paine could only make conjectures about how ravaged the man was now and how much more desperate he'd become for that cure. What the man had been willing to engage in twelve years ago had thoroughly shocked Paine at a time when he thought he was an unshakable, jaded youth. Paine could not bear to envision what the man would be willing to do as his desperation grew exponentially over the years.

Julia had to be protected at all costs.

The force of that realisation was jarring. He had not felt the need to safeguard anyone to that extent for years, maybe not ever, certainly not a woman. But for whatever unexamined reasons, Julia brought out the need in abundance.

In his years abroad, he'd become a businessman, keen at assessing risk and profit. He seldom started a venture without an eye for how it would end. With Julia, it was different. The wealth of risk was there, as it was in any venture, but the profit was veiled at present. Still, with an intuition born of experience, Paine knew he had to see this through to whatever conclusion lay ahead. It wasn't enough that the passionate, curious, Miss Prentiss had to be protected. If it was, he could fob her off on people more sociably suitable than himself. He could probably talk his Aunt Lily into taking her. No, Julia had to be protected by him. For that to happen, he had to make himself respectable again. There were two ways to respectability: money and connections. Paine had both if he chose to use them.

Paine lowered his feet and got back to work. The first

was easy. He had a shipping fortune at his disposal. From the stack of letters on his desk, there were many people in need of funds who cared far less where the money originated.

Many of the letters were from highly placed men appealing for a private loan to tide over ageing estates and emptying coffers. That would help with the second requirement for respectability—connections.

Those connections might take more time than he had and Paine had a better card to play, if he dared. His brother was the Earl of Dursley. They had been close once. His scandal with Oswalt had put a rift in that relationship, but perhaps it could be redeemed. He'd been disappointed that his brother, Peyton, had not written to him since his return. He'd loved his two brothers dearly. It looked like he would have to make the first move in that regard. Paine picked up his pen and began to write. The first letter was a long-overdue missive to his brother. The second was a terse note to one of his most trusted employees, Brian Flaherty, who was charged with the mission of seeking out news of Mortimer Oswalt and whether or not the man was hunting down his errant betrothed.

'Damn it, that's the fourth one.' Paine gave his cravat a hard tug and gave up. He'd tried for twenty minutes to fashion a *trône d'amour* knot. He was supposed to be at the hell by eight. At this rate, he wouldn't make it until midnight and all he had to show for his delay was an ignominious heap of crumpled lengths of once-pristine linen on the bed.

'Here, let me try.' Julia rose from the low bed where she sat watching him go through his *toilette*. She was dressed in his robe, fresh from a lazy bath, her hair still up in pins. She drew another length of fabric from the drawer and draped it around his neck. Standing in such proximity, he could inhale the delicate scent of her. Tonight, she smelled divinely of English lavender. If serenity and softness had a scent, this would be it. Somehow, the smell suited her to perfection.

She reached up to straighten the linen length and the overlarge robe gaped, affording him an unadulterated glimpse of her breasts. Blood heated in his groin instantly. After all their love play this morning and the night prior, he thought he'd be at least momentarily sated, that his body wouldn't be capable of rousing again so thoroughly or so soon. Evidence to the contrary made an auspicious tent in his dark trousers. Apparently he was wrong.

Intent on carrying out the intricacies of the knot, Julia was oblivious to his new state. Beyond a terse 'Keep your chin up', the linen held all her concentration. 'Make a single knot, place one end of the fabric over the knot to hide it, spread the remainder out and turn down into the waistcoat.' She bit her lower lip adorably while she muttered the 'recipe' for his knot, competent hands deftly shaping the fabric and smoothing it beneath the claret silk of his waistcoat.

'There.' Julia said with satisfaction, stepping back to survey her work. 'Much better.'

Paine peered into the looking glass above the cabinet holding his personal accessories. 'This is not the *trône d'amour*.'

'No. That was half your problem.' Julia flounced smugly on to the bed, a smile twitching at her lips, unaware how the robe strategically gaped. 'Your cravats aren't nearly starched enough for that knot and rightly so. Minimal starch in the cravats is all the rage these days.'

'How do you know so much about men's fashion?' Paine cocked his head to study the innocently provocative woman on the bed. She could rouse him without effort as the simple act of tying his cravat had proved.

'Three male cousins, two of whom fancy themselves to be pinks of the *ton*.' Julia gave him a wide smile. 'You need a valet.'

'I have a valet.' It was embarrassing to admit how heavily he'd come to rely on his valet, Jacobs, in the year he'd been home. During his sojourn abroad he'd managed to dress quite well on his own. But it had been out of the question to send for Jacobs with Julia present. He'd sent a note earlier in the day to Jacobs at his Jermyn Street rooms, telling the valet to stay away.

The fewer people who knew about her being here, the better. Until he could ascertain the current level of gossip surrounding her disappearance, it would be best to keep her hidden. That was why he felt it was so imperative he spent the evening at the club. The way Julia was looking at him right now though, he wondered if she'd ever let him leave.

She rose up on her knees on the bed, her eyes dancing with light mischief. 'I said the cravat starch was *half* of your problem. Do you want to know the other half?'

'Absolutely,' Paine sensed a game afoot and stepped towards her in anticipation of her gambit. In China, girls learned the art of seduction from pillow books, but Julia had unerring instincts that couldn't be taught when it came to arousing a man. 'There's an ancient Chinese proverb that says "learning is a treasure that follows its owner everywhere". He encouraged in husky tones, 'I think you'll find me an excellent student.'

'Then I feel compelled to tell you that the other half of your problem was your trousers. They were *and* are too tight.'

She said it with such straightforwardness that Paine did not immediately understand until her hand reached for him, cupping him through his trousers. He gasped, the friction of the cloth against his member creating an exquisite set of sensations that made him simultaneously want to end and prolong the moment.

There was nothing for it. He'd be of no use at the club walking around in this frustrated state all night. The club's legitimate owner would have to make do without him tonight, at least for a while.

'Take my trousers off, Julia.' He managed a hoarse whisper and, in terms of words, that was all he managed for a good long while.

Chapter Six

By midnight, Paine realised he wasn't going to the club. It wasn't too late to go. Indeed, midnight was considered early among those who frequented the hells. The real action and serious gambling would just be getting under way this time of night. If he went, he could still hear all the news about town. The truth was, he didn't *want* to go. The thought of leaving Julia and the warm bed for the dingy hell was vastly unappealing. For the first time in a year, he had somewhere else he wanted to be.

Julia stirred in his arms, her naked form pressed against him in reminder that he did not make it a regular practice to hold sleeping women at length after the act. 'Tell me about yourself,' Julia murmured, obviously unaware that that type of question after lovemaking was far too smothering. Countless times that question served to be a conversation ender, not starter, with him.

But miracles seemed to be in endless supply that evening. Not only did he not want to go to the gambling hell, he actually wanted to talk. Paine absently stroked a length of her hair. 'What do you want to know?'

'I want to know why you choose to flaunt convention, why you run a low-level gambling hell when you could move among high society, I want to know….'

'Whoa, one question at a time!' Paine protested, but only in jest. He found he didn't mind her curiosity. She was quite astute to pick up on the little contradictions of his world.

'The *ton* likes to ignore my money because it comes from a shipping business I ran for ten years in Calcutta. You and I know both know how working for money is frowned upon. But such narrow-mindedness works out because, as it happens, I like to ignore them.' Paine gave a little laugh, smiling in the dark. 'What about you, Julia? Do you like the *ton*nish world?'

'I haven't had much experience with it,' she admitted with a sigh. 'I should like to try a taste of it, though, just for fun, without the pressures of the Marriage Mart.' She spun him an innocent fantasy of waltzing in a fine ballroom with a dashing hero of a man, drinking champagne and wearing a beautiful gown. 'You must think me a foolish girl for thinking such things. I try to be practical, but every once in a while it's nice not to be.'

Paine chuckled and tightened his grip about her

shoulders. 'Not at all, my dear. It's perfectly fine to have dreams.' It was a girlish fantasy, but he found he wanted to give it to her, hero, gown, waltz and all.

'Enough about me, Paine. This was supposed to be about you. Was shipping one of your dreams? Is that why you were in India?'

The vixen was clever. She'd noticed the shift in conversation and had redirected it back to the original topic. Her comment also reminded him just what an ingénue Julia was. She hadn't been in town long enough to hear all the sordid details of his exile, only the more romantic rumours of his exile. She was young and untouched in so many ways. His thirty-two years seemed eons from her innocent nineteen.

Paine shifted his position for more comfort, rising up on an elbow so he could look at her while he spoke. 'I suppose you could say that. Shipping was a necessary dream. I am the third of three sons. You know *that* story—eldest gets the title, second son gets the military commission, third son gets the church or whatever else he can muster up. Well, it was obvious at a young age that I would never suit the calling of a church—something to do with getting caught with a village blacksmith's daughter when I was twelve.'

'No!' Julia gasped in mock surprise.

'Your lack of faith in me is touching. I must add in my own defence that there was some hope I might become a missionary. I did love to travel. I spent most of my school days poring over atlases and studying geography.' Paine drew down the bed sheet covering Julia and traced a delicate circle around the aureole of a breast. 'I think if my tutors had impressed upon me that more of the world went topless than naught, I might have gone the missionary route,' he said in seductive tones.

'You would have been a horrible missionary.' Julia laughed.

'Or a very persuasive one,' Paine whispered, tracing a ticklish line to her stomach. 'Have you ever read the Song of Solomon?'

Julia batted at his hand. 'Stop it. You're getting off track again. So you went to India and became a shipper?'

'Hmm.' He was losing interest in the story. Julia's body was far more entertaining. He could not recall the last time he was so captivated. 'In short, I ran an export business for ten years. I travelled the breadth and depths of India in search of rarities. I even went to China once. I would have gone to Burma if the war in 1824 hadn't closed down the borders. I sold the business, though, when I came back, and banked the profit.'

'What made you decide to come back?'

'I don't know. It just seemed like it was time. I realised that if I could build a business and thrive on my own, I could certainly handle any repercussions, if any, from the duel with Oswalt. Usually, the police are too busy with real crimes to worry about cases of the Quality fussing over honour.'

Julia opened her mouth to ask another question, but Paine silenced her with a finger to her lips. 'That's enough questions about me, my sweet. The less you know about me, the better.' At some point, part of him feared Julia would realise the kind of life he'd have led to acquire the knowledge he had and then she'd be completely appalled by the man she'd associated with. 'I have a better idea. We can play forfeits. We can each ask a question and the other can decide if they wish to answer the question or pay a forfeit to forgo the question,' Paine suggested. 'I'll go first since you've have your questions already. How did you come to live with your aunt and uncle?' It was admittedly a highly personal question, but Paine found he wanted to know everything about her and not because he was risking so much for someone he knew so little about. He wanted to know everything about the delectable Julia Prentiss.

'That's an easy question, so I'll answer it,' Julia said, rolling on to her back. 'My parents were killed when I was small in a freak boating accident. I've been with my father's family since I was five.' She looked over at him, her gaze intense and demanding of his attention. 'You don't know them. They're very good, very simple people. Whatever they've done, or whatever comes out of this mess with Oswalt, I want you to know that. What my uncle is attempting to do with Oswalt is appalling, but he's not a practical man. The world does not always deal fairly with philosophical men like him who love their theories and ideologies more than the realities of the day.'

'You don't have to defend them, Julia. They've certainly not defended you,' Paine shot back, unnerved that, even at this late date, Julia's goodness would try to countenance such inexplicable behaviour.

'Now it's my turn,' Julia said, setting aside the brewing quarrel regarding the culpability of her uncle. 'How many women have you been with?'

Paine groaned. 'What kind of question is that?'

Julia gave an insouciant shrug. 'My question. Are you refusing to answer?'

'Absolutely—a gentleman never brags of his conquests.' Paine put on a great show of gentlemanly affront.

Julia scooted towards him, a hand caressing his chest. 'You will pay the forfeit? Anything at all that I want?'

'That was the rule,' Paine drawled, his curiosity piqued at wondering what the inquisitive Julia would demand.

'Very well.' She put on a show of thinking, then said at last, 'Teach me the sutras.'

The request stunned him. 'Why ever would you want to learn that?'

'Why should you be the only one who knows the secrets of pleasure?' Julia challenged, smiling.

The minx thought she'd got the better of him and maybe she had, but not in the way she most likely thought. He guessed she'd meant to shock him. But the shock was the idea of Julia using such techniques with another man besides him at some point in a far-off future. 'These are intimate skills, Julia,' Paine warned. 'The sutras are about more than studies of sexual congress. They're about managing marriage and love quarrels as much as they are about the physicality of lovemaking.'

Even as he recited the admonitions his own teachers had given him, he knew Julia would heed them as much, or as little, as he had. In the beginning of his education, he'd seen them only from the English perspective of positions and sexual prowess. It had been much later before he'd begun to see them in the Hindu way, in the sacred way of being an exalted religious expression of oneness—the whole point of life.

'You agreed to a forfeit. Are you reneging?' Julia pressed.

'All right, I'll tell you about Kama.' Paine relented. Kama could be used by anyone for establishing peace of mind, it needn't be only sexual in orientation, although it was hard to remember that with Julia snuggling against him in expectation.

'Kama is the experience of enjoyment through utilising all five of the senses,' Paine said in a low voice.

'Ah, like the oranges this morning,' Julia said.

Paine chuckled softly, pulling her closer to him. 'Yes. Intercourse should be an experience of sights, sounds, scents and touches. A good lover sets the scene, from his own grooming to the place where he intends to be with his partner. A good lover is concerned about trust on all levels. Without trust, sex cannot attain its sacred plain.'

'Your sheaths,' Julia put in quietly, lying content in his arms, happy to listen to him carry out his forfeit. 'They're about trust.'

'It is a lover's duty to ensure a fulfilling sexual experience. If either partner is worried about the after-effects of their liaison, then the experience is minimised,' Paine said simply. These lessons had become so ingrained in him that he couldn't remember thinking otherwise. But hearing himself speak these lessons out loud reminded him how foreign these practices might be to someone else and a thought occurred to him.

'If you hadn't found me, Julia, where would you have gone?'

'I'd thought of a brothel,' Julia said sleepily. 'I am glad I found you, though.'

'Me, too,' Paine whispered as he felt her drift off into a contented sleep. And in truth he was. He'd had relationships with many women, most of them far more experienced than Julia. With them, no matter how short their acquaintance, he tried to obey the teachings of the sutras. He would not wish any of them subjected to the rigours of Oswalt's perverse demands.

It was a long while before he joined her in sleep, his mind racing about next steps. What would Oswalt be doing? Where would he be looking? What would the man do once it was clear Julia had disappeared from the usual avenues?

'Are you complete idiots? How can one innocent bit of muslin, who has never been up to town and has no friends here to speak of, give every last one of you the slip?' Oswalt bellowed to the panel of henchmen sitting in his offices on the London docks.

He jabbed a rough hand at one of the men. 'You, tell me again everywhere you looked.'

The big man named Sam Brown began his recitation one more time. Oswalt leaned back in his chair, hands intertwined over his belly. He did nothing to disguise the fact that he was furious. The girl was gone, completely vanished. How the hell had his crafty plan gone so drastically awry after having gone so smoothly?

He'd expected she would run. She'd shown far too much spirit to mildly abide by her uncle's wishes. He'd seen it from the start and he'd counted on it. She would run. He would drag her home in disgrace and make an agreement with her uncle to marry the disreputable piece of baggage before a scandal could erupt. All this benevolence in exchange for returning already advanced funds—funds he knew Lockhart couldn't repay. Then he would spring the trap that would net him Lockhart's ship in repayment of the loan. The cargo from the Americas was valuable, but that wasn't the reason he wanted it.

It was the first stage in the ruination of the poor, un-suspecting viscount. The second stage would follow in quick succession. Once bankrupt, the viscount would be stripped of everything but his title. The crown couldn't take the entailed estate, but anything else that wasn't nailed down was vulnerable to the creditors in payment. It wouldn't be long before the already pinched viscount would be stripped of anything of value. His estate would be worthless. That's where he came in. Oswalt would be waiting to redeem the estate of his beloved bride's family with his wealth. Oh, yes, he'd be waiting with his new bride, the viscount's luscious niece, in tow. Marriage to Julia would ensure he'd get the estate and look bloody honourable doing it. Julia's marriage to him would allow the Lockhart lands to stay 'in the family'. Such a noble act on behalf of a peer of the realm and years of economic servitude for the crown would surely help him clinch his long-coveted knight-hood. The king couldn't overlook such generous favours.

Certainly, he could still move forwards with some pressure to retrieve the funds from Lockhart, but without the girl, he'd look like the opportunist he was. The girl made him look noble.

Oswalt cracked his knuckles with relish. He felt

better thinking of the elaborate plot he'd concocted. The plan had been meticulously laid out. He had no feud with the viscount; the man was simply vulnerable, a veritable chicken waiting for plucking. It was hardly Oswalt's fault the man was in debt up to his eyeballs and, while sharp at the ideologies of politics, less astute when it came to personal economics.

The man would have made a good professor of philosophy, but Lockhart was out of his depth here. Oswalt knew. He'd hunted this sort of prey among the nobility before. It served those peacocks right for treating him with disdain all these years just because his money was earned instead of inherited. If Lockhart wasn't careful, he just might find himself bereft of his three sons and looking to Oswalt and Julia's children as legitimate heirs to the title.

'Where do you suggest we look next, boss?' The big man's question interrupted Oswalt's daydreaming.

'Try the ships. She might think to flee to the Continent.' Oswalt edged a piece of dirt out from under a shabby nail with another equally ragged nail. 'Try the gambling hells, too.' If she'd been foolish enough to go to ground in the darker sections of London, perhaps the gambling hells had word of it.

He hadn't sent men to those places earlier because it seemed unlikely Miss Prentiss would find shelter there. According to his logic, she would have been more likely to seek out her one friend, Elise Farraday, or attempt to go back to the country. But since Elise had told the viscount she'd not seen her friend and the posting inns reported no one who matched Miss Prentiss in description or situation, he was forced to expand his search.

He was also forced to consider the risk that if his intended had tried to lose herself in the slums of London, she might have also lost her virginity. He grimaced at the prospect. 'Try the taverns and whore-houses; maybe she fell into trouble,' he added as an afterthought. The idea brought a leer to his dry lips. If he didn't need a virgin so badly, it would serve the beautiful Julia Prentiss right to be subjected to such embarrassment after shunning him so overtly in front of her uncle.

Once he had her back, he'd teach her how to be humble. His groin stirred at the thought, numerous images passing through his mind. He dismissed his men with bags of gold for bribes and drinks and spent the rest of the afternoon lasciviously contemplating all the different ways he'd instruct the errant Julia Prentiss in the art of humility.

Chapter Seven

'What do you think, monsieur? *La fille est très belle, n'est-ce pas?*' the petite French dressmaker trilled for the countless time that afternoon.

Julia grimaced at the sound of the woman's ingratiating, high-pitched voice. For the past three hours, she'd been reduced to the role of a doll, standing at attention, draped in fabrics and pins in the middle of Paine's spare bedroom. The woman had immediately recognised Paine as her benefactor and had ceased asking for anyone's opinion but his. Indeed, Paine had been in charge all day, a fact that was growing increasingly annoying.

They'd slept late and, after breakfast, Paine had decided it was time to remedy the deplorable condition of her wardrobe. Actually, there was no 'condition' to remedy since she technically had no wardrobe beyond the robe of Paine's she'd worn for the better part of two days.

Two days! Those days seemed to have flown by, melding into each other, and yet two days hardly seemed enough time to countenance all that had passed between her and Paine. She felt she'd known him for far longer than the space of a few days. She twitched and the dressmaker reprimanded her.

Julia rolled her eyes and appealed to Paine. 'How much longer will this take?'

Paine ignored her. *'Non, le rose, madame.'* He gave a dismissing wave to the length of soft green muslin Madame held up to Julia's hair and gestured to a rose-coloured swatch instead.

'Ah! Très bien, monsieur!' the woman exclaimed. 'You have an excellent eye for women's clothing.'

Julia fought the urge to childishly stomp her foot. With all the aplomb she could collect, she said, 'I think we have enough for today.' She tossed her head and stepped down from the impromptu dais of a large square ottoman.

The woman gasped. She appealed to Paine. *'Monsieur*, we are not finished.'

Julia thought for a moment Paine would call her back, but he merely laughed, spearing her with a gaze that held myriad messages.

Julia waited for Paine in the sanctuary of his extraordinary bedroom. This gold-and-crimson room had become her refuge. It was shocking to think of how little she'd been out of this room in the past two days, how little desire she had to leave this room.

But the dressmaker's visit was a sharp reminder that she had to do more about her situation than sit in Paine Ramsden's bedroom. The dressmaker was also a reminder that she'd uncharacteristically let someone else take the reins. Since she'd landed in Paine's arms, he'd decided everything, from the course of action to be taken with Oswalt to the very colour and type of dress she'd wear. Was it really a good idea to let a virtual stranger plan her future? Aside from the pleasure he gave her, what did she know about him?

In some ways, Paine Ramsden was more than a stranger. Not even the rumours she'd heard about him had been accurate, so she didn't have gossip to fall back on. Paine Ramsden was a conundrum; for starters, it seemed unlikely that a purported gambler would bother buying property and devote the time needed to turn it into a business venture. Such effort spoke of long-term commitments, something she didn't associate with gamblers who didn't look further than the turn of a card or the throw of the dice.

Further confusion arose from his foreign but noble outlook on intimate relations—an outlook that permitted copious amounts of sex, but with a strong sense of ethics that was currently lacking among members of the English *ton*.

The concept was intensely juxtaposed to that of the hypocritical *ton*, making it impossible for the English mind, steeped in virginal traditions, to countenance.

Julia doubted the rakes peopling the *ton* had the scruples to which Paine ascribed.

At the core of her conundrum was the reality she'd personally encountered in Paine. She'd deliberately gone looking for a man who wouldn't take an interest in her affairs after the initial act was done. Instead, she'd found a man who had his own reasons to stay interwoven in the current events of her life. In a city of thousands, she'd managed to find the one man who wanted revenge on Oswalt.

Julia did not fool herself into thinking that Paine allowed her to stay out of any romantic attachment. He let her stay because she could assist in his retaliation. She was useful to him for that reason alone.

The rest of it—the love play, the instruction in intimate arts—meant nothing particular to him. He was a man used to a different code of conduct, a different code of honour. The English gentleman's code of honour abhorred the deflowering of virgins. Apparently, Paine's foreign codes didn't abhor the deflowering so much as it abhorred a poor bedding.

It would be too easy to misunderstand his intentions, to view his actions through English eyes. She must be careful to remember how Paine saw the world or else she'd start entertaining impossible notions about a future with Paine Ramsden—a man who would be easier to love than he would be to forget.

She *would* have to forget him. Eventually, this gambit

would end in some fashion and she'd have to move on. Paine Ramsden certainly would. He'd go back to his cryptic lifestyle, his exotically conducted affairs and forget about the viscount's niece who had begged him to deflower her. The vision was a difficult one to stomach.

Downstairs, a door shut at the back of the house, signalling the dressmaker's departure. Within moments, Paine's footfalls sounded on the steps and shortly afterwards the bedroom door opened.

'Julia, love, you have the patience of a flea!' he proclaimed in high spirits. 'That is Madame Broussard, the finest dressmaker in the city by many accounts. One does not order her about like a common servant. She might leave pins in your gowns.'

Paine came to sit beside her, pulling the tails of his shirt out of his trousers' waistband. 'But you were right. That was enough for the day. I didn't think I could stand another minute of looking at your delectable body clad in nothing more than a shift. I thought my trousers would burst.' He tugged on her hands. 'Come, relieve me, Julia. I'll show you "the splitting of the bamboo". You'll like it.'

He looked boyish and carefree; it took an enormous amount of will power to resist. 'Wait, Paine.' Julia shook her head. 'We need to talk. It's been two days and I'm no closer to knowing what my future holds than I was the night I walked into your club.'

Paine shrugged and lay back on the pillows, hands behind his head. 'Go ahead, then, talk,' he offered expansively.

'What's the meaning of all this?' Julia began. 'What's the purpose of all the gowns? Why am I staying here? What's to become of me? This is not what I had planned at all.' She could hear the frustration rising in her voice and resented it. The last thing she wanted to do was sound like a hysterical girl.

Paine tried for humour. 'Well, I will want my robe back at some point in the future.'

'Not funny. Really, tell me, what am I doing here?'

Paine sat up. 'You are staying safe until I have all my pieces in place, Julia. Oswalt is dangerous. We cannot rush out and challenge him. He's too smart for that. I have asked my investigators to make inquiries about Oswalt's business. We need to know what he is up to and plan accordingly. I've asked for inquiries about your uncle, too. I know you say he's an honest fellow, but I am a bit more cynical.'

'Inquiries! I did not give you leave to pry into my family's private matters,' Julia protested, further exclamations silenced by the soft press of his finger against her lips.

'As for the dresses,' Paine went on, overriding her dismay, 'we'll need the backing of the *ton*, some of them at least, for what I have planned. I mean to reclaim my good standing.'

'Good lord, that could take years!' Julia cried without thinking.

Paine chuckled. 'Again, your trust in me is overwhelming, my dear. I think you'll see it will only take a matter of weeks.'

'And you'll be wearing the dresses while you reclaim this good standing?' Julia probed wryly, not following his logic in its entirety.

'You'll be by my side, Julia. You're the key to my reform. The influence of a good woman's love is a powerful source of conversion.'

'I haven't converted you,' Julia said carefully. A man who knew such colourful expressions and methods for lovemaking like 'splitting the bamboo' was in no way reformed. 'When did you decide on this story?' Here was yet another example of Paine Ramsden's managing ways.

'Yesterday afternoon when I was taking care of some correspondence, I started thinking about it. Today, somewhere between the blue silk and the green muslin, it all seemed to come together. The *ton* will like the story, it's a fairy tale come to life and it will make a good explanation for how I turned up with you.'

Paine's eyes glinted with the excitement of the drama. 'We'll tell everyone it was love at first sight. When I saw you, I knew my erring days were over. It's a plausible reason for being together and it will give me a valid excuse to keep you close. Once Oswalt learns that you're with me, the game will be fully engaged.

He'll stop at nothing to have you back. We just have to draw him out into the open and expose him for what he is.'

Julia recognised the plan wasn't quite that simple. They needed the *ton* to accept them, or rather to accept Paine, so that there would be support for exposing the issues with Oswalt. That support would be needed to bring Oswalt down. Apathy could be a powerful non-weapon. If no one cared enough to buy into their cause, the status quo would remain the norm. That norm would see her wed to Oswalt, the contract with her uncle upheld. For Julia, that outcome was unacceptable.

'And until then?' Julia asked, moving back towards the bed.

'Until then, all we have to do is pretend we're in love.' His eyes were mesmerising in their persuasion. Who could resist those blue eyes, dark with desire? 'Are you ready to split the bamboo?' he whispered, nipping at her neck with soft kisses.

'I see this has nothing to do with trees,' Julia managed to flirt between kisses.

'No, not trees, love, but it has everything to do with your deliciously long legs.' Paine moved and knelt before her on the bed, running a hand down the length of one leg and gently lifted it over his shoulder. 'Make your legs into a raised V for me, Julia. We'll start with the "yawning position" and take our "bamboo" from there.' He leaned forwards to kiss her mouth. 'And no quips about the "yawn" being boring. I assure you it is not. In fact, it's quite exciting.'

'Why?' Julia murmured.

'You'll find out,' Paine offered in cryptic reassurance.

After that, she had no more thought for questions. Julia gave herself over to Paine's exotic instructions. In the wake of his persistence and passion, Julia found it wasn't hard to convince herself his plan made sense. Neither was it hard to do her part and pretend she was in love with him. As he knelt before her and showed her how to alternately raise her legs to his shoulders, thus 'splitting the bamboo', she suspected she was already half way there.

There was no question of Julia going to the gaming hell with him, although it was the devil convincing her of that. He might have been able to take one night away from the club, but he could not afford to be absent another night. Not only would it deprive him of valuable information, but his absence was sure to be noticed. Julia had finally consented to be left behind on the condition that he bring her back a wig.

Thinking of her saucy demand as he left brought a smile to his lips even now. Bringing Julia with him had a certain appeal. He might even teach her a few of the club games. Just the thought of Julia's bosom leaning over the dicing table stirred him and he'd only been gone from her an hour. Paine set the tantalising image aside. Tonight, he had work to do, work that mattered to him and to Julia.

John, the doorman, was waiting for him when Paine arrived at the club shortly after eight-thirty. 'We all missed you last night.' He gave a short nod to the group of dandies led by Gaylord Beaton, talking too loudly in the corner. 'They want to play faro with you. The bunch of them came in last night.'

Paine nodded, sizing up the rowdy group. He'd bet they would be in more sombre spirits by midnight. He'd hoped the earlier loss at Commerce would have taught Beaton a lesson about playing beyond one's means. Apparently not. 'Anything else?'

'The gel that came looking for you has a man looking for her.' John lowered his voice. 'That man over there has been asking about her. She matches the description he's been giving, anyway.'

Paine's eyes narrowed, taking in the burly, unkempt man by the wall, slumped over a glass of cheap brandy. 'What did you tell him?'

John shook his head. 'Nothing. I didn't like the looks or smell of him. The gel doesn't fit with him, so I thought the worst.'

'You're right about that. The girl's from a good family. Until I instruct anyone otherwise, we've never seen her. Make that clear to everyone—the dealers, the bartender, the other girls.' Paine bounced on the balls of his feet, organising the evening's business in his mind.

'John, send a bottle of our best brandy to the dandies with my compliments. I'll join them for faro at ten. I'll be in my office settling accounts until then. When Brian Flaherty comes in, I want to see him directly.'

Flaherty was a stocky Irishman with a balding pate and good humour in spite of his dark career as a private investigator. In the past year, Paine had come to trust the Irishman implicitly when it came to the business of the gambling hell.

The man was a veritable bloodhound, able to sniff out the backgrounds of Paine's sundry clientele. No credit was extended, no deal struck, without Flaherty's stamp of approval. The man's ability for research had saved Paine countless pounds. Tonight, Paine was hoping Flaherty had information regarding Oswalt and his search for Julia.

'The man is definitely looking for her,' Flaherty said, easing himself into a chair in Paine's office. 'Oswalt has his men everywhere. The three coaching inns I asked at indicated others had inquired about the same girl early yesterday. The good news is that it appears he didn't think to start searching gaming hells and other such establishments until tonight. That means he's still guessing with nothing substantial to go on,' Flaherty reported.

Paine nodded. He'd expected as much, but it was good to have those suspicions confirmed. 'And the uncle?'

Flaherty shook his head. 'I am still working on that. It's hard to say. Oswalt had visited the uncle, but to my knowledge the uncle has not been asking around for the girl except for inquiries at the Farradays.'

'Thank goodness for that at least.' Paine sighed. He'd take all the luck he could get. He'd hoped the man had enough sense to keep Julia's disappearance quiet and it seemed he had. If no one was aware of her disappearance, it would be far easier for her uncle to cover it up, explain it away with a believable story, or even with Paine's story that he and Julia had fallen in love at first sight. As things stood currently, only Julia's family and Oswalt knew she was gone.

Paine preferred it that way. 'Can I trust the uncle?' Paine mused out loud. The man had shown surprising discretion so far. Perhaps he'd judged Barnaby Lockhart too harshly, too soon. He'd thought he might go to the uncle and assure him of Julia's safety.

Paine also had other reasons for seeking out Uncle Barnaby. Paine wanted to 'help' him concoct a safe story that explained Julia's absence. It would be easy enough to use the sick relative in the country story and neatly tack on that while there she encountered him, under the watchful eye of chaperons, of course. Romance bloomed, allowing their 'courtship' in London to take place upon her return.

Paine most definitely wanted to have a hand in that alibi if he could manage it. Julia's situation demanded concentration if one was to avoid a scandalous misstep. It could not be left to an amateur.

So far, his luck was holding. The uncle hadn't raised the hue and cry. But his silence wouldn't last long. Even if the uncle didn't say anything, people would be asking for Julia. Like any busy débutante, she was no doubt committed to events ahead of time. When she didn't appear at the places she was expected, people would miss her and her uncle would have to explain. Paine wanted an alibi in place before that happened.

As much as Paine wanted to pay Uncle Barnaby a visit, Paine worried that Oswalt's hold on the man would be too strong for the keeping of any secrets. The last thing he needed was to face Oswalt's henchmen in an unequal fight. It was a daunting reality to acknowledge that he was literally the only person standing between Julia and Oswalt. If he fell, Julia would be entirely at the man's mercy.

Flaherty affirmed his misgivings. 'No, the uncle is under too much pressure. He sees Oswalt as his only way out from under the burden of his debt. Already, Oswalt is bargaining for the girl's return. He says he'll marry her anyway if she's found, but he'll pay less than the originally promised sum. If she doesn't reappear, he is seeking a return of the funds he's already advanced.'

Paine's eye brows perked at the mention of a new

deal brewing between the uncle and Oswalt, his brain working quickly to assimilate the new details. 'Is there a chance the uncle can pay?' He didn't believe there would be, but he had to be certain.

'I don't think so.' Flaherty rummaged through a battered black bag at his side and pulled out a sheaf of papers. 'Here's what I managed to get from the uncle's solicitor.'

Paine took the sheaf and whistled. 'Your skills never cease to amaze, Flaherty. I don't want to know how you managed this.' He quickly scanned the documents, records of the uncle's latest finances.

The outlook was dismal, but not unexpected. Viscount Lockhart's pockets were to let except for the ship that Julia had mentioned. If Julia didn't return, the family's collapse would be immediate. The ship's cargo, should it return, would be used to pay back what the family owed Oswalt. There would be nothing left over. If Julia returned, there was no telling how far the reduced sum would go in alleviating the family's financial concerns. Paine wagered it wouldn't go far enough. Oswalt wanted something that the viscount's financial viability blocked.

'Help me think, Flaherty.' Paine drummed his fingers on the desk. 'Why would Oswalt go to all this trouble to ruin a man who is already on the brink of it? He's deliberately pushing Lockhart over the edge. He's singled Lockhart out for a reason.' Paine rubbed at his brow, gathering his thoughts. 'Flaherty, look into Oswalt's business dealings and, while you're at it, find out what cargo Lockhart's ship is carrying. There might be something telling in that. Let me know when you have news.'

Paine had a feeling that marriage to Julia was merely part of a larger plan Oswalt had set in motion. She was one of many steps—a critical step at that if the amount of manpower behind his search for her was any indicator—but Paine had no idea what that larger game might be, only a feeling that if Julia wasn't found, Oswalt's game might be hampered. Oswalt was a man who didn't like to be thwarted. It made him an exceedingly dangerous opponent. If Oswalt felt cornered, he would become more volatile. On the other hand, he might also become more desperate and that could work in Paine's favor.

He would also send an anonymous note to Uncle Barnaby, letting him know Julia was safe and that he should give out the story she was tending a sick relative in the country if he wanted to minimise scandal. He wanted to do more, but under the circumstances, the meagre effort would have to be enough.

There was nothing to do now but reassure and wait. He would reassure Julia that he'd taken some short-term steps to alleviate her uncle's worry and to pre-empt the potential scandal. Regardless of his thoughts on the worm her uncle was, Julia obviously regarded him in a more friendly light. And he would wait; wait for the responses to the letters he'd sent out; wait for Flaherty's news regarding Oswalt's pursuits. Then there would come a time of action.

Between now and then, he would skin the young bucks waiting for him at the faro table and teach Julia to gamble. The thought of the last brought a lingering smile to his face.

Chapter Eight

'I'm ready,' Julia said with a touch of uncertainty at the top of the stairs. She nervously smoothed the skirts of the deep rose evening gown Madame Broussard had delivered earlier in the day. The gown was of the first stare of fashion, far beyond any of the pale, virginal gowns in her débutante's wardrobe at home. There was no disputing the quality of the gown with its exquisite tailoring and stitching.

'How do I look?' She moved slowly down the stairs, highly conscious of the plunging neckline and the way the gown clung to her silhouette. Perhaps the colour was too bold after all? She would never have dared such a bold colour either. She suspected only Paine Ramsden would have the audacity to pair the rose with a cinnamon-haired girl and carry it off. She had to admit the shade Paine had chosen complemented her hair rather than clashed. Not that it made any difference tonight. Her auburn tresses were securely tucked up under a black-haired wig.

Julia reached the bottom of the staircase and gingerly touched a gloved hand to her head to check her wig one more time. 'Say something, Paine. Do I look all right?' But she already had her answer. Apparently the gown achieved its desired effect if Paine's intent gaze was any indicator.

His eyes were hot; the wolfish smile spreading across his lips were approval enough. There was a certain thrill in earning the approval of a man like Paine Ramsden. He didn't have to say anything. She knew with her new-budding woman's intuition that he liked what he saw—that he desired her.

'You're absolutely ravishing, Julia. I can't decide if you're Snow White or Red Riding Hood. You look like a fairy tale come to life, even with that wig.'

Julia gave a faux-pout. 'Little Red Riding Hood? That makes me sound like a child.'

Paine leaned close to her ear and nipped the tender flesh of her ear lobe. 'No, not a child, Julia, a delicious ingénue,' he drawled. 'When I look at you, I see an intoxicating mixture of innocence and sensuality, a lady about to awaken to the pleasures of the world.'

Warm heat rushed to Julia's core at the images his low tones conjured. There was no doubt as to what those worldly pleasures might be and how they might be provided. The man flirted so well, it was impossible not to be taken in. 'Then perhaps you are mistaken. I am neither Snow White nor Red Riding Hood, but Sleeping Beauty.'

Paine laughed near her ear, enjoying her witty efforts. 'If you're Sleeping Beauty, what does that make me?'

Julia bit back the first reply that sprung to her lips— that he was the prince come to awaken the princess with love's first kiss. That would never do for a man like him. It implied too much. 'Why, that's easy,' she said instead. 'You're the wolf. You're always the wolf.'

Paine stepped back, his eyes dancing. 'Then let's away to my lair.' Her answer had pleased him. Julia wondered if the banter had been a test of sorts to make sure she wasn't entertaining any romantic notions.

The idea to go with Paine had been an exciting prospect in theory. Dressing up in a low-cut gown, donning a wig and becoming someone else altogether for the evening had been exhilarating—right up to the part where they arrived at the gambling hell.

Paine's coach lurched to a halt and Julia's stomach did a lurch of another kind. 'Are you sure no one will recognise me?' she asked tentatively. Paine had explained to her that Oswalt's man had come the night before asking about her and that it was possible the man might come again once Oswalt knew this hell was Paine's territory.

Paine offered her another round of reassurances and leaped down. He turned to hand her out of the carriage. 'Remember, Julia. This is not a fancy place. You'll stand out like a diamond among coal. But we're counting on that. If Oswalt's man is here, there's nothing better for throwing him off the scent than a glimpse of my dark-haired lady throwing dice. He'll report back to Oswalt that the woman with me didn't resemble you in the least.'

He shot her a dazzling smile, meant to reassure. 'It'll be fun, Julia. Relax. Tonight, you're not Julia Prentiss, you're Eva St George, an actress with many talents.'

That made her smile. Julia summoned her courage, telling herself she was on the brink of a grand adventure. When would she have the chance again to visit a gaming hell? As Julia Prentiss, the niece of a viscount, such behaviour was beyond the pale but as the embodiment of the fictitious Eva St George, anything was possible.

An hour later, she was fully into her role as the adventurous Eva St George. She stood at the head of a crowded hazard table, giddy with the thrill of it all. It was her turn to act the part of the caster. She jostled the dice in anticipation. Near her ear, Paine offered a running litany of instruction.

'Call your main before you throw, that's any number you choose between five and nine. If that number comes up, you win the stake. If you throw a two or three, you lose—it's called "throwing crabs." If neither the main nor the crabs comes up, it's your chance and you neither win nor lose on it.'

'Seven!' Julia called out, tossing the ivory cubes on to the green felt table. A six turned up first and she bit her lip, relieved to see a one showing on the other cube. 'I win!' Julia cried.

The men gathered around the table laughed good naturedly at her excitement. She picked up the dice again, prepared for another round. Paine bent over and blew on them for luck, taking a fair amount of ribbing from the other players.

'Lady Luck is supposed to blow on the dice, Ram,' one of them shouted.

'Are you kidding?' another joked, 'With Ram's luck, I'd let him blow on my dice any night of the week.'

Julia called a six and threw her main. 'I won again!' In her enthusiasm, she flung her arms around Paine's neck and pressed close against him. 'I love this game!' In reality, she thought she'd love anything that kept Paine by her side, whispering in her ear. The combination of his dark evening wear and the scent of his spiced soap was intoxicatingly potent. Tonight, he exuded a commanding aura of urbane control and powerful masculinity. He was a man in charge. He could just as easily have come from an elite club or *ton* ballroom.

Paine responded to her embrace wholeheartedly, sweeping an arm about her waist and capturing her upturned face with a full-mouthed kiss that had the table whooping. 'Let's see how that helps your luck,' Paine said with a grin, releasing her and handing her the dice. 'Third time lucky.'

'Looks like she already got lucky,' someone at the end of the table hooted.

Julia blushed. The public display from Paine had been unexpected until she remembered who she was supposed to be. A seasoned actress would not balk at such a display or at any comment made about it. Eva St George would take such a moment in her stride. Julia Prentiss would have to, too.

As he stood beside her, Paine's hand settled at her waist, steadying her as if he guessed her reaction. 'You're doing fine, quite convincing actually,' he whispered near her ear.

She threw again and the table cheered.

The raucous laughter coming from the hazard table held Sam Brown's attention almost against his will. There was a boisterous crowd tonight. The noise made it hard to concentrate on surveying the rest of the club. He'd been here the prior night, too. He'd spent that night in vain. No sign of his boss's girl had materialised. Yet, he had a hunch that someone here knew something. The glint in the big doorman's eye suggested as much. The doorman had been too quick to dismiss his questions and deny knowledge of anyone meeting the girl's description. So, with nothing else to go on, he'd come back to wait and to watch.

From his small table against a back wall, he had a clear view of all the comings and goings in the place. Technically, no one was going to slip past him, but his attention kept drifting back to the hazard game. A whoop of excitement carried over the general commotion, followed by applause. The sea of people around the hazard table shifted. He caught a glimpse of a nattily dressed man in dark evening clothes and a stunning dark-haired woman dressed in a striking rose gown, leaning over the table with the dice.

The man, he recognised from the prior night. The man had been alone then and not dressed as formally as he was tonight. Still, it was the same person. His face, with its elegant cheekbones and aristocratic flair, was quite memorable.

A serving girl in a provocatively low blouse passed his table. He grabbed her arm. 'Another brandy,' he ordered, tossing a coin on her tray. He jerked his head towards the hazard table. 'Who's the gent?'

'That's Paine Ramsden.' The girl sighed, her voice full of an annoying touch of hero-worship.

He grunted, scoffing at the girl's obvious infatuation. The handsome coves had it too easy. 'Is he bleeding royalty, then?'

'He is to us. He runs this place. He comes in every night and handles all the business personally.' She smiled, but he knew the smile wasn't for him. She was remembering something about the god-like gambling-hell owner. Well, at least she was willing to talk about the object of her adoration. It was more than what he'd got out of anyone else—another telling sign that something simmered beneath the surface here. Everyone was too close-lipped.

He smiled back at the girl and nodded, encouraging her conversation. She leaned towards him. 'He's not royalty, but there's a rumour that his brother is an earl.' She sighed again. 'Just think, the brother of an earl rubbing shoulders with us in our part of the world. Who would have thought?'

The girl moved on, her stock of facts about Ramsden exhausted. But she'd given him plenty to chew on. Who would have thought, indeed? What was the brother of an earl doing managing a cut-rate gambling establishment? The place wasn't a place the Quality would frequent. He could see first hand that the people here were from London's underbelly, rough men, men of disrepute—the dandies in the corner being an exception. But Sam could imagine why those toffs had come. No doubt they were looking for the adventure and excitement they thought hobnobbing with the lower classes could provide.

The girl returned with his brandy and set it down. 'What about the woman with him? Do you know her?'

The girl shook her head. 'He's always got a pretty bird on his arm. Some of the other girls say she's an actress.'

He nursed his brandy and stared hard at the

handsome couple. He could tell, even from a distance, that Ramsden was a charismatic man, but the real reason everyone flocked to the table was the woman. The deep hue of her gown was a siren, drawing men to her from across the bleak, colourless hall. Her laughter kept them. She was enthralled in the game, her excitement over winning as genuine as her disappointment when the dice betrayed her.

The man finished his brandy and edged closer to the crowd, hovering on its rim, studying the woman. Someone in the group called out, 'Come on, Eva, roll a good one!' She held up the dice for Ramsden to blow on for luck. She tossed and won. The group cheered. 'Hurrah for the St George luck!'

Eva St George. Now he had a name and an occupation. That would be something to go on. But what? According to the serving girl, it wasn't unusual for this Ramsden to have a woman by his side. There was nothing to suggest a connection between this couple and the lost girl. Another wasted evening and an unusual incident of his hunches failing him.

He gave the happy table a last look and was about to call it a night when he felt a discreet presence at his elbow. A well dressed young man with slightly dissipated features stood next to him.

The young man stared ahead at the game in progress as he talked, making no attempt at eye contact. 'Are you the man seeking information about a girl?'

He eyed the newcomer, sizing up his potential. 'Yes. Do you know something?'

'Do you have the means to pay?'

He nodded. 'But only for good information. I've got a nice knife in the ribs for liars. Meet me in the alley out back and we'll see what you've got.' He hadn't survived this long as one of Oswalt's henchmen for believing every tip he received.

The young man waited out in the alley for him, clearly nervous. Good. It gave him a chance to assume the upper hand. 'All right, tell me what you know. I have a fifty pounds if your information is good.'

The young man brightened at the prospect of money. Excellent. The buck could be bought.

'The girl was here a couple of nights ago. She wore an aquamarine silk dress and had reddish-brown hair.' The boy blurted his information quickly. 'Can I have my money?'

He narrowed his eyes. 'Not so fast. Why should I believe you? Perhaps you overheard me describing her.'

The boy swallowed hard, his Adam's apple bobbing. 'I saw her with my own eyes. I was sitting at a table, playing Commerce with Ramsden himself. He went to the door and met the girl. Then he took her back to his office. Ramsden didn't return that evening or the next.'

He nodded. 'Very good.' He'd noted the hardness to the boy's voice when Ramsden's name was mentioned.

It explained much, like why the finely dressed young man was out in the alley talking to the likes of him. He turned friendly. 'Did Ramsden clean you out?'

'Yes.' A sigh followed. 'I didn't think I'd lose as much as I did, but Ramsden has the devil's own luck. If the pater finds out I've lost my quarterly allowance already, I'm in the suds.'

He smiled in the dark. From the sound of it, this wasn't the first time this bucko had had a run of bad luck. 'How much do you owe Ramsden?'

'A hundred pounds,' the lad said dejectedly.

'Tell you what, I'll give you a hundred pounds—fifty for your information tonight and there's another fifty in it for sticking around the club and letting me know if the girl resurfaces.' He tossed a leather purse full of sovereigns at Beaton. 'There's good money in information,' he assured the lad.

'How shall I contact you?'

He clapped the boy on the shoulder with false bonhomie. 'Don't worry, I'll find you.'

From the hazard table, Paine covertly watched Gaylord Beaton re-enter the club after a ten-minute absence. It took all of his will power to refrain from dragging the boy outside and doling out the pummelling he deserved. The boy was a poor loser and a stupid one at that. After losing at Commerce, followed with a losing streak at faro the other night, the boy hadn't learned his lesson about playing within his means. Paine knew the loss had cost him dearly. He'd hoped it would teach the boy to keep away from the tables.

The lesson hadn't taken and now the boy was bent on revenge, no doubt seeing Paine as the arbiter of his ill fortunes. Unfortunately, the boy wasn't all that good at skulking. Paine didn't have to ask John where the boy had gone. He'd tried too hard to slip out into the alley unnoticed by the back door.

Paine could guess, too, who he'd met out there. Oswalt's man had been back. He'd had his eye on him all night. He'd watched the man chat to the barmaid. In spite of his best efforts to keep Julia's appearance at the club secret, it appeared the secret was starting to surface and his connection to Julia along with it. It was bad luck that Gaylord Beaton had been at the club the night Julia had shown up and that he'd found the courage to share that information with Oswalt's henchman.

Paine grimaced at the consequences. By dawn, if not sooner, Oswalt would know he ran the club where Julia was last seen. Oswalt would correctly surmise that Julia was with him, knowing that he'd not let an innocent loose to be caught in Oswalt's clutches. The only secret that hadn't been exposed was that Julia was the dark-haired woman with him.

The disguise of Eva St George had been a resounding success on all levels. At times, Paine had struggled to remember the woman beside him was the gently reared niece of a viscount. Julia's *joie de vivre* was utterly convincing. But it would not hold. The henchman might not have put two and two together, but Oswalt was clever. He'd see through the disguise and the coincidence that two new women had shown up at the club within two nights of each other, especially after he searched the playbills of London and determined there was no actress named Eva St George currently treading the boards.

Paine shot a look at Julia, laughing as she tossed the dice. He didn't want to alarm her. She was having so much fun. The men around the table were utterly charmed. But he needed to call an end to the evening. He only had a handful of hours to get Julia to safety, somewhere where she could be protected.

He was a loner, used to relying on himself. It was rather difficult to think of anyone or any place where he could take Julia. But one place did surface, as hard as he tried to fight it. He could take her home. Not to Jermyn Street or to the anonymous town house on Brook Street, but to his family home, the seat of the Earl of Dursley, deep in the sheep country of the Cotswolds.

He hadn't been there for twelve years, and he'd left in disgrace, but it was still the one place he thought of when he thought of being safe. Between the influence of the Earl and the thick sandstone walls of his home, Julia couldn't be safer, no matter what kind of reception he himself would receive from his brothers.

He sighed and edged to Julia's side, placing a possessive hand at her waist. He murmured something into her ear about leaving. It was time. The prodigal was going home.

Chapter Nine

Something was amiss. Paine's playful whisper in her ear about going home didn't match the iron grip he had on her waist as he guided her to his carriage parked in front of the hell. That was odd, too. When they'd arrived, they come in the back door and left the carriage in the wide alley.

'What's happened?' Julia asked the moment the carriage door was shut behind them. 'Why are we parked in front?'

'Because I wasn't sure who was waiting in the alley for us,' Paine said tersely.

Julia didn't need further explanation. She knew what that implied. She swallowed hard. 'Oswalt knows.'

Paine gave a short nod. 'He will know shortly. Gaylord Beaton, one of the dandies who comes slumming, went outside with Oswalt's man. I don't have to be a fortune teller to know what transpired. Beaton was here the night you came to the club. He's been losing heavily. I am sure he saw this as a prime opportunity to get a little of his losses back and some revenge against me as well.' Paine sighed. 'Oswalt will put the pieces together when his man gives him the news.'

'Then Oswalt will come looking for you.' Julia supplied the rest, concern evident in her tone. This was the very scenario she'd wanted to avoid. She didn't want anyone entangled in her problems. She'd sought Paine out because he wasn't likely to take an interest. But just the opposite had occurred. She didn't want him to become a casualty of her folly.

'Don't worry,' Paine said. 'He's got to find us first.'

'Where are we going?'

'We're going to my family home in the Cotswolds. I don't know what kind of reception we'll get, but I know my brother won't turn us away. We'll stop at the house briefly, just long enough to pack a few supplies, no more than an hour. I don't know how much time we have before Oswalt sounds the hunt.'

Julia didn't like the grimness in Paine's tone. At the house, she tore upstairs with single-minded efficiency, throwing necessities into the first satchel she could find. A travelling valise was right where Paine had said it would be. She dragged it out from under the low bed and stuffed a few items of clothing for them both into it. Paine was downstairs furiously dashing off notes.

* * *

He'd said no more than an hour at the house. She thought an hour was too much. Julia dashed downstairs fifteen minutes after going up them with a jumble of cloaks and a spare blanket draped over her arms, the valise in one hand, the small satchel full of toiletries in the other. She couldn't attest to how well the garments she'd haphazardly packed would hold up, but at least they'd be clean and warm when they needed them.

Paine looked up at the sound of her racing feet on the steps. 'I am just finishing a note to Madame Broussard about your clothes,' he said, too casually for Julia's taste.

'My clothes? How can you think about something like that at a time like this?' Julia scolded, breathing hard from her exertions. 'Let's go. Hurry.' She hated the desperation welling in her voice, but there was no hiding it. She was scared.

Paine came to her, placing a hand on each arm. 'Everything will be fine. I will not let Oswalt lay a hand on you, not even a finger. But for me to be successful, we can't let Oswalt drive us off course from our plan. When we return to London, you'll need those clothes for all the events we'll be attending. I rather Oswalt not get wind of this residence because a delivery boy comes poking around with trunks of lady's clothing and starts asking questions because he doesn't know where to leave them.'

Julia hardly heard the last part of his rationale. Her mind was still stuck back on the 'for me to be success-ful' part. 'That's just it. I don't want you to be success-ful. I didn't want anyone involved at all and now you're in this up to your neck and we're racing off to impli-cate your brother, the earl, too. Why don't we just drive over to the Buckingham Palace and involve George IV, too?'

'Well, if you thought it would help,' Paine drawled, sending the last of his quick missives.

'Arrrgh! Men!' Julia stamped her foot in irritation. No, that wasn't nearly strong enough for what she was feeling. How could he be so calm when Oswalt could be out in the streets looking for them already? Men had no sense of righteous, warranted, fear.

Paine came around from his desk. 'I am sorry, Julia. I shouldn't have joked. It was poorly done of me.' He drew her into his embrace. 'Go to the carriage. The coachman is hitching up my travelling team. You can get in and arrange the luggage.' Paine kissed the top her head. 'I'll be there in a minute.'

Julia nodded, offering Paine a tremulous smile. He was doing his best to be strong. She should do the same. But she knew Paine was worried too. She'd felt the hard steel of a pistol at his waist when he'd held her. She didn't have to be told that it would be a mad dash to the Cotswolds and a dangerous one at that. It was at least two hours until dawn. Thank goodness for the full moon. It would be the only thing keeping them on the road instead of in a ditch. But, Julia rationalised, any head start would be valuable.

Sam Brown gave his boss the news over breakfast in the 'white room' of Oswalt's London town house. In the five years he'd served in Oswalt's employ, he'd never come to the house or any of the man's residences. All their business was done in the dock offices. He wished they were there now. He much preferred the plain plank floors and the inevitable dirt to the starkness of this room. The room made him overly conscious about the city mud on his boots.

The use of so much white was an odd choice for décor in a city well known for its abundance of soot. But he'd heard talk among the other men about Oswalt's unusual penchant for purity. This was the first time he'd seen actual evidence of it.

He stood at attention, making his report and trying not to worry about what was on the bottom of his boots while Oswalt cut into the thick sirloin with relish. 'The club she was last seen at is owned by a cove named Paine Ramsden. I saw him last night. He's a right handsome ladies' man. I wouldn't be surprised if—'

'What did you say?' Oswalt's fork stopped halfway to his mouth, his eyes going hard.

'I said the girl was spotted at a club operated by a Paine Ramsden,' Sam repeated hesitantly, shocked by the vehemence of Oswalt's response. He had not thought his boss would take the news so poorly. All the others had reported nothing. He had a lead to offer. To his way of thinking, the boss should have been jubilant to have some news at last, a place to begin the search and a name to go with it.

Oswalt's fork clattered on to the white china plate, the sirloin forgotten. 'She's with Ramsden?' he growled.

'I don't know that, sir. My informant said only that he saw her the night in question.'

'Who's the informant? Anyone we know?'

'None of the usual.' Sam Brown knew the boss was referring to the regular snitches they bought information from when the need arose. 'This was a blue-blooded buck who'd lost his father's allowance. He was scared and ready to talk. I found out his name is Gaylord Beaton. He saw her go into the back room with Ramsden and she didn't come out. But that doesn't mean she's still with him.'

Oswalt brought his fist down on the white tablecloth. 'Of course she's with him, you dolt. Where else could she be? She went into his office and didn't return. No one else has reported a sighting. He's probably spirited her away somewhere.'

'It's just that he was with a different woman last night at the club and no one has seen the girl since,' Sam Brown said nervously, twisting his cap in his hand. He seldom had to argue with his boss to make a point. But he'd yet to see his boss so upset over an individual that logic risked being overlooked.

'Who? Who was he with last night?' Oswalt shouted, his eyes glinting.

'An actress, Eva St George.' Sam Brown was doubly grateful he'd been astute enough to pick up that information last night.

'She had black hair and didn't match the description of your girl. She was definitely not a débutante. Her gown was cut low, she wore cosmetics and she and Ramsden were quite affectionate in public.' He shifted his feet, awkwardly remembering the very passionate, very public kiss Ramsden had given the woman and how the woman had responded wholeheartedly, clearly enjoying it. From what he'd heard of débutantes and high-society ladies, they never enjoyed it.

'Really? What else? Tell me about it—their "affection", as it were.' The boss seemed over-eager for a detailed accounting of the couple's intimacies.

Sam did his best, thinking the request one of the queerest requests ever made of him. 'I don't know how to describe it, sir. She leaned into him and he pulled her so close it was hard to tell where one began and the other ended. They looked like they were in love, sir. That's why I didn't think there was a need to look into the woman's background further.'

'More's the fool you,' Oswalt sneered. He raised his bushy eyebrows. 'An actress? Are you sure about that? Have you checked the playbills? What role does she have? What theatre does she work at?'

Sam Brown didn't like to be treated as an idiot. He was good at his job. Oswalt would never have hired him otherwise.

The boss was apoplectic by this point, his face red. 'Perhaps the woman wore a wig. Did you think of that? I bet that's what the conniving bastard, Ramsden, did—passed her off as someone else beneath our noses!'

'I'll go back to the club and when they turn up again tonight…' Sam began.

'Why wait until tonight? Find out where he lives and check his quarters,' Oswalt demanded. 'If he saw you make contact with anyone, or if the informant—this Gaylord Beaton—was seen, your hand's been tipped. With luck, you'll take him by surprise, maybe even *in flagrante delicto*. You'd better hope so, because if luck fails, it'll be a race to the Cotswolds.'

Sam was relieved to see some of the anger ebb from Oswalt's features. His boss calmed down considerably once the man started to plan. 'Why the Cotswolds, sir?' Sam ventured to ask. He couldn't imagine why a man about town with one foot in the underworld and one arm around a gorgeous, willing actress would happily head to the bucolic Cotswolds.

'Because that's where his brother, the earl, lives. The family seat is in Dursley.' Oswalt's piggish eyes narrowed. 'If we don't catch them on the road, there'll be no getting to them once they're under Dursley's jurisdiction.'

'Seems like you know the family pretty well,' Sam hedged, wondering how his boss had come to know so much about a family of peers.

Oswalt leaned back in his chair, hands folded across his corpulent belly. 'You could say I've had dealings with them before.' His interest in the sirloin returned, the crisis had passed. He jabbed his fork into a fresh piece of meat. He waved it at Sam before taking a bite. 'Mind you, I won the first encounter and I'll win this one, too.' The gleam in his eye suggested he was looking forwards to the challenge laid down before him.

There were more questions Sam would like to ask, but didn't dare. There was a deeper game in play than Oswalt was letting on. The name, Ramsden, had upset his boss greatly, more so than his men's inability to unearth any useful information on his escaped betrothed. One thing was clear. His boss knew and disliked Paine Ramsden. There was a bad past between them. That much was obvious, although the reasons for it were not. Now there was bound to be a bad future, too, since the boss's coveted virgin bride had given him the slip and fallen right into Ramsden's hands. There was no denying Ramsden's attractiveness to the opposite sex. Sam Brown thought it highly likely that the boss's bride wasn't a virgin any more. Perhaps that was what had the boss worried.

Sam Brown turned gingerly on his heel, careful not to leave behind any more markings on the carpet than necessary, and careful not to think too much about why his boss wanted a virgin bride so badly. The men had talked about it, speculating that Oswalt had the pox, that his physician recommended a virgin to cure it.

Like many of the rumours surrounding Oswalt, that one, too, was nothing more than drunken conjecture over ale in the dockside pubs. As such, Sam Brown didn't have to regard it with any amount of seriousness. There were many things in his dealings with Oswalt he was careful to treat in the same manner, for fear of looking too deeply into the issues that paid him a handsome salary.

After all, he was not paid to think, not in that vein, anyways. He was paid to act and, right now, he needed to round up a few of his trusted men to search out Ramsden's residence and if needed, track the man and his actress to the Cotswolds.

Chapter Ten

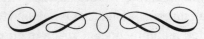

Julia dozed fitfully, her head bumping against the carriage wall. The coach was well equipped enough with its squabs and padding to minimise the constant jounce of the road, but she wasn't. Paine had encouraged her to sleep, but sleep was impossible. Her mind whirred with the unreality of it all.

Tomorrow was the fifth day. If she'd stayed in London with her aunt and uncle, she'd be facing Oswalt and his physician. The thought made her shudder. But was this any better? She'd run away in the hopes of simply losing her virginity to the one man of her meagre acquaintance immoral enough to take her maidenhead and not think twice. Her plan had succeeded in terms of achieving her goal, but her plan had been naïve, not nearly enough to stop Oswalt if Paine was to be believed.

Apparently, she *did* believe him. That was what contributed most to her restless napping. In four days, she'd come to rely on Paine Ramsden, a dark rake, as a man of honour. She trusted him with her future and that of her uncle's. That trust was based on precariously little beyond instinct. Instinct had convinced her that her best hope in eluding Oswalt was to take Paine's advice and not return to her home. That same instinct now had her making a mad dash across country before dawn in the hopes that his family would take them in and cloak them in protection.

Instinct had led her down a slippery slope with Paine Ramsden and not all of it was about her problems with Oswalt. For better or worse, she'd allowed herself to see Paine as more than a means to an end. She had yet to decide how foolish that choice had been.

She had known girls back home who had become infatuated with young men from the village and in their infatuation had constructed entirely unrealistic pictures of the objects of their affection, only to be disillusioned later when their fantasies failed to come true. Had she done that with Paine Ramsden? In her panic, had she been so desperate for a hero that she'd fashioned one out of whole cloth and put the guise on Paine, determined to make it fit?

The mistake would be an easy one to commit even without the duress of her situation. He was sinfully handsome and had all the makings of a Gothic hero: a man with a scandalous past, a man decent women were warned away from, the perfect creature waiting to be redeemed by love's healing power.

The bit about 'waiting to be redeemed' was the problem. Julia couldn't imagine Paine waiting for redemption, no matter what story he'd concocted to tell the *ton* about them. She shot a look at Paine from beneath her eyelashes. He wasn't asleep either, although his eyes were shut. There was a tenseness to his body that belied his otherwise restful repose. He was waiting for something right now, but redemption wasn't it.

No, Paine Ramsden seemed quite content with his life, sutras and all. When she'd walked into the gambling hell and seen him striding towards her, all causal confidence in his rolled-up shirtsleeves, he'd seemed a man who was supremely at ease in the world around him. He'd found his place. Julia thought it highly unlikely that anything or anyone could entice Paine to give that up. 'Normal' living would hardly be appealing to a man who enjoyed 'splitting the bamboo'.

Perhaps normalcy was the reason behind his aversion to the *ton*. Such a lifestyle like the one available to him as a traditional younger son was bound to be too confining for a man of his ilk, its rules too foreign to him. The choice to remain aloof from society had also forced him to stay aloof from his highly respectable family. A difficult choice, and not all that different from the choice she'd recently made.

Of course, she might be reading too much into that in her desire to see the similarities between her and Paine. Again, the niggling worry arose that she was fashioning a hero out of a man who did not wish to be cast in that light. He simply might not like his family. The choice to remain aloof might have been an easy one.

She knew very little about his family besides the few facts floating about the *ton* that new-come débutantes were allowed to hear and the information she had read from a dry page of *Debrett's*. His brother was the Earl of Dursley, of course, and Paine was the third of three sons. On top of that, there was the scandal that seemed to follow Paine everywhere like a calling card. Julia had known precious little of the details when she'd decided to seek Paine out, only that he had been involved in a quarrel twelve years prior over the virtue of a woman. Julia did not know for sure. The quarrel had escalated into a duel and become a public spectacle. The rest was murky after that. She knew only that Paine had been exiled when the duel had been exposed to the authorities. Since then, she'd learned from Paine that the quarrel had been with Oswalt.

She wondered what it was costing him now to go home and face his family. Certainly, he'd made something of himself during his time abroad. But the past was a potent demon and it could not be easy. Yet, he'd done it without any hesitation for her sake. She had not suggested it; indeed, she hadn't even been fully aware of the imminent danger she faced in London.

Julia gave up any pretence of resting. She sat up straight against the leather cushions. 'Why did you do it?' she asked.

Paine's eyes opened quickly, alert and blue, giving every indication that she'd been right. He hadn't been sleeping either. 'Do what?'

'Decide to go home.'

'There was nowhere else to go. The decision was painfully easy,' Paine said bluntly. 'I could think of nowhere safer than my brother's house.'

'Will he be glad to see us?' Julia queried, wanting to know what kind of reception they'd get.

Paine gave a wry smile. 'In his own way, I expect he will be. Don't worry, Julia. He'll love you.'

'What will you tell them about me?'

'I shall tell them the truth, although I doubt my brother will be glad to hear of my latest run-in with Oswalt.' Paine's face was grim. 'But he'll help us.'

'Oh,' Julia said quietly. She'd thought for a moment he might tell his family the story they'd made up about love at first sight. It was surprisingly disappointing to hear the real truth spoken out loud. But she nodded as if that was the tack she'd expected all along.

Paine didn't seem inclined to pursue the conversation, so Julia forged ahead on her own. 'What's your brother like?'

'Which one? I have two you know. Peyton, the earl, and Crispin, who is also older. I imagine it's quite possible that they'll both be at home. Crispin despises the Season and Peyton won't come up until the end of June. He puts it off as long as he can. At least he used to.'

Julia experienced a moment of fear. What if they'd come all this way and the earl wasn't home? 'Is there a chance your brother has already left for London?'

Paine shook his head. 'No, a note I'd sent earlier to the town house was returned and my footman said the knocker wasn't on the town-house door. I'd sent out two notes, just to be sure—one in town and one to the country.'

Her momentary fears were eased. But other concerns presented themselves. 'So, I am going to a bachelor estate and setting up house with three brothers.' Julia tried to make light of it. She felt ridiculous for suddenly worrying about propriety at this late date. Technically, she'd broken every rule a débutante could break. It was entirely illogical to be concerned over such a little thing now. Still, old habits died hard.

Paine laughed. 'Peyton has convinced our Cousin Beth to take up residence. My Aunt Lily tells me that Beth runs the house these days and Peyton finds the arrangement much more amicable than finding a bride to do it.'

Julia thought of the tall, poised older woman Paine had been escorting the night she'd seen Paine from a distance at the ball. That must be Aunt Lily. She and Paine had the same raven-dark hair and had looked congenially at ease with one another. 'Why doesn't he marry? Cousin Beth can run the house, but she can't provide him heirs.' Most men she'd encountered put a supreme importance on producing a successor for the family.

But Paine dismissed the concern. 'Perhaps Peyton hasn't met the right woman yet. No matter, Crispin is an admirable heir in that case. The family will go on.'

Paine leaned forwards and pulled back one of the curtains, assessing the growing light. 'We'll be able to stop soon and refresh ourselves,' he said, clearly changing the subject. Julia had to content herself with what she'd learned, although the answers he'd given had spawned more questions.

Other than Aunt Lily, he'd apparently not made any contact with his brothers in the months he'd been in England. She wondered why. It was obvious he held them in affection and he was interested in what his family was doing. Was this lack of contact reciprocal? Had the earl tried to contact Paine? Surely he knew Paine was back. It seemed unlikely to Julia that Aunt Lily would let such a thing go unnoticed even if the earl didn't make a habit of coming up to town.

The sun had been up for two hours when they stopped at an inn to break their fast and change the horses. Paine reserved a private room for them so they could eat in quiet and with as little attention as possible. Julia's gown was wrinkled, but the colour and cut would still stand out. At Paine's suggestion, she kept her dark wig on. At least now the innkeeper and his wife could deny in all truth that a cinnamon-haired woman had passed that way with a man of Paine's description.

Julia felt better after washing her face and hands and eating. She saw to the packing of a hamper in the kitchens while Paine dashed off another note and sent it with a rider.

'Who's the note to?' she asked coming up at Paine's side in the stable yard.

'My brother. I thought we'd better tell him we were coming. He doesn't like surprises.' Paine smiled and tried to tease her, but Julia missed nothing. There were lots of reasons beyond the obvious why Paine would want his brother on the lookout. If Oswalt's men caught up to them and they failed to arrive on time, Dursley would come looking for them. That could hardly be what Oswalt's men preferred.

Julia hoped it wouldn't come to that. She knew her etiquette well enough to know that Paine was a mere mister, the title of 'Honourable' only applying as a written heading. Tangling with him was one thing. Engaging in a violent act against the Earl of Dursley was another.

Paine handed Julia into the coach and took his place on the top of the box to give the coachman a break. They couldn't afford the luxury of stopping for sleep and the coachman couldn't drive for ever. A man could be pushed no more than a team of horses without risking the safety of the journey. Such action would be complete folly. It would do no good to outrun Oswalt's minions only to be caught by the side of the road with a broken carriage wheel.

Paine clucked to the team and slapped the reins. It would be a tiring two days on the open road. Part of him longed to be inside the coach with Julia to distract him. He would have given a monkey to know what she'd been thinking about so hard this morning. Her eyes had been shut, but he could practically have seen the wheels of her fast-moving mind whirling at top speed.

While he was flattered to think those thoughts might have been about him, he hoped they were not. He was dangerous for Julia. Usually he limited his relationships to women who understood the game, women who were satisfied with the temporary pleasures he could give them, women who knew that, like all games, theirs would come to an end. Julia Prentiss was a different kettle of fish, which was the exact reason he felt so compelled to protect her, even to the point of going home to face Peyton and all the things he had to apologise for.

Whether she would admit to them or not, or was even aware of them or not, Julia had expectations. She needed a hero right now and he was more than glad to oblige for the short term. But he wasn't capable of being her hero for longer than that. There was too much restlessness in him. Paine already knew he'd leave England again. Maybe not tomorrow, or next month, but eventually within a few years he would leave again. There was a huge world to explore and Britain was well placed to conduct those explorations. Julia had grown up in the country. She would want a husband who was stable, reliable, able to stay in one place and put down roots.

Whoa. Paine jerked on the reins, avoiding a near run-in with the ditch on the side of the road. Husband? When had he gone from short-term hero to husband? Commitments didn't get any more long term than that. He couldn't be anyone's husband, especially not Julia Prentiss's. She would give him all her trust, all her passion, all her heart and he would hurt her. She deserved more than a restless man. Before he could consider being a husband, he had to find peace for himself. Maybe that peace was in Bombay, or Burma, or in some mystical place he had yet to explore.

Maybe it's with her. Maybe she brings you peace, a tempting voice quipped in his head. *That's why you showed her 'splitting the bamboo' and the 'yawn.' You know that position lets each lover view the other's reactions without any obstacle. The position renders you emotionally exposed. That's why you climax so intensely with her and her alone. Go on, slay her dragons and win the fair maid's hand.*

Paine yanked hard on the reins, pulling the coach away from a deep rut in the side of the road. Lucifer's bells, he was going crazy! He'd nearly wrecked the coach with thoughts of playing husband to the delectable Julia. Now, his mind had wandered from eastern sexual sutras to the chivalry of England. What was he thinking?

Oh, he knew *what* he was thinking, and he knew what he *ought* to be thinking. He ought to keep his thoughts on the tasks at hand; goodness knew there were several of them more worthy of his time than impossible fantasies about peace and Julia Prentiss.

London was already seven hours behind him. Tomorrow's sunset would see them on his brother's doorstep. He was cognisant, too, that the game with Oswalt was irrevocably in motion now. Tomorrow would see him and Julia at Dursley, a day closer to both a reunion and a reckoning that had been twelve years in coming.

Paine drove all afternoon. The idea of a reunion with his brothers, coupled with the soft rolling green hills, proved to be too potent of a temptation to resist, making it easy to indulge the memories he loved so well.

Around him, waving fields of golden summer wheat not yet knee high spread like a haphazard quilt, so similar to the landscape near his home. In his mind's eye, he saw three boys rollicking in the fields, trousers rolled up and fishing rods slung over their shoulders. A stranger would not see much difference in them. Not much separated them in physical appearance except for their stair-step height. All had jet-black hair and blue eyes that sparked with constant mischief.

Those had been halcyon days when they'd lived as brothers and friends under the spell of an English summer. Each year upon year, it had always been that way for as long as Paine could remember. The tutors dismissed for the warm months and the boys free to roam at will. Paine was six years younger than his oldest brother. He'd thought such summers would last for ever.

But they ended when he was eight and Peyton left for school that autumn, leaving a huge chasm behind. Peyton had been the mortar that bound all three of the boys together. Without Peyton, he and Crispin were lost. Peyton had been the one to create their fantastical adventures, to lead the way on their expeditions. He'd been the one, because of his age, to act as both brother and father in the absence of a real father who lived almost exclusively in London.

Paine recognised now that, if his father had been home more often, Peyton wouldn't have been allowed to attain the ripe age of fourteen before going off to school. Most heirs were long gone from the family estate years before then. Still, everything had started to change the day the coach pulled out of the drive, taking Peyton away.

He didn't want to think about those dark days today, not with the sun shining on a perfect mid-morning summer. He wanted to be a boy again, innocent and fresh-come to the world. Not too young, though—not so young he couldn't celebrate this glorious day with a maid.

Paine laughed out loud, startling the horses. If it was his fantasy, he would do it right. He'd be sixteen and only modestly experienced in the ways of the world and flesh. Yes, he'd be sixteen and in love—a pure, unadulterated love with a girl as pure and curious as he was. She'd be a country girl, of course, so they could pack a picnic and hike through the woods to a field of wild-flowers. They'd lay out their picnic of brown bread, a cheese wheel and a jug of cold ale on an old faded blanket. There'd be no need for chaperons or fancy delicacies or mating games with intricate negotiations.

Paine thought of Julia, snug in the carriage. Of all the women he'd known, she'd perhaps like such a picnic best. Certainly, she was by far the most innocent he'd ever known. It seemed something of an irony that she'd come looking for him to ruin one of the qualities he admired about her most. He knew as she did not that innocence was more than the physical manifestation of her maidenhead. He'd met virgins who weren't innocent in the least. She'd meant for him to take her innocence and now, he'd wound up protecting it. He would fight Oswalt with every weapon at his disposal before he'd let Julia see what that man could do. He would examine the reasons for such motivations later.

Chapter Eleven

When they stopped for a short lunch in the afternoon the next day, Julia begged to ride up on top with Paine. She'd had enough of being cooped inside with a snoring coachman. The man had driven through the night for them and deserved his rest. Julia wasn't convinced, however, that it entitled him to expose her to such a noise.

She was also convinced that they'd eluded Oswalt. There were only two hours to go until they arrived at Dursley. The fear that had formed a continual knot in her stomach since London was starting to unravel.

Julia was contemplating the pleasure of a hot bath and cooked food when the shot rang out. Julia screamed. Shards of lacquered wood grazed her cheek from the impact of a bullet piercing the side of the coach. The horses whinnied in fright, galloping recklessly down the rutted road, dragging the coach behind them. The strength of Paine's arms were the only barriers between the horses and certain doom if the carriage veered into the ditch. At this speed, even a shallow ditch would cause the vehicle to flip, flinging its occupants to imminent injury or death.

'Julia, how many are there?' Paine shouted over the jangle of the coach, all his attention focused on keeping the coach on the road, on keeping them alive.

Julia clutched the seat rail and hazarded a quick backwards glance. 'Four.'

'Get down!' Paine shouted as another shot rang out.

'Julia, listen to me. We'll have to stop the team. I can't hold them for ever; if they keep running, it's only a matter of time before a corner is too sharp or we hit a rut. At this speed, we die most assuredly. When I stop the coach, you get down and run for the trees. Just keep running. Stay under cover and keep your sense of direction. You'll run into Dursley Hall.'

'Where will you be?'

'Here, fighting them off. Then I'll catch up.'

'Four men?'

'Don't fight with me over this, Julia. It's you they want. The last thing I need is to have my concentration divided between you and them. I can't fight you both. It only takes one man to swing you up on his horse and ride off while the other three keep me busy.'

Paine sawed hard on the reins, bringing the frightened team to a stop. 'Go, Julia!'

Julia tumbled over the side and ran for the woods, hoping Paine was right and that no one had seen her yet. With luck, Oswalt's men would assume she was inside the carriage. The shots that had been fired hadn't necessarily been aimed at the driver.

Julia gained the thick copse that grew near the road side, worry for Paine filling her. *The shots had been aimed at Paine.* Julia's hand flew to her cheek where the wood shards had scratched it. At a distance and with the blur of motion, the men had no way of knowing Paine was the driver. They'd assume Paine was in the coach with her and, as the gentleman, he'd be riding with his back to the box, facing backwards.

Paine's words came back to her. *You're the one they want.* That had made logical sense. Oswalt wouldn't want her dead. He needed her definitely alive. But Paine was expendable and, given their history, perhaps it was even preferable that Paine was dead.

She turned to look back. One man lay still on the ground, probably from Paine's single pistol shot before he'd got too close. Another grappled with Paine on the narrow box seat. Paine drew back his arm and delivered a debilitating punch to the man's jaw, sending him staggering off the edge. But two men remained and they'd had time to get into position. One of them had drawn a knife.

Julia watched in horror as they dragged Paine off the high seat, one of them swiping at Paine with the blade. The trio hit the ground, Paine rolling free of the punches they threw. He reached swiftly into his boot to withdraw his knife. He crouched, arms held wide, ready to fight, but he was already bleeding. In the close confines of the box seat, the blade had found purchase.

Julia could see a slow stain forming on his arm—the right arm that held his knife. The steel blade Paine possessed suddenly seemed inadequate to her. How could such a thin piece of steel keep those burly men at bay? How long would Paine's wounded arm hold out? Where was the coachman? Surely he hadn't slept through all the commotion and the bone-jarring ride? He should be out there, helping Paine.

One man moved and Paine stabbed with his knife. The man danced away. The other one feinted, drawing Paine's attention. Julia bit her knuckles. This could go on for ever and, if it did, Paine would come out the loser.

Julia glanced around and picked up some rocks, an idea taking shape. Decisively, she ripped the silk gown, tearing it above her knees. Now she could run and, now, thanks to summers spent roaming the estate with Cousin Gray, she had a weapon.

Julia crept quietly to the edge of the trees, careful to stay hidden so that a flash of colour from her vibrant gown didn't give her away. She was close enough to recognise one of the men as the man from the club and close enough to hear the ragged banter exchanged between the men and Paine.

'What do you want with me that would be worth

dying for? I'll get one of you before you get me,' Paine argued, invoking his wit as a weapon.

'We want the chit with the cinnamon hair. You have her. The boss wants her. The boss *owns* her. We've come to reclaim stolen property.' The big man's tone was menacing.

'I don't have her. You can check the coach, but there's nothing inside except my dead coachman,' Paine replied.

Julia blanched at the news, thinking of the bullet that had pierced the side of the coach. The men confronting Paine were not bothered by the results of their errant bullet. 'That bullet was for you, Ramsden. If you'd been where you were supposed to be, this would all be over now.' The smaller of the two men lunged for Paine, opposite side to the hand that held the knife.

Julia fought back a gasp. It would be difficult for Paine to reach across his body and make an effective effort with his weapon. Instead, Paine kicked out with his leg in a fluid movement Julia had never seen before. The sweep of his leg caught the man at the knees and brought him to the ground. Quickly, before the last man could react, Paine delivered a sharp jab to the downed man's abdomen, rendering him temporarily useless.

But Paine wobbled as he spun to face the last man and the man saw it for what it was—weakness that would only grow with time. He had only to wait and he would be victorious. He'd used his comrades and their failures to take Paine's measure. He'd seen Paine's arsenal of wit and strange, foreign moves. Now Paine was exposed.

He charged Paine like a bull, head down and fast for a man so large. His head caught Paine in mid-torso, the impact taking Paine to the hard ground and causing the knife hand to release its grip. The knife spun out of reach on the road.

Julia went into action, loading one of her stones into the hastily fashioned sling from her torn dress. She could hear the grunts and yells of the men's fight, Paine taking the brunt of it in his weakened state.

She had more rocks at her disposal but her first shot would be her best shot, full of surprise. She edged closer to give herself better range. The man reared up over Paine, giving her a clear target without the risk of hitting Paine instead. Julia cocked the sling and called out, using her voice as an additional distraction. It worked. The man kept his head up, glancing about to find the source of the sound. With dead-set determination, Julia fired the sling. The stone found purchase in the centre of his forehead. He slumped forwards.

Paine oomphed at taking the burden of the heavy weight and shoved at him, quickly gaining his feet, then looked around warily for the unexpected assistance. Julia rose up out of the brush and strode towards him. 'Paine!' She ran the last of the short distance.

'You? It was you?' Paine asked, his expression

inscrutable, taking in the pink sling dangling in Julia's hand.

'Don't be mad. I looked back and saw those four men coming after you. I couldn't let you face them alone.' The words came out in a rush.

'Shh, Julia.' Paine's face cracked into a smile in spite of the bruises it had sustained. 'I'm not mad. I'm amazed. I am sure Madame Broussard would be. I'm not certain she ever envisioned her precious satin being used in such a manner.' Paine took the sling from her hand and held it up, saying with an amount of jocularity, 'Yes, I think this just might be the most expensive sling shot in the world.'

'Well, it won't last for ever. Let's get going.' Julia insisted, tugging at Paine's hand. The scene of such violence was starting to unnerve her.

'Wait, Julia, there's time for this.' Paine pulled her back to him and kissed her hard on the mouth. 'I was never so glad to see someone as I was to see you come out of the woods, striding like an avenging tree nymph,' he whispered. 'I do believe you saved me today.'

'And I will continue to do so,' Julia said with a bravado she didn't feel. She trembled, fighting back the shock that threatened to settle over her now that the ordeal was done. But Paine still needed her. 'Sit down and let me tend that wound. It's a nasty gash, Paine. I don't like how it's bleeding.'

Paine sat on the carriage step without complaint. It

worried Julia that he'd given into her request so easily. Part of her had hoped he'd protest, declaring the wound only a 'scratch'. But anyone could see it was more than a scratch.

Julia bit her lip and gingerly probed the cut through the slashed fabric, wishing she had some medical skill, but beyond a few instances of cleaning up minor hunting accidents, she was vague on what should be done. Well, she would make do with what she knew and rely on common sense for the rest, she told herself steadfastly.

Fortunately, there was water in the coach from the last coaching inn where they'd taken on some provisions. Julia tore the tails of Paine's shirt to make a rag and some spare wadding. She poured water in the rag and sponged the affected area.

'Wounds always look better after they're cleaned.' Paine said, far too cheerily.

'Hmm,' Julia answered noncommittally. She wished she could agree. The wound did look cleaner, but it also looked more vivid. The bleeding seemed to slow. As long as the bleeding stopped, she could bind the arm. Otherwise, the blood would make the bandage sticky and hard to remove, not to mention painful. She took the second length of cloth and began to bind his arm.

'Ouch!' Paine winced as she pulled the cloth tight.

'If it's not tight, the binding won't do any good.' Julia said firmly, tying a knot high on his upper arm. 'That should hold. At least the fabric will keep the wound clean between now and reaching Dursley.'

Julia stood up, breathing deeply to steady herself. The sight of gaping skin was not one to which she was accustomed. Lord willing, it would never be a sight she would count in her repertoire of regular experiences.

She turned her attention to the coach and the horses and the carnage around them. The remaining men were still out cold, but it had been a while. 'Paine, will they wake up soon?'

Paine grimaced. 'Get a shirt from the valise. We'll rip it into shreds and bind them. It won't prevent them from following, but it might slow them down.'

Julia followed the instructions, nervously watching while Paine toed one of the unconscious men in the stomach. There was no reaction. With Paine's injured arm useless, it was up to Julia to bind the men's arms and legs.

She stared at them and then at Paine. He'd risen and was trying to mount the driver's bench. It took him three awkward tries to pull himself up with one arm. She made a quick decision, one he wouldn't like. But there was no choice.

Julia scrambled up beside him and picked up the reins he was struggling to grasp in his good hand. 'I'll take those. You're in no shape to drive the coach.'

'We're not walking to Dursley,' Paine retorted.

'No, we're not walking, you stubborn man. I'm driving,' Julia informed him of the decision she'd made.

Paine snorted. 'You don't know how to drive a coach and four.'

Julia looked straight ahead down the empty road, her tone determined. 'No, I don't. But I think this is the perfect time to learn. I do have some experience with a pair. Now, this rein here—I take it this is for the lead horse?'

'Julia…' Paine protested.

'Paine, you can't drive and we must continue. You can't be so dense as to ignore the realities of our situation. If we stay here, we're literally sitting ducks. Any mile we make it towards Dursley is a mile closer to safety and whatever help your brother can offer,' Julia argued. But Paine didn't like being weak or being bossed about.

She softened her tone and tried a different tack. 'I thought you were magnificent today.' She leaned closer and managed a kiss without falling off the narrow seat. 'You did your part today to keep us safe. Let me do mine.'

'Well,' Paine said reluctantly, 'if you insist. I'll let you drive.'

Julia doggedly gripped the reins that separated the narrow box seat from the ground several feet below. Her shoulders and arms ached from the strain. She needed all her strength to keep the team of four on the road as the coach bounced towards Dursley Hall. They had conquered Oswalt's men, managing to subdue them. Once they recovered they would have to spend precious time regrouping, redrafting their plans. It was unlikely Oswalt's men would catch up to them before they reached Dursley Hall. But that victory had been accomplished at a great price.

The coachman lay dead in the carriage and Paine was wounded. The cut must be a burning torture on this rutted road. Beside her, grim-lipped and pale, Paine had his eyes fixed on the road before them, watching for any sign of trouble as a way of staying alert.

A man dead and another wounded. All because of her. Julia could not overlook the facts. Her mad scheme to elude Oswalt had led directly to the coachman's death. She had meant to be smart in outwitting Oswalt's perverse desire for a virgin bride. At the outset, she'd honestly believed she was only risking herself. The falsity of that belief had been made painfully clear to her today.

'Are we still clear?' Julia asked, trying to make conversation, fearing Paine might lapse into unconsciousness if she didn't keep him engaged.

Next to her, Paine dared a glance backwards, checking to see if Oswalt's men had caught up and were even now darting out of the woods that lined the road.

'Nothing. We're safe,' he breathed.

'How much farther?' she asked. It seemed she'd been driving for ever. Time had become meaningless. Darkness would settle shortly and she feared that the most. If they were far enough from Dursley Hall, perhaps Oswalt's men were waiting for the light to fail. In the dark, she and Paine would be hard pressed to out-manoeuvre them again.

'Just two miles.' Paine grimaced, turning paler than he had been. 'Julia, listen to me, there'll be a turn in the road, it marks the entrance to the Dursley parkland. Turn and then head straight, the road will lead you to the hall.'

Just two miles. Julia said the words over in her head like a Catholic litany. They had to be the longest two miles she'd ever travelled. Then, just when she thought they were safe, five riders loomed in front of them as they neared the turn in the road.

Five magnificent dark horses spanned the road like a barricade. Julia felt her panic rise. She would never make the turn or be able to crash through them and remain unscathed. Her skill was only hours old. Julia fought back her terror, but she couldn't refrain from the scream that bubbled up in her throat.

Paine laughed beside her in spite of his injury and weariness. 'Don't be frightened, Julia love, it's merely my brother. We're safe now.'

Julia's fear turned to relief. At last, she could lay down her burden. She pulled the carriage to a halt with the last of her arms' strength.

A black-haired man rode up and smiled up at Paine. 'Welcome home, little brother. Somehow I am not surprised you've returned with a beautiful woman at your side and the hounds of hell at your heels.'

'Crispin—' Paine's voice was full of emotion, although he couldn't speak more than the one word.

'He's hurt,' Julia broke in, eager to get Paine off the road and to see the journey completed. 'I can drive the team well enough if you can manage the leader on the turn.'

'Where's Peyton?' Paine managed.

'Waiting for you at the house with Cousin Beth.' The brother called Crispin tossed the words over his shoulder as he edged his horse up to the where the leader stood, blowing hard after the run. 'No more questions until we get you settled. The lady's given her orders,' he joked, but Julia thought she sensed worry in his voice.

Paine did look quite awful with his myriad cuts and bruises, the ragged bandage on his wounded arm showed signs of new bleeding—bright red blood still damp to the touch. Remnants of their encounter on the road and two days of unending travelling had worked great changes in Paine's appearance. No one would guess the man beside her had been turned out with sartorial elegance two nights prior.

Julia knew without the benefit of a looking glass that she appeared no better than Paine. The expensive silk was ripped and stained beyond repair. Her hair hung tangled and matted from wind. But just as she knew how awful the pair of them appeared, she knew his brothers wouldn't care. There'd been abject devotion in Crispin's eyes and underneath his teasing words of welcome.

Beside her, Paine tried to slip off to sleep or into unconsciousness—she couldn't tell which. She elbowed him gently. 'Don't you leave me now. Your brother will never forgive me if you arrive asleep after a twelve-year absence.'

'How do you know?' Paine mumbled, his speech slurred with exhaustion.

'Because he's coming down the lane right now,' Julia said, unable to hide the smile from her voice. Crispin had led them around a bend in the road and the house came into view as they gained the drive. Two figures stood on the wide steps, dark in the fading light. At the sight of them, one of them started moving.

Nearing the figure, Julia could see he was running, a swift, athletic sprint. When he was close enough he called out, 'Crispin, is it them? Paine? Paine? Is it you?'

The voice roused Paine. 'Julia, stop the carriage. Help me down.'

Julia protested, 'We're nearly there. Can't you wait until we reach the steps? You're in no shape, Paine.'

'Please, Julia. I want to get down and meet him on my own feet,' Paine persisted, his tone sharp and surprisingly alert.

Julia pulled on the reins, calling to Crispin to halt. She helped Paine steady himself. His injured arm made his descent ungainly, but he had his wish. Then Peyton had him wrapped in a brotherly embrace that nearly moved Julia to tears.

'Paine, you're home, at last. Thank God. I thought I had lost you for ever.'

Paine murmured something Julia couldn't hear and sagged in his brother's arms, spent at last. She watched Peyton and a footman haul Paine indoors and presumably upstairs to a chamber to rest. She felt bereft. The one person she knew in this strange place could be of no assistance to her now.

'He'll need a doctor. There was no time to stop on the road and nowhere to stop, in any case,' Julia said to no one particular, feeling at loose ends.

'He'll be fine.' A woman of middle years with dark hair and kind eyes spoke in soft tones, coming up to the carriage. 'Crispin!' she called out. 'Come help Paine's lady down.' The woman turned a gentle smile in Julia's direction. 'I'm Cousin Beth; you're in good hands now. Don't worry about a thing. We'll get you settled in no time. There's nothing wrong with Paine that rest and good cooking can't cure and you, too, for that matter. You look as if a meal and a long sleep would be welcome. I'll send for the physician from the village.'

She meant her words kindly, but she could not dispel the loneliness that swamped Julia. Julia let Crispin swing her down from the high seat. She let the eminently capable Cousin Beth lead her through the house to a beautifully appointed lady's chamber. She was appreciative of the friendly welcome, but she desperately wanted to be with Paine, even if it was to watch him sleep.

Only now when Paine was out of her reach, did she fully realise how much she'd come to rely on him—not simply for protection, but for companionship. In a short time he'd become her buffer between herself and the world.

Chapter Twelve

Cousin Beth's prediction proved unerringly true. After seventeen hours of sleep and poultices, Paine looked and felt immensely more like himself, with the exception of a stiff arm. Peyton and Crispin had rummaged their wardrobes for spare clothes to replace the tatters he'd arrived in. They were all of a similar build and the fit was good. The few personal effects Julia had grabbed at the Brook Street house were laid out on the dresser. He recognised his comb and his razor.

Out of curiosity over what had become of the rest of the clothes Julia had packed in the travelling valise, Paine opened the wardrobe and peered inside. Paine laughed to himself. It was empty except for his trousers, hopelessly wrinkled and entirely unsuitable for wearing. He remembered then that his shirt had gone for a good cause. He hoped Julia had been as fortunate with a makeshift wardrobe as he. Whatever she'd packed for herself was probably in the same wrinkled state his own clothes were in. But he did not doubt Cousin Beth's efficiency in managing every detail. He was certain suitable clothes had been found for Julia as well.

The sight of his crumpled clothes brought an image to mind of Julia upstairs in the Brook Street house, madly opening drawers, rummaging for clothes. At first, the image seemed humorous and touching. Even in her haste, Julia had thought of what he might need—the comb and razor were evidence of that. Then, the image lost its warm edge. His Julia should never have to flee in the middle of the night. His Julia should never have to know the fear she'd known during their flight from London. A fierce protectiveness awoke within him. *His Julia.*

Paine took a final quick look in the long mirror. He would do. A shave would be nice, but he didn't want to take the time. He wanted to see Julia. Paine felt he had been somehow remiss in his duty to her. She was his to look after. He'd left her alone in a house of strangers to find her own way. Not that there was much need for worry. Peyton wouldn't let her go wanting. Neither would he let her out of his sight. Paine had been very clear in the note as to the dire situation of her circumstances.

Thoughts of Julia, of wanting to assure himself that she was well, propelled him downstairs in his borrowed clothes. The sun was up and it was mid-morning of what promised to be a glorious May day. Voices floated out of the breakfast room, Julia's among them, chatting and laughing with his brothers, and Beth was joining in the light banter around the table. It was an easy sound, a comfortable sound, one that made Paine smile.

Julia had the seat across from the door. She spied him immediately, a brilliant smile lighting her face upon seeing him. 'Paine, you're awake.'

He could have basked in the sun of that smile all day. Paine couldn't recall the last time a woman had smiled at him with such genuine warmth that had nothing to do with wanting something from him.

'How are you feeling?' Peyton was all concern from the head of the table.

'Quite well,' Paine assured him, suddenly feeling awkward in his brother's presence. He had much to reckon with in regards to the family and Peyton. He fought the urge to shift from foot to foot like an errant schoolboy called on the carpet instead of a thirty-two-year-old man with a self-made fortune. Paine turned from Peyton and busied himself at the sideboard, filling a plate with the traditional breakfast offerings that had adorned the Earl of Dursley's sideboard since he could remember. There was a quiet joy in lading his plate with sausages and eggs and a stack of buttered toast—the comfort foods of his boyhood.

He took the seat across from Julia, feeling conspicuous. The happy chatter he'd heard coming down the stairs had faded away, replaced with silence while they waited for him to be seated.

Paine unfolded the square of linen next to his plate. Perhaps the reckoning would come now at breakfast. He rather hoped not. He'd prefer to explain things in private with Peyton. He didn't relish the idea of being called to the carpet in front of Julia. He'd come to like the idea of being her knight in shining armour, a hero instead of the dark rake.

Having to explain the last twelve years to Peyton in front of her would tarnish his image. A year ago, he wouldn't have cared what someone thought of him. But in the time they'd been together, it had suddenly come to matter very much what Julia thought.

'It will be a fine day,' Peyton began, drawing everyone's attention easily, falling back on the faithful topic of any English conversation. 'The weather is perfect for taking Julia out and showing her the estate.'

'I'll have Cook pack a hamper if you like, Paine. You can pick strawberries. They're in full fruit right now,' Beth suggested eagerly.

Julia beamed at the idea. 'I'd love to see everything,' she exclaimed excitedly and then sobered. 'But it can wait. I don't want to take you away from your brothers. There must be a lot to talk about.' She meant it kindly. Paine knew she had no idea just how much there was to talk about.

Peyton was quick to assure her. 'There will be time to talk later.'

Paine felt a flicker of anger lick at his conscience. He could make his own decisions. He wasn't the baby brother any longer. He didn't need Peyton's permission to show Julia around.

He tamped down his temper, disappointed that the old kernel of his discontent was still there, so readily accessed at the smallest provocation. He'd come home to keep Julia safe. He knew the choice would mean making amends and explanations. He could not let himself be angered so easily or Peyton wouldn't see him as a changed man, a man who knew the world.

'Then, we'll go,' Paine offered with a tight smile, but he felt Julia's eyes linger on him as if she could see the turmoil beneath his seemingly easy acquiescence.

Dursley Park was easily several times larger than her uncle's modest estate. Julia marvelled at the sheer vastness of the parkland, the immense stretches of green, manicured lawn reaching up to the woods that bordered the southern flank of the house. Paine told her the woods were full of bridle trails leading out to various follies. There would time to explore those later. Today, they were headed to the west side and the grain fields that beckoned with an undulating golden wave in the light breeze.

Paine drove them about in a plain pony cart pulled

by a cob, the sleeves of his linen shirt rolled up past his elbows, the steady, slow pace manageable with one hand on the reins. He was jacketless and the shirt was open at the throat. He exuded a natural male beauty in his simple attire. Julia thought she could stare at him for ever. She might have continued casting covert glimpses at him from under the brim of a borrowed straw riding bonnet if he hadn't caught her.

'What is it, Julia? You're staring.'

'I was thinking how you look today reminds me of the first night I saw you. You had your sleeves rolled up then, too,' she stammered, embarrassed at being caught in her perusal.

'A whole week ago,' Paine said wryly.

'A lot has happened since then,' Julia replied, struggling to keep her gaze fixed forwards. She was reluctant to talk of the business between them on such a lovely day, but it seemed dishonest not to acknowledge it. 'I never meant for it to come to this,' she said quietly. It had to be said. The guilt of it all was too much to bear silently.

She felt Paine's eyes on her. 'How much have you told Peyton?'

Julia shook her head. 'Hardly anything. I wasn't sure what you wanted me to say. I thought you should be the one. I wasn't sure…' she faltered, repeating herself. She was entirely out of her depth here. She did not know the extent or quality of Paine's relationship with his family. She had not meant to involve an earl in her plan or to even develop an association with Paine Ramsden that went beyond one night.

Paine pulled the cart over to the side of the path they'd followed and jumped down. 'No more talk of such things. Today is for us.' He came to her side of the cart and swung her down.

The easy grip of his hands at her waist felt welcome. She'd missed his touch while he'd slept. She'd missed his presence. Of course, she couldn't tell him that. This thing between them was strictly business. That he gave her pleasure, that he stirred longings in her, was not part of their agreement, merely a by-product. A shared by-product.

Mutual attraction might not be part of the contract, but it had developed. Julia took comfort in that. Whatever his emotional attachment to her was, she knew Paine desired her physically. When this was over, such knowledge would have to be consolation enough.

Paine's hands stayed at her waist long after her feet found the ground. He pulled her to him, causing her head to arch back to look up at him. She revelled in the feel of his body, hard and muscular against hers. Without hesitation, he took a swift kiss, bending with expert precision to avoid the brim of her hat.

When he pulled back, he was all carefree boyish charm. 'Where did you get such a contraption?' He made a gesture towards her hat. 'Tell me you didn't pack it all the way down from London?'

'No, it's an old hat of your Cousin Beth's. Do you like it?' Julia did a pirouette.

'Absolutely not. It's awful, just awful!' There was laughter in his voice. 'Peyton needs to give Cousin Beth more pin money if she's been reduced to such a travesty.'

Paine held out his hand. 'Here, take my hand. I don't trust you can see the path plainly with that thing on.' He kept her hand gripped in his own. With his other hand he swept up the hamper and led the way to a shady spot. Julia was thankful for the strength of his hand. She would have tripped without him to steady her on several occasions. The terrain was uneven and awkward to traverse in Beth's slightly too-long skirts and slightly too-big shoes. Still, Julia was grateful for Paine's cousin's generosity. Otherwise, she would have been tramping the countryside in a torn silk evening gown.

'We're here,' Paine exclaimed at last, dropping the hamper and blanket.

Julia looked about her, trying to grasp what 'here' was.

'Take a deep breath and just listen,' Paine coaxed softly.

Julia did as instructed, the allure of the place becoming immediately apparent. The scent of summer wafted gently from the fields behind them, the sound of a nearby creek mixed with the errant chirps of meadow birds filled the air. She didn't have to open her eyes to know it was summer.

'We can pick strawberries later.' Paine grinned and pointed to a patch. He spread the blanket. He sat down and began to tug off his boots.

'What are you doing?' Julia asked.

Paine chuckled. 'Getting comfortable. Sit down, Julia. Take off your shoes. We can be ourselves.'

His good humour was infectious. Julia plopped down and took off her shoes. 'I think your sutras would like this place. The site appeals to all the senses.'

'You're a quick learner.' Paine said, stretching out beside her. 'Although I think the sutras would prefer fine furnishings and music to our ragged blanket and chirping birds.'

'I like our setting. It's simple,' Julia said, casting a coy glance sideways at Paine. She would have to store up all the images of him she could. She would have to share him with his brothers, and then with society, if their plan were to succeed. And that success would be the end of their association. She'd once thought it would be a facile trick to walk away from him. But she'd never dreamed a man like him existed.

Julia tossed her shoes aside and reached for her stockings. Paine's hand stopped her before she could roll them down.

'As I recall, you like to have me do this for you,' Paine whispered huskily, his eyes glinting with mischief. His hands reached up beneath her skirts, skimming her hidden curls as he grasped the top of each stocking.

Julia bit her lip against the sensual play. She knew she was damp when he reached for the second stocking. It was embarrassing to note how wanton she was with him. 'Paine…' she began uncertainly. 'We're outdoors.'

'On the contrary, nature is the perfect place for this. The sutras suggest that male and female take inspiration from nature for inventing their own love-play,' Paine whispered in his low, seductive tone. He pushed back an errant strand of hair from her face. 'There are several positions named for animals: the mare, the elephant, the blow of the boar, sporting of the sparrow. The list is quite extensive.'

Julia blushed furiously. 'You have the most scandalous conversation of anyone I've ever met.'

'Hush, Julia.' Paine rose up over her, turning his attention to her face. His hands crept to the bow that secured her hat. 'We'll have to get rid of this monstrosity.' He untied the hat and tossed it aside. 'It's far too hard to kiss you with this thing on.' He kissed her hard on the mouth, easing her gently back on to the blanket, his body covering her. 'That's known as the "kiss that kindles".' He nuzzled the side of her neck. 'What shall we try today?'

Julia struggled a bit, pushing him away long enough to speak. 'You don't have to do this, Paine. You've held up your end of the bargain. I am thoroughly ruined. You don't have to continue your instruction.' Indeed, she didn't want him to, not if that was all it was—lessons conducted much in the fashion that one might receive a piano lesson.

'I thought you liked my "instruction".' Paine reared back slightly.

'I do,' Julia stammered. How could she explain she didn't want to be the student, but a partner, an equal, without driving him away? Such an implication would send Paine fleeing, validating everything he believed about virginal débutantes and their obsessive goal to capture a husband.

'I'm sorry. I was cow-handed in my approach a moment ago,' Paine said, his gaze studying her, no doubt seeing more than she wanted him to see. 'I want to do this and you want this, too.'

Julia felt her face burn, knowing he had not over-looked the effect of his hands on her legs, knowing he had proof that his actions had aroused her. She returned his gaze, seeing in his eyes the rise of his desire. It was enough to convince her he understood her dilemma. There was something else in his gaze, too, she couldn't name—perhaps a desperation that had clawed its way to the surface. But she couldn't imagine what a man like Paine Ramsden had to be desperate about. He bent over her, taking her mouth in a long, searching kiss, until her body gave him compliance.

He shouldn't have done it, Paine thought ruefully. He lay on his back, one hand thrown over his eyes against the sun, on the blanket next to a dozing Julia. He told himself she'd been a willing participant in what had transpired on the blanket. But the argument was a weak one, only a technical justification at best. She was an innocent, untouched by any but him. He was experienced in the art of pleasure and arousal. He'd known he could easily coax her submission. He'd used her own body against her. In truth, she'd hardly had a choice.

It wasn't that the coupling hadn't been enjoyable for her. It was just that he had done it for the wrong reasons. He'd wanted her from the moment he'd seen her in the breakfast room and so he'd taken her with no regard for the uncertainties surrounding them.

Her requirements of him had been met. She was thoroughly ruined in both reality and circumstance. No well-bred young lady put herself in the hands of Paine Ramsden for a night, let alone an entire week spent in his company, a week that had her visiting gaming hells and making a mad dash across country unescorted. They had not spoken of continuing their sexual relationship beyond the confines of the agreement. There were many things they'd not talked about and should have. Their association was quickly spiralling far beyond the parameters of their original intent.

Certainly, acting as her self-appointed protector hadn't been part of the deal or even discussed. Yet, the role had been implicitly affirmed. That was at the core of what bothered him. He had brought her here to

Dursley Park for her own safety because it was the right thing to do.

He didn't want Julia thinking that she had to pay for his favours, that his protection was bought only with the currency of sex or that she would suddenly find herself set adrift if she failed to comply with his wishes. His pride couldn't bear such a notion. More importantly, his honour would not tolerate it. For a man believed by many to have very little honour, the thought was humbling.

Yet, he had perpetrated the act with utter careless-ness, all in the name of selfish need. He'd even gone so far as to couch it in terms of 'education'. Julia had seen right through that ruse, just as he'd immediately seen her reasons for refusing to accept it under the guise of such educational experience. She was not mentally or emotionally equipped to transmute their congress into simple terms of physical gratification and leave it at that. He was partly at fault. He'd not given her the tools to adjust her way of thinking. Instead, he'd prattled on about the Hindus seeing sex as a sacred expression of religion. Now, he was facing the consequences. Julia wanted him as more than a tutor in the sexual arts. Worse, he could not, should not, allow her to believe more was possible and yet he craved her.

He wanted her with a desire so intense he'd been willing to put all other considerations aside, pride and honour be damned, just to caress her body, to be inside her again, to feel the hot pulsing rush of his seed and know that the shuddering release of his climax would bring the exquisite peace he'd mysteriously found with her.

No matter how short lived that peace was.

He would need her again.

Already his coveted peace was slipping away. He'd expected it would. The eastern scholars he knew in India had taught that only true peace came from within. No one could give peace to another, at least not permanently. One had to find permanent peace from within oneself. They'd also taught him the key to such peace started with forgiveness of oneself. Paine often doubted he'd ever be able to do that. Julia's purity was a stark reminder of how far he'd fallen.

He thought of the story he'd fabricated to explain Julia's association with him—that her love had reformed him. It made a nice fantasy to ponder, starting with the bit about her falling in love with him. A gently bred girl like Julia would come to rue the day she fell in love with a man like him. She'd been very clear the night she'd come to him about why she was there. He was the most immoral man she could think of, who would do what she asked, all because he lived by a different code she could not completely understand.

Still, she'd put her trust in him. She'd followed him to the country and she'd fought beside him on the road. She never doubted his ability to protect her and when she turned those green eyes on him, they were not full of calculation, proving she no longer thought of him as only a man to stand to stud. The thought gave him some hope and, in his experience, hope was a dangerous thing, especially for a desperate man.

Beside him, Julia stirred, her hair loose and warm from the sun. She was beautiful and he felt his body surge, wanting to take her again and lose himself in her. But he was a man of honour now, and he could not justify such selfishness again.

'How long did I sleep?' Julia asked, raising up on one arm.

'Not that long. A half-hour,' Paine said carelessly. He reached for the hamper. 'Hungry?'

He waited until they'd finished off the picnic before bringing up the subject plaguing him. He smiled as Julia wiped her hands on a cloth napkin. Even outdoors with bare feet she had good manners. He'd known from the first she was a lady, a real lady.

'Julia, we have to talk about our future,' he began.

Julia looked up from folding her napkin, a small frown knitting her brow. 'I thought we'd agreed not to talk about Oswalt today.'

Paine shook his head. 'This is not about Oswalt. This is about us. You and me.' He rushed on before she could break in or misunderstand him. 'I must apologise for what happened on the blanket. We should have talked about this before anything like that happened. Our agreement has been fulfilled and I don't want you to feel obligated to have sex with me as any further part of our relationship.'

He felt awkward saying the words with Julia. In the past, he'd talked about sex quite conversantly with numerous women. In his past liaisons, such negotiations had been commonplace.

Julia coloured at his frankness. Then she surprised him, putting her hand over his where it rested in his lap. 'You have done me an enormous service by bringing me here. Without knowing me, you have offered yourself as my protector. It never crossed my mind that you were a man to provide those services and expect an exchange of favours.'

'Perhaps it should have,' Paine said wryly. 'You know what I am, how I live. I'm a dark rake. I sleep with hundreds of women and play in the underworld. I am thoroughly debauched by the *ton*'s standard.'

Julia gave a soft laugh. 'So they all say. I am hard pressed to believe it. They don't understand you.' She looked down at her lap, biting her lip in contemplation. 'Paine, I owe you an apology. I came to you for sordid reasons, but even so, you've treated me with far more respect than what I reserved for you. I looked at you through society's eyes and I misjudged you.'

'And now, Julia? What do you see?' He was heady with desire, swamped by it, in fact. He exhaled heavily, fighting her effect on him. She had no idea how much he wanted to wrap his body around her.

She reached up to stroke his cheek. 'I see a good man who hides his true self from others.'

There it was.

Was it possible that in one sentence, she'd seen what everyone had missed? Julia made him think the impossible—that he could be saved, drawn back from the abyss, that perhaps he could offer her more than he thought.

He wrapped a strand of her heavy hair around a finger. 'Why do you think that is?' he mused.

Julia shrugged. 'I don't know. I am sure this good man has his reasons.'

'No, that's not what I meant,' Paine whispered. 'Why is it that you see a good man when everyone else sees a rake?'

Julia tilted her head and gave him a contemplative smile. 'I'm not the only one who sees it. Your family sees it, too.' She tugged at him. 'Now, make love to me because you want to. No more talk of agreements, Paine.'

Chapter Thirteen

Peyton was waiting for them, for him, when they got back. Paine hid a smile. Peyton wasn't overtly waiting for them in the foyer, that wasn't his style. But he'd been on the lookout for them. The sudden hustle of servants upon their return indicated as much. Paine would have bet good money he'd barely turned into the stable yard before news of his return reached Peyton in the study.

The door to the study was open. It would be difficult to get by there without being seen. This was, of course, what Peyton had planned. Paine turned to Julia in the wide main hall and nodded towards Peyton's open door. 'I need to see my brother. Will you excuse me?' There were many things he and Peyton had to talk about. He wasn't ready to have Julia hear the family laundry aired and he wasn't sure how diplomatic Peyton would be about it. But he was ready to face it, armed with Julia's confidence and a new sense of hope.

Paine saw Julia up the stairs and then strode towards the office, prepared to reconcile with Peyton for the first time in twelve years.

Peyton looked up from the papers on his desk at the sound of footsteps. 'Paine, you're back. Did you have a good time?' he asked as if he hadn't known they'd arrived twenty minutes before.

'Yes. Julia is upstairs, resting. I thought we could talk. There are things that should be said,' Paine said, taking charge of the conversation.

Peyton nodded. 'Would you like a drink?' He motioned to the polished cabinet that displayed a series of cut-crystal decanters.

'No, thank you,' Paine declined, taking a chair across from the expansive desk, marvelling at Peyton's nervousness—Peyton, who had always been decisive and in control.

'You've changed so much, Paine. I can hardly take it in when I look at you,' Peyton began. 'You're a man now. It's hard to countenance that my baby brother is two and thirty.' He shook his head. 'I still think of you as much younger. But you're a man full grown...'

He foundered there and Paine knew Peyton was thinking of the long years in exile when there'd been no letters from India assuring him of his brother's safety and well-being; of the long months Paine had been home in London, but sent no word.

They stared at each other, lost in awkward silence. Paine shook his head and shrugged. 'I should have written, but I didn't know how. I'd been so foolish, so stupid. I didn't know even where to start. I was a complete disgrace.' Or even if his brother would want to hear anything. Peyton had been so angry, Paine was sure his older brother would be glad to simply have him out of the way, no longer a blight on the family name.

'My sentiments, exactly, only about me. I have regretted my behaviour, my choices, every day since you left. I was so stupid, so foolish, a complete disgrace.' Peyton used Paine's words and gave a sad smile, one that showed the deep brackets at the corners of his mouth. For the first time, Paine was struck by the amount of time that had passed and how close he'd come when they'd been attacked on the road to not having this moment with his brother at all. Perhaps he was still foolish.

'I want to hear what you've been doing, how you've spent your years,' Peyton said.

'I'm sure you can guess most of it,' Paine said, reluctant to roll out his accomplishments like a litany and even more reluctant to share his sins. The East was a different world, half a globe away. He wasn't sure Peyton would understand what it meant to move in that world.

'Please tell me,' Peyton asked softly. 'Ridiculous pride has kept us from communicating too long.'

It was all he needed to let the stories come. Once he started talking, Paine was surprised how easily the telling came. The wanderings into strange countries when he had no sense of direction, setting up the shipping business when he found he needed a purpose, selling the shipping firm when he'd made his fortune and decided it was time to come home. There were other stories, too, that tumbled out. Stories of the people he'd met, the cultures and lifestyles he had encountered, the beliefs that had challenged him in his own thinking. Long shadows were falling outside on the lawn when he finished.

Peyton looked impressed. 'It seems you've come full circle then, Paine. Home again with a fortune at your disposal and years of hard-won wisdom. What are your plans now?'

'I own a gambling hell, which I am sure Aunt Lily told you.' He saw Peyton trying not to wince at the mention. He moved on. 'I recently bought a house in Brook Street that I want to turn into a hotel.' Paine held Peyton's gaze. 'There are things to do, however. Oswalt is still a menace. That comes first. Then we'll see.'

Peyton raised his dark brows and steepled his hands. 'And Julia Prentiss? How does she fit into all this? Is she a pawn or something more?'

Paine heard the challenge in his brother's voice and he clenched his jaw to hold back his rising temper. Peyton was trying to see him as a new man. But he couldn't expect Peyton to change over night. To him, he would probably always remain the little brother in some capacity. 'She came to me, if that's what you're asking. I didn't go looking for a chance to get at Oswalt.'

'But you certainly didn't turn her away once you heard she was connected to Oswalt.' Peyton's challenge was no longer veiled.

'How could I? I of all people know what Oswalt is capable of. I could not turn my back on her, especially when I have the means to stop him.'

'Do you? Have the means to stop him? You thought you could handle him the last time, too. You were lucky you weren't killed.' In his temper, Peyton had risen behind the desk to his full height.

'I'm not a naïve stripling about town these days,' Paine warned, gaining his feet to match his brother. 'I know how to handle men of his ilk.'

'No. You have come here for my help. If you want it, you'll let me handle everything,' Peyton insisted, eyes flaring over being gainsaid.

'I didn't come home to let others fight my battles,' Paine growled in a near shout.

'For once, can't you do what you're told?' Peyton barely refrained from yelling.

'Why? I won't hide behind you or anyone else.'

'Because I can't stand to lose you again. Because I need to make it up to you.' The admission tumbled out of its own accord, bringing the brothers' argument to a halt. The tension dissipated.

'I should never have let you go the first time,' Peyton said quietly, years of remorse clear in his eyes. 'I thought taking on Oswalt would teach you sense. I never dreamed it would lead to a duel, that it would come to a head over a woman. But you and your misplaced chivalry wouldn't hear otherwise. By the time I realised what was really happening, it was too late to protect you. It won't happen again. I didn't mean to fight with you, Paine. I only meant to say I was sorry.'

Paine sank into his chair, trying to absorb it all. 'All these years, I thought you were ashamed of me. I couldn't face you afterwards, knowing that I'd disappointed you.' All this time, he'd not once thought that Peyton had anything to apologise for.

Peyton shook his head. 'I won't fail you again, Paine. This time, we face Oswalt together. Tell me what you have planned.'

And just like that, he was absolved.

Paine was at peace and he savoured it, even though he knew it couldn't last long. He let himself bask in the knowledge of his brother's love and Julia's honest affection. It would only be a matter of days before the fruits of his hastily dashed notes in London would arrive at Dursley Park.

Within a week, Flaherty's news would catch up with him, giving him insight into why Oswalt was after Julia's uncle and what the bastard planned next. Mail would also arrive regarding the business loans he'd proposed to influential members of the *ton*. Soon, the plan would be in motion. They would return to London and the issue with Oswalt could be resolved, leaving Julia free of the man's shadow.

Free to do what? He hadn't been able to adequately answer his brother's questions regarding Julia. In terms of his feelings for Julia, he feared he'd picked the very worst time to fall in love. But what else could it be when the thought of her being free to pursue another caused his stomach to churn?

Paine's short idyll lasted approximately a week and a day; the end heralded by a note from Flaherty that arrived neatly tucked inside a trunk full of Julia's clothes from Madame Broussard. Julia discovered the letter while shaking out the last of the gowns from their meticulous tissue wrappings. It fluttered to the floor, the plain brown-paper envelope a stark contrast in a room filled with a riot of flounces and lace.

Julia bent and scooped up the envelope, concluding immediately that the note was not an additional note from Madame Broussard, whose correspondence had been on top of the tissue wrappings and strongly scented with lilacs. She turned the envelope over, noting the masculine scrawl.

She doubted the letter was for her. First, this letter had been secreted in the trunk in such a way that implied the writer was worried about discovery. Second, the letter was clearly not for her. No one would know where to send a letter for her. No one knew she was with Paine Ramsden, and certainly no one knew she'd visited Madame Broussard's. No one would know she was expecting an order of clothes.

Only Paine knew. Julia smiled to herself over Paine's consideration for her. In the rush of their departure from London, he'd thought of everything, dashing off that note to the dressmaker so that Julia would have her gowns, at least enough of them. The rest—her evening gowns and fancier town dresses—would be waiting upon her return.

She didn't have to be a mind-reader to deduce that the note she held probably had something to do with when that return would occur. That return worried her immensely. Going back to London would force her to deal decisively with Oswalt as well as bring her association with Paine to a head. Once her situation with Oswalt was resolved, she reasoned that her situation with Paine would be dissolved as well.

More than that, her future, whatever it would be, would begin when they returned to London. There was her family to consider in all this. What were they thinking right now? Did they miss her? Worry for her? Understand why she had taken such drastic action? Would they receive her when she returned and give her a chance to explain? She'd known when she embarked on this mad scheme that after she was ruined, she might very well be turned out of the family. She'd known it was a very real risk she was running. Still, she wanted a chance to explain.

Who knew one simple envelope could cause such turmoil?

Julia made a face at the envelope. There was nothing for it. She had to go and find Paine.

She found him in what had become his customary place—sitting at the long table that dominated the length of the book-lined library. She could easily understand the appeal of the room. The far end was graced with floor-to-ceiling windows that provided both the ability to flood the room with light and the ability to soothe an agitated guest with a view of elegant expanse of verdant grass.

Paine was dressed casually in a lawn shirt and paisley waistcoat, a simple cravat tied at his neck. The ledgers in front of him held all his attention as he tallied columns and wrote sums. Peyton was with him, sprawled on a leather couch near the windows, immersed in a book.

A peaceful scene. Julia hated to interrupt it. She'd much rather stay buried in the country with Paine at her side. However hard it had been for Paine to come home, the choice had served him well. She still didn't understand all the dynamics behind his separation from his brothers, but it was easy to see he was loved here and forgiven.

She bit her lip and felt her cheeks heat at the thought. Since the picnic, they'd been together every night. Peyton had given them separate rooms, but that hadn't stopped Paine from visiting after the house quietened. She looked forwards to those hours spent in the dark, when Paine was by turn both lover and teacher. Even now in the bright light of the afternoon, she was nearly giddy with anticipation of the evening ahead at the very sight of him.

Julia pushed the door fully open and stepped into the room.

'Hello, Julia.' Paine looked up from his ledger before she'd had time to speak. Was he that aware of her presence that he could sense when she was in the room? It was a novel fantasy. 'How are your dresses? Don't tell me you're done trying them on already?'

'They're lovely. But, no, I haven't tried any of them on yet.' Julia approached the table, aware that Peyton surreptitiously watched them from the couch. 'This came for you. It was tucked inside the trunk.'

Paine took the envelope and studied it. 'Thank you. It's from Flaherty, one of my investigators. I've been hoping to hear from him.'

'Is it about the club?' She asked as he scanned the note.

'No,' Paine said without looking up.

Julia waited, hoping to hear more and feeling left out when nothing more was forthcoming. 'Is it about my uncle?' she pressed. Paine had mentioned such an inquiry before.

Paine looked up from his perusal of the letter. 'No, not directly anyway.' He smiled, but Julia was not fooled.

'I will not be treated like a child, Paine. If that note concerns me, I want to know what's in it.' Julia could feel her temper rising. The blackguard was trying to dismiss her.

'Julia, there is no need for you to worry,' Paine said pointedly, looking up from the document in irritation. 'Everything will be taken care of.'

Peyton rose from his couch and came to stand behind Paine, reading the letter over his brother's shoulder. Paine made no attempt to shield the letter from his brother's perusal. That was the final spark that ignited her temper.

'I see. Only men are allowed to worry.' She placed her hands squarely on the table and leaned across it. 'Well, that's not good enough, Paine. There is every need for me to worry. A coachman is dead and my uncle faces financial ruin, all because of me. You cannot fob me off with a smile and false assurances. I am in this up to my neck.'

Peyton eyed her speculatively, seeming to weigh the situation. 'I suspect your uncle faces more than financial ruin, Miss Prentiss.' He nodded towards the note. 'Let her read it, Paine. It's best she knows the worst straight away. Sugar coating never makes things better in the long term. I'll ring for tea and have a footman search out Crispin.'

Paine gave a tight laugh. 'Tea and Crispin? Speaking of "sugar-coating", dear brother, is that your way of calling for a family meeting?'

'Why, yes, it is.' Peyton said without prevarication.

'I don't really understand any of this,' Julia said, waving the now well-worn and -read note in her hand. Tea and Crispin had arrived and the letter had been passed about. It was thankfully short, but informative. 'I'm not sure what marriage to me has to do with the cargo on Cousin Gray's ship.'

Paine spread his hands on his thighs and drew a deep breath. 'Those two occurrences are not linked to each other, but they are both linked to a larger plot.'

'Which is?'

'That's the part that is still unclear.' Paine looked at her with his sharp eyes. 'What is clear though, Julia, is that you're in danger and your family is in danger when it comes to Oswalt. He's convinced your uncle that they're on the same side, that you're the enemy. In reality, your aunt and uncle are in as much danger as you are, although it's a danger of a different sort.'

'Oswalt can't marry them.' There was a touch of acid to her tone. Paine had let her read the letter from Flaherty, but he was still trying to protect her by speaking in vagaries. He knew more of the puzzle than he let on.

Paine stood up and began pacing, making his familiar gesture of riffling through his hair as he spoke his thoughts out loud. She would have found it endearing if she hadn't been so annoyed with him. This was her plan, her choices. How dare he exclude her?

'Here's the story we know so far,' Paine began. 'Oswalt makes a habit of ruining noblemen. Usually—in fact, always—it's ruination of a financial sort. He likes the challenge of the chase. That's what makes the situation with your uncle so difficult. There's no money to speak of, except for this potential cargo, and there's no challenge—the two things Oswalt traditionally thrives on. Bottom line, Oswalt is not after your uncle's money.'

'But the cargo is valuable,' Julia cut in. 'Uncle Barnaby says it will cover our debts.'

'Certainly that's true.' Paine gestured to the letter Julia held. 'Flaherty confirms that the indigo and cotton carried on the ship will be valuable to your uncle. However, Oswalt is a merchant. He has a fleet of his own ships at his disposal. He doesn't need to go after your uncle's cargo. He could have one just like it with less risk and more efficiency.'

'Then why?' Julia furrowed her brow. Admittedly, her sheltered experiences with the world provided little for her to draw on in terms of options. 'If he doesn't need money, what does he need that my uncle has?'

'That's the question we are trying to answer,' Peyton put in, reaching for another sandwich from the tea tray. 'Can you think of anything your uncle might be dabbling in? Investments? Agriculture?'

Julia shook her head. Nothing came to mind. 'I can't think of anything he's mentioned over dinner. Most of our dinner conversation is about his Parliament work.'

'Could that be it?' Paine asked slowly.

'I see what you're thinking,' Crispin spoke up in excitement. 'Perhaps Oswalt wants a voting politician in his pocket. If he financially bails out Julia's uncle, the viscount will feel beholden to him.'

'That wouldn't last long,' Peyton mused cynically. 'That's a fairly terminal exchange of goods and services.'

'Not if Oswalt married the viscount's niece. Then he'd be in the family and the expectation could go on indefinitely,' Paine pointed out.

'And cure his pox at the same time,' Crispin added flippantly from his corner, forgetting his present company.

Julia sucked in a quick breath. 'Pox?'

'Crispin!' Paine shot his brother a quelling look.

Crispin shrugged, unapologetic. 'Everyone knows.'

'I didn't know!' Julia cried in a choked voice. 'Did my uncle know?' she whispered, unable to keep the horror from her face. The more she knew about the backdrop against which her wedding contract had been negotiated, the darker it became.

Paine shook his head and reached briefly for her hand in a comforting gesture. 'I don't know.'

'Sorry,' Crispin muttered into his teacup.

'Let's focus on one issue at a time.' Paine resumed

his pacing. 'Perhaps Oswalt is playing for the right to pull the puppet strings in Parliament. Are there other ideas? What else does the viscount have that Oswalt would want?'

'Land? An estate?' Peyton suggested.

It was Julia's turn to respond. 'My uncle's estate isn't nearly half as big as Dursley Hall. It's hard to believe anyone would go to so much trouble for a small manor when there are larger prizes out there. Besides, Oswalt couldn't get the estate anyway. It's not for sale. It's entailed. Surely a master planner like Oswalt would know that.'

'That's it,' Paine pronounced, hardly needing a moment to think. 'He's after the title.'

'Paine, that's an enormous leap of logic,' Peyton cautioned.

'I don't see how he could get it.' Julia agreed. 'Titles are bestowed by the Crown and my uncle has an heir. Why, Oswalt isn't even related.' A hand flew to her mouth. 'Yet. Marriage to me would change that. Children of ours might inherit if Gray or the others don't marry. But it seems unlikely that all three of them wouldn't produce a single son between them.'

Paine shrugged. 'There are other more direct ways to get a title than staking it all on a roll of the genealogical dice. Oswalt could be made a knight,' he put in. 'Perhaps the king would knight him as a favour for saving a peer financially, especially if he was already married to that peer's niece. The king might even see that Oswalt is named the trustee for the estate since it's his money propping it up and he would have a connection by marriage.

'I'll have Flaherty dig around and see if Oswalt's put a petition in motion to that end. Additionally, perhaps Oswalt can argue years of economic servitude to the Crown. There's no contesting that he's made money for the empire.' Paine's eyes assessed her face and she felt herself smile in spite of herself.

She felt better until Crispin said, 'There's always murder, too. He could simply marry Julia and then arrange to have the three brothers encounter untimely demises.'

Paine and Peyton shot him quelling looks, but the damage was already done. Julia blanched at the blunt assessment. It was what she'd been thinking. Was Oswalt capable of seeing three young men dead? What kind of tortured soul could wilfully engineer such atrocity? Julia shivered at the thought.

'None the less, all this speculation assumes the ship comes back,' Paine continued, trying to gloss over Crispin's blunt assessment. 'Need I point out that Oswalt's job is much easier if the ship doesn't return? Without the cargo, the viscount owes creditors *and* Oswalt.'

'Gray's ship will come back. He's never failed,' Julia said with grim conviction.'

'Ship or not, the most important issue now is what

we will do about Oswalt, assuming that our assumptions are correct.'

'That's simple,' Paine ground out. 'We go back to London and expose him before he can act on all the machinery he's put into motion. Once the *ton* gets wind of his conspiracy to undo one of their own, society will do the rest.'

'Exposure will require proof. There will be an element of risk,' Peyton reminded the group sternly.

'Anything worthwhile contains risk. I am well aware of the risks involved when dealing with Oswalt, probably better aware than most. That makes me eminently capable of seeing this situation resolved to my satisfaction.' Paine spoke confidently, refusing to be cautioned.

Julia gave him a searching glance. There was so much she didn't know about his past with Oswalt. His motivations for so fully engaging Oswalt were more than a fleeting concern. Although it was flattering to believe that he did all this on her behalf as her champion, reality suggested there were other, stronger forces at work that prompted his choice.

Paine needed her protection as much as she needed his. Oswalt was dangerous to them all. Around her the men talked of risks and benefits, but she'd had enough. She had to end this before another man, one she cared for immensely, ended up injured or dead. She had to get away from Paine Ramsden for his sake.

Julia stood up and smoothed her skirts. Her voice

was firm as she made her pronouncement. 'Gentlemen, I thank you for your input and your services. It has helped me see the situation I face and, in part, the situation I created when I left my uncle's home. It is also clear to me that I cannot in good conscience continue to implicate others in a web of my own making. Tomorrow, I would kindly request the use of a travelling coach so that I can return to London.' She turned to face Paine directly.

'I am afraid we can't let you do that.'

Julia looked around in confusion for the voice. She'd certainly expected to hear those words of refusal, but she'd expected Paine to be the one to say them. The feminine tone came as a complete surprise.

Julia stared in amazement as Beth set aside her needlework and rose from the chair she occupied near the work table. Julia had been so wrapped up in the discussion over Oswalt's motives, she hadn't heard or seen the woman come in. Beth gave her a kind smile and moved to stand beside her, tossing Paine and his brothers a scolding stare. 'Shame on you all, you can't simply ride back to London and declare war on Oswalt. Think about what it will mean to Julia. She'll be beyond the pale if she shows up in your company.'

'We'll be discreet, Cousin,' Peyton began in a placating tone. 'We'll take her to Dursley House where she'll be well guarded, and we'll be with her whenever we're out.'

Beth gave an unladylike snort that made Julia like the woman immensely. 'Just like a man, even a well-meaning man. Men don't have to think of these things, so they don't,' she said dismissively. 'How will you explain Julia's return? Especially, how will you explain why Julia is at Dursley House and not back with her family? And who will be at Dursley House? She can't stay there with the three of you! She needs a chaperon, a very formidable one at that. What would the *ton* say if they knew she was living with three men? Have you thought of that?'

Julia smothered a giggle. In spite of the seriousness of their circumstances, there was a modicum of hilarity behind watching the Ramsden brothers shuffling from foot to foot, staring at each other, waiting for one of them to pick up Cousin Beth's social gauntlet. In truth, there was no arguing with Beth. She was entirely correct. They had analysed Oswalt quite thoroughly, but had not addressed the immediate concern of what to do with Julia.

'Point well taken, Cousin,' Peyton said after a bit more shuffling and staring passed between the brothers and they somehow decided Peyton got to eat humble pie because he was the eldest and the earl. 'You're precisely right, as always, about these matters. To start with, I'll write to Aunt Lily. She's in town and can take up residence at Dursley House immediately. That will provide Julia with an appropriate chaperon. A chaperon doesn't get much more proper than the Dowager Marchioness of Bridgerton, fondly known as our father's sister or Aunt Lily.'

Beth would not be satisfied with half-measures. 'That's a fine beginning, but what about the rest? I think it will look exceedingly odd for her to stay with friends with her family so close at hand, mere streets away.'

This was more difficult and for a while Julia thought there was no viable explanation. Surely she wouldn't have to return to her uncle's home? She wouldn't be safe there for a moment and all this would have been for naught.

'If Julia and I were engaged,' Paine offered slowly, giving the impression that they were hearing his thoughts the instant he thought them, 'we could say I wanted her to meet my family and get to know them without the bother of commuting between homes, that I wanted her to spend as much time at Dursley House as possible with my Aunt Lily, since Aunt Lily will be handling the bulk of the wedding plans.'

It wasn't a perfect explanation, but it was all they had and it did make sense. After all, Julia's aunt and uncle didn't move in the same lofty circles as the Earl of Dursley. Commuting between the grand town house of the earl and the shabby, only marginally acceptable neighbourhood occupied by Julia's family could be viewed as commuting between levels in the social hierarchy and that was awkward for everyone in the *ton*.

'Julia's presence at Dursley House suggests that my

marriage has my brother's full support and, by consequence, that Julia has my brother's full support,' Paine
said, his conviction growing as his thoughts came together.

'Well,' Beth said hesitantly, 'it might work, but
people will still look askance at the speed of such a declaration.'

'If they do, I doubt they'd dare to speak such a thing
out loud. Peyton here will burn their reputation to a cinder,'
Paine said jokingly, but knowing very well that Peyton
held power amongst the *ton* and few dared to cross him.

'I believe Paine is right in this case, Beth. If people
believe I support the match, they might question in
private, but won't dare to breathe a scandalous word in
public,' Peyton averred. 'Now that's settled, I think we
should proceed to dinner and celebrate an engagement.'

'It's just pretend,' Julia blurted out.

'Don't let anyone hear you say that. Our success
depends on our believability,' Paine scolded and Julia
sensed the scold was not a tease. He was in dead earnest,
as they all were.

That decided it. She had to put a stop to these mad
schemes. They risked too much for her and she was cognisant of it to the extreme.

'I cannot let you all do this. It is too much to ask and
it is not your concern, not really. I never meant for this
to go so far.' Julia turned to Paine. 'Paine, you are
chivalrous to a fault and for that, I relieve you of all obligation with my thanks.'

She saw his jaw tighten as she swept past him to the door, but to his credit he did not explode. To her surprise, he actually let her leave the library and make it up to her room. It was disappointing, but for the best. She'd expected him to rant or at the very least follow her upstairs and make an effort to protest her request. But he did none of those things. Yet. Or, perhaps like her, he would soon realise just how out of control things had got and that severing ties with her was in his better interest.

Chapter Fourteen

Upstairs, Julia folded a few gowns back into the tissue paper and placed them in the trunk she'd so recently unpacked. When she'd gone downstairs to give Paine the note, she'd known the missive's contents would dictate their return to London. But she had not planned to so abruptly sever her ties with Paine. Then again, she had not known the full danger of her situation. She bent over the trunk and heard the door open behind her.

'Obligation has nothing to do with it,' Paine drawled. 'You cannot relieve me from that which was never a duty.'

Julia turned from the trunk, summoning her resolve. She couldn't extricate herself from this web, but she could set Paine free. Her growing feelings for him dictated she do as much. 'Don't do this, Paine.'

'Don't do what?' Paine lounged in the doorway, leaning against the white frame and looking somewhat intimidating in his maleness in her feminine abode.

'Don't confuse reality with fantasies and suppositions,' Julia said meaningfully.

'Perhaps you're the one doing that,' Paine returned, coming to take the clothes she held from her hands. 'The reality is that you are in very real peril from Oswalt in every way possible, both physically and socially. The fantasy is that you think you can go back to London alone and manage to untangle his deceits.'

Julia shook her head, finding his closeness intoxicating as always. 'Please don't try to seduce me out of this.' She sounded like she was begging and she was. She had no idea what she would do in London, if her uncle would even listen to her and believe her claims, if he would protect her from Oswalt.

Paine's eyes were intent on hers; her resolve all but collapsed at what she saw in them. 'Paine…'

His mouth took hers softly. The kiss was slow, kindling a heat in her that would not be rushed. This would not be a frantic, desperate coupling. Nor was it a farewell. Nothing in his demeanour suggested he felt it would be the last time for them. This was a lover's seduction of a beloved partner and she revelled in it.

Paine unhooked the buttons at the back of her dress, pushing the gown off her shoulders to the floor, his mouth intent on hers. He guided her back to the bed, sweeping away the piles of new gowns with his arm. He eased her back, leaving her only long enough to strip out of his clothes. Then he joined her on the bed, lowering himself over her, fitting himself between her thighs. His slow thrusts were as powerful as any of the more heated couplings they'd shared. Julia found herself powerless to resist the call to pleasure he offered. She fought his temptation valiantly. She knew why he did this.

'Paine, I can't allow this,' she tried to argue between languorous kisses.

'This is not about rules and contracts, Julia.' Paine stared down at her. 'This is an aide-mémoire. When you came to me, you became mine to care for.' His phallus, rigid and warm and deep inside her, could not have been a more potent reminder.

Paine was gone from her side in the morning as usual. Julia took it as a good sign from the fates. It would be far easier to leave without having to face him. Facing him would mean a quarrel and she'd learned last night that Paine didn't fight fairly. Still, she was exceedingly grateful to have one last night with him. What Paine did not understand was that her feelings for him were nearly as hazardous to her as the situation with Oswalt.

Julia rang for a maid and laid out clothes for travel.

She would send the maid for a footman to carry her trunk and to see to the coach.

Although it was early, a maid appeared promptly and hurried off to carry out her orders. That made Julia suspicious. The earl's cousin ran an efficient household, but Julia had expected some resistance since it had been plain that her solution was not welcomed by the stubborn Ramsden brothers. Perhaps the maid had gone to inform Paine instead.

Julia dressed hurriedly, pushing aside her qualms. She didn't have time to create conspiracies out of whole cloth—not when she had a very real conspiracy to unravel back in London. When the maid returned with a footman, Julia half-expected to see Paine follow her into the room. She experienced a twinge of disappointment when he didn't.

Without questions, the footman shouldered the trunk and politely inquired if that was all. He and the maid left the room and Julia swallowed hard. All she needed to do was walk downstairs to the coach. No one was going to stop her. She should be exuberant. She held her head high, although there was no one to see her this time of day except the servants, and swept down the stairs.

Outside, the sun was just up, heralding a good day for travel. The horses stamped in the crisp air. The coachman, dressed in Dursley livery, touched the brim of his hat when he saw her. Julia nodded. She took one last look at the house and stepped inside the coach. Paine would thank her later for this.

'Beautiful day for a drive.' The object of her ruminations was sprawled on the seat of the roomy coach, impeccably turned out in riding gear, Hessians and a well-tied cravat, the clean smell of his morning *toilette* subtly filling the carriage.

Smiling would definitely hurt her position. It would be hard to convince Paine she was angry with him, but she found herself smiling nevertheless.

'Happy to see me?'

Julia settled on the front-facing seat. 'I asked for a loan of a travelling coach and driver so that I could leave this morning.'

'And my brother has graciously supplied all that you asked.'

'That's an understatement. I didn't ask for company.'

'Aha, but you didn't not ask,' Paine countered smoothly.

Julia frowned. 'How is that? I don't think that's even a grammatically correct sentence.'

Paine's eyes were dancing in jest. He warmed to his game. 'You didn't not ask,' he repeated. 'You merely said you would be returning to London. You never stated we couldn't come along, or specifically that I couldn't come along.'

Julia grimaced. 'I said you were relieved of obligation.'

'But that doesn't mean I can't come. It only assumes that I am not obliged to come or that I was obliged to do anything in the first place, which I've already pointed out that I was not.'

'You're being obtuse. It was implied that I wished to return alone,' Julia snapped.

'And I *implied* that I disagreed with that choice.' Paine smugly rapped on the coach. 'Let's be off!'

'You're insufferable,' Julia huffed, although inwardly she wasn't nearly as upset as she appeared because, at that moment, the carriage door opened and a smiling Cousin Beth poked her head in. 'Good morning. Be a dear, Julia, and move over.'

'What is this, Beth?' Paine protested, his surprise at her appearance evident.

'A young woman of virtue can't ride around the countryside in a carriage alone with a man,' Beth scolded. 'You might have played fast and loose with the rules to this point, young man, but, from here on, it's by the book.' Beth took a seat next to Julia and took out her knitting. 'I'll have a nice scarf by the time we get to London,' she said with far too much cheer.

Paine groaned. 'Now who's being insufferable?'

'That makes two of you,' Julia replied stiffly.

The house disappeared behind them and Paine leaned forwards. 'You cannot tackle Oswalt alone, Julia. It is the height of foolishness to think so.'

'So you've said. You seem quite certain of that.

Would you care to tell me why? It's a long ride to London—days, in fact—and I think it's time I knew what it is exactly that lies between you and Oswalt.'

Beth looked up from her knitting. 'Yes, Cousin. Tell her. She has a right to know.'

The sharp eyes that pierced him from across the carriage were acutely reminiscent of the way Julia had looked at him that first night in his office when she'd put her request to him. She'd given him that same unwavering gaze, so forthright, so honest and so bold that he'd known there would be no refusing then. And he knew it now. It was an ironic quality of hers that she possessed such an abundance of feminine beauty and none of the covert wiles that usually went with such attractiveness. Nothing escaped her notice and nothing was safe from her comment.

Julia tapped a foot impatiently, her eyebrow giving a supercilious quirk. 'You may begin.'

'Why should I tell you at all?' Paine protested. He seldom shared his past with anyone; now, he would have shared it twice in quite recent times—once with Peyton and now with Julia.

Julia narrowed her eyes. 'You should tell me so I can determine if I will let you meddle in my business.'

Paine would have teased her if she hadn't looked so serious. 'Meddling, is it?'

'Yes. Meddling. This was my problem from the first

and it's still my problem, even if the parameters I thought I was dealing with have been a bit altered in their scope,' Julia insisted. 'I say who has access to my life.'

'You'd better decide I do. You will need me before this is over.' Paine matched her blunt tone.

'Convince me.' Julia sat back against the seat and crossed her arms, challenging him to deny her request.

She softened slightly for a moment, becoming the image of the Julia he liked best—the Julia that moaned beneath him on the picnic blanket, who thought he could slay dragons, who brought him his secret peace. 'Come, Paine, how awful could it be?'

He gave a small smile at that. 'It could be pretty awful, Julia.'

'Let me be the judge.' She leaned forwards, all rapt attention.

Paine drew a deep breath. 'I was a rowdy youth. I ran with a fast crowd of young bucks when I came up to town. Most of the people in my set were younger sons and rather cynical about their lot in life. It became the trademark of our group that we flaunted the fact that we were the spares and in some cases, like mine, the spare to the spare. We were "non-essential" to our families so we lived hard, pushing convention as far as it could be pushed with outrageous feats: races, affairs, bets and dares.'

Julia made a quizzical frown. 'I can't believe Peyton made you feel that way.'

'Of course not, not directly, but Father had done the job for him. By the time Peyton was earl and I was ready to storm around town, I felt pretty "non-essential". Peyton was head of the family, Crispin was doing a stint in the military as an officer—and a fine officer he was, too, I might add. Then there was me. Peyton sent me to Oxford. I think he hoped I'd find direction there. However, I finished with no particular purpose in mind, although I received a first-class degree in the classics and loved history. Peyton wanted to set me up as an estate manager on one of the smaller family properties, but I wasn't interested in land management. Without any direction and with too much time on my hands, I was a prime candidate for falling in with that crowd.' Paine chuckled. 'It's amazing how clear the pattern seems from a distance of years.'

'That's understandable. You're not the only young man to run into that sort of trouble,' Julia offered sagely.

'Trouble with your cousins?' Paine probed.

'The two younger ones are something akin to hellions. I wouldn't be surprised if their antics have heavily contributed to the family situation these days.' Julia dismissed the subject, wagging a finger at him. 'You won't get off that easily, Paine. Now, you said you pushed convention as far as it could be pushed. Go on.'

He didn't mind her direct probe this time. Now that he'd started talking, it was easier to continue. 'Yes, I pushed convention and one day it pushed back. There was a…um…"party" for gentlemen only at an estate out in Richmond, far enough out of town to avoid real trouble or censure.'

'Party, Paine? Don't mince words. What kind of party?' Julia pressed, sensing his hesitation.

Paine cast an uncomfortable look at Cousin Beth, who looked back blandly.

'Don't mind me. I've seen more than you think, Paine. I am not so shocked by the world as you might think.'

'It was an orgy. Do you know what an orgy is?' Paine asked, shifting in his seat with acute embarrassment. If they were being blunt, he might as well ask.

Julia blushed. 'I have some idea.'

Paine nodded. 'Well, this was worse than the usual masked *demi-monde* affair, if that's what you're thinking of.'

Julia bit her lip and shifted uncomfortably. He felt ashamed for having brought it up. He easily forgot she'd only seen parts of his world for a few days. It was a sharp reminder of the type of life he'd been leading, so far away from the standards of the *ton*.

He went on, wanting to get the next part over with, to spare her. 'The gathering was to be held at a place Oswalt owned. Peyton encouraged me not to go when he heard about it. Apparently, Oswalt had acquired the property from a baron in a card game. Peyton felt it was wrong to attend an event at a place acquired in such a manner by such a person. But I didn't listen.

'In all honesty, I didn't fully understand the depth of depravity that would be on display there.' Paine waved a hand negligently. 'I thought it would be high-class prostitutes and a few wild moments in the dark. At that time, it seemed like a lark.'

He shook his head, trying to shake off the memories of the altar-like marble block set up in the ballroom, surrounded by candles and silken ropes, and of the young woman Oswalt had forcibly bound to the altar and then begun accepting bids for public congress with her.

Paine could not look at Julia or Beth, who helpfully kept her eyes on the knitting needles, as he spun his morbid tale. He'd thought it was a game at first, that the woman was a high-paid prostitute hired to play the role of sacrificial virgin. Although telling himself that did not make the spectacle any more palatable. Then it had become clear to him that the woman was not there of her own accord.

'I thought someone would speak up, someone close to Oswalt, who would carry some sway with Oswalt. Surely all these men gathered wouldn't condone such an act. But no one did and the girl was clearly terrified.' Paine swallowed hard here. 'I pushed my way through the crowd and demanded this activity be halted. I had stupidly thrown off my mask in my outrage and Oswalt merely laughed at me. He said, "Or what? You'll tell your brother, the earl?" Well, I was on the outs with Peyton, knowing he was displeased with my choice to attend in the first place and my pride was stung that Peyton had been right after all. I could not settle for such a remark that night. I threw down my glove and challenged him to a duel in front of everyone.'

'That's very noble of you,' Julia offered softly.

'No one else thought so. I wasn't the only nobleman or nobleman's son in the crowd that night. No one wanted breath of their attendance reaching the proper circles of high society. When it became known that the girl was the daughter of an unremarkable merchant, it was implicitly decided that the event simply didn't exist, it hadn't happened. No one ever spoke of it. No one acknowledged what I had seen. The event suddenly became nothing more than a squabble between me and Oswalt over a girl of questionable background, hence questionable virtue. The girl was ruined from the gossip and I was expendable as a third son whose brother had already inherited the title.'

'And the duel?' Julia asked, expectantly. At least she hadn't completely shunned him yet. That was a good sign.

'It happened. Almost. I was determined to see it through, even though I knew what had happened to the social understanding of the events. But either London society or Oswalt himself decided that the duel would not take place. Suffice it to say, someone tipped off the authorities.' Paine shrugged. 'You know the penalty for duelling.'

'Exile,' Julia supplied. 'But what happened to Oswalt?'

'Nothing. I think he bargained with the authorities

to overlook his participation in the duel. When the authorities showed up, Oswalt pressed for exile as my punishment. The outcome was decided so swiftly, Peyton could do nothing in time to intervene. He had left a few days prior to attend business at an estate not too far from London. But it was far enough away that he didn't get the news in a timely fashion.' Paine shrugged. 'Not that I would have wanted his assistance. I was too stubborn then.'

'Just then?' Julia teased.

'Vixen.' Paine smiled. 'That's the story. I think Oswalt feared what would happen if I stayed in London and had a chance to rally support and re-introduce the issue, so I had to be sent away.'

'That's awful.' Julia sighed, worry shading her eyes.

'It's the truth. I want you to know that this incident with your uncle and Oswalt is not an isolated occurrence. The man has been ruining peers, quietly and subtly, for years. He's been preying on innocent girls for much longer than that.'

'I can't believe no one has done anything about it.' Julia shook her head in disbelief.

'That's society's way. If we talk about it, it gives the problem validity. If it's ignored, then it must not exist.' Paine spread his hands on his thighs. 'But it's not my way, Julia. That's why I want to help you.'

Julia smiled at him gamely. 'And that's why I'll let you help.'

'*Let me*, is it?'

'Yes, *let you*.'

Paine pulled out his pocket watch and flipped it open. 'And my brothers, too, I hope?'

'Why is that?' Julia eyed him curiously.

'Because, by my calculations, they're an hour behind us on the road.'

Julia shot him a considering look. 'I was never going back alone, was I?'

'No, you never stood a chance,' Paine confirmed, although the reason that was true was the reason he was hesitant to acknowledge, even to himself. The idea that he should at last find himself falling in love was too new, too foreign to his way of thinking. He would need some time to get his metaphorical hands around the distinct possibility that Julia Prentiss had permanently garnered his affections.

Chapter Fifteen

Dursley House glittered a regal welcome in the summer twilight after a dusty, jouncing two-day journey back to London. Inviting as the town house looked, Julia also found it imposing, with its four storeys of long elegant windows. Dursley House on Curzon Street was an enormous step up from the home her uncle had rented on the fringes of Belgravia, which was still a respectable location, but just barely.

Julia tossed Paine a longing glance as he helped her down from the carriage. She knew it was important for her to be at Dursley House, but it didn't stop her from wanting to be alone with Paine. She'd much rather be at his Brook Street property, just the two of them, where they could shut out the world. She wondered if he felt the same.

Paine seemed to read her thoughts. 'We have to think about your reputation,' Paine said seriously in a tone that caused her stop and stare. When had he become the arbiter of the moral code? It certainly hadn't been last night at the inn. He'd hardly waited a decent interval before showing up in her room, although he'd been very quiet so as not to wake Cousin Beth in the antechamber or Peyton next door.

'My reputation?' Julia had to remember to shut her jaw. 'I thought the whole point was to *ruin* my reputation.'

'It was, but we can't openly flaunt society while we're living under my brother's roof. Remember, for the public we're a case of love at first sight. My Aunt Lily will be in residence at Dursley House with Cousin Beth, so everything will look legitimate, less like a bachelor household.'

They climbed the steps and were greeted by the butler at the door. Peyton and Crispin entered behind them, Peyton making a low-voiced inquiry of the butler as he passed. Aunt Lily met them in the large foyer, looking for the world like an efficient hostess instead of a woman who'd been uprooted from her London residence that morning to see Dursley House opened and ready for five impromptu guests that evening. She was indeed the woman Julia had seen with Paine earlier and Julia liked her immediately. She seemed the complete antithesis of her own aunt, who worried and fussed herself into a state over unplanned happenings.

'Aunt Lily, thank you for coming. May I present to you Miss Julia Prentiss?' Paine made the necessary introductions.

Aunt Lily fixed Julia with a gimlet eye and a slow inspection. Julia imagined the woman was weighing whether or not she was worth the trouble of moving residences. It seemed that even the brothers held their collective breath. At last, Lily spoke. 'So you're the gel that has Paine running in circles. That boy's a lot of trouble. Are you sure he's worth it?'

'Julia, Aunt Lily will show you to your room. You can freshen up. A maid will see to the unpacking,' Paine said before Aunt Lily could impugn him further.

Aunt Lily shot Julia a conspiratorial glance. 'Just like a man. Paine has no desire to stand in the foyer and be taken to task by his aunt any more than he wants to hear your answer to the question. But you can tell me upstairs if the boy is worth all this fuss. Come with me, dear. I'll show you to your room and you can enlighten me as to what is *really* going on. Dursley's note made a lot of demands, but little sense. You come, too, Beth. At least I'll get sense out of you.' She shot Peyton a quelling look and Julia fought back the urge to laugh at the Ramsden brothers being taken to task like errant schoolboys.

'I hope you will find everything to your liking,' Peyton put in. 'Tell Aunt Lily if there's anything you need. I've instructed Cook to lay out a light supper in the dining room in an hour, if you'd like to join us.'

To their credit, Aunt Lily and Beth sensed Julia's need to gather her thoughts and they didn't stay long in

Julia's chamber in spite of Lily's comments to the brothers. Julia was certain the two women were down the hall right now, exchanging news, and was glad for the privacy to settle into her new rooms.

Julia's room overlooked the gardens and the open windows caught the scent of the climbing roses that grew below. As town gardens went, Dursley House boasted quite a large one by urban standards.

She was glad for it. The trees and the greenery blocked out the city din and provided a soothing calm. Her nerves were on edge at the thought of being back in town. She would have preferred going to Paine's house and being alone with him in his exotic bedroom. Perhaps he would have, too. She was starting to understand what had goaded his passionate display at the inn. It was doubtful he'd be able to come to her room as long as they stayed here under the watchful eyes of Peyton and Aunt Lily, who occupied the room next door to her. It was all part of her 'protection'. Paine had made it clear that he didn't want her left alone at any time and Peyton had staunchly supported his brother's wishes.

In his residence, there would be just the two of them and a handful of day servants. Here, she was surrounded by him, his brothers and the family servants, whose loyalty was unquestionable. If need be, Dursley House could be her fortress.

She appreciated their efforts to see her well guarded.

But it was both stifling and unnerving. Peyton was probably downstairs now, meeting with the staff, coaching them about their latest guest.

Julia leaned out the window to inhale the roses. She closed her eyes and breathed in their peace. She would need the peace of the garden in the weeks to come. Paine's arguments of propriety and protection aside, there were other reasons they *had* to be at Dursley House. Dursley House was about status. She and Paine needed the credibility of the Dursley name behind them for their plan to succeed.

Paine waved up at her from the terrace, looking casual and fresh in a clean shirt and breeches. 'Julia, come down!'

Had it been an hour already? Julia changed into a simple yellow-sprigged muslin from Madame Broussard's in record time and flew down the stairs. The brothers were waiting for her in the drawing room. 'I'm sorry to be late,' she apologised.

'You look lovely. The yellow becomes you,' Paine said, coming to stand next to her and lifting her hand to his lips in a soft kiss. The gallant-suitor act startled her for a moment until she remembered the plan. Ah, the play had begun. She must remember to play her role as well. That would mean no sparring with Paine or arguing in public or private.

Beyond them in the dining room, dinner had been set

out on white cloth-covered tables lit with candles, footmen waiting to remove the covers. Peyton and Aunt Lily led the way. Paine offered her his arm for the short distance and she smiled up at him as they walked. 'This is a nice fantasy,' Julia said, hoping to convey to him that she understood his behavior and that she would act her part. Paine merely smiled. He pulled out her chair and seated her, letting his hands linger on her shoulders before taking the chair next to her.

After a short round of small talk, while the covers were removed and the footmen departed to let them eat in privacy, Peyton turned the conversation immediately to their mission at hand. Julia suspected this was the very reason they'd chosen to dine informally inside instead of outside on the terrace, enjoying the summer evening. Here, they could serve themselves and not be interfered with; indoors, they wouldn't risk the sound of their conversation being carried to unwanted ears.

'We've arrived without mishap.' Peyton raised a glass of the excellent white wine served with the fowl. But there was no rest for the weary. They'd barely taken two bites before Peyton raised their business.

'I have already met with the staff here at Dursley House and given them my strictest instructions regarding Julia. They are not to discuss her presence in this home. To do so will result in being dismissed immediately. Additionally, I have instructed them that Julia is not to leave the house without one of us with her plus an appropriate escort of footmen. Is that clear, everyone?' Peyton fixed them all in turn with his regal stare before continuing. 'Preferably, I'd like Julia to stay put. As soon as Oswalt knows the knocker is on the door, there's no doubt he'll set men to watching the house as a precaution. None the less, we will not hide like scared rabbits. Tomorrow, we tackle the *ton*. We need to talk about that.' He turned to Lily. 'You've looked over the invitations—which gathering do you recommend?'

'Invitations already?' Julia broke in. 'We've only been in town a few hours.'

'I had the knocker go up on the door before I even arrived,' Aunt Lily said as if another eight hours' notice made all the difference. The message was clear. The Earl of Dursley was a sought-after commodity.

And why not? Julia couldn't help but cast a glance at the man who sat at the head of the table. He was an older, more mature image of Paine, who was nigh on irresistible with his good looks. It had not occurred to her before just how much of an eligible *parti* Peyton Ramsden would be for the matchmaking mamas. Stable, wealthy, titled and handsome—all eminently desirable and rare characteristics to find in a marriageable man. But not for her.

Julia dropped her fork in a clatter at the realisation. Paine had ruined her for other men, even handsome look-alike peers with titles and money.

'Do you have something against the Worthington soirée, my dear?' Lily inquired innocuously from across the table.

Worthington soirée? Was that what they'd been talking about? Julia feigned attention. 'No, of course not. It should be a lovely evening.'

'Do you have something to wear?' Peyton, always the detailed planner, asked.

Julia didn't get to answer. 'Another trunk arrived from Madame Broussard's today. I put it in her room,' Aunt Lily supplied.

Julia smiled to herself. She'd seen the trunk, but hadn't had time to open it. Apparently she didn't need to. The efficient Aunt Lily probably knew the contents of the trunk down to the last button. She was getting used to the Ramsden way of managing everything and everyone. It was even starting to be entertaining, watching them try to manage each other. She would have to pick her battles and they would have to learn that Julia Prentiss could manage things, too. The Ramsdens weren't the only capable people in the world. She would miss them when all this was over and that was a sobering thought indeed.

Plans were laid quickly after that and Julia was careful to pay attention lest she become swept away in the ardent wave of Ramsden plotting. In the morning, Paine would go over to Brook Street and check on his house. She and Aunt Lily would pay calls on some of

Aunt Lily's more influential friends at their at-homes and attend a ladies' lunch. That evening, they would make their 'grand' entrance into society at the Worthington soirée.

'What about my family?' Julia asked as the planning session drew to a close. 'There's a chance we'll run into them or a chance that they'll hear of me being in town.'

'There's every chance of that. We're counting on it,' Peyton offered, pouring the last of the wine.

'The servants won't talk, but we can't really hope to keep your presence here a secret and, truly, there's no point in making this covert. After all, we'll be out in public. We *want* to be seen together,' Paine said. 'As soon as your uncle knows you're with us, I'll pay him a visit.'

Julia didn't like the sound of that. It sounded exclusive and very Ramsden-like. 'I want to be with you when you visit. I want them to know I chose this and that I am fine. They've probably been worried to death.'

'We'll see, Julia. I won't have you put in unnecessary danger,' Paine said tersely. He pushed back and rose. 'Time for bed, I think. Tomorrow will be busy and today was long.'

Julia rose to go with him. 'You did that on purpose,' she scolded in a low voice as they exited the dining room.

'Did what? Excuse myself from the table?' Paine said obtusely. 'I tend to do that on a nightly basis.'

'Absolutely. You did it so I couldn't respond to your dictates about visiting my uncle.'

Paine glanced over his shoulder, then, apparently satisfied with what he'd seen or not seen behind them, pulled her into a dark corner of the terrace. 'You're a horrible minx to try to out-think,' he teased, attempting to steal a kiss in the shadows.

Julia put him off, twisting her head out of reach. 'No. You are not going to distract me with kisses either.' Although she wasn't at all sure of her ability to live up to that claim of resistance. 'I am not going to be left out of the visit any more than you were going to be left out of my return to London. Promise me, Paine, that I'll get to go with you.'

'All right, I promise as long as there's no danger to you.' Paine sighed in exasperation. 'Bargaining with you is the devil, Julia. May I have a kiss now?'

Julia leaned into him, arms around his neck. 'I thought you would never ask.'

'Yes, you did.' Paine gave a low laugh in the summer darkness before he claimed her lips with a kiss that Julia thought might be quite the best goodnight kiss in the history of goodnight kisses between two people who were only pretending to be in love.

Julia stood in the long line of guests waiting to be introduced at the Worthington soirée, grateful for a few moments to gather her thoughts and happy to let the others handle whatever greetings or conversations came their way as they waited in line. At this moment, the managing tendencies of the Ramsden brothers was a very welcome trait.

The day had been a whirl of activity. She had not expected otherwise. But Julia had not been prepared for how draining the routine would be. Just changing her gowns had been a tiring chore. She'd dressed in a muslin morning dress for the calls they'd paid before the lunch. Lily had rushed her home between calls and the luncheon to change into something 'fresh' although she'd only worn the gown for three hours. Then there had been another change so she could be seen driving with Aunt Lily through Hyde Park at the crowded hour before returning home for dinner and to dress for the soirée.

Four dresses! And Lily had overseen each choice with military precision from slippers to bonnet. No detail had been overlooked. Her own aunt hadn't paid close attention to her wardrobe at all as long as the gown was considered fashionable. But then, her aunt was not Lily Branbourne, Dowager Marchioness of Bridgerton and a Ramsden by birth.

Lily had expertly shepherded her through the day, introducing her to influential women, including a patroness of Almack's. Lily had not forgotten, as the cadre of Ramsden males had, that Julia was new come to town and there were protocols to follow. Julia had barely been presented at court and had her own comeout before the trouble with Oswalt began. Lily understood all that implied. She'd gone so far as to warn

Paine that Julia could not yet dance the waltz since Almack's hadn't given her permission.

Paine had protested the notion, but had earned himself nothing but a sharp rap on the knuckles from his aunt's ivory fan.

Paine's own news for the day wasn't good. His venture to the Brook Street home had been dismaying. The home had been burgled. The few pieces of furniture the house possessed had been broken, the elegant yin-and-yang cabinet vandalised, its contents shattered on the floor. Paine could not discern if anything was missing and he reported that he doubted anything was taken.

The Ramsden brothers concluded that the break-in had been designed to scare or perhaps to catch. Somehow, Oswalt had figured out where the discreet residence was and was sending the message that he meant to flush Paine out. There was nowhere to hide.

Fortunately, hiding wasn't part of the plan. They meant to go about in plain sight. Julia spread her own fan and waved it delicately to generate a little air. The evening was warm and standing in line was warmer still. She was glad Lily had suggested the light gown of 'changeable' pale pink silk adorned with ribbon instead of the one Julia had favoured with heavier beading.

'You look lovely,' Paine whispered in her ear. 'I don't know how you manage to look both sinful and innocent at the same time. I want to devour you.'

'There'll be none of that, Paine, my boy,' Aunt Lily scolded, stepping in. 'It's our turn. Behave.'

Her tone was censorious and a sharp reminder that tonight wasn't only about Julia. It was about Paine returning to the fold with the backing of his brother's good graces. In order for them to put a stop to Oswalt's manoeuvrings, Paine had to be accepted back into society.

They were announced to the hostess and Julia fought back the impression that the announcement had been louder than anyone else's and that everyone stopped their chatter to stare at them.

'Everyone is staring,' Julia whispered.

'Of course they are. They're wondering who the beautiful woman is on my arm,' Paine encouraged softly. 'We want it this way. We want to be noticed.' Further conversation was impossible as they approached their hostess. Paine turned on his considerable charm, bowing gallantly over Lady Worthington's hand and they were through.

'See,' Paine said once they entered the ballroom, 'Ramsdens don't skulk. We don't have to slither in and be ashamed of anything.'

'Then we've succeeded,' Julia shot back. It was clear the clusters of people standing near the entrance to the ballroom were indeed staring at them. She kept her head high and dared a smile at one or two who were brazen enough to meet her eyes.

'Keep moving,' Paine counselled through a smile as he acknowledged an acquaintance here and there in the crowd. His hand never left the small of her back and Julia welcomed its light pressure, its warm reassurance while they navigated the crowd.

'Here. We'll stop here. This will be a good place to make our own,' Peyton said at last when they gained a spot near a pillar along the side of the ballroom. Within moments, people seemed to sense that the Earl of Dursley was ready to 'receive'.

People who had watched his progress from the reception line through the ballroom began to make their way towards them. Julia's fear that they'd be shunned was quickly dispelled. Within minutes, they were surrounded by mothers wanting to introduce daughters to Peyton, men wanting to meet Paine and women hoping to do more than meet him, Julia thought uncharitably. Everyone wanted to hear Paine's story.

The evening served as a pattern card for the evenings that followed. The Ramsden brothers were seen at every affair of merit hosted in Mayfair's ballrooms over the next few weeks, squiring about the sparkling Julia Prentiss with the redoubtable Aunt Lily close by. The story of Julia and Paine's supposed country romance was on the lips of every worthy gossip. Aunt Lily's chaperonage lent the tale credibility. The twosome had met during Paine's reunion with his brothers recently and had become quite taken with each other. Aunt Lily claimed having introduced them at a family dinner.

As June lengthened towards midsummer, everywhere they went, crowds surged around them. But Julia wasn't naïve enough to assume the sycophantic crowd around them meant Paine had been welcomed back. It was too soon. That judgement would occur later and the verdict would start trickling through Mayfair. As would the verdict regarding herself. Had she 'taken'? How much people liked her would hugely affect how willing they'd be to accept her story without probing too closely. But there were good indicators success was assured. She'd even survived Almack's and now had permission to waltz.

Standing next to her at the Hatley rout, Paine shook hands with a gentleman. 'I'll be staying at Dursley House. Please feel free to call and we can discuss business more thoroughly.'

'That sounds promising.' Julia nodded after the re-treating figure of the gentleman.

'Yes. I've found business loans can be one way of restoring my reputation,' Paine said. 'They're starting up the music. Would you dance with me? I seem to recall dancing with a gentleman at a fine affair was on a certain Julia Prentiss's wish list,' he flirted lightly, offering his arm.

'You remember that?' Julia placed her hand on his sleeve, fighting a blush. She remembered that, too, but more vivid than what she'd said was what they'd done.

'Yes. And…' Paine's eyes twinkled as they took their places in the forming sets '…I remember other things we did that night, too.'

Crispin claimed her for the second dance, but the third dance was an energetic country dance and Julia was glad for the rest. The ballroom was warm and she was desperate for a cool breeze.

Paine read her need immediately when Crispin returned her to their court. 'Perhaps you'd prefer a stroll on the terrace,' Paine suggested.

'Just the terrace, Paine,' Peyton cautioned quietly from his side. Julia stifled a laugh. There they went, managing each other again, or at least trying to. She appreciated Peyton's reasons for it, though. They were close to success, close to laying Paine's dubious past and rowdy youth to rest. An amorous blunder now could easily put paid to their hopes.

'Just the terrace, Peyton.' Paine grinned and whisked her away.

The terrace was disappointingly crowded, but the cool air was a relief. 'I think it would be all right to walk in the gardens,' Paine suggested. 'I'll be glad when all this nonsense is over and I can kiss you when I like,' he whispered in her ear.

Julia silently agreed with that sentiment. As expected, he'd been unable to come to her room and, with all eyes on them, their opportunities to be together were severely curtailed.

The gardens were better. They were less populated and Paine adroitly found them a bench by a quiet fountain surrounded by tall hedges.

'You've been here before,' Julia said, suspicious of the ease with which the place had been located. It was well hidden enough that the casual wanderer would be unlikely to come across it.

'Yes.' Paine put an arm about her waist and drew her close. 'I can safely kiss you here.'

'Paine, you know the rules,' Julia protested. 'The evening's been going so well, I don't want to jinx it.'

'We won't get caught. Besides, anyone who catches us would have plenty of explaining to do as to why they were out here, too,' Paine reassured her, sweeping her into his arms for an impromptu waltz before she could marshal another argument. 'I've wanted you so much. It's killing me not to be able to touch you.'

Julia stumbled a bit as she tried to find Paine's rhythm. 'This is not at all like dancing with my cousins.'

Paine laughed. 'I should hope not!' He pulled her tight against him and swung a tight turn around the fountain.

'Paine, there's supposed to be distance between us,' Julia gasped, but her gasp had little to do with outrage and everything to do with the excitement of being in this man's arms. With him, even a simple dance was an adventure.

'I wonder why this dance is so scandalous. I mean, the way they dance it inside. It's just a pattern of circles and turns,' Julia mused out loud, finally falling into Paine's rhythm with confidence.

'My dear, don't you know? The waltz is a metaphor for sex.'

'I don't believe you. I think you're just making that up to shock me.' Julia laughed.

'No, watch and learn,' Paine drawled, his eyes turning dark with seductive intention. He slowed his pace, making their steps deliberate. 'The woman is in pursuit, that's why the woman is always dancing forwards, as it were. It's a chase. If we dance too close together, you can feel me through my trousers, even my most intimate parts. That's why those prim matrons in there insist on distance. But out here, we don't have to worry about such nonsense.'

'Do you know everything about sex?' Julia flirted, knowing he was dangerously aroused, but not caring. She was desperate for him after weeks of denial.

He danced her against a hedge and kissed her hard on the mouth. 'I've wanted to do that all night.'

'Devour me, you mean?' Julia managed between kisses. The truth was, she wanted to devour him, too. She'd missed his presence in her bed.

'I want you, Julia.' Paine placed a line of hot kisses down the column of her neck. Julia arched against him, a moan escaping her lips. She made a valiant bid for sanity. 'I don't think this happened to Cinderella when she danced with the prince.'

'Oh, you don't, do you?' Paine whispered huskily. 'You might be surprised. Perhaps the prince knew how to do the "twining creeper".' He lifted her skirts, baring her thighs to the summer night. 'Let me do this for you, a little of our own magic before midnight.' His hand found the nub nestled in her nether curls.

He stroked.

She closed her eyes and gasped at the intimate invasion, but she was unable to fight it. His touch was exquisite, inviting her to take the pleasure he offered. In a few moments, he would let her soar. She was nearly there. Then suddenly he stopped.

Her eyes flew open in indignation. 'Paine, why did you—?'

'What was that you said about us waltzing?' Paine grumbled softly to her, shielding her long enough for his deft hands to adjust her skirts.

'I said it would jinx things,' Julia said, still confused as to the abrupt interruption in their interlude.

'Looks like you were right.' Paine shifted from his protective position enough to reveal their unwanted guest.

They were no longer alone. Crispin Ramsden stood in the little entranceway to their hiding spot, having the decency to look uncomfortable.

Chapter Sixteen

'You were supposed to stay on the terrace,' Crispin ground out once he recovered his senses.

'I am not a toddler in leading strings,' Paine retorted, pushing Julia behind him in a belated attempt to protect her modesty. 'What are you doing out here? Did Peyton send you to keep track of me?'

'I wish it were that simple.' Julia did not miss the import of the gaze Crispin sent Paine.

Paine didn't miss it either. 'What's happened?'

Crispin held out a note. 'It's from your man, Flaherty. Apparently, he found this so important that he came here and left it with a footman.'

Paine took the note and unfolded it, reading slowly. 'It's worse than we thought. Oswalt has indeed managed to have his name put forwards for a knight-hood. It seems that he means to bankrupt your uncle's

estate and then prop it up financially. Flaherty specu-
lates that he might even ask to be given custody of the
estate when he's awarded his knighthood. It's not an
uncommon practice for bankrupt estates to be given
over to a trustee for financial management. It's a long
shot, but we should be prepared for it. The estate's only
protection is its entailment. Still, in terms of custody, it
might not be enough.'

Paine swore low under his breath. 'It's too audacious.
It's not chivalrous. I can't believe the crown would reward
such blatant chicanery. He won't get away with it.'

'Yes, he will,' Julia said softly. The ramifications of
the note were enormous. 'If he marries me, the request
for guardianship will look benevolent. He can argue that
he wants to manage the estate for me, with an eye to the
future heirs. His guardianship keeps it in the family. No
one will ever connect him to being the cause of my
uncle's debts. On the surface, he'll look like an angel,
having offered my uncle a fair settlement for me, and
for tiding the family over during difficulties. It won't
look like it's his fault the family continues to sink into
bankruptcy.'

Julia fought the urge to sway. She grabbed on to
Paine's arm. 'We have to tell my uncle. He must be
warned about Oswalt's intentions.'

'I'll go tomorrow,' Paine promised.

'Correction, *we'll* go tomorrow,' Julia contradicted.
The garden had lost its magic, the glitter of the evening

had paled against the reality facing them. Crispin sensed it, too.

'We've accomplished enough for an evening. I'll tell Peyton to send for the carriage. We can respectfully leave,' he said quietly. 'I'll see you both inside in a few minutes.'

'It's bad, isn't it?' Julia said once they were alone.

Paine nodded slowly. 'I had hoped against hope that you were merely an accessory to Oswalt's master plan, whatever it turned out to be. I had hoped your ruination might save you from him.'

Julia took his hand. 'We did our best in that regard.' She tried for levity, but this was too serious. She didn't have to be told that she'd been upgraded in Oswalt's plan from a virginal accessory for a debauched man's cure to a key lynch pin. If Oswalt meant to seize the estate ostensibly on her behalf, he'd want her, virgo intacta or not.

Paine paced the length of Peyton's room. It was well past the time to be in bed, but he was restless, his body full of energy with no outlet and his mind a riot of options he repeatedly sorted through and discarded. 'What would you do, Peyton?' he said at last, halting briefly in front of the fireplace.

Peyton waved the question aside. 'That's irrelevant, Paine. You're not me. I can't advise you in this.'

'That's no help,' Paine snarled.

'Not my fault.' Peyton straightened up from his slouch in the big wing chair by the window. 'What do you want to do, Paine? She came to you for one thing and you've done what she asked. You don't have to do any more.'

Paine furrowed his brow. 'Are you suggesting I should just walk away?'

Peyton gave a casual shrug. 'There's really only two choices here, you know. You can walk away or you can stay with her.'

'I know that and I can't walk away. She'll be ruined or sacrificed to Oswalt's cause or both,' Paine protested. The option to leave Julia to her fate was reprehensible. 'I've squired her around the *ton*, declared to have feelings for her.'

Peyton nodded. 'It was part of the plan. Julia agreed to it, knowing full well those declarations were not necessarily real. She seems to be a smart girl, Paine. She knew what she was doing.' Peyton splayed his fingers on his thighs in thought. 'But if letting Julia find her own level is so unpalatable to you, then your choice is clear. You see this out. But have you thought what that means or where that ends? I should ask what your feelings are for the girl. Do you like her?'

'Yes. I like her a great deal.' Paine let out a breath. He supposed that was the real issue he'd been contemplating since Flaherty's news had arrived. He couldn't lose Julia. He wanted Julia for his own. This was the conclusion he'd been dancing around all night. He didn't want to go back to a life without her in it.

'You'll have to do more than make her your mistress,' Peyton cautioned.

'Of course,' Paine shot back, irritated that Peyton thought so little of him that he had to be reminded of a gentleman's duty. 'I'll ride to Lambeth Palace for a special licence as soon as the hour is decent.'

'Then congratulations are in order. You're about to become a married man,' Peyton offered.

If she'll have me.

He parted from Peyton, his mind lighter. The thought of a special licence did bring a sense of peace. He had a path to follow now, a path that led to Julia if he was successful. But he was not naïve enough to think a piece of paper would solve all their problems. Unless the contract between her uncle and Oswalt was broken, no one would legally recognise his marriage. And then there was Julia's own reaction to the situation. Would she want to marry him? Would she understand he wanted to marry her for reasons that had nothing to do with the conundrum they found themselves in?

'The chit was seen at the Worthington soirée!' Oswalt threw down the note he'd received from Julia's uncle in disgust. He strode back and forth in front of the line of his assembled henchman, including Sam Brown. The office at his dockside warehouse was warm and fetid, crowded with the men who worked for him. They were shuffling their feet nervously and twisting their caps. As well they should be.

They'd failed miserably. Of the men who'd ridden with Brown to catch them in the Cotswolds, one still limped, one still had an arm in a sling and the other would bear a life-long scar from his run-in with Ramsden's knife. The others had failed to confirm Julia's return to London except for noting that Dursley House had started sporting a knocker on the front door.

'Damn you all! What do I pay you for if some incompetent nincompoop finds her first? How is it those milksop cousins of hers noticed her before you did?' Oswalt ranted.

After a long silence, Sam Brown stepped forwards. 'With all respect, sir, the likes of us aren't invited to those functions. It's one thing to get inside a gambling hell, but it's mighty awkward to skulk about a ball without drawing undue attention.'

Oswalt grunted at that. 'Still, it shouldn't have come to this. We should have been able to snatch her out of Dursley House.'

Emboldened by Sam's report, another man stepped forwards. 'We have men watching Dursley House all day and all night. She hardly leaves; when she does, she's with the Ramsden brothers and those burly footmen of the earl. We're not afraid of a fight, but it has to be one we can win. No point in losing.'

Oswalt had to concede the man made sense. 'We need an equaliser, then. Keep your posts, men. Watch Dursley House. I want to know the minute they leave. We'll follow them everywhere and look for our chance. There's a bonus in it for the man who captures Julia Prentiss. Everyone is dismissed. Brown, fetch my personal physician immediately.'

In the empty office, Oswalt sat behind the desk, marshalling his thoughts. The game was just about over and just in time, too. He needed Julia Prentiss brought to him before the solstice. Julia and the Ramsdens would get restless, secure in their own safety one of these days, and he'd be waiting to pounce on the opportunity. More than that, he'd be ready.

The door to the office opened a half-hour later. 'You wanted to see me?'

Mortimer Oswalt looked up from his papers. His physician was here. 'Yes, I need a poison ring, preferably by tomorrow and something discreet for a knife blade as well.'

Julia felt she'd been gone from her uncle's house for much longer than weeks. She stared up at the town home on the outskirts of Belgravia, waiting for Paine to instruct his tiger. Fine living with the Ramsdens had ruined her much more quickly than she'd have thought possible. The house looked shabby in little ways. Weeds pushed up between the cracks in the steps leading to the door and the windows looked drab in comparison to the tall windows and elegant curtains of Dursley House.

'Are you ready?' Paine took her arm. 'You can wait with the carriage. My tiger can drive you to Bond Street and you can shop.'

Julia gave him a sharp look. 'I am not about to go shopping while my future is on the line.' She fidgeted with the fringed edge of her summer shawl. She didn't know exactly what that future held. Either way— winning her freedom or being forced to marry Oswalt— she and Paine would part ways. Even her coveted freedom seemed to pale against the thought of saying farewell to Paine. She'd have to go away and make a new, quiet life some place where her behaviour in London would be overlooked or, better yet, never heard of. She'd known, or imagined she knew, what the consequences would be for her choice to seek ruination. But her feelings for Paine Ramsden had not been factored into the equation then.

Well, she had made her choices and there had been no going back for quite some time now. She'd best get on with it. Julia squared her shoulders and gave Paine a confident smile. 'I am ready.'

The viscount was stunned to see them. Aunt Sara couldn't decide what to do first, swoon or order tea. Their mere arrival threw the household into an uproar. Julia gave Paine an apologetic look.

'Where have you been? Your cousins say they saw

you at the Worthington soirée in the company of the earl, while we've been here at home not knowing you were even in the city!' Uncle Barnaby said gruffly once the excitement subsided and the four of them were seated with teacups in the small drawing room.

That news surprised her. She hadn't seen her cousins that evening and it struck her as odd that they would have spied her, but not approached her. If they'd really been worried, wouldn't they have rushed over and greeted her? Worse of all was the realisation that, if her cousins knew, Oswalt knew. Julia tamped down her growing anxiety.

'I've been with Lady Bridgerton,' Julia said smoothly, laying out the story she and Paine had practised. It wasn't a complete lie. She had been with Lady Bridgerton, just not for as long as her aunt and uncle might be concluding. 'I have decided that I will not be marrying Mortimer Oswalt.' She couldn't repress a smile as she made her announcement. It felt good to confront the issue at last. She felt powerful. Although she knew this time it was the presence of Paine Ramsden that gave her the power. But she had an ally and that made all the difference. They couldn't force her to marry Oswalt now. They couldn't lock her in her room.

Aunt Sara wrung her hands at the news. 'Oh dear, don't you understand? You can't decide that on your own. What's got into you, Julia? You used to be a nice biddable girl. Now, you've refused a marriage your uncle has arranged for you and you've run off without a note for weeks at a time. We've been worried to death.'

In truth, her aunt did look as if she'd been concerned. The woman looked tired and was more nervous than usual. Guilt for that gnawed at her. 'I didn't mean to hurt anyone, I simply needed time to sort through my feelings.' Julia said.

'Who is this young man?' Aunt Sara turned to Paine.

'I am Paine Ramsden. I'm Lady Bridgerton's nephew,' he added politely.

Uncle Barnaby set down his teacup, eyeing Paine in much the same way one views a venomous snake. 'Julia, what you've done is of the gravest nature.' He, too, looked as if worry had taken a great toll on him. 'We have a contract with Mortimer Oswalt. He's paid for every gown upstairs in your wardrobe. He expects a gently bred bride. I have given him my word, and you've destroyed his faith in me.'

'Then break the contract, Uncle,' Julia answered unswervingly, bringing the topic around to the point they needed to discuss. This part of the conversation would not be pleasant and it would be entirely too blunt, but there was no other way.

As expected, Uncle Barnaby's watery blue eyes bulged at the mention of breaking the contract. He began to sputter. 'A betrothal contract can't just be broken! Do you know what that entails? I'll have to reimburse Oswalt for all his expenditures on your behalf, Julia, and for funds he's already advanced the family on the understanding that you would soon be wed.'

'You could just return the money,' Julia probed, hoping to determine her uncle's exact level of indebtedness to Oswalt.

'Silly chit! Oswalt was right. These kinds of transactions are too complicated for the female brain. The money has been spent. We had to have something to live on until Gray returns and Oswalt's money seemed good for spending. After all, it was an advancement on what he owed us. We didn't have to pay it back. It was ours.' Uncle Barnaby's weak chin trembled. 'At least it was ours until you ran away and Oswalt started asking for the funds back. Now, we owe him Gray's cargo unless you marry him.'

Julia swallowed hard. She'd heard Paine explain this aspect of Oswalt's plan to her on more than one occasion, but hearing the despair in her uncle's voice was difficult to bear, especially since he saw her as the cause of their woes.

Her aunt piped up cheerfully from her corner, 'All is well now, Barnaby. Our Julia is home and she can woo Oswalt back.'

Julia folded her hands in her lap and stiffened her spine. 'I am afraid that's not possible any longer. He stipulated in the contract that he wanted a virgin bride. Those terms no longer apply to me.'

Aunt Sara gasped. Uncle Barnaby's eyes flew to Paine. 'You're a black-hearted scoundrel, taking advantage of a girl about to be married. You're worse than the rumours.' He shook an ineffectual fist in Paine's direction.

Paine ignored the older man's rant and jumped into the conversation for the first time. 'What Julia hasn't mentioned yet is that we came here to warn you about Oswalt. He's planned this all along. He meant to ruin your finances, which were precarious at best. He meant to push you into irrevocable debt.'

'Balderdash. He's got no reason to do that. You can take your lies elsewhere,' Uncle Barnaby stammered.

'He's got every reason.' Paine carefully laid out Oswalt's plot to the best of his most recent knowledge. 'You cannot doom Julia to that life. You have to stand up to Oswalt and put a stop to him once and for all. You're not the first nobleman to fall victim to his plots.'

'Don't listen to him, Lockhart. He's a lying cockerel only seeking revenge for an old perceived insult,' a voice said from the doorway. All heads swivelled to see the newcomer who'd not waited to be announced.

Mortimer Oswalt stood there in a garish mockery of fashion, dressed in a tangerine afternoon suit of China silk, more appropriate for an engagement at court in the last century than a call at the shabby Lockhart residence. Julia sucked in her breath and compulsively grabbed Paine's hand.

'I'd call this a fortuitous happenstance if I didn't

know better.' Oswalt waved a beringed hand. 'But I do know better, thanks to the men I have watching Dursley House. Imagine my elation when they informed me you were headed in this direction. I had to see Viscount Lockhart today and this makes the visit so much better.' He advanced with mincing steps. 'Ah, Julia, you've returned. I knew you would once the guilt over deserting your guardians prevailed. I am looking forwards to our nuptials, my little virago.' He reached into a pocket and withdrew a tin of snuff. The gaudy ring on his middle finger flashed.

'Ramsden, I'd heard you'd got yourself entangled in this little mess.' He sniffed, sneezed, and gave a satisfied sigh. 'I think it's Ramsden's perfidy we should be discussing, not mine, Lockhart, and we would have that discussion if I didn't have distressing news to share, which is the reason I've come by. There was word today down on the docks that the ship, *Bluehawk*, has foundered at sea off the coast between France and Spain. The *Bluehawk* is your son's ship, is it not? I thought you should hear the news from a friend first.'

Aunt Sara swooned.

Julia jumped to her feet. 'You lie!' She turned to her uncle. 'Don't believe him. He could tell you anything. There's no way to verify it.'

Mortimer laughed, a hoarse, evil sound that sent shivers through Julia. 'Whatever Ramsden has been teaching you, it hasn't been manners.' He stepped towards her and Julia flinched involuntarily. Paine rose beside her, lending her the strength of his presence.

'So you like them wild, Ramsden? All those savages you bedded from your time abroad, no doubt. Well, I'll make a lady of you yet, Julia. Have no worries on that account.'

Julia's skin crawled. 'We'll be going.' She had to get out of this room. Oswalt radiated malevolence.

'Not so fast, my pet.' Oswalt said, motioning for his henchmen to approach. 'I think, under the circumstances, I'll ask permission to keep my bride-to-be under lock and key until the ceremony, which will be very soon and very quiet out of deference for the family during their mourning.'

'I don't know…' Uncle Barnaby sputtered.

'Yes, you do,' Oswalt sneered, all veneer of friendship gone from his face. 'You know Julia's marriage to me is the only thing that will keep your family financially viable.'

'I won't go with you,' Julia protested.

'Wants are of no consequence. That's what my men are for. Men, help Miss Prentiss to my carriage. You three, handle the arrogant Mr Ramsden for me. You know what to do. I believe you have a score to settle from the Cotswold road with the gent.'

Julia screamed and grabbed up the nearest vase, hurling it at the closest attacker. Various parts of the tea set followed in quick succession. All to no avail. In the end, there were more men than tea sets and thin china shards were no deterrent to men used to knives in London's dark alleys. The men seized her roughly by the arms and hauled her towards the door.

She dragged her heels and screamed for Paine, but Paine was fully engaged with three burly men, warding off snaggle-bladed knives with a delicate chair. He was doing well, having survived thus far with only a streak of blood showing on his arm. Then, suddenly, for no explicable reason he collapsed on the floor in a dead heap.

A man stood over Paine, knife ready to deal a final blow. Julia screamed again, fear for Paine giving her more strength. Oswalt called him off. 'Let's go. He can't follow us if he's dead. We want him to live a while longer.'

'Uncle! Help me, stop him,' Julia cried a desperate plea, swivelling her head around to the corner where Uncle Barnaby had retreated during the fight. Surely, now at the last, when all the masks had been pulled from the vileness of Mortimer's scheme, her uncle would do something! But the shock of losing Gray had numbed him completely. He huddled in the corner, helpless and ineffectual.

'Uncle!' she cried once more, thrashing in the grasp of her captors. But she knew, even as she called for him, she was entirely on her own.

Oswalt was not amenable to her pleas. 'I'll silence the bitch myself.' He advanced on her. Julia anticipated a blow to the head. Instead, she saw it coming too late.

He grabbed her hand and scratched it with the ring he wore. The sensation rendered her senseless, no matter how she tried to fight the descending darkness in her mind.

Sam Brown didn't like the way events were developing one bit. He dutifully deposited the unconscious girl in the small chamber on the top floor that Oswalt had set aside, but he didn't like it. Swindling a weak viscount was one thing. They'd done that often enough in the past. But involving an innocent girl was beyond the pale in his book.

He sought out Oswalt, finding him in the large office on the second floor.

'Is it done?' Oswalt barked when Sam Brown came to the door.

'About that, boss…' Sam Brown began. He did not make a habit of questioning Oswalt. 'What are we doing with her?'

'*We're* not doing anything with her. I'm marrying her tonight.' Oswalt stopped long enough to cough, a harsh racking sound. He spit into a brass spittoon. 'Once I marry her, all my problems will be over.' He coughed again.

Sam noticed the papery quality to Oswalt's sallow skin. He had not realised how frail the man had become. 'You've got Lockhart ruined. You don't need her.'

Oswalt eyed him curiously. 'Is a pretty face all it

takes to turn your head these days, Sam? Time was when you were immune to that.'

Sam shifted from foot to foot. 'Time was, I only dealt with the coves you were culling and it was good sport,' he dared bravely.

'Today's not the day to get squeamish. I need her to secure the knighthood and, more importantly, I need her for my cure so I can live long enough to receive that title.'

'Your cure? You can't believe all that Druid nonsense about restoring your potency,' Sam blurted out.

'Druid nonsense?' Oswalt snarled. 'It's hardly nonsense. It's the reason I've lived so long as it is in spite of my affliction.'

Affliction, hah. Oswalt's ailment was more than a minor affliction. It was pox at best, syphilis at worst, Sam Brown mused, and it would kill the young girl upstairs in a slow torturous death that was unworthy of her.

Oswalt waved him away. 'Back to work, Brown. There's plenty to be done before tonight. Send my physician in on the way out.'

Sam Brown grunted. He'd been lucky Oswalt hadn't taken his head off. What had he expected to accomplish? He hadn't really expected to dissuade Oswalt. He knew the man was intractable once he had made his plans.

He found the forest crone Oswalt loosely titled as 'physician' and went outside to the lawn where workers were erecting a large slab. He didn't like to think what it was going to be used for. Oswalt had taken great relish in outlining what would be done to purify his bride on that slab. The description had turned Brown's stomach.

No, he didn't like the direction Oswalt's plot had taken. He was a straightforward man who liked direct action. He didn't mind ruining the viscount, who was most likely ruined already by the hand of his own stupidity. Brown didn't mind picking a fight with coves like Ramsden, who knew the rules and the consequences for living in the stews and hells. He hadn't liked 'cheating' with the poisoned blades and he certainly didn't approve of what was being done to the girl.

Sam Brown glanced at the sky, tracking the sun's descent. He had a few hours left in which to do some thinking.

Chapter Seventeen

Paine woke slowly, struggling against the intense fog that swamped his brain. He could hear Peyton and Crispin. Peyton was angry. He could hear his brother's cold 'earl' voice berating some unfortunate soul. Why would that be the case? Where was he? Wherever he was, it was hard and felt like a floor.

'Paine?' That was Crispin. 'Are you coming around now?'

Paine found the strength to push his eyes open and then wished he hadn't. The room swam. Crispin's face appeared in his line of sight like a mirage on the desert. Was he ill? He didn't recall being sick earlier. 'Help me sit up.' His tongue felt thick.

Crispin supported him on one side to hoist him up. Paine gave an involuntary groan at the motion and tried to push with his arm on the other side. His hand made contact with a sharp shard of something. It felt like china.

'Julia!' Full cognisance flooded back. Paine forced his eyes to stay open in spite of the dizziness. He grabbed at Crispin's coat. 'Julia's gone. Oswalt's taken her. There were men, too many of them.' He was babbling, letting the last moments of consciousness tumble out in no particular order.

'Hush, Paine. It's all right.' Crispin soothed him like he had when Paine had fallen out of a tree in their youth.

Paine pushed at his brother. 'No, it's not all right.' The dizziness was slowing, less crippling now. They were still in the viscount's drawing room. He could make out Peyton with Lockhart in another corner. So that was who Peyton was giving a tongue-lashing to. He didn't pity the man at all. Whatever Peyton did or said to the man wouldn't be any less than he deserved. The coward had let Oswalt forcibly remove Julia from the house.

Peyton spied him and abruptly left the trembling viscount to come to his side. 'Peyton, tell me everything. How did you know to come?' Paine pressed, sparing his body no discomfort as he fought to recover.

'Your tiger came for us when he saw the men go into the house. He counted up numbers and realised he'd be of more use coming to us.'

'They've taken Julia. Oswalt has her. He means to marry her,' Paine said. 'I have to find her.'

'I know.' Peyton paused.

'Tell him everything.' Crispin urged when it seemed Peyton wouldn't say anything more.

'What?' Paine swivelled his head between his brothers as they shared a silent communication. He paid for the effort with a sharp bout of dizziness.

Peyton went on. 'Julia fought them. She didn't go easily. The viscount says they had to drug her, too, before they reached the carriage.'

'The bastards!' Paine wanted to explode with anger; anger at the men who did Oswalt's bidding, anger at the viscount for putting them all in this situation, anger at himself for having failed Julia.

'Calm down, Paine. You can't help Julia if you aren't thinking clearly or if you make yourself sick. The drug will wear off shortly. It's already been an hour.'

Paine touched his arm where one of the men had nicked him. The ugly blade had slipped through Paine's chair-shield only briefly. At the time, Paine had thought he'd been clever to avoid a larger slice from the wicked blade. But a larger slice had not been necessary.

'The blade was poisoned?' Paine asked.

'It seems to be the case,' Peyton concurred. 'The viscount said you collapsed suddenly and without reason. Oswalt probably had the blades rubbed with a topical poison.

Paine nodded. That made sense. He'd encountered several types of poisons in the East that could be used in that manner and bring about the desired result. As a merchant with far-reaching trade interests, Oswalt would have knowledge of and access to such a commodity.

'Have some tea. It will help settle your head and your stomach.' Crispin handed him a mug, probably wrested from the kitchen staff. It was thick and large, not at all like the dainty teacups Julia had thrown at Oswalt's men.

The thought of her brought the guilt back in full force. 'We have to get to her fast.' The words were inadequate to express the fears rioting through him. It brought him physical pain to think of Julia suffering the effects of the drug while being alone in the hands of her enemy. *Julia, I am coming.*

'Do you know where they might have taken her?' Crispin asked after he'd had a chance to drink some of the strong tea.

'I have an idea,' Paine confirmed, calling over to Lockhart. 'Lockhart, does Oswalt still have his property in Richmond?'

'Y-y-yes. I believe so.' Lockhart was rooted to his chair across the room, looking utterly immobile except for the movement of his mouth.

'That's where they went,' Paine said confidently.

'B-b-but he's got a house in London. It's closer. Are you sure?' Lockhart took that unfortunate moment to speak up.

Paine lashed out. 'Yes, I am goddamned sure of that.

I was unaware I had asked for your opinion or that you were even capable of formulating one of your own.' He pushed to his feet, spoiling for a fight now that the tea had quelled the last of his ill effects.

'Paine,' Crispin warned *sotto voce* at his elbow, a gentle hand on his arm. Paine was unsure if the gesture was meant to restrain him or offer balance if he wobbled. 'The man's lost his son and his livelihood all in one day. He's in shock.'

Paine shook off Crispin's touch and sat back down. 'Get him a drink and get him out of here, then. His valet can see to him,' he growled.

Peyton barked an order and the valet came to fetch the viscount.

'I love her, you know,' Paine said as the viscount neared the door. 'I mean to marry her when all is settled, if she'll have me.' He had the special licence in his pocket to prove it. He'd interrupted the archbishop's breakfast for it just this morning.

But he didn't think the archbishop minded too much by the time their business transaction was done. Paine had his paper and Lambeth Palace had a new illuminated map of India from Paine's own collection of atlases. It was one of his favourites, acquired from a Hindu map-maker in Calcutta. The Archbishop was thrilled at the prospect of sending missionaries to all the secret, heathen kingdoms on the map. Paine could care less what the Archbishop did with the map. The only soul he wanted to save was Julia's and he would have given anything in his possession to do it.

'It's been two hours since they took her,' Paine said restlessly.

'You're sure it's Richmond?' Peyton queried.

'Yes. Oswalt could have had me finished off during the fight—a lethal blade or a stronger poison would have done it. He meant for me to live and he means for me to find Julia. He knows I'll guess he went to Richmond.'

'All right, we ride and then we wait,' Peyton said. 'We wait for the cover of darkness and make our move then, unless there is good reason to move sooner. We'll stop at Dursley House and collect my footmen. They'll be useful in a fight, but we'll still need every advantage the darkness can provide.'

Paine nodded. Peyton was right, but it was six hours until dark and it seemed an eternity to wait. Foolish bravery would earn Julia nothing.

They collected Peyton's footmen and set out the short distance to Richmond. Paine rode with grim determination, the sound of his horse's hooves pounding out the litany that rang through his mind: *Julia, I am coming.*

Paine would come. *He would.* Julia paced the confines of the tiny attic room she'd been stuffed in. It was windowless and eight feet wide—not that she could pace the whole eight feet, given that the slope of the roof line prohibited anyone over three feet tall to access the last few feet.

She sat on the little cot, the room's only furnishing, and sighed. She was glad for the privacy she'd been afforded so far. She'd been terribly ill when she'd woken up. She much preferred panicking alone than in the company of her captors.

Now that she felt better, she could take stock of the situation. It was probably an intended side effect of the drug that one couldn't think clearly for quite some time after waking up.

Once her head had cleared, her first thought had been for Paine. He was alive. She knew that much. Oswalt had spared him for that purpose. That worried her. Oswalt *wanted* Paine to find her. That meant Paine knew where she'd be even though he'd been unconscious and unable to follow them. She wondered if they'd gone to Richmond. Paine had mentioned Richmond as the site of his first encounter with Oswalt.

Paine would come. Oswalt would use her to trap him. How convenient it must be for Oswalt to play two games at once—the game with the Lockharts and whatever lingering end play he thought he had with Paine over the old quarrel.

Maybe he wouldn't come, her devil-side argued. Why would he? Perhaps right now, he was cursing her for bringing him into such a mess. Sex was one thing. Dying for it was quite another. He'd promised her pleasure. He'd promised nothing else. He might decide he'd done enough for her. And he'd be right in that conclusion. He'd rescued her from Oswalt once already. He knew how Oswalt thought. He would know this was a trap simply because Oswalt had left him alive. He would know Oswalt wanted him to come. Paine was a stubborn man. He wouldn't come just because someone wanted him to.

Julia stood up and resumed pacing. There it was—for all his manipulations, Paine was the one person Oswalt couldn't manipulate. He could not ensure Paine would come, only that he had all the information to come if he chose to. She smiled at that. It would gall Oswalt no end if Paine didn't come. She would remember to take comfort in that little prod when the time came.

At least that was settled. He wouldn't come. Paine was too smart. She'd better stop counting on him to join in her rescue and start thinking of how best to rescue herself.

Unfortunately, she had none of the traditional escape routes at her disposal. All the captured heroines in the Minerva Press novels had secret passageways hidden in their fireplaces or bedsheets for ropes. Hah! That made her snort. Bedsheets were the least of her worries, not that she had any on the bare cot. She needed a window to start with.

For good measure, Julia went to the wood door and tried the handle. It was locked and a guard shouted back at her. Well, that was to be expected. Oswalt knew she wouldn't sit by passively and let her fate play out on its own.

The handle turned and Julia retreated to the cot. She should have spent her time looking for something to craft into a weapon. She recognised the guard as one of the men from her uncle's house.

'Good, you're up and around. The boss will be glad to know it.' He held out the long box he carried. 'The boss says for you to put this on.'

Julia didn't move to take the box. 'What is it?'

The man sneered. 'It's a wedding gown. You have a half-hour to dress. Boss wants the ceremony to take place at sunset.'

'And if I don't?' She gave a haughty toss of her head. This man would know that she was not cowed by his bulk or brashness.

'Then you can attend your wedding naked.' He threw the box on the cot next to her.

'Get out. The clock is running,' Julia ordered in a last attempt at bravado.

He snorted. 'You can be high and mighty now—it won't last much longer.'

The door shut and Julia sighed. She might have done better to probe for more information instead of antagonising the guard. Why sunset? At least she had confirmation of what was going to happen to her. She was going to be moved to another place. Sunset wouldn't matter in this windowless room.

Compliance was her best option at present. She'd learned through unfortunate consequences the foolishness of her resistance at the house. If she'd gone willingly, she would have kept her consciousness. Perhaps she could even have attracted attention or called out for help. Unconscious, she made things easy for Oswalt.

Anxiously, she lifted the box lid. The gown was more of a robe than it was a dress: a sleeveless, shapeless robe of white silk. In the bottom of the box was a girdle of twisted gold set with gems every few links and two large gold arm bracelets set with turquoise. The ensemble looked like something a Druid priestess might wear, like something she'd seen a history book before regarding early Britons.

The notion sparked something. Druids. Midsummer. The solstice. She frantically tried to recall the date. Oswalt's idea of a wedding was becoming clear. She was certain today was June 21. It explained the odd gown and the desire to perform the wedding at sunset.

'Fifteen minutes!' the guard shouted through the door.

She needed to hurry. She didn't doubt the guard would make good on his threat to haul her downstairs naked or that anyone would mind terribly much.

Julia dressed swiftly, trying to push her thoughts away from the impending events and what they meant. The horror was too overwhelming. If she dwelled on them, she'd be paralysed with fear. She needed to stay alert, she needed to look for any opportunity to run or to defend herself. She bit her lip. She hoped she had the courage to do whatever needed to be done and, if there was a chance to kill Oswalt and free herself, she hoped she had the courage to take it.

The guard came for her as she was fastening on the last of the bracelets. He brought friends. Two of them. She was sandwiched between them as he led the way to a room two flights of stairs down from the attic.

'Where's Oswalt?' Julia asked, quietly looking about her during the walk, remembering corners and turns, anything that might prove useful in the future, but the house was unhelpfully blank. She wondered if Oswalt had done that on purpose. No pictures or colours on the walls that might provide a visual memory—what was it Paine had called it? An *aide-mémoire*? 'No, don't think of him,' she cautioned herself. Thoughts of Paine would only bring tears.

'It's bad luck to see the bride before the wedding.' The guards laughed at their joke. 'You'll be seeing him soon enough.'

They led her into a bedroom done in stark white. The large poster bed was white, the coverlet on it was white satin. The curtains were white. *Ah, good*, Julia thought. *A window and bed sheets*. Things were looking up.

One of the guards seized her hands. 'What you are doing?' Julia cried, shocked by the swift movement.

'It's orders. You're not to be trusted.' He looped

tight cords of twine about her hands and bound them to the bed post.

'Please…' Julia protested against the indignity. But the protest was merely for form's sake. These men would not be swayed by any gentleman's code of honour.

One guard jerked his head towards the window. 'You've got nothing to complain about. You've got a view of the ceremonies. You can watch them set up for the wedding. The physician will be here shortly to keep you company.'

The horror was real. Julia fought despair. Being left alone was a certain torture of its own. Too much time to let her imagination run riot. But Oswalt was a master at this. He knew exactly what he was doing. She couldn't give in to the terror. He couldn't make Paine come and he couldn't make her be frightened.

The sky became her enemy as the sun inched closer to the horizon. Nature's hour glass. Someone came to set out lanterns in the yard below. It wouldn't be long. A half-hour, maybe a few minutes more.

The door opened. Julia couldn't turn to see who was there. An ancient crone older than Oswalt himself came into her line of vision, crabbed and wrinkled. 'Hello, dearie, I'm the physician. I'm here to check, shall we say, on the status of things?' Julia fought the urge to cringe. Oswalt must be mad to call this forest witch by such a title.

A movement caught Julia's eye out on the lawn. It

was slight and then gone, but she could have sworn a man with raven hair had looked up at her window, studying it before blending back into the lengthening shadows. Paine had come—maybe. It was the only scrap of hope she had at the moment and so she clung to it. If Paine was down there, looking for her, she could endure a little while longer.

Chapter Eighteen

Paine drew back into the shadows of the lawn. He was certain he'd seen Julia in the upstairs window. Crispin confirmed it, tossing him a robe and hood as he returned from his short reconnaissance mission. 'I overheard some of the guards talking. The location sounds right. Put these on.'

'Druid robes?' Paine asked, shaking out the garment.

'For the ceremony. We'll blend in,' Peyton said, slipping into another set.

'How did you get these?' Paine asked, slipping on the robe.

'Let's just say three men have a little less to wear than they did a few minutes ago, but I doubt they'll be missing their clothes for a while,' Crispin said with relish.

Paine grimaced. 'How many people will be here?

We'll stand out if it's only a handful. Oswalt expects us. He'll be on the lookout for anything out of place.' He didn't like the idea of waiting that long, not only because of the torture of watching Julia engage in this ritual and being unable to help her, but also because they would be enacting their rescue surrounded by many people who would have other interests to support.

He glanced at the sky, streaked pink from the setting sun, and made a decision. 'I am going up after her now. We haven't the same odds of success if we wait.'

'We're coming with you,' Crispin put in.

Paine shook his head. He couldn't risk his brothers. 'No. You stay hidden here and proceed with our plan if I don't succeed, and get Julia away from here.'

'Better hurry, then.' Peyton nodded to the lawn where people dressed as they were in robes started to mill about.

The sight made Paine's skin crawl. He put on his hood to obscure his identity and set off in the direction of the house. *Julia, I am coming.*

His plan had certain merits. The house was busy with last-minute preparations. Guards were distracted, checking in guests and stabling horses, even though it looked to be no more than fifty men were expected. Better yet, everyone looked the same in their robes and hoods. Paine fully understood why no one would want to be openly associated with such an event. Most were on the lawn, however, making his movements more obvious and suspect the closer he got to the house.

Paine used the back entrance and went up a servants' stairwell, counting landings as he went and trying to outguess Oswalt. What did he think the plan would be? Would he be anticipating an attempt before the ceremony or during? He gained the landing and stepped out. The hall was deserted. Had this been too easy or just natural since Oswalt didn't want his guests prowling the house? Either was a viable option. Paine surreptitiously checked the pistol and knife beneath his robe. It was comforting to know the weapons were there. He only hoped he'd be able to get to them fast enough.

The window he glimpsed her in had been towards the middle on the right. Paine began trying door handles. One of them gave. Warning shivered down his spine. This was too easy. While he had the chance, Paine slipped the pistol into his hand and eased the door open slowly, not sure what he'd find.

'Julia?' He dared a whisper, but there was no doubt it was her. Even in the fading light, her auburn hair was unmistakable, hanging loose down her back in thick waves.

She struggled to turn, a little screech escaping her when she saw the hooded figure. 'It's me, Paine,' he assured her, finally seeing the reason she hadn't turned fully on his entrance. 'The bastard bound you.' Paine pulled his knife free and sliced the ropes. 'Are you all right?' He took a precious second to hold her once the ropes fell away.

'I am more scared than hurt,' Julia confessed, sinking into the safety of his embrace. 'Paine, Oswalt expects you to come. He'll be looking for you. We have to hurry.'

She no sooner spoke when the door handle turned. 'Hide, Paine,' she whispered fiercely.

The idea was distasteful to him, but he ducked swiftly down on the far side of the bed, tense and waiting for the time to strike.

'I see the crone left you untied. Unwise of her.' That was Oswalt. Paine tightened his grip around both of his weapons. If Oswalt was alone, he wouldn't get a better chance to strike.

'My man is here to take you down, my little virago. But first we have things to talk about.'

Paine could practically hear Julia flinch. He imagined Oswalt's hand with its yellow nails stroking her cheek.

'I am no good to you, Oswalt. I've been with Ramsden. You need a virgin,' Julia argued defiantly.

'I know, but since I have assurances you are not with child, you can be purified. Do you see everything out there? You have an excellent view. The high priest will do the ceremony in front of that altar block. Afterwards, you'll mount the block for an old purification ritual. It can only be done on midsummer. Would you like to hear about it, my dear? I think it will go quite far in restoring you to a more biddable nature. Perhaps you would prefer to be surprised? You look lovely.'

'Don't touch me,' Julia snapped. Paine quietly cheered her bravado. Julia had confessed how much the proceedings had unnerved her, but still she found courage to fight back.

'I am surprised that your gallant lover has not ridden to your rescue. He's leaving it rather late, isn't he?' Oswalt mused cruelly.

'He's not coming. It was never more than business between us,' Julia said staunchly. 'Why should he risk so much for me?'

Oswalt chortled. 'Firstly, because you're a lovely bit of baggage, enough to muddle any man's mind, especially a rutter like Ramsden who thinks primarily with his cock. Secondly, aside from his feelings for you, he detests me and blames me for his exile. This would be a grand opportunity to strike back for all those wasted years.'

'They weren't wasted. He became a man of self-made wealth,' Julia retorted. 'Perhaps he's outgrown the need for revenge. Certainly that should be a relief to you. You won't have to fight him a second time. You've had your victory.'

Paine wanted to applaud. His Julia was turning out to be a fine interrogator. Even under pressure, her bold manner had Oswalt's hackles up and the man couldn't resist the urge to brag.

'My dear wife, I've decided exile isn't good enough for Ramsden. He must die. I can't afford to have him live with all that he knows. And since I am to be married to you, I would find it deuced uncomfortable to have him lurking around, insane with jealousy over my good fortune.'

'You can hardly call this wedding legal. The church will never recognise it,' Julia pointed out.

'We'll have the small ceremony I promised your uncle in a few days once the shock starts to settle regarding Gray's ship. Just think of all the good you'll be able to do your family in their time of crisis.'

There was a length of silence, a squirming sound from Julia that caused Paine to grit his teeth and then a resounding crack. 'I told you to take your hands off me!'

That was his cue. Paine leaped from behind the bed, thankful the light was behind him. 'Let her go!' He levelled the pistol at Oswalt and hefted his knife with the other. There were just the two of them—Oswalt and the guard. The guard he recognised from the club, the one who had bribed Gaylord Beaton. The man held a pistol like his own.

Oswalt grabbed Julia as a shield. 'I doubt your aim is that good in the dubious light,' Oswalt sneered, 'None the less, I am delighted that you came.'

'Sam, bring our guest downstairs. I want him to have a front-row seat for my nuptials. Then afterwards, take him out and shoot him. That is, unless you'd prefer to be shot beforehand.'

Paine shifted his pistol's focus to Sam Brown. He could shoot the man accurately at this distance. If he could shoot, then so could Oswalt's guard. He doubted he could dodge the bullet at such close range. And the pistol fire would bring too many people to Oswalt's aid.

He gave Julia a look, hoping to convey to her his choice. If he could bring the big man closer, he could deal with him more effectively, perhaps be able to use his knife. Paine made a show of lifting his arms in surrender and placing the weapons on the ground.

Oswalt ordered the man to pick up the weapons. 'We don't want him getting them back.'

The big man moved forwards, stuffing his own pistol back into his belt, clearly confident in his bulk to sustain him in a fight should Paine choose to play the hero.

Paine chose his moment carefully. When the big man bent over, Paine landed a hard kick to the man's nose, sending blood spurting everywhere. The man writhed on the ground, clutching his broken nose.

'Now, Julia!' Paine cried, lunging for her before Oswalt could recover the situation.

Julia brought her foot down on Oswalt's instep. It was enough to cause the older man to release her. Oswalt drew a knife and Paine threw Julia behind him, careful to keep the door at his back. If nothing else, he had to secure Julia's escape.

'Do you know what's on this blade, boyo?' Oswalt advanced. 'A little equaliser—after all, you have years of youth on me. I can't possibly match physical strength with you.' Oswalt waved the knife blade.

'This isn't a drug. This afternoon, you were lucky.

This will kill you. It's made from cobra venom among other deadly things and cost me plenty for an ounce. It won't take that much to kill you. All I have to do is throw it.' Oswalt weighed the blade. 'I've been practising.'

Paine flexed his shoulders, covertly assessing his height. Julia would be safe. He was too tall for Oswalt to accidentally hit her instead. He could charge Oswalt and hope the poison acted slowly enough that he'd be able to take the feebler man to the ground before the poison claimed him. Pinned beneath his strong form, Oswalt would be unable to go after Julia. It would give her a slight head start, enough time to get to Peyton and Crispin. She didn't know they were there, but they'd be watching for her.

'No, Paine, you won't die for me,' Julia said behind him as if she'd read his mind.

'Oh, this is so touching,' Oswalt mocked. He lifted the knife and Paine sprang into motion. This would be resolved once and for all. Paine leaped for Oswalt, making a sprawling target as he flew for the man's throat.

Several things happened at once and the world slowed.

Julia screamed.

The knife sailed through the air. Paine braced himself for the jarring impact. There was no way the knife would miss him at this range. But miraculously it did, falling to the ground. An explosive sound rang out and

Oswalt fell to the ground beneath Paine's weight, but he was dead already, a bullet through the back.

The door crashed open and the world sped up again, revealing Peyton and Crispin, pistols drawn and hoods off.

'Paine, are you all right?' Julia rushed forwards as he gained his feet, quickly taking in the events.

'I'm fine.' He gestured to the knife. 'Don't touch it. It's loaded with poison.' He was alive. The thought rocketed through him like liquid lightning. Then he saw the reason. Sam Brown's one hand held a smoking pistol Paine recognised as the one he'd laid down earlier. The other hand still clutched his nose.

'You fired the shot?' It made sense. Peyton and Crispin had arrived too late and from the wrong direction. In his arms, Julia trembled, quickly reaching the last of her reserves. 'I am grateful.' *Not to mention perplexed.* 'Why did you do it?'

Sam Brown got to his feet awkwardly. 'He was a bad man. I've worked for bad men before, but he was the worst. I didn't understand just how corrupt he was until recently. What he planned to do to your young lady and what he planned to do to her family wasn't right. They'd done nothing wrong, they were just vulnerable, and I don't hold any truck with preying on the weak. It was different before when it was those who deserved to be swindled out of a few pounds.'

Paine wasn't sure he completely agreed with Sam

Brown's entire code of ethics, but he was grateful the man had seen fit to act on his behalf.

'All I ask is that I be allowed to disappear, go make another life somewhere, an honest life. I've tired of this one,' Sam Brown asked humbly.

'Absolutely, after one more duty,' Paine agreed. 'We still need to get out of the house. We have horses waiting. Ensure our safety.'

Dressed once more in their hoods, and with Julia between them, Sam Brown escorted the Ramsden brothers to the edge of the property without mishap, stopping only once to explain to guards that they were escorting the long-awaited bride.

They mounted up on their horses, Julia riding in front of Paine. 'What will you do now?' Paine asked Sam Brown.

'I'll go back to the house and tell the guards to disperse the crowd, that Oswalt has died.'

Paine threw the man a leather purse. 'This is to thank you for your silence.' He wouldn't suggest this was to buy the man's silence, that was too risky. He didn't want the man to think he could set up a lucrative blackmail scheme in the future, no matter how reformed he thought he was. But he did realise the man could tell everyone that the bride had escaped, rescued by the Ramsden brothers. That would cause a riot of scandal if it ever got out. It would only take one brash braggart admitting to being there for everything to become well known.

Peyton seemed to realise it as well. 'There's a ship I know of leaving for America. A man who works hard can make a good life there. I'll arrange for your passage. It sails at dawn with the tide.'

Negotiations were complete. There was just one more negotiation Paine had to manage and that was with Julia. It took all his will power not to blurt out his proposal and rush her off to a vicar immediately before further time passed. He would wait until her mind was at ease. She'd endured too much in one day to fully appreciate his proposal. The last thing he needed was for her to feel he was offering out of a sense of obligation or pity. When he proposed, he wanted her to know it was out of the only thing that mattered—his love.

Chapter Nineteen

The family held their collective breath for the next three days. Sam Brown had boarded the boat to America and they waited to see if any hint of scandal regarding the odd doings in Richmond circulated the *ton*. In spite of Julia's ordeal, Aunt Lily insisted the family make a showing at one fashionable gathering each night. She argued that nothing would set tongues wagging faster than being absent from events three nights in a row during the height of the Season.

It was a compelling argument, especially since they'd made such a showing once the Season had hit full stride. They couldn't let those newly established inroads go to waste. Paine admired Julia's strength. Each night, she donned a new gown, looking more beautiful every time. She smiled and she danced, keeping up a happy front. If anyone inquired about the Lockhart ship, she simply said, 'We have no confirmation that the ship sank or that there were no survivors. Until we do, I prefer not to believe the worst.'

She told the truth, as best as they knew it. The day after their return from Richmond, Paine had paid a visit to the viscount, encouraging him not to announce the loss of the ship until it was a certainty.

He wasn't afraid to admit he had sound reasons and selfish reasons for it. He'd sent Flaherty to search out any truth to Oswalt's announcement. Flaherty had found nothing substantially reliable to bolster the rumour. There had been some trouble off the coast of Spain. Other sailors reported a heavy storm, but no one could agree on whether or not the *Bluehawk* had been affected.

Selfishly, Paine didn't want another obstacle put in his path when it came to marrying Julia. A mourning period would have to follow if Gray was announced dead. That could very likely come to pass, but he wanted Julia firmly wedded to him before that happened. He'd gladly spend six months quietly living outside of Society's eye tucked away with Julia. But he doubted he'd survive another six months unable to claim her. The viscount had been happy to follow Paine's lead. Recent events had upended him completely and destroyed his desire to take any action.

Aunt Lily's insistence bore better results than antic-ipated. Not only was the *ton* pleased to welcome back

Dursley's brother, but requests for business assistance came flooding in in response to many of the letters Paine had sent out a few weeks prior and through the connections he'd established at the gatherings. There was even talk of Paine heading up an investment group at the Bank of London. As a third son, dabbling in commerce was highly acceptable.

There only remained wooing Julia to complete Paine's happiness. He knew she was inwardly worried over her cousin Gray, and that mentally she was grappling with the horrors of her brief captivity, but he could wait no longer.

Paine patted his pockets for the fifth time in as many minutes, waiting for Julia to come downstairs. The weather was brilliant and he was taking her driving. Yes, all three items were there just as they were a few minutes ago and a few minutes before that.

'I'm ready,' Julia called from the top of the stairs, a bit breathless from rushing. 'I couldn't find my parasol right away.' She waved the pale green parasol to illustrate her point.

'You'd be beautiful without it.' Paine smiled up at her, enjoying the sway of her hips beneath the thin summer muslin gown as she came downstairs. The mint colour of the gown and the forest green grosgrain trim complemented her colouring splendidly.

'You're too kind,' Julia teased, putting her hand on his sleeve. 'Where are we off to?'

She sounded like his Julia, but when she looked up at him, her eyes were still haunted. They didn't sparkle like he knew they could. Not yet. They would again, though, he vowed. He'd spend his whole life devoted to seeing that they did.

'Someplace wonderful,' Paine said mysteriously.

They drove through Hyde Park, Paine cheerfully nodding to passers-by and stopping to talk with new acquaintances. Julia sat patiently beside him, acting the part of a banker's wife perfectly, offering intelligent conversation when needed. A banker's wife! The thought filled Paine with schoolboy giddiness. Who would have thought twelve years ago, or even a year ago, that he would find his inner peace with a wife and a career, with being restored to family and to society—things he'd thought he could live without?

Paine turned out of the park on to a quiet tree-lined street. The street was wide, clean and empty, untroubled by the traffic from the park. A few, large town houses dominated the area. It was clearly a wealthy and exclusive neighbourhood, perhaps not for peers, but for a different type of wealth and power—new wealth and power, the kind that would matter more as England grew into its age of industry, an age that Paine could see already on the horizon and heading towards its zenith.

'Where are we?' Julia asked, looking about at the impressive buildings.

Paine brought the carriage over to the kerb and jumped down. 'Come and see this place with me, Julia. I need to take a look at it.'

He helped her down and produced a key—item number one—from his pockets.

He swung the front door open and waited anxiously as Julia gazed around the wainscoted vestibule, her eye caught by the enormous brass chandelier overhead. 'It's fabulous.'

'I think you should see all of it before you decide that.' Paine chuckled.

Julia walked ahead of him, eyes wide open, taking in the rich soft tones of the walls done in creamy shades of winter wheat. She gave an audible 'aaahh' at the sight of the dining room. 'That table must seat fifteen people!'

Paine grinned at the sight of the polished mahogany table he'd ordered a week ago, anticipating such a reaction. 'Actually, it seats twenty.'

'Twenty?' Julia commented in awe. She mounted the stairs, her hand trailing on the carved banister. 'There's been such attention to detail.'

She sailed through the bedrooms, noting how large and airy they were, how well appointed the views out of the private sitting rooms were where they looked out over the gardens in the back.

When they reached the last bedroom, Paine blocked the way, an arm across the shut door. 'I have to ask you something before you go in there.'

Julia eyed him suspiciously. He pressed on. 'Would you like to live here?'

Julia's eyes went wide with confusion instead of the surprise he'd hoped for. 'You want to buy me a house?'

'Actually, I *bought* you a house, this house if you like it. The moment I saw it, I could see you in it. I could see you at the table presiding over dinners, I could see you walking in the garden, picking lavender. When I saw you in the vestibule, I knew I was right.'

Julia was nonplussed. 'I don't need a house. I don't need one this big. It's awfully large for one person and I certainly won't ever have twenty people over for dinner at one time.'

She was rambling. Maybe that was a good sign. She was usually so logical. 'Well, I'd probably have twenty people over for dinner on occasion and you wouldn't have to live here alone. I'd like to live here, too, with you.' Now he was rambling and probably making a muck of things. Paine drew out the second item from his pockets, this one a legal document in a slim leather case. He gave it to her.

'What's this?' Julia said slowly.

'It's the deed to the house. It goes with the key.' Good lord, that sounded dumb. Of course it went with the key.

He'd better get on with it before all his faculties fled. Paine took her hands, gripping them firmly. 'I want to marry you, Julia. I want to marry you and live in this house and raise children with you. Would you consider having me?'

'Marry me? When did you decide this?' Julia stammered, unsure how to respond.

'I think I decided it weeks ago when I first met you. I never believed in love at first sight, or really even believed in love until you, Julia. You've reformed me. I don't think I can afford to lose you.'

'You were always going to lose me. Keeping me was not part of the deal, Paine. I don't expect for it to be part of the deal now. I've overstayed my welcome and you needn't feel obliged. I admit I am at sea over what to do now.' Julia disengaged her hands and began walking down the hallway.

'I didn't think everything would turn out so well. I thought I'd be publicly ruined and shunned, sent off to the country. I had planned for that in my own way. I rather thought it would all be simpler. I didn't bargain on all the, um…shall we say "adventure"? Perhaps for you, these past weeks have been quite ordinary, but for me… Well, I've got nothing to compare them to in my heretofore very common life. You've done well by me and you don't need to feel obligated to save me.' She turned her sad green eyes to him.

It occurred to him that she'd been contemplating this all week. While he had been contemplating how to propose, she'd been contemplating how to say goodbye, how to free him.

He went to her, putting his hands on her shoulders, ostensibly to steady her, but perhaps to also steady himself. He was not going to lose her. 'This is not about obligation, it's not about passion, although we have quite a lot of that, too. This is about love.

'I have fallen thoroughly in love with you, Julia. You have brought me peace for the first time in my life. I need you and I want you and, at last, I have something to offer you in return. I've got a desk at the bank now, a home that's not my brother's, a fortune for you to spend.' He laughed a little at that. 'I even have a title.' Paine pulled out the third item from the inner pocket of his jacket. He gave Julia the folded piece of paper. 'Read it, it's a letter from the king.'

Julia scanned it. 'Oh my, Paine, you're to be knighted. Sir Paine Ramsden.' She read further. 'For invaluable service to the crown. Whatever did you do?'

'The crown needed to be aware of Oswalt's treachery against members of the peerage. There were many people, his Majesty included, who were glad to have certain issues, as it were, resolved. You'll be Lady Julia Ramsden. I am worthy of you now.'

Julia's eyes watered. Damn it. He hadn't meant to make her cry. She was supposed to jump with joy, preferably right into his arms.

'You were always worthy of me, Paine,' she whispered. 'When I started this, I was looking for the most dishonourable man in London. I never thought he'd turn out to be the most honourable.' She bit her lip and smiled through her tears. 'I don't suppose you have a ring in those pockets, do you? You seem to have everything else.'

Paine laughed. 'I most certainly do.' He pulled out the fourth item, a small velvet box from one of London's finest jewellers. He went swiftly down on one knee and flipped open the box lid. 'Marry me, Julia.'

Julia feigned contemplation, tapping a finger against her chin. 'If I do, will I get to see what's behind the door?'

'Vixen!' Paine slipped the ring on her finger, a brilliant emerald surrounded by a band of tiny diamonds. 'It's from my own collection. I had it set especially for you.' Paine rose and reached for the door.

Julia laughed when she saw the room. 'You've been busy.'

Paine swept her up into his arms and carried her to the low bed. It had been restored, along with the cabinet. It would take time to fix this room up to his expectations, but he couldn't imagine him and Julia sleeping in any other bed. The need to have her was suddenly swift and urgent as it coursed through him.

She read his need and reached her arms up to draw him down to her, kissing him deeply. 'Did you bring a sheath?' Julia murmured, lifting against him.

'I brought something better,' Paine said next to her ear, nibbling and sucking at her earlobe.

'What could be better?' Julia said, on the brink of losing all reasoning.

'A special licence.'

She laughed softly, her breath warm against his neck. She shifted her body to accommodate him, taking him between her thighs. 'You once said I was like the Sleeping Beauty—come awaken me with love's first kiss.'

He didn't have to be asked twice. Julia Prentiss was his happy ever after.

Epilogue

Champagne flowed freely in sparkling crystal glasses at the Ramsden wedding breakfast a month later. Surrounded by the Ramsden clan, Julia thought the wait had been worth it. True, Paine had a licence that could have enabled them to marry sooner, but Aunt Lily had argued again on the platform of good form. In the end the argument had made sense. After working so hard to erase the questions of Paine's past, it made little sense to scotch those efforts with a rushed wedding and all the speculation that would ensue.

Beside her at the head table, Paine drank yet another toast to their happiness, one hand surreptitiously under the table on her leg. Watching him recite his vows at St George's this morning, one would never have guessed that a mere three months ago he'd been a confirmed bachelor with no thoughts towards being redeemed. Today, he was a man resolutely in love with his wife.

Julia knew the look on his face well because it was the same reflection she saw in the mirror when she looked at her own. She had never guessed such happiness was possible. It seemed a far cry from the darkness of Oswalt's proposal.

The only minor crimp in her bliss was that her aunt and uncle were not here to share it with her. Although Paine had taken charge of her uncle's finances and seen the family through the financial aspect of their crisis, no amount of money could compensate them for the loss of Gray. While there was still no confirmation of a body, the Lockharts had given up hope that Gray was still alive at this late date and had retreated to the country to mourn in private.

Still, looking around her, Julia felt she had a new family now in Aunt Lily, Peyton and Crispin, men who Gray would have liked immensely as brothers-in-law.

They were talking with Lily and Beth when Crispin tapped Paine on the shoulder. 'Excuse me, but there's someone at the door. I need you and Julia to come with me.'

Paine and Julia followed Crispin to the door where Peyton already stood waiting. 'Julia, this man says he knows you.' Peyton stepped aside to reveal the late-come guest.

He was dressed in worn clothes hardly befitting the

heir of a viscount, but Julia recognised him immediately. A hand flew to her mouth and she clutched Paine's arm to steady herself, hardly daring to believe the sight before her.

'Gray! You're alive. How?' The shock of seeing him was so overwhelming she couldn't organise her thoughts into any coherent pattern.

Paine laughed softly at her surprise and urged her forwards. 'Go to him, Julia. See for yourself that he's not an apparition.'

Julia needed no further prodding. She flung herself into Gray's arms. 'I can't believe you're safe after all this time.' She stepped back to look at him and then hugged him again, unable to decide if she wanted to hug him or look at him, to see that he was all right.

'You're here, you're really here. You're not dead!'

Gray hugged her tightly. 'I am really alive, although it was close. Thanks to Ramsden and Dursley here, I have returned home.'

'Oh my goodness, your parents, your brothers are going to be so thrilled. You don't know what this will mean to them!' Julia's happiness over seeing Gray ebbed a bit and she lowered her voice. 'They aren't here, you know. They're in the country, mourning you.'

The look on Gray's face was grim, too. 'I rather suspect they will mourn me when I get done with them. I can't believe what they attempted to force you into, my dear cousin.'

Julia cast a glance back at Paine. 'It's all in the past, Gray, and it's brought me this wonderful man. He's taken care of me and the family.' She motioned to Paine. 'Paine, come and meet my cousin, and, Cousin Gray, meet my husband. Then we must talk. You must have so much to tell.' She was still giddy with the surprise of seeing him.

'There is, but I have it on good authority that the most exciting tale to tell is yours and I want to hear all of it. I came to celebrate with you the moment I stepped foot in London. My story can wait.'

'All tales can wait until you've had a chance to change. Come with me,' Peyton offered, 'I am sure there's some clothing upstairs that you can make do with.'

Peyton hurried Gray off to clean up, leaving Julia and Paine alone in the entry. 'Did you do this, Paine?' Julia inquired, studying her new husband thoughtfully.

Paine had the good grace to look sheepish. 'I have some connections in the shipping industry and I put them to work. I was suspicious that nothing had turned up, especially since the coast of Spain is notorious for bodies washing ashore. Sure enough, someone recalled a man of Gray's description when he passed through a remote sea village. I sent Flaherty after him.'

'It's the best wedding gift ever. I could not have asked for more,' Julia said, tears in her eyes. 'I was going to wait, Paine, but I have a gift for you, too.'

Paine protested. 'I have everything I want, Julia.' He moved to pull her into his arms.

Julia twined her arms around his neck and pulled him close to whisper in his ear.

'I stand corrected,' Paine said, his voice trembling slightly. 'I only *thought* I had everything I wanted. When, my dear, do you think the gift will arrive?'

'Around February, in time for Valentine's Day,' Julia said softly.

'And to think this all started because you needed to be ruined and I needed to be redeemed. I think this has ended rather well.'

'Ended?' Julia laughed up at him. 'This is only the beginning. Happy ever after is only for fairy tales.'

* * * * *

REGENCY

Collection

*Let these sparklingly seductive delights whirl
you away to the ballrooms—and
bedrooms—of Polite Society!*

Volume 1 – 4th February 2011
Regency Pleasures by Louise Allen

Volume 2 – 4th March 2011
Regency Secrets by Julia Justiss

Volume 3 – 1st April 2011
Regency Rumours by Juliet Landon

Volume 4 – 6th May 2011
Regency Redemption by Christine Merrill

Volume 5 – 3rd June 2011
Regency Debutantes by Margaret McPhee

Volume 6 – 1st July 2011
Regency Improprieties by Diane Gaston

12 volumes in all to collect!

MILLS
BOON

www.millsandboon.co.uk

REGENCY

Collection

*Let these sparklingly seductive delights whirl
you away to the ballrooms—and
bedrooms—of Polite Society!*

Volume 7 – 5th August 2011
Regency Mistresses by Mary Brendan

Volume 8 – 2nd September 2011
Regency Rebels by Deb Marlowe

Volume 9 – 7th October 2011
Regency Scandals by Sophia James

Volume 10 – 4th November 2011
Regency Marriages by Elizabeth Rolls

Volume 11 – 2nd December 2011
Regency Innocents by Annie Burrows

Volume 12 – 6th January 2012
Regency Sins by Bronwyn Scott

12 volumes in all to collect!

MILLS
BOON

www.millsandboon.co.uk

"To say that I met Nicholas Brisbane over my husband's dead body is not entirely accurate. Edward, it should be noted, was still twitching upon the floor…"

London, 1886

For Lady Julia Grey, her husband's sudden death at a dinner party is extremely inconvenient. However, things worsen when inscrutable private investigator Nicholas Brisbane reveals that the death was not due to natural causes.

Drawn away from her comfortable, conventional life, Julia is exposed to threatening notes, secret societies and gypsy curses, not to mention Nicholas's charismatic unpredictability.

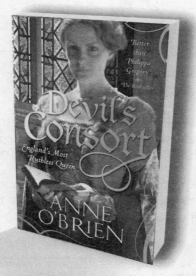